jaxon publishing
Copyright 2001 by Jacquelyne J. Scott

All rights reserved. No part of this publication may be reproduced or transmitted in any form or by any means, electronic or mechanical, including photocopy, recording, or any information storage and retrieval system, without permission in writing from the publisher.

Requests for permission to make copies of any part of the work should be mailed to:
jaxon publishing
227 e. ontario #11664
chicago, il 60611

Library of Congress
Cataloging-in-Publication-Date

Scott, Jacquelyne Jermayne
Snapshots, is love picture perfect/jacquelyne j. scott
p. cm.

ISBN 0-9676646-1-6

jacket cover by francelli p
layout by Dockett Graphical Productions
Printed in the United States of America
Second edition
Originally titled Snapshots, a love story

First and foremost,
I want to thank my Lord and Savior Jesus Christ,
without whom I would be nothing...at all

*You may have loved and lost
and there are some things you may never get back
but as long as you have your dignity
you have enough gas to back out the driveway
and start the journey all over again...*

In loving memory of my grandparents
who raised me and taught me
the value of self-discovery and the real power of love

Snapshots

Snapshots

Their lives could be watched like a movie. It could have been a fresh, new, Hollywood love story, with many twists and turns. To people looking on, things for Dante and Gabrielle seemed to be so perfect that it would have to work out. But even when things seemed their worst, people still hoped that the best would come; Dante and Gabrielle, explosive yet enchanting, were meant to be. But, Dante was so wild and unpredictable that no one knew his next move, and though you hoped for the best, it was hard to tell how things would turn out in the end.

From the beginning, Gabrielle Davis, a soft spoken, small town girl, and Dante Jackson, a second round draft pick in the NFL came from different experiences, that formed them into different people.

A quick snapshot of Gabrielle's early life would show a puffy cheeked, brown skinned girl, with short twisty pony tails, hopping up and down her front stairs. You could have seen her progress through the stages with her two best friends, Michelle and Yvette, as they played baby dolls, then Barbie dolls, rode bikes, had slumber parties, or hung out at the local pizza place. They did these things well into junior high, but by high school, things had begun to change.

Gabrielle was outgoing in class, but in other settings, she was soft spoken, if not shy. She was an ordinary brown skinned girl with high cheek bones, thick eyebrows and slanted eyes. Her legs and behind were proportional to her body, yet they were bigger than her top. Her hair was thick, and medium length and she tried to do a lot of different things with it; but this was for herself, because in their town, no boys were interested in a brown skinned or dark brown skinned girl with short or medium hair.

Michelle was different; she was a hit, and always had been. She was tall, slim, and light skinned. She had hazel eyes and Sandy blond hair that reached nearly to her behind. She was like Vanity 6 in high school, and then she was Apollonia when Purple Rain came out.

Yvette was the same complexion as Gabrielle. They were about the same height, 5 foot 3, and had the same body type, except Yvette was a little more petite. The difference was, boys accepted Yvette just as much as they accepted Michelle. That wasn't too rare, because even though boys didn't like the brown skinned, short haired girls, Yvette was lightning; the boys wanted to see her flashes and try not to get struck; Yvette was a challenge.

That wasn't Gabrielle's personality, so she submerged herself in the books. Not only because boys weren't interested, but more so because she wanted to go to college, and she knew that a scholarship would be the only way. Her mother, Danielle, had worked hard for everything she got in life. She had Gabrielle at 16, got little to no assistance from her parents, and had to make it in the world on her own. Though Gabrielle's mother adored her only child, she taught her the same hard work ethic, and made it clear that at 18, Gabrielle was on her own. That was two more years than Danielle had gotten, and she would be sure, at 34, to resume her own life. That wouldn't be too late for her to enjoy herself.

So Gabrielle made it through high school and went to college, a shy girl, working hard for everything she got, and knowing that if she made it, she would have to make it on her own.

But for Dante, things had been much different. Dante seemed to have started off as a playboy.

The first snapshot Gabrielle got of his early life was of a time when he was six years old, out in the backyard behind a tree, lying on top of a girl with his hand up her dress. His mother, Mrs. Jackson, had been standing on the back stairs calling out to him, when his eldest sister, Pauline, pointed her in his direction. Dante's mother walked behind the tree and stood over him and his playmate with a switch in her hand. One hand was on her hip, and the other one was ready to start the whipping. She called his name one more time, and he looked up, trying to explain that they were just playing hide and go seek. Then he jumped up, trying to dodge his mother, who was asking 'seek what?' with every stroke of her switch. She wasn't waiting for him to give an answer; instead, she was making up the answers for him each time she swung.

Dante's days growing up in Dallas were full of a lot more hard times than Gabrielle's. The Jacksons were lower middle class, but with seven of them in the house, it seemed that they were poor. Dante was the second to the youngest, with an older brother, two older sisters, and one baby sister. They were all closely knit, but Dante seemed to always outshine everyone.

Dante wasn't the smartest in school; Pauline, his oldest sister, was that. He wasn't the most athletic; his older brother, Torrence, played almost every sport. Yet, there was something shining in Dante. His personality was so outgoing and full of life that it seemed he could one day be some sort of celebrity. He was always playing jokes and games, maybe he'd be a comedian or an actor. His father never encouraged it, so his mother never spoke on it, but everyone knew in their hearts that Dante was headed for some life in the spot light.

Early in life, Dante perceived his own proclivity for greatness; and one day at the dinner table, just out of no where, he announced to his parents that he was going to take care of them. Dante's father had just worked his fifth evening of overtime, and was too tired to do anything but look at Dante puzzled. His mother was silent, until Torrence told Dante he: *Shoots off at the mouth too much*; Pauline defended him saying he was: *just a baby*; Erica, his second older sister told him not to forget her; his baby sister said nothing; but his mother told the rest of them to be quiet. Then looked directly at Erica, as if the commotion was her fault, and said sharply: "We're just fine. And no one will need to take care of anyone."

Mrs. Jackson had a way of changing the focus to someone else when in reality it was Dante who started it. There was no real favoritism, in her eyes; still, Dante was her *baby*.

He knew that, and even though the conversation was supposed to be over, Dante re-asserted his statement by saying: "Just watch. One day I am mama."

His father looked over at Dante again, and his mother nodded to say: 'Okay, Dante.'

She wanted to get Dante quiet because she knew that in a minute Mr. Jackson would take over, and Dante would be in real trouble.

From the earliest part of Dante's life, his mother coddled him and his father chastised him. His father's stern discipline sometimes seemed too severe, so Mrs. Jackson intervened when she could, and Mr. Jackson sometimes let her. But, when it was time, he was usually the only one who could and would straighten Dante out.

Torrence seemed most frustrated that Dante got away with everything. And for some reason, that day at the dinner table, he felt a little threatened by Dante's prophesy that he would be the one to *make it big*. It seemed like after Dante's middle school promise, he and Torrence stopped being companions and became rivals.

But, by the time Dante entered high school, Torrence was no competition. Torrence had left for college with an athletic scholarship but lost it after smoking, then selling marijuana. When he came back to Dallas, he took hustling to the next level, and caused many problems in the Jackson's good Christian home.

There were constant confrontations with Torrence. Dante had gotten bigger, and was continually finding himself verbally and physically between Torrence and someone else in the house. That only created more animosity between the two brothers. And, added to that, Dante's athletic potentials were flourishing. His coaches believed in him, and his personality captivated them. They worked hard to make sure Dante would get priority in whatever deals and scholarships were coming in.

His peers adored him equally. His charismatic personality always made him the life of any event or activity. People loved to see him coming because he was fun, humorous, and full of life. He seemed to need all the attention and feedback people gave him; in the early days he used it to build confidence; later it turned to conceit.

No matter what he became, he had always been sensitive, caring and genuine. When he was in high school, girls were starting to notice him more as boyfriend material, rather than just a fun and funny buddy, and everyone seemed to vie for his attention. This continued to his college years where he had so many choices between hanging with his frats, teammates or the countless girls who fell into his charms. By the time he went pro, this was taken to a new level. He had the means and mannerisms to lift almost anything, and place it under his wings.

When he met Gabrielle, things were a little different.

# # #

Gabrielle had left Kenosha and was a sophomore in college in Minnesota. She had a full scholarship that paid her classes, room and board, but she worked part time in a department store to cover her smaller expenses.

She was at work the day she met Dante. He had come in the store on the ground level, and had purchased several different things. He had ladies' clothes in one bag, men's clothes in another. He had made it to the top floor, where Gabrielle was ringing out a customer. As with everything she did, Gabrielle was focusing her attention on her task. Dante noticed her, and tried to make her look at him. He swivelled his neck from side to side, made funny faces, and then paraded back and forth through the aisles.

Snapshots

She tried not to notice, but at six foot six, three hundred twenty pounds, and Hershey's kisses dark brown, he was hard to miss.

Her customer was an older white woman, who looked the wealthy part but was checking to make sure every sale item had been rung in correctly. She asked that Gabrielle check back through a few things, and when she saw there was a mistake, and that Gabrielle's attention was elsewhere, she demanded to see the manager. Gabrielle tried to explain, but when the manager arrived and took over, she was in trouble. The part that had most upset the customer was that 'if this gal hadn't been so busy laughing about my questions, maybe she could have gotten the sale items correct.'

It wasn't that Gabrielle was laughing at the woman; Dante had tripped in one of the aisles while he was trying to get her attention, and she had shaken her head and laughed. Now that the manager was taking over the transaction at another register, Dante stepped forward and leaned on her counter.

"Hey, how you doing, Miss lady?" he smiled.

"I was just fine until you got me in trouble," Gabrielle replied.

"What I do?" he asked and leaned back. "Hey I was just trying to get a fine lady to see my way."

She couldn't be mad at him; he was too congenial. And, he had made her blush. She was *fine*?

But she couldn't forget herself. She had to let him know she was slightly upset.

"Well, you made me lose my commission," she replied.

"Oh is that it?" he said, waving his hand as if it were nothing.

"That's enough," Gabrielle began. "I'm in school, you know, those things do help."

"Oh come on baby; you ain't hurting for nothing. I can see that. You all good."

She looked at him for a moment, then shook her head. He looked back at her, then tapped his hand on the counter two times, as if to say: *Check you out later* and then walked off.

She couldn't believe it. He was so rude. There were a few things now that she would like to tell him about himself for coming over there, making all that commotion for her, only to walk off as if nothing had happened, or as if that had been his goal, to make her get in trouble and...

Just when she had been thinking of all the things she could say to him now that he was gone, he walked back up and dropped an arm-full of clothes at her register. She was in the women's department, so he had collected things that were nice, some things that were sexy, but they were all different styles and all different sizes.

"What is this?" she asked, wanting to be a smart alack and finish with 'some racks you've messed up and want to see me have to go back and fix?'

But she wouldn't have ever said that to a customer. Besides that, before she could finish her snide thoughts, he interrupted.

"This is your commission baby," he smiled.

"What?" Gabrielle asked.

"It's your commission," he said proudly. "I messed you up, and now I'm going to make it up. Double time. That lady over there wasn't bringing you no commission. And look at her; she's still over there fussing. Probably trying to get even more of a deal."

Gabrielle didn't know what to say, so she said nothing. And she couldn't figure out where Dante was coming from, so she just stared into his face. *A man's eyes will tell you everything.* Her mother had once told her. *And most of them are saying, I'm no good.*

Dante interrupted Gabrielle's thoughts and said: "Ring me up, baby. I got to head out of here to practice."

Gabrielle had been in a daze thinking of Dante's actions and her mother's words. But Dante was now hurrying her, so she rang up then bagged his things.

Dante walked away from her counter with even more bags; he had so many he could have fallen over, but he knew how to balance things. He got back to the bottom floor and made one more stop at the jewelry counter and picked up a few small items; then he got into his truck, parked right outside the door. There was a slim, model type girl waiting in the passenger's seat. She took some of the bags from his hands then leaned over and kissed him when he sat down.

"What took you so long, baby?" she moaned.

"Oh, you know I had to get the right pieces for my boo," he said.

Dante never felt that he owed an explanation to anyone because that was just how he *carried things*. But he gave this girl one

Snapshots

to make her feel like he answered to her.

While the two of them drove off, Gabrielle was in the store receiving a written warning from her manager. He was scolding her about their high customer base, and warning her that she would need to be far more professional and less flirtatious if she was going to keep her job there.

Flirting was furthest from Gabrielle's mind, and when her shift was over, her manager, the job, and the incident would be wiped out too.

She went back to the dorm to study for the night. It was Friday night, and perfect. She wouldn't even have to leave out of Cheston Hall.

The girls who were usually screaming up and down the halls with water balloons, plans for raiding other dorms, or some other drama, would be gone tonight. They'd be out partying which meant Gabrielle wouldn't have to head out to the library for peace and quiet.

She organized all of her books and materials on her bed, changed into her shorts and a t-shirt, and got ready for the peace that would be coming in about a half an hour. But just when she had lain down on her bed, Cassandra and Angelique burst through her door.

"Get up girl. You got to get up."

This was Cassandra. She had slapped Gabrielle on the back of her shoulders, and then bounced down on her bed.

"You have got to go out with us tonight girl. The Ques are having a party and I heard it's going to be off the hook!" Cassandra finished.

Angelique was still standing in the door way, waiting to turn right back around. She knew Gabrielle was not going out. Gabrielle never went out, no matter how appealing they made it to her.

Gabrielle kept her face in somebody's history, English, biology or whatever kind of book.

"You are not going, right Gabrielle?" Angelique rhetorically asked.

"Of course she is! This is a Peaches Holland event, and all Peaches' parties are in there," Cassandra answered.

Gabrielle rolled over and sat up in a butterfly position. "Really, I can't. I have a test in the morning, and I have so much studying to do."

Cassandra smacked her lips, and hit the bed. "Study, study, study, that's all you do."

Under her breath Angelique directed a comment to Cassandra:

"Do it, do it, do it; that's all you do."

"What? What did you say?" Cassandra asked point-blank, after she had marched right into Angelique's face.

Fearing Cassandra's tone, Gabrielle tried to intervene. "Guys, guys, now come on."

"No, no, no," Cassandra began looking back over her shoulder to Gabrielle, then back to Angelique. "What did you say heifer?"

Angelique would not back down, and stated:

"You heard me."

Cassandra reached one of her long arms out to the side and grabbed a pillow from Gabrielle's roommate's bed and slapped Angelique over the head.

"Oh, it's on now," Angelique replied and grabbed one of Gabrielle's pillows.

Angelique and Cassandra pillow fought all through the tiny dorm room. Gabrielle tried to break them up, but they only drew her into it. The only thing that stopped them was Gabrielle's roommate. She was a lanky, super-studious looking girl who walked in, just in time enough to get hit, so hard that her glasses flew off her face. It was her shock, not the pillow stuffing or books that were everywhere, that made the girls stop.

They collapsed on the bed laughing, then the three of them began to clean up the room, and apologize to Gabrielle's roommate. When they were finished cleaning up, Cassandra and Angelique refused to leave until Gabrielle agreed to go out with them.

chapter two

The two of them crossed the campus nearly dragging Gabrielle to the car. She was still trying to back out and head to the dorms. Cassandra wasn't concerned with Gabrielle's protests about having to study. Gabrielle was so smart she could sleep through the next three years, and still graduate with honors. Cassandra was more interested in Gabrielle's outfit.

"Where did you get that? They sell that kind of freak gear at N&M's?"

"No," Angelique answered for Gabrielle. "You know one day I had to take Gabrielle's conservative behind to *The Hook Up* so she could be sexy like yours truly."

That became a new complaint for Gabrielle, how uncomfortable she felt in the outfit. But they had made it to the parking lot, where a few of the Ques, including Cassandra's ex-boyfriend Mark, were standing outside drinking and trash talking each other. When Gabrielle approached, Mark stepped away from his crowd of friends.

"Uhhn baby, mmmph. Don't you look good," he said, eyeing her up and down.

"Yeah, all that junk in the trunk back dere boy. She know she fine," one of his frats called out from the back.

"And more than that..." Mark said, then put his hand around her arm. "Cute face, nice body, mmm, what I could do with you."

"You can get your hands off of me," Gabrielle asserted, and tried wiggling her arm from his.

Cassandra snatched Gabrielle's arm from Mark's hand. Gabrielle would have told him about himself, but Cassandra had already taken over where Gabrielle left off.

"Yeah, well she wouldn't have anything to do with you," Cassandra said, squinting into his face.

"And, I don't need to do anything else with you, since I've had it every way I possibly could have," Mark shot back at Cassandra.

She hollered back an expletive to him, and his response was: "Only if you do it with your lips again."

Cassandra started yelling out insults to Mark; but worse than that, she was also walking back toward him, fingers pointed and ready to really fight. No surprises, they had gone there before. Her swinging, him trying to hold her down; but, Cassandra wasn't easily managed.

Fortunately Gabrielle and Angelique were able to cool things off briefly. They pulled Cassandra to the car while she was screaming things at Mark, and then shouting at them to let her go.

Once they made it to the car, things could have cooled down, but Cassandra started talking about what a dog Mark was. Instead of just agreeing with Cassandra, as Gabrielle was doing, Angelique put in her two cents. She told Cassandra that of course Mark was going to disrespect her since she had continually disrespected herself. While Cassandra and Mark had been dating, Cassandra had compromised herself in private and in public giving him whatever he wanted, when and how he wanted it. So, Angelique was quick to point out: "When a woman disrespects herself, she can't expect a man to do anything but treat her how she treats herself."

Cassandra couldn't believe, and didn't bite her tongue to say that Angelique had a lot of nerve giving out morality speeches...especially since Angelique was messing with one of the biggest hustlers in their home town, DC. As far as Cassandra was concerned, Angelique had to be doing a lot more freaky things than she was.

The argument got so intense that Gabrielle wondered how Cassandra and Angelique could remain friends. They argued like this with each other at least once a week.

But Cassandra and Angelique were peas in a pod. The minute they got to the club and valeted the car, all was forgotten. The three of them found an empty table, but Cassandra and Angelique dropped off their coats and disappeared into the crowd.

Gabrielle couldn't believe it. They had drug her all the way out, away from her studies, and now they were just off, gallivanting around the club with each other. After thirty minutes of this, she started to leave. She would just get up, get a cab and head back to the dorms, but something distracted her thoughts. It was a guy, standing a little ways from her, but flexing his muscles and directing all his silly behavior her way. When she didn't notice him at first, he moved a little closer from the distance, and began parading back and forth, flexing his muscles, and pausing to smile. It was Dante.

She looked at him and smiled. He bobbed his head and motioned his arms asking: *Can I come over there?*

Gabrielle only moved her lips to say: *Sure.*

He read them, and walked over to her table.

"Hey, how come you sitting over here alone?" he asked.

She shrugged her shoulders, then smiled slyly. "I don't know. I guess it's because you're not sitting here with me."

"Oh...well then..." Dante began.

She had caught him off guard. So to cover up his surprise, he became theatrical.

May I? he gestured as he began moving each of the coats.

"Sure, go ahead," Gabrielle told him.

After he had moved the coats, he pointed to the seat closest to hers and made the *May I?* gesture again.

She nodded her head yes. He pulled his chair in really close to her and she pushed him back from his shoulders.

"Whoa baby, you're kind of strong."

"Yeah right," she replied. "You're just silly," she paused, then said: "You were voted class clown, right?"

"How'd you know?" he said playfully, then continued, "And you were voted most finest thing on the face of this earth."

"Oh, you're funny," she said a little snappy.

"Well...." he said.

"Well what?"

"Well, were you?" he asked.

"No. Far from it," she replied.

"Well you should have been," he said. "I know a lot of brothers out there would love a girl like you. Fine, smart, and got a nice body. Shoot, baby, you're prime time."

Gabrielle was a little shocked by how much he complimented her, especially, as the night went on and she saw that some of the prettiest girls continually stopped by to speak to him, ask if they could sit at the table with him, drop off phone numbers or sent him drinks. Some girls were sophisticated with it, most were blatant, but he respectfully declined them all. He directed all of his attention to Gabrielle.

The hostess, Peaches, had stopped by numerous times to offer Dante a variety of things, and ask if he was okay. He made sure to answer everything as *we* for him and Gabrielle. Peaches understood that Dante was representing Gabrielle as his girl, not just some groupie that had parked next to him. So, she made sure she was extra careful to continually offer drinks to Gabrielle, ask to show her around to the beer gardens, and invite her to play cards. But Dante answered *no* for everything Peaches offered Gabrielle, and assured Peaches that Gabrielle wouldn't be going anywhere. Gabrielle told Dante she liked *his nerve* saying what she would or wouldn't do; nevertheless, she stayed seated with him the entire night.

In addition to all the females that continued to stop by the table, quite a few guys were coming by *just to holler* or *give big ups* to Dante.

Gabrielle didn't want to inquire about all the attention he was getting. He had been polite to the people who stopped by, but he kept everyone to a minimum, telling them he was just cooling out and wanted to *parle* with his *girl*, that being Gabrielle. He never admitted to being a local celebrity; he just explained that these people knew him from *around*. But, Gabrielle had heard his name enough to know that he was the one in *prime time* around here.

He was Dante Jackson, the most promising offensive left in the League after just one season, according to the announcers. And, after just two years, he was headline news as the most productive player that had ever graced Minnesota's roster. According to the people in the club, he was the playboy who could show up in the most common clothes, flashiest cars, and take home the prettiest girls. To his teammates and home boys, he was the life of the party; and to Gabrielle, he was fully attentive with genuine conversation and interest in her.

They enjoyed each other's conversation throughout the night. Dante took all Gabrielle's questions in stride, even when she put him on the defensive. She had brought up their department store experience and asked him if he'd had a chance to deliver all the clothes he bought for his different girlfriends. He told her that she needed to get it right. He didn't have a lot of girlfriends. He didn't have any girlfriends. All that stuff he had bought when he was in the store was for his mother and sisters down in Texas, 'since they don't have that type of stuff down there.'

She didn't believe him, so she gave him an evil, and *are you sure?* eye.

Snapshots

He continued to ask her: "What...? What...?" Then finally sunk back in his chair, smiling straight at her, but somehow looking at her from the corner of his eyes.

He was playful and funny, and maybe even a little sly, but there was a lot about Dante that Gabrielle had begun to like. He was able to talk seriously about college, and how much he respected her goals of becoming a writer, especially since he had wanted to become a veterinarian, but left school his junior year to enter the draft. He was level headed about the attention people gave him, and seemed to take it in stride.

And, when the Ques came out to step, Gabrielle saw another side of Dante. He was loud, boisterous, and he could really dance. He threw his arms in the air a few times. And once, he even got up from the table and started *dogging* with the line, right from where he stood.

When he sat back down, Gabrielle asked if he was a Que. He rolled up the sleeve on his t-shirt and showed her the double-horse-shoe-brand on his left arm. He was indeed.

When the step show was over, Dante went out to greet a few of his frats and exchange comments about how *bad* his own line used to be. Cassandra and Angelique returned to the table. Cassandra's attention was fully on the new guy she had met, and Angelique had simply grabbed the coats from the table and told Gabrielle that she was going to get the car; they were ready to go. With that, Angelique was headed for the valet. Cassandra was lagging a little ways behind her, with her arm in the guy's arm. She turned around just slightly to tell Gabrielle, she better hurry up or Angelique would end up leaving.

Dante had made it back to the table in time enough to hear that.

"Oh, boo, you better hurry up and catch your friends," he said.

"Well, I'm not ready to go just yet," Gabrielle answered.

"Well boo, they might leave you, and I...I just don't want you to be left here without a ride. I mean, I'm riding with my boys and all."

"I know how to catch a cab," Gabrielle said, snapping at him a little, but smiling.

"Oh, no, I mean. I'm just saying. There ain't no reason for you to stay here and all. I mean, I have your number; I'ma give you a call."

"What?" Gabrielle asked. She couldn't believe his nerve and made sure he knew it.

"Listen, I didn't come here with you and I didn't ask to leave with you, so if there's someone else you've got waiting for you, you can go on. You don't have to put it on your boys. I'm not asking you to sit here with me."

"Whooooa. I was just saying," Dante replied, making a 'slow down' motion with his hands.

"Well don't say anything more," Gabrielle returned.

Somehow Cassandra had realized that Gabrielle had not caught up to them, and she walked back over to remind Gabrielle to come on.

"Y'all can go on and leave me," Gabrielle announced to Cassandra, who looked puzzled that Gabrielle, who didn't want to come, now didn't want to leave.

Cassandra realized Dante Jackson was standing there as if he were waiting.

"Oh..." Cassandra said, looking at Gabrielle, as if to say: *You're leaving with him. I see why you waved us off.*

"No, I'm not," Gabrielle snapped her answer to Cassandra, who was even more puzzled by Gabrielle's saucy flavor.

Cassandra looked at Dante as if to ask what was going on. Dante simply shrugged as if to say he didn't know what was going on.

Gabrielle barely looked over to him, but she rolled her eyes at him just the same.

"Well then, let's go Gabrielle. You have a test at 9 in the morning."

"Cassandra, leave me!" Gabrielle demanded. "I can take a cab."

"Oookay! I was just saaaaying..." Cassandra began.

"Alright, well, I am just telling you," Gabrielle returned.

Cassandra was getting impatient. She had a cute guy waiting on her, and Gabrielle standing here with an attitude.

"Gabrielle, let's just go. You know you have a test..."

"Look, leave me!" Gabrielle demanded.

Cassandra said nothing more. She threw up her hands, shook her head, and walked toward the door.

"Aggressive!" Dante said, smiling and shaking his head. He had placed his hands on the table and looked like he was ready to sit down.

"For real, I told you. You can leave too," Gabrielle said with her arms folded.

"Baby, you sound tough, but I'm three hundred and twenty pounds. I don't think you can make me."

Gabrielle softened and agreed. "Okay, maybe you're right. But I bet I can make you do one thing."

"What is that?" he asked poking out his lips a little.

"Go get me a drink," she replied.

"You want a drink?"

"Is that a surprise?"

"Yeah, you don't strike me as the type."

"What's that supposed to mean?" she asked.

"I mean, you don't seem like a party girl. You seem kind of sa'ditty, kind of bookish."

"And what's that supposed to mean?" she folded her arms again, but playfully.

"Oh, nothing. I'm just a country boy. We can take shots for breakfast, but someone like you who..."

"Who what?" she seemed ready to demand.

"Look. Nothing," he said playfully, "I'm not getting ready to get into it with you again. I was just getting ready to say, my mama and sisters would have a fit if they thought I was out here corrupting someone as sweet as you. But I'm not saying nothing else. You a feisty thing. I'ma just go on and get your drink like you told me to."

He got up from the table pretending to bow to her as he continued to back away.

She laughed and smiled with him as he made a scene. But, as soon as he turned around to order her drink at the bar, she slipped away through the crowd to the outside of the club where she hailed a cab and went to the dorms.

chapter three

The next morning the phone woke Gabrielle up. She rolled over and answered it.

"Hey, what's up sunshine?" Dante began.

"Who is this?" Gabrielle asked.

"You know who this is. How you gon' play me last night?"

Gabrielle did not reply.

"Ey, I know you hear me. How you gon play me?" Dante asked again.

"Look, I know I don't know you all like that, but I guess I know enough to know that I wasn't the only female in there you were kicking it to or whatever. And I was just letting you know, you could go on and do your thing. I didn't want you thinking you had to be obligated to me."

"Ho, ho, hold it now. Me and you are supposed to be bigger than that...besides, a good old fashioned country boy like me. I didn't even feel right keeping someone like you out that late; there was too many hooligans."

Gabrielle didn't buy it, but replied "Yeah..."

"Yeah," Dante continued, "I told you. My mama and sisters would be all over me about corrupting someone wholesome and sweet like you."

Another: *Oh yeah* came from Gabrielle.

"Yeah. Serious. Besides that, I didn't want none of the hooligans there, besides me, to be talking to you."

They laughed a little, then Dante told her that she better get off the phone because she had class soon. He told her to just put on some clothes and hurry over to her class, since it was 8:45 and she had a test at nine. That hurried Gabrielle out of the bed, down the hall to wash up and get dressed. After she got back and grabbed her books, she ran out the door.

As soon as Gabrielle opened the dorm door, Dante was there holding a breakfast carry-out box in his hand.

"Hey!" Gabrielle gasped, shocked to see him.

"Hey you," he replied.

"What are you doing here?" she asked.

"I've been here all this time. I was waiting in my truck for you to come out for class, and when I didn't see you, I just had to call from my cell phone to wake you up. Plus, I had brought you breakfast."

He opened up a tray with muffins, eggs, ham, and an orange. She grabbed the orange and told him she had to run. He asked her to at least take a muffin, then lifted one out. She bit into the muffin, staring him in the face, then put it back in the tray. She turned back around quickly, waving a short goodbye, then ran to class.

He watched her jogging down the side walk. Finally he waved a small goodbye, though she was already gone. When he got back in his truck, the 'Old School Flashback' was playing on the radio. It was "Weak at the Knees" and the appropriate verse was on: *"Well I heard that you were hard to satisfy, mama, and I heard other men tried and were denied..."*

He took out the muffin and licked it where she had bit.

"Mmmmm," he groaned.

Dante pulled away from the campus, but had driven right into Gabrielle's life.

chapter four

Before they even knew it, Dante and Gabrielle were becoming continual parts of each other's lives. He was dropping by campus to bring her things or take her to work. Even though he rarely went to the library when he was a student himself, he was periodically going with Gabrielle. He helped her look for books, or lifted her to the shelves when she couldn't reach some of them. He'd visit with her in the parlor at her dorm, since male visitation wasn't allowed in their rooms. When the dorm got too noisy for her to study, or the parlor got too crowded from people finding out he was there, he started taking her to his place. Other than work or class, Gabrielle was with Dante: at his apartment, practices, or games. When the holidays came and she went back to Kenosha, they called each other every day. Dante called Gabrielle when he was finishing weight training, leaving work, in the hotels or airports when she couldn't make it to his away games.

They were an item. Everyone knew that, even though some people weren't too crazy about it.

Cassandra and Angelique rarely saw Gabrielle any more. The three of them were no where near as close as she, Michelle, and Yvette had been, yet Cassandra and Angelique had been friends with her since freshman year. It was the two of them who started bringing Gabrielle out of her shell.

Freshman year, they had invited Gabrielle home to D.C. with them. They took her to Shockwaves, the hottest D.C. salon, and had Terry give her a cut and style that made everyone compare her to Toni Braxton. Cassandra and Angelique, two pretty brown skinned girls, helped Gabrielle realize her own beauty and sex appeal when they took her home to D.C. and introduced her to their male friends.

The city guys were different. They had an appreciation for girls like Gabrielle. City guys liked nice bodies, and girls who kept their hair and nails done, wore nice clothes and shoes. And since Gabrielle had entered college, became friends with Cassandra and Angelique, and started working in the department store, she met every criteria that made the guys *eww and ahh*. Angelique assured

Snapshots

Gabrielle that these "big time hustlers' words meant much more than those hickey sticky little country boys who used to tease" her.

To be sure, Gabrielle had reveled in all the appreciation that the new people showed for her appearance, but she was still a plain girl at heart. So by sophomore year, she had let her hair grow back to medium length, and she usually kept it pulled back in a neat ball. She still kept her nails and toes painted, but instead of acrylics and designs, she did her own manicures and pedicures, and kept the nails painted clear.

Furthermore, she developed a deeper sense of appreciation for Michelle and Yvette. Even though they had gone separate ways during high school, they had always remained friends. And they were the kind of close knit friends that made them family, so even distance and time didn't make them feel as if they had been apart. They would always be able to pick right back up from wherever they had left off. They had grown up together, and they were more like sisters than friends. Michelle and Yvette had never thought about bringing Gabrielle's looks out. They had never seen each other as anything but the same little friends who had sat at Gabrielle's dining room table eating African grilled cheese sandwiches (which meant her mother had sliced them diagonally), or at Yvette's house visiting with her mom, brothers and sisters and taking in all the drama that came with that scene.

All of Gabrielle's friends had been good to her, and brought out the best in her from their own hidden talents, but after an incident with Cassandra and Angelique, Gabrielle longed for summer so she could go home and catch back up to her real friends.

Gabrielle had been so busy with classes, work, and Dante that she hadn't chatted with Cassandra and Angelique for months. But one day during late April, Cassandra and Angelique were in the department store shopping while Gabrielle was there to check out her work schedule. They almost didn't see each other; Angelique was picking out some shoes when Cassandra made a loud appeal for her to: 'Look who's here. Gabrielle.'

While Cassandra was dragging Angelique from the shoes to speak, Gabrielle was trying to explain to her manager that he had given her too many hours; she would have finals in less than three weeks. He flipped the schedule down and gave her a look that said 'Well missy, you don't have to work here.'

As he walked off, Cassandra followed him with her eyes, then neck. She was just about ready to say something to or about him when Gabrielle said how glad she was to see them.

"We're glad to see you too," Angelique replied.

"And she wouldn't have seen you, or even the king of Spain unless he was in those shoes. I had to drag her over here," Cassandra started.

"Oh stop!" Angelique began. "Anyway, Gabrielle knows how I am living for these banging shoes; and Jay-El has not been sending me money like he used to; so when it comes girl, I got to get out here and get what I can."

"What was that all about anyway?" Cassandra continued to Gabrielle.

"What? Oh...the manager?" Gabrielle asked.

"Yes girl. He needs to be unbothered; was he giving you the business, and for what?" Cassandra ran on.

"Oh, it's nothing big. Just my schedule," Gabrielle answered.

Angelique almost dropped her purse, but re-composed herself. Cassandra didn't have as much couth.

"Schedule. I know you're not still working here. Uhn uhn. Girl no. I thought you were in here just shopping like us," Cassandra began.

Angelique looked at Cassandra with a *shopping like us?* look, since Cassandra wasn't buying anything.

"Chile please. You can't be still working and you're with one of the most paid players on the team. No. What's the deal with that? And you practically living with him? We don't ever see you. I thought it was because you were with Mr. Jackson, not Mr. N&M's."

Cassandra would have kept going, but Angelique interrupted with: "Cassandra, please."

This gave Gabrielle a chance to speak.

"It's no big deal. I mean, I'm just working for my own money. What Dante makes is his. I have just always been independent."

Gabrielle was stammering over her words, but she didn't have to say too much more because Angelique interrupted.

"I know that's right girl. You got to be these days."

It would have seemed genuine, but Gabrielle saw Cassandra and Angelique slip snickering looks to one another.

Snapshots

"I got to go," Gabrielle responded and began walking away.

She vaguely heard them saying things like: *You take care girl* and *Well, alright then.* But when they had walked further away, she could hear them getting louder saying: *Uhn uhn, girl no.* That went on until maybe they made it back to the shoe department.

It might have been longer than that, but Gabrielle was out of the City Center's doors and getting into Dante's truck, well rid of her college friends' jeers.

"What's the matter boo?" was Dante's first question when Gabrielle got in the truck. She told him that nothing was wrong, but by the time they got back to his apartment and she hadn't hugged, kissed, or been playful with him, he knew something was wrong. And when she was supposed to be in the back bedroom studying, but came out and laid across his lap on the couch, he was sure something was bothering her.

"Boo, you've got a lot of studying to do. What's on your mind more than your school work, and even more than me?" he ended playfully.

She sighed and stared over at the game he was watching for a while. He played in her loose hair, smoothing it back with his finger tips, then gently turned her face toward him.

"What's wrong boo?" he asked again.

This time she looked toward the ceiling and thought she was making a full explanation.

"It's nothing. It's just that girls are so petty and jealous."

He wanted more than that, so she told him about the run in she had with Cassandra and Angelique; and he reminded her of what she already knew, not all girls were like that.

He also told her that sometimes people don't even realize they're making mistakes that will stick in someone's head like this was doing to her. She agreed with him, but said she still couldn't wait to get home to be with her real friends. Dante told Gabrielle she wasn't going anywhere until she had aced her finals. He lifted her from the couch and patted her butt to send her back to the guest bedroom.

A few hours later, he went to the kitchen to make her a sandwich, then headed down the back hall to peek in on her and make sure she ate. Gabrielle was sprawled across the bed, face down and asleep with all her books and materials scattered over the bed and floor. He cleared a couple of the books that were close to her side and then sat next to her. That didn't wake her, so he rubbed her back. When his touch didn't get her up, he bounced up and down while seated on the bed. That made roller coaster, if not seismic waves, and she woke up, shocked that she had fallen asleep.

"See boo, now, I'ma hafta come down on you. Get up. Get your sandwich, and let's get in these books," Dante said, passing her the sandwich, then picking up books and starting to quiz her.

The study session paid off. Less than three weeks later, Gabrielle was at Dante's house collecting many of her clothes and things so she could pack for the summer and head home. She heard him come in the apartment, drop the keys on his coffee table then fall down onto the couch. This was typical after a day of off season conditioning. He was exhausted and lying down on the couch. But when she sprang out into the den, kissed him on the forehead, and waved her grades in front of him, he sat up and pulled her beside him. He told her while kissing her cheeks then lips how proud of her he was.

"Now, you can go home. Even though, I don't want you to," he said to her.

Dante was just romancing her, she knew. He was going home to Dallas himself for a few weeks after mini-camp was over. He wanted to spend some time with his family before training camp started.

After Gabrielle had packed her suitcase at Dante's, they went to the dorm to pick up the rest of her items. She and some dorm mates dragged her trunks through the halls. Dante waited in the parlor, and after asking her and her dorm mates (who were huffing and puffing) if they were okay, he lifted one trunk over his head and started walking toward the truck. Gabrielle and another girl were pushing the other trunk, but they were far behind him. He peeked back a few times and kept teasing by asking if she was alright.

chapter five

Along the ride to the train station, Gabrielle gave Dante several instructions about storing her things at his place. It didn't seem like she stopped giving him instructions until they arrived at the station and she asked him what all he was supposed to do. When he ran the list back to her, she simply stated, 'okay' and hopped out the truck.

"Uh, excuse me," he called out to her, as she headed toward the station.

She turned her face back toward him, smiled, but kept walking.

"Gabrielle! Gabrielle..." he began hollering out the window. "Don't make me get out of this truck, Gabrielle," he playfully warned.

She kept walking across the island, and started slightly running, knowing that he would soon be behind her. True to what she had expected, he had come jogging behind her.

"Hey girl. Hey..." he said as he caught up to her.

She turned around, and looked at him confused. "You talking to me, Mr.?"

He frowned at her a little, but then smiled. "You know you forgot something, right?"

"Did I?" she pretended.

"Yeah, and if you make me get my truck towed, all your things are going to be in somebody's junk yard."

"Hmm. Well maybe, I do remember what I forgot."

"Good," he said, waiting for her to jump up to try to kiss his lips; instead, she slapped him on the butt, like he had done to her earlier when she was struggling with one of the trunks. She got ready to run off after that, but he reached out, grabbed her by the waist, pulled her into him to kiss her goodbye.

"Make sure you call me when you get there," he told her.

"I will," she called back as she ran into the station.

chapter six

Gabrielle didn't realize that getting home would make her forget so many things about school, including her promise to call Dante as soon as she got there. But it couldn't be helped. Things were somewhat out of sync when she arrived at the station on the outskirts of her town. She had walked around the lobby looking for her mother. She didn't even have her phone card with her, so she couldn't make any calls. Just when she thought to call Dante collect, Michelle came into the station dragging little Michael by the hand, and carrying Michellene in her arms.

"Girol, I am so sorry," Michelle began after kissing Gabrielle on the cheek.

"Your mom had called and asked me could I make it out here to get you, because her car is in the shop. I couldn't leave MJ and Michellene with Michael because he had a case to work on, so at the last minute I had to get them ready and drag them along. And this one..." Michelle said pointing to little Michael.

"Oh, he's a cutie pie," Gabrielle began. "Give Ti Ti Rielle kisses," she continued, leaning toward Michael, who moved away from her and closer to his mother.

Michelle pushed Michael back toward Gabrielle.

"Boy you are not shy. Give Gabrielle a hug, boy."

"Oh, he's okay," Gabrielle said reaching out for his hand, which he snatched away.

Michelle and Gabrielle were walking toward the car and catching each other up on things. Little Michael started interrupting them and talking to Gabrielle.

Gabrielle didn't get a chance to talk much about Dante, because Michelle was busily talking about Michael, the condo he had bought, and how well things were going for them.

Gabrielle was happy for Michael and Michelle. They had been together since Michelle was a senior in highschool, and he was beginning law school. In the mean time, they had moved in together, had children and though they weren't married, and Michelle hadn't mentioned if they ever would be, they were still together, and things were going well.

When they made it into town, Michael and Michellene were sleep. Gabrielle wanted to see Yvette, so they stopped by her mother's where she, her daughter Jasmine, her brothers, sisters and mother were living. Gabrielle and Michelle took one child each and headed up the front sidewalk.

They could hear an argument from outside. It was Yvette, yelling at her brother, asking what he had done to make her baby cry. Her brother, rebellious and fourteen, thought he was grown enough to tell Yvette that: *ain't nobody done nothing to Jasmine; she just spoiled as...*

Yvette interrupted him right there to call out to her sister who was hanging clothes in the back yard with her own daughter and Jasmine sitting in the grass. Her sister called back, nonchalantly, and said that Jasmine was upset over a popsicle.

That was enough for fireworks from Yvette. She had paid for those popsicles and *wasn't none of these crumb snatchers going to be eating up Jasmine's stuff and then acting like Jasmine didn't have a right to cry.*

Her mother came upstairs, with the usual: *Vette please.* Yvette's mother had stopped asking: *What's this all about?* years ago, because she knew with Yvette, it didn't matter. Any argument was a good argument, as long as it got her heart rate up.

This is what Gabrielle and Michelle walked in to. No surprises. When Gabrielle gave an excited: *Hey girl* and hug to Yvette, and Yvette responded with a dry repeat, Gabrielle took Yvette's face in her hands, and asked her: "I can't get no more love than that?"

"Aren't you in college?" Yvette said. "Why are you coming home with these double negatives? And how long are you going to be here anyway? I heard you have some boyfriend now. You better not be having sex."

She had to be a smart alack, but that was Yvette; she had been quick with her tongue ever since they were kids.

They all made it to the front porch, where they had been meeting up with each other on every break since Gabrielle had left for college. They talked and caught up with what had been going on since Christmas; Michelle and Yvette had been left in the dark about Dante updates since Gabrielle *didn't even bother to write any more.* Yvette's words.

They couldn't get too far into what was going on with

Gabrielle, because Ollie, Jasmine's father was riding down the street on the passenger's side of his friend's hooptie. When he called out: *hey baby girl* to Jasmine, Yvette lit into him. She told him that he wasn't Jasmine's father. He told Yvette that he would get out the car and beat her narrow black behind. When Yvette asked him: "Why, cause I'm telling the truth? You ain't bought one pamper, one barrette, one shoe out of a pair for that matter. You ain't done nothing. You ain't nothing."

He replied with what he knew would really enrage her; he leaned out the window laughing, and blew Yvette a kiss, then reminded her that Jasmine was still his 'baby girl.'

Yvette ran off the porch and lifted a brick from her mother's flower garden and flung it at the car. The guy slammed on the breaks, and Ollie jumped out.

Yvette was already yelling: "What nigga? What? What you gon do? You gonna hit me? Come on. If they won't get you for child support, they need to get you for something, and I wanna be just that chick that makes them come."

Ollie had no intentions of hitting Yvette. He just liked to antagonize her. It was that sassy part of her personality that first attracted him to Yvette anyway. So after standing for a minute and squaring her down from a distance, he laughed and pointed to her. Then told Jasmine he'd be back for her later. By then, Jasmine was crying and lying her head on Michelle's lap, and Michael was clutching Michelle's other leg. Yvette made her last statement to Ollie.

"You're a sick nigga. You are. You are. I wish you would just stop coming around here."

No one had tried to calm Yvette down. They knew after all these years that she was going to be her own way, and she would settle herself. When she did, they picked right back up where they had stopped. Although briefly into the conversation, Michelle threw in how Yvette shouldn't make scenes like that in front of Jasmine, who was still leaning onto Michelle.

"Don't worry about mine Michelle. You got enough to worry about on your own," Yvette retorted.

"Alright now," Gabrielle began. Then they went back and forth about who was right or wrong from Michelle's comments, until they found their way to more pleasing topics. By the time they realized they were having a great time, the kids were really ready for bed, and Gabrielle realized she needed to hustle home and meet Dante's next call. For sure, he had called a few times.

chapter seven

Danielle, Gabrielle's mother, was at the back of the house with her live-in boyfriend, Reggie. They were having coffee. It didn't matter that it was nearly midnight, Danielle drank coffee around the clock; it was probably from years of working the swing swift. She heard Gabrielle dragging her suitcases along the hardwood floors in the hallway, and motioned for Reggie to go help her. Reggie walked the suitcases through the kitchen then up the stairs to Gabrielle's room, and set them outside of her door. Danielle waved Gabrielle over to the table, then stood up partially to hug and kiss her daughter.

"Well, where have you been, Miss Danyella Davis?" her mother asked. She knew that Gabrielle had been with her friends, but she also knew if she called Gabrielle's middle name, Danyella, Gabrielle would know that she was a little upset with her for not coming home first.

Knowing that her mother was upset, Gabrielle just shrugged. Her mother continued: "Where's Michelle anyway? How come she didn't come in and speak?"

"Well, she had the kids; they were asleep, plus she had to get back to the city," Gabrielle answered.

"She had the kids? Michael usually keeps them when she has something to do."

Gabrielle explained that he had a major case he was representing, and needed them to go with Michelle. Danielle talked about how Michelle had really hit *the big time*, with her attorney boyfriend, new condo, children, and the good life they had. Danielle was equally impressed that Michelle had him *wrapped around her fingers*. Michael was a provider and watched the kids whenever Michelle needed him to, if he wasn't on a case.

Gabrielle challenged her mother about what was so good that Michelle had landed a life where she was just basically living off of someone else, a man at that. She and her mother had argued about this before. Her mother always ended the discussion with her absolute: "Michelle's making it. She could have ended up with somebody who wouldn't have done anything for her. Men out here don't want to take care of children and a family. They're looking for someone to take care of them. Michelle was smart enough to pick someone who did it all. Most of these guys have their picks and choices of all kind of girls who put up with everything. And they could make a baby, run off, come back, whatever. But Michelle has a good man that stayed with her. And that is a rare find."

Her mother could have gone on praising Michelle further, but the phone was ringing, and Reggie was on his way to work. Danielle walked him to the door, and Gabrielle ran up the stairs to her room to get the phone.

It was Dante. He fired off a line of questions about where she had been and why she hadn't called, and if she had a man at home that made her forget all about him. They teased and played on the phone until they both nearly fell asleep. Then he told her they better get off the line. She figured it was because he had an early morning strength training. She didn't know he had a 2 a.m. beep on the other line. They cut the conversation short that night, but talked every night while Gabrielle was at home.

Gabrielle spent three weeks running in and out of the house with Michelle and Yvette. They were at the park, the mall, the skating rink, getting ice cream, a backyard cookout at Yvette's. They were having so much fun with each other and the kids that they talked about all the lost time they had missed by going separate ways in highschool. This was Michelle's doing.

One night they left the kids with Yvette's mom, and went to a local bar to have a few drinks. Yvette could have two or three drinks and be fine. Gabrielle wasn't a drinker, and Michelle shouldn't have been either.

Mid-way into Michelle's first drink, she went melodramatic on them about how they 'used to play dolls and hopscotch, oookaaay...' She remembered when one of them dropped tabasco on her lips because she was the first to fall asleep at one of the slumber parties. 'Nobody was mad.'

They didn't get mad about anything in those days—not with each other. So, Michelle just needed to know "What in the world happened? How did things change so much in highschool?"

Gabrielle and Yvette assured Michelle that they hadn't changed; it just seemed like they got into different things.

"It's still one love, and you know that Michelle. Ain't nothing changed because we are all still here together." That was Yvette, sobering the moment.

Gabrielle was unknowingly encouraging it by still trying to comfort Michelle. But that's not what Michelle really wanted. "Michelle, just wanted to go on and on and on about something," and Yvette "didn't even feel like hearing it," so she put a stop to it.

The minute Yvette did, the music hit Michelle. It was the early 90's, but the d-jay liked to "take the turn tables back," especially toward the end of the night. "You've Got the Best of My Love" had come on. Michelle got onto a new subject of how they better not ever let 'no man use them' especially Gabrielle since she 'got in the game late and ain't never had a man before.'

Gabrielle knew that she didn't know a lot; she was: "...naive and this was her first go round, but she had somebody good, plus she had common sense, and she had goals of her own, nobody was getting in the way of that." Those were Michelle's words. After she said that, she pointed, first to Yvette then to Gabrielle saying: "Cause you my girl, and you my girl, and any nigga ever get over on you, he's mine."

Yvette was rolling her eyes, but Michelle thought she had their full support and continued: "I mean it. I mean it. Y'all know that right? Y'all my girls and I got your back."

Once again, Gabrielle had gotten drawn into Michelle's drama by agreeing with her; Yvette flat out said: "That's it. I'm ready."

Michelle wanted to order one more drink before the bar closed, but Yvette was heading things up, even though Gabrielle was driving.

"We're leaving Michelle. Now, you can stay down here if you want to, but we're gone," Yvette demanded.

For a minute, Gabrielle had stood in the middle of them, Yvette leaving the table, and Michelle still seated. She wanted to tell Yvette that they couldn't just leave Michelle there, but Yvette called Gabrielle one more time, then pulled her hand and they walked away from the table. Michelle was still there, trying to wave the bartender over for 'a little drinky drink drink.'

This was a part of their relationship Gabrielle had never seen. They hadn't hung out as teenagers, so as a young adult, she was a little confused. But Yvette knew what she was doing. She knew Michelle well. As soon as she and Gabrielle were unlocking the car, Michelle was making her way toward them, first telling them how she couldn't stand them, and then getting in the car saying how much she loved them.

During the ride home, Michelle had fallen asleep, and it was decided that they would just head to Yvette's. Once they made it there and into the house, Michelle wanted coffee and breakfast. That was reasonable. It was nearly 4 a.m., so they worked together making breakfast, then reminisced and enjoyed themselves. By 7 a.m. they were lying over each other on the living room couch and floor. Even though it seemed like old times, they woke up with one thing that had changed. Kids. They were looking for mommy, cereal, or the bathroom. Jasmine and Yvette were in the kitchen, and Michelle was propping Michael on her lap to give him a kiss and to tell him to go get 'Che Che', his baby sister, from upstairs.

The morning scene lead to their last controversial topic: when was Gabrielle going to have kids. This question was of course initiated by Michelle. Yvette had made it back into the front, with Jasmine following behind, carefully balancing her cereal, because she knew her granny would not want spills on the carpet.

Yvette was totally against Gabrielle even thinking about kids. The conversation was more between Yvette and Michelle who felt life didn't stop after children, and that plenty of people finished college with a kid, or two. Yvette didn't care about any of that. She told Gabrielle to take care of 'number one' and not to start with any children. Michelle said that with the right man, kids and family could be perfect. Yvette seemed to be telling the entire household that you can't pick a perfect man, because the same one in an Armani suit or Versace shades would be spending his money there, and not on a gallon of milk. And that college degrees, good families, nice clothes or cars don't show a man's true value.

Michelle felt Yvette was just hostile because Ollie was such a bad seed, but that Yvette had known that in the beginning.

Yvette guaranteed her that 'I'ma take care of mine; that ain't no problem' and that Jasmine had never wanted for a thing in her life, but that was because Yvette could provide it. She told Gabrielle to make sure she could take care of herself first so she wouldn't have to worry about the man being good or bad, 'regardless.'

Snapshots

What confused Gabrielle most was why Michelle and Yvette were going back and forth about her having children. Gabrielle had already decided for herself. She was going to complete her creative writing degree first, then think about children and marriage or however the combination would come. Right now, she was just glad that she had half of college out of the way. So that settled the conversation down. And when they parted for the day, they all double kissed each others' cheeks and things were back to normal.

When Gabrielle walked into the house, her mother was on her way out to work. She patted Gabrielle's face to hers and told Gabrielle that she should think about spending some of her time with her mother. Then Danielle informed Gabrielle of something she already knew, Dante had been calling all night. But it was day time rates now, and Gabrielle better just call him later or wait for him to call again.

As soon as her mother was pulling out the driveway with Reggie, Gabrielle sent Dante a sky page. It took him a little while, but he called back from the weight room. He wasn't just telling her how much he missed her and asking where she had been all night. She had expected that, and she even expected him to request that she give him the number next time or page him so he knows she's alright.

She was in Kenosha, she reminded him. She could sleep outside all night naked, and the most someone would do would be to put some clothes on her and take her home.

That lead him to a brief diversion of asking her what she had on, and if she would go up to her room and take it off. When she screeched at him: *Dante, I'm at my mom's*, he was semi-apologetic, and said: *"I know boo."* Nevertheless, he got right back on the subject by asking when she was going to be there at his house. They talked about how she had three more weeks in Wisconsin, and the fact that he was going to Dallas for at least a week to visit his family before camp started. He told her that his plans to go to Dallas had changed, and that he wanted hers to change too. He wanted her back in Minnesota with him, immediately, and he said everything he could to convince her to come back.

And his last line: "Boo, I'm lonely," confirmed her arrival.

When Gabrielle had spent two full days with her mother, Danielle knew something was going on, so she asked Gabrielle. Danielle was astute, but Gabrielle was also obvious.

She asked if Gabrielle was going back to be with 'that guy', something that Danielle didn't seem too thrilled about. Gabrielle denied that, and said she had a lot of paperwork in order to renew her scholarship, and she had to start getting some things in order, maybe do community service or go to some meetings as part of the scholarship renewal.

It all sounded made up because it was. Danielle explained to Gabrielle that as long as she had no ties to a man, she shouldn't chain herself. Gabrielle almost wanted an explanation, since her mother seemed to adore Michelle's situation; nevertheless, she realized that her mother admired some things for other people, but aspired for Gabrielle to live her life differently.

Just the same, when Michelle and Yvette pulled up in the driveway, Gabrielle had her mother helping her carry her things to the car. She promised her mother that she had legitimate reasons, but Danielle simply told Gabrielle that she was grown now, so whatever she was doing, she was the one who would have to deal with it. She stood firm in what she had taught Gabrielle growing up, once she was eighteen, she was responsible for herself. Danielle was perfectly fine with Gabrielle's decisions so far, and felt sure that Gabrielle would continue to do well. She gave her daughter a tight hug, fared her well, then reached in the car to speak to Michelle and Yvette. When they backed out the driveway, Danielle stood watching for a moment, then headed back in the house.

The ride to the train station seemed longer than it was. Unbelievably, they were engaged in another dispute. Yvette had spearheaded this one. She raked Gabrielle over the coals for cutting the visit short, and asked every question about who Dante was and who he thought he was. Gabrielle promised that she'd be back soon. Maybe a week or two after the 4th.

Gabrielle rode back to Minnesota with pleasant thoughts. Her friends were really her friends. They had experienced such a good time together, and they were as close as ever, just like sisters, just like always. And her mother had shed some insight on her feelings about Gabrielle being mature enough to make the right decisions. This was something Danielle hadn't done before.

Danielle had always been a hard worker and provider. She had always wanted the best for Gabrielle and set high expectations for her. Gabrielle usually lived up to them, but Danielle never praised

Gabrielle for the things she was just expected to do. She rarely even talked to Gabrielle about her feelings or pride in what she felt Gabrielle could do. She spent most of her life working and trying to take care of them. So, this felt good. Gabrielle had gotten a rare, warm moment with her mother, who told her she had pride and confidence in her abilities.

And to top it all off, Dante was missing her. She had friends who would always be there, a mother who believed in her, and a man in her life that was absolutely adorable and wonderful. He couldn't make it through a day without calling her, and now he couldn't make it through the summer without seeing her.

So, she was going back, heading to home away from home, Dante Jackson.

chapter eight

In Minnesota, the train station was full of people coming and going; it was close to the 4th of July. Gabrielle put her bags on a cart because she knew Dante would be outside. He couldn't come inside the train station. He had finished his third year with the team, so they had just re-negotiated his contract. His salary and signing bonus had been in the paper and on the news, so he couldn't get people to give him any space. He told her as many guys as girls kept coming in his face.

She had teasingly asked him about the girls, and he told her, in his serious but smooth way: "You know I don't be entertaining that biz."

As much as she loved what he said, she loved the way he said it. He had a lot of heart, a lot of personality, and was bubbly almost all the time, but he was also smooth, and she liked that in him.

Even though she knew she was meeting him outside, when she got out there, she stood looking all around. He wouldn't come in, she knew that much, but he also wouldn't be late; she thought she knew that much.

Dante was sitting on the passenger's side of his truck talking to a rookie team mate. He checked his watch and wondered what was taking Gabrielle so long. He looked out to his right and saw her looking around from the curb. He had forgotten; he had gotten rid of his Land Cruiser and bought a new Hummer. She didn't know that, and he jumped out to go get her. When he got over to her, he picked up her bags, pecked her lips and asked: 'Hey girl, you didn't see me?'

She told him of course she didn't. He pointed to the new truck and told her that's where he had been. When she told him that she hadn't even looked into that, he felt good. Lots of girls that he knew would have stared through the tint if the windows had been up, just to see who was in that Hummer. He smiled and hugged his arm around Gabrielle's shoulders. Not only was she not scoping out that truck, but she obviously wasn't looking at any guys; that's the way he took it.

Dante introduced Gabrielle to Lawrence; he was a rookie

Snapshots

from just outside of Dallas so Dante had taken Lawrence under his wing. Lawrence had gotten picked up in the seventh round, so it would be a long while before he'd be driving like this. Dante had an 850ci and motorcycle as well, so he didn't mind letting Lawrence sport his Hummer around town. The only thing Dante was telling Lawrence about the truck right now was how to navigate it to Gabrielle's dorm. That started an argument. It was playful at first, then heated.

Gabrielle informed Dante that she could not stay at the dorms; she thought he knew that. When he asked what she was talking about, she jokingly repeated 'whatchewtalkinboutGabrielle?' When he turned around to the back seat and told her he really wanted to know why she wasn't staying in the dorm, she almost blew up.

Gabrielle didn't know why he was having such a problem with her staying at his place, since she had been practically staying with him all of the last semester. Plus, she had stored her things at his place for a reason, because all but one dorm was closed during the summer, and she couldn't stay there anyway because her scholarship was only for the academic years. To top it all off, he was the one who called with: *Gabrielle I miss you. Gabrielle I'm lonely*, and she could have still been at home if he wouldn't have been begging her to come back. Now, he didn't even want her at his place.

Dante made sure that Gabrielle knew, he didn't have to beg for anything. That was first. If he could have gotten in a word earlier while she was complaining, he would have offered to pay for her a room in the dorm: *It couldn't have been more than what, a thousand?* So he told her that, secondly.

Just when she got ready to shoot off another argument from that, he interrupted with: "Besides all that, I got my boy staying here with me. This is my homey from D's up."

That lead Gabrielle into questioning how he would tell her she couldn't stay because he had a friend there. Lawrence repeatedly told Dante that he could leave, and just stay at the team's complex, but Dante kept waving him off, and trying to tell Gabrielle they'd figure something out. Her solution was simple. "Take me back to the train station Dante. I can go home for all of this."

"Then what's going to happen to all your stuff at my house? I'll just throw it away," he said teasing her.

"Well then you just do that," she shot back.

Maybe Gabrielle had spent too much time getting argument lessons from Yvette, or maybe Dante had just never given her a reason to confront him in this manner. But it didn't matter. She was fuming, and she was letting him "have it."

Dante just leaned back in his seat and kept giving Lawrence directions on where to turn. Gabrielle was staring out the window, so mad, that she didn't even realize Dante was giving Lawrence directions to his apartment complex.

chapter nine

With the three of them staying in the apartment, Dante made some modifications on Gabrielle's conduct there. Even though Lawrence was staying at the far opposite end of the hall and had his own bathroom, Gabrielle wasn't to use the third and common bathroom; she could only use the one in Dante's master bedroom.

Lawrence was on a pre-camp rookie training schedule, so he was out of the house far earlier than Dante, even still, Gabrielle could not walk around in her typical thong and t-shirt because 'Lawrence could accidentally forget something and come back.'

Dante was so over protective of Gabrielle when it came to her being around his single friends that he almost seemed to be insane. He knew she wasn't interested in those guys, but one time when she told him that, he said very sharply that it didn't matter, because she: *didn't know how those niggas are.*

There was no real logic behind his argument. Even though some of the guys would switch up with the hottest chicks, compare notes, only to talk about them and throw them away, Gabrielle wasn't a hot chick. Furthermore, they were right in Dante's home. With all Dante's hospitality, he couldn't have thought Lawrence would take that for granted. And moreover, Dante should have known her well enough to realize that she wouldn't have matched any other offers that his team mates or anyone else could make. He was her first love and she was head over heals with him. He knew that.

But Dante's argument wasn't based on Gabrielle or Lawrence's behavior. It was grounded in his own knowledge of himself. Though he didn't say this to Gabrielle, he knew there were certain temptations where he *couldn't help it*. But, moreover, he just really wanted to make sure that she was all his, always. Still, it wasn't his style to explain that. When the thoughts rushed into his head, he just started making demands.

He would have continued arguing with Gabrielle, but she walked back toward his master bedroom and shut the door. He opened it and continued arguing for a moment, but when she was looking more disappointed than angry, he stopped.

Later he crawled across the bed, where she was sitting up and reading. He laid diagonally across the bed and placed his head on one of her legs then looked up at her and asked: 'You mad at me boo?'

She shook her head no, but he kept telling her that she was. It wasn't until she started stroking his eyebrows and forehead, that he knew she wasn't mad. But those actions lead to others, like him lying her back and kissing all over her face.

He normally just ran his finger tips through her hair, but he was rubbing her head, and grabbing all the parts of her body he loved. It had been so long since he made love to her. Going beyond two days was like a drought. Sometimes he and Gabrielle had spent an entire day, throughout the apartment having passionate and creative venues; but since Lawrence had been staying with them, Dante kept his and Gabrielle's love making to a minimum. He didn't want Lawrence to get any ideas.

Still, he missed making love to Gabrielle. She was a great lover. Even though he was her first, and he had to be patient and teach her things in the beginning, she was creative enough to almost blow his mind at times. She was a writer, and her imagination went far beyond the pen. He couldn't forget the day that she had lain him across the bed on his stomach and rubbed his entire back down, from head to foot she massaged him. And when she had warmed him up just enough, she turned him over and placed cold pineapple rings around the center of his body, and gently went around in circles, biting them off.

When he flinched from how cold the pineapple rings were, she assured him, she'd warm him up in a minute, and she did. She drizzled heavy drops of hot fudge at the tip of his center, then made him feel warm all over. She was the most creative lover he'd ever had.

Today, he didn't make love. He was in need, so he was greedy for her whole body, and after he took her all in, he fell over on his back and put his arm around her. He patted her on the stomach with his other arm, and told her: "You're getting a little chunky there aren't you boo?"

They talked about that for a minute, but then the subject changed to some of the things that they would have to do over the next few days.

Snapshots

Lawrence was moving out. He was heading back toward Dallas for the last few days before camp. He was homesick, so he wouldn't be back until the day they all left for Mankato. In the mean time, Dante was going to limit the number of times and the number of friends who just came in and out visiting. During the Season and the early off season, it seemed like Gabrielle and Dante only saw his friends here or there, sometimes at the apartment, but most times when they went out to eat or had a few informal get togethers. However, with the arrival of the new guys, it seemed like Dante was playing host and big brother constantly. The guys were there playing video games, having rap sessions, giving and getting advice about other players' moves, different team strategies, who gives the best comps, and girls.

The first two topics were discussed at a bare minimum; comps was a hot topic, since they always seemed to discover some new place that was offering them a deal; but, girls and their conniving ways was the hot topic, especially for veterans, those who had lived enough of their lives in the club to have seen it all. They loved to school the rookies on the kind of girls to watch out for.

When it came down to it, the only way to know if somebody truly had your back was to: *Go back to those days in college and find that girl who really stayed down for you.* Or better yet, some of the guys talked about ...*those days in the hood when you didn't have nothing, and going pro was a dream for you and a joke to others. That girl who was with you then, like in high school; she was down.*

They couldn't find girls like that now. And it was most likely because they never gave the decent girls a chance.

If they saw a moral looking girl in the club, they by-passed her. They wanted to have the best time with the hottest looking girls, yet they complained how women weren't about anything. It was almost paradoxical that the guys picked the girls who seemed easiest, but then complained that the women out there didn't have substance, when that wasn't what they were looking for in the first place.

Even when they met pretty girls who had goals and ambitions and probably would have been decent partners, they rushed her into bed with the promise that everything would still be *all good* between them. Of course, the guys didn't stay with the girl much longer, and the excuse was: "She was just looking to get some too, otherwise she would have waited."

Dante never let Gabrielle stick around when he was *parlaying with the fellas*. She didn't want to either. She hated those discussions, and she could hear them even when she was closed away in the bedroom. Dante never seemed to say much about women, or maybe he kept his voice lower, but when they got heated enough, Gabrielle could hear his team mates' conversations through the closed door.

They could be upset because a girl had been talking to one of them, then the next week (after he had dumped her) he saw her with a bigger named teammate or an NBA player, entertainer or baller. She was a groupie then. It didn't matter that whoever she was with had pursued her, just like the guy before; she was the scandalous one.

They didn't all have bad things to say. Some of the guys would chime in: "That's why I'm glad I just went on and got married." Or, "That's why I got my same girl from home." If she wasn't there, he'd be sending for her in a little while.

The guys never really seemed to give new girls a chance. There was always something wrong with that girl, and there was always an excuse waiting for her. They could dress it up differently. It could start off: "You seem to be nice and all. You're attractive, have a good head on your shoulders but I can't be sure if you're really after me or my money. I have to have someone who I know will have my back."

Many of the guys had no intentions on even giving the girls a chance to show them that much. So the bottom line of their excuse, no matter how they altered the words, came down to: "There's only one woman I trust, and sorry, it's not you."

Gabrielle had gathered that about the other guys, and a few times she thought she heard Dante concede to some of those common experiences with them. She wondered how he felt about their relationship.

She and Dante could get into discussions about many things, but whenever she asked how he viewed her, he only had one line:

"Oh, you straight; you straight with me."

She wanted more than that. She asked him if he saw her the way his friends saw some girls. He told her that first of all she shouldn't be in his conversations, and that secondly she couldn't compare the situations. She was his girl, and those girls his team mates talked about were *just out there*. Some of them were in school, some of them had good jobs, some of them had a kid, or a man already; but none of them were relationship material.

Gabrielle wondered if Dante saw her as relationship material. She hadn't been with him any of those days when he was "in the hood" nor had she been his girl in college. She hadn't known nor stuck by him when he "didn't have anything" so she wondered if he was just passing time with her before he would go back to his college or hometown girl.

She was ridiculous, he told her. He had been with her for nearly a year now, hadn't he? Didn't she know anything from that? She was with him almost every night and day. She hadn't seen or heard about anyone else, wasn't that enough? All his friends knew who she was and that he was crazy about her. He didn't want anyone else around her long enough to think about having her; what more did she need from him? He obviously appreciated her, otherwise he wouldn't have kept her around this long.

Those were argument words. Who did Dante think he was to say that he had kept her around? She demanded an answer for that. He smoothed it over by saying that both of them had a choice. He respected the fact that she wouldn't have stayed around if she didn't really care about him too. So it was settled. Either of them could have left the other, but they had stayed together; that showed something.

This was Gabrielle's first relationship, so she didn't want to over react, or be petty, but she felt that he could have done a better job at making her feel at ease. She wondered how other guys resolved situations like this, but he told her that she couldn't compare him to how anyone else would handle things. Different people handled things differently.

Furthermore he told her that her friends 'couldn't speak on' his 'situation.' He said their lifestyles were too different to compare.

Some parts of his statement sounded right; but Gabrielle learned to divide what he had said. Careers and lifestyles didn't determine behavior. As long as people were human, there were some good actions or terrible mistakes that any of them could make. He knew that deep down inside, and she learned that, the longer she stayed with him.

chapter ten

There were only a few more days before Dante would be departing for camp. He had finished planning out their agenda for the next few days, and the last thing on the list was to attend a charity basketball game at one of the estates that Peaches had rented out.

Peaches ran a not for profit organization that put on a myriad of events that interspersed athletes from NFL, NBA and MLB with any of the public who were willing to pay to attend the events. Most of the proceeds went to charity.

Dante was always one of the featured attractions for these events; so, he and Gabrielle had attended quite a few, but Gabrielle was never enthusiastic. Today was no different. Dante was getting himself dressed, and patting her on the butt as she went between their bedroom and bathroom back to the walk-in closet, trying on different outfits.

"Boo, what's wrong with you?" Dante asked after her fourth outfit was lying across the bed. "Nothing looks right to you, and everything is fine. I liked all the ones you put on," he said.

"They just feel funny," Gabrielle whined. "And they look funny. They look tight."

Dante would have disagreed, but he did think she was getting a little chubby, so he used this moment to remind her. "Well boo, I did tell you, you are getting a little big. Maybe you need to start doing some exercise."

When Gabrielle looked ready to burst into tears, he paused, but decided to continue.

"I mean don't get me wrong, I love a girl with a petite body and junk in the trunk, but you don't want to let it get too out of control. You are short now. So you got to remember that."

Gabrielle was getting ready to fire a line of questions, but he stopped her quick and cold.

"Look Gabrielle, just get dressed. We'll worry about the weight thing later. We got to go, alright?"

He wasn't really asking a question; he was telling her. So, she put on the first, most free-flowing dress she could find, and they sped to the game in silence. Gabrielle had made Dante late, and she could tell he was upset. When they pulled up, he told her to park the car, then he jumped out and headed inside.

Peaches greeted him at the door, and told him not to worry that he was late because a few other players had gotten caught in some traffic. He still wanted to go upstairs and get changed for the game. He was a natural competitor, and wanted to practice some of his basketball shots before the others got to the court anyway.

Peaches encouraged him to head off with her; there were quite a few girls who wanted to meet him. They had actually bought the roof top VIP seating so they could mingle with him over hors d'oeuvres. He told Peaches that he was there with his girl, and wasn't interested in meeting any girls. He asked her to just be on the look out for his girl because he was going to get changed.

Gabrielle arrived at the door a little while afterwards. When Peaches opened the door, she asked Gabrielle for her pass. Gabrielle explained that she was there for Dante, and didn't have a pass. Peaches told her that there were many girls there for Dante, but if she wanted to meet him, she needed a ticket for the game, and a VIP pass to go to the roof. Peaches had not forgotten that Dante said his girl was coming, but Gabrielle was dressed too plain and looked too ordinary to even seem like Dante's type. So Peaches continued telling her that if she didn't have a ticket, she couldn't get in, because the event was sold out.

Veronica, who was the wife of one of Dante's teammates, luckily was passing by when she saw Gabrielle and walked over to the door to speak to her. She told Gabrielle to come on in, and up to the roof with her. Dante and Altruis, her husband were already on the court. Peaches asked Veronica, surprisedly if they knew each other. Like a quick breeze off a duck's back, Veronica answered yes, then walked away with Gabrielle.

Gabrielle walked up the stairs telling Veronica how Peaches wasn't even going to let her in, even though she had seen Gabrielle and Dante together at many of these events. Gabrielle wondered if maybe Peaches wanted Dante for herself. Veronica explained that Peaches was just phony; she was the type that could be your best friend only when she sees who's on your arm.

Veronica told Gabrielle, not to get her wrong; she didn't put anything past any women. She and Altruis had been married for years, still women constantly approached him, thinking that maybe they could get his money or time. But according to Veronica, what those other women just didn't know was that she had his wallet and she was the watch; so Altruis didn't have any money or time.

Veronica was funny and sassy, and she knew that she had put Gabrielle more at ease; but, she wanted to pass along something she had learned years ago. "You can't worry about who's after him. You have to know Dante well enough yourself to trust that he won't stop for them."

Veronica and Gabrielle had made it to the roof and were resting on the ledge and looking down. Dante happened to look up and see Gabrielle. He waved and blew a kiss. Gabrielle smiled down at him. Dante was sweet, and he was good to her. She knew him well enough. She felt sure of that.

Altruis, Veronica's husband came upstairs before the game to get his good luck kiss from 'Roni.' He never started a game without it. He wasn't as superstitious as most of the players, but he did keep that one ritual. Dante bounced around on the court, practicing spin moves and dunks for a while, and the three of them watched him. He was an entertainer for sure. He was rolling his arm out to some of the kids who were standing near the court. He was pretending to offer them the ball, then taking it and driving to the hoop.

"That Dante is a character," Altruis laughed.

Altruis had been in the League nine years, with the same team. He was a right tackle, but he still advised Dante on things related to the team, business, and Gabrielle. He had been over there during one of the rap sessions, and he had told Dante what a good girl he had in Gabrielle. Gabrielle didn't hear Altruis' comments, nor did she hear Dante reply that she was average, "just like any other girl out there." She was sweet and all, Dante had told him, but he wasn't getting too serious about anyone. He was just enjoying his time. None of the things he had in Minnesota would last forever.

When Dante looked back up to the roof and saw the three of them standing there, he grabbed a kid off the side line, and told him to "hold it down" for him. The little boy stood at the three point line, trying to shoot from the same spot where Dante had been. Dante shook his head vigorously in disbelief. He put his hands on his hips and leaned over the boy asking what he thought he was doing. Before the boy could answer, Dante theatrically grabbed the boy's arm and moved him directly in front of the basket and told him:

Snapshots

"Now, you shoot."

Dante jogged off, and the people near the sidelines continued laughing as the little boy looked around asking: "Where did he go?"

He spotted Dante and got ready to chase him. He yelled for Dante to "get back here, you." But Dante pointed the little boy back to the court, then he ran up the stairs, two at a time to get to the upper deck.

He joined the threesome of Altruis, Roni and Gabrielle. They talked for a while. Peaches was circulating the roof top, introducing the people she felt deserved to mingle. Later on she walked over to Dante's party. She spoke to everyone by name, then paused because she didn't know Gabrielle's. Dante introduced Gabrielle as his girl, and Peaches was so flattered to meet her. Once Dante was standing with Gabrielle, Peaches remembered (all of a sudden) "Oh yes, I do see you two together." She looked at Dante for approval then emphasized: "All the time."

Gabrielle was naive enough to let her mouth drop almost wide open. Roni would have cut her eyes at Peaches, but, instead she gave Peaches an overdone smile. Peaches notified Altruis, Dante, and the other guys on the roof that the game would start soon.

Gabrielle was glad that Veronica was there. She was sure Roni was the only genuine female in the crowd.

chapter eleven

Gabrielle was exhausted by the time she and Dante had made it home. She didn't want to fall right to sleep when they hit the bed. This would be their last night together before he left for camp, but she was truly fatigued. The air was thick and warm. Dante wasn't crazy about air conditioning, so the window was cracked and he was staring out in the blue-blackness of the night, with Gabrielle lying at his side; he held her and stroked her then ran his fingertips across her eyelids, and just as he had intended, he woke her up.

He started off by asking if she had a good time tonight. She turned over to face him and told him of course she did. She leaned her face into his chest and kissed his left side. He was distracted. He wanted to bring something up to her, but she was licking the brand on his arm and pinching his nipple at the same time, and he loved that. He let her go on with the kissing and touching for a while until he stopped her to ask if she would promise to do something for him while he was gone.

She told him that she would do anything for him, and he said he knew that. He proceeded with his question which was an appeal for her to lose some weight for him. She protested that she had only gained about five or ten pounds, and nobody even knew it. He wouldn't have even known if she hadn't told him. He kept saying,

"Oh I knew. I knew. I just didn't want to say nothing."

But that was a lie. Dante always said what he felt, even if he changed later by saying it wasn't what he meant.

Gabrielle was even more upset when Dante told her to forget about losing the weight; he told her point blank:

"Look that's cool. If you don't have any self-esteem about yourself or just want to let yourself go like that, that's fine with me. Shoot. I'm just trying to help *you* out."

Gabrielle sat up in bed a little. She couldn't believe that Dante was getting that upset over some weight loss. She really didn't look bad at all. Just her hips were spreading and her behind was sticking out a little more. She wondered if someone had said something about her weight that made him embarrassed, or maybe he had seen someone slimmer and sexier he liked, or used to be with. She didn't know what to do. Her instinct was to cry. But that confused her, because she rarely cried over major things, let alone something as small as this.

She toughened up by thinking what would her friends do. Michelle would call him on it. She would ask if he had seen someone else he liked. Yvette would have cursed him out. No, she would have done both, called him on it, then cursed him out. Just because he had to run around for a living and work out all day didn't mean she had to. And he was 320 pounds, what difference did it make if she was 115 or 125. If he saw someone who weighed 100 pounds he should go after her, because Gabrielle was made up of all the right stuff, inside and out and didn't need to get rid of any of it. That's what Yvette would have said. But this was Gabrielle, and all she could do was ask Dante what he wanted her to do.

He told her again, but this time while hugging and squeezing her into him, that he wanted her to just lose a little weight. He asked her 'please' and when she said okay, he asked if she was sure, and if she was mad at him. She told him of course not. Then he was somewhat playful again. He told her that she was still looking good, and that he saw a few of his boys checking her out today. She rolled out of his arms and turned over to her side and mumbled that she didn't want anyone but him. He rolled her back over to him, and repeated it as a question: "You don't want nobody but me?"

She looked down toward her feet, then back up to his face and shook her head no. He responded with kisses all over her face: "I know you don't boo. I know you don't."

He rolled on top of her and made himself even warmer when he placed his body within hers. They were one then; it really felt like it.

chapter twelve

Dante left for Mankato, and he was back to himself. He was missing Gabrielle "all day long." He called and passed every night with her on the phone until curfew came, and they shut the phones off. She was driving out there for brief intervals when he had insomnia because he hadn't been able to touch her for days. So, one morning when the phone rang at 6:30 she picked it up talking to Dante, telling him that she had just left, so he couldn't be lonely already. But it wasn't Dante on the other end of the line. It was Yvette.

Gabrielle was so excited to hear from her friend. Yvette hadn't written in the longest, and since Yvette "did not like to sit around talking to girls on the phone," Gabrielle was elated to get her call. Yvette killed the spirit by firing off questions about where Dante was, why he made Gabrielle come back there when he knew he was leaving, and why Gabrielle wasn't at work. Didn't Gabrielle think that Jasmine and the rest of them wanted to spend more time with her? No, she just had to go back to Dante, and now he wasn't even there.

Gabrielle answered Yvette's questions one at a time. The toughest one to explain was why she didn't have a job anymore. As far as Yvette was concerned, if Gabrielle didn't have a job, she had nothing to do for the next month of the summer, and she could be right back there with them. Gabrielle told Yvette that being in Minnesota was necessary, because she had to go back and forth to see Dante. But explaining the job situation was uncomfortable. Gabrielle moved slowly back to that, but Yvette warned her that she was waiting. So Gabrielle flashed back to a few days before Dante was leaving for camp.

He had decided to take her shopping and buy a going away gift for her. They went to her department store, and he asked her to pick out a few things in the jewelry case that she liked. The sales clerk, Sheila, knew Gabrielle worked in the store, so she let Dante and Gabrielle view several pieces at a time and she even stepped away from the case.

Gabrielle decided on the jewelry she wanted, but Sheila was still gone, and Dante was parked illegally. Since he had frequently purchased jewelry from the store, he took the items to another clerk who was getting ready to clock out for the evening. She had made large commissions off of Dante in the past, so she re-opened her register, made the sale, then locked up her co-worker, Sheila's case. Sheila returned and didn't wonder how her case had been locked up; she only noticed that a set of the jewelry was gone.

When Gabrielle went to work the next day, Sheila saw the jewelry set first, Gabrielle in it next, then the manager, immediately. Without thinking that it could have been purchased, since she hadn't made it back in time for the sale, Sheila assumed it had been stolen.

She told the manager the story of how she had trusted Gabrielle with several pieces out at a time. She wouldn't have done it with any other customer because she knew it was against the rules, but since Gabrielle was an employee, she trusted her. The manager absolutely understood her case.

The manager called in Sheila, the security staff, and Gabrielle to question her about the merchandise. He asked her to remove the jewelry so they could run the serial numbers, but Gabrielle told him there was no need to check; the jewelry was from there. They told her maybe it was all a misunderstanding, and that all they needed was the receipt. She didn't have that, so she said she would have to call Dante, who had bought it. If she would have been thinking, or even if she had known how drastically Dante's temperament could change, she would have been quick enough to tell them to check last night's sales. But she called Dante, explained the situation, and asked him to bring the receipt.

Dante arrived immediately. He had come quickly, parked his truck recklessly on the sidewalk and bolted into the doors of the store. He came in clouding the entire store with gusts of rage and sparks of hostility.

Gabrielle's effeminate floor manager assured Dante that all he had to do was just show them the receipt. But Dante's eyes flew wider and redder, and he told them:

"I don't have to show y'all nothing." And when it seemed that they were going to speak, he continued: "You can pull out your surveillance tapes, go through the register tapes, do what ever you got to do, but me and my girl are out of here."

The store manager now spoke up and told him that they would need the receipt or the merchandise back, then stuck out his hand for one or the other. Dante grabbed Gabrielle's hand and pushed past the manager's. Security looked as if they would step in his way. But Dante just breathed out long and slow: "Dog, I'm telling you, you better get out of my way." He spoke to the three security guards as if they were one. So the manager waved them off, and pressed for the police. He sent for last night's sales receipts, but wanted to make sure Dante and Gabrielle didn't get away before they found out for sure whether or not he was telling the truth.

The two of them had made it as far as his car when a few officers were arriving and advising Dante that he couldn't leave just yet. Dante's arms flew into the air and came pounding down on his truck.

"What is this man? What is this?" he started demanding.

Then he asked what could they do to him, and used a slew of expletives to say that he hadn't stolen anything.

Gabrielle was in tears by then. She was just sure they were going to arrest him, or shoot him or anything. A few of the officers seemed ready, as if he were a wild elephant on the loose, and they wanted to tranquillize him.

Dante kept saying that they knew who he was, and that if he had stolen anything they knew where to find him, right at the stadium. One officer was able to calm him down briefly, and fortunately, one of the managers was walking toward them with the register tape. The manager was apologizing all over himself, but Dante just stormed into his truck and tore off with Gabrielle. One officer mumbled about how they should pull him over for speeding or having been parked on the side walk, just to mess with him. But God was on his side that day. Dante would have exploded by then.

That story was enough to satisfy one question Yvette had earlier; Dante was crazy. Yvette told Gabrielle that she needed to leave him alone. But Gabrielle knew Dante too well. He would never lose his temper like that on her.

Yvette still said that she was worried about Gabrielle being out there with a 'maniac like that.' So Gabrielle told her if she was so worried, and missed her so much, she should just bring Jasmine and come on out there. Yvette hemmed and hawed but Gabrielle convinced her, and in a couple weeks, she and Jasmine were at the train station and climbing into the 850ci, which Dante had left for her since she couldn't manouevre his Hummer.

Yvette had planned to stay for a week, but after the first two days, their visit was cut short. They had been out grocery shopping because Yvette didn't want Jasmine eating out any more. Jasmine was used to at least one home cooked meal a day. So they lugged the groceries into the apartment, but Gabrielle dropped a bag of them on the floor when she noticed the bedroom door open, and that Dante was stretched across the bed. She called out his name, walked in the room and closed the door behind her.

Dante never came out of the room. Gabrielle came out once to get the door for their food delivery, but then she spent the rest of the evening consoling Dante. He had gotten cut. In addition to an injury he had aggravated, the team assessed that he was becoming too much of a risk. Gabrielle only knew of a few of Dante's explosive times, but the team knew of many.

Dante had been going through changes with the team. For a long time Dante had been equivalent to the guy in the "red shirt," which meant that in many ways, he was untouchable. Those perks were usually reserved for the premiere running backs, some wide receivers, and of course the quarterback. Still, Dante had been getting his share of the perks, since he was their guy. But the past season, he had been a distraction, late to meetings, confrontational with teammates, especially in the locker room.

Behind closed doors, it was almost expected that some of the more flamboyant players would jeer some third string or inactive players who bragged or complained about winning or losing a game that they hadn't even played in.

But Dante took things to another level. Especially when one of the corner backs, AJ, who had been activated from the practice squad had made an extra dirty hit on T-Dub, Dante's old college teammate. AJ had taken down, then elbowed T-Dub right around the pelvis area. The refs didn't call it, and AJ wasn't fined.

Back in the locker room, AJ bragged on it. This got Dante heated because T-Dub had been his teammate, room mate, and frat brother during college. They were boys and brothers, so Dante began attacking AJ about the hit.

Dante started off saying the refs didn't fine AJ because with a practice squad salary, he couldn't afford to pay it; but then Dante also charged at AJ. This was partially because AJ commented that Dante and his former college teammate T-Dub must have been more than just room mates, and that next time Dante should kiss T-Dub where it hurt (right at the pelvis).

The locker room had first lit up with laughter that AJ had enough heart to "come for" Dante, but then things turned chaotic when Dante took a running charge toward AJ, especially over an opposing team.

Newly activated, practice squad or not, a teammate was a teammate, and Dante's actions were bad for morale. Sometimes the coaches could overlook team squabbles during camp. When teammates were vying for spots, things could get a little heated. But, the fact was, Dante had exploded during the season, and even during camp he was showing signs that he would continue.

The team wasn't going to pay him to give them a hard time, no matter how good he was. They had written conduct into his contract for incentives, but with the attitude he was developing in camp, they weren't going to see him through a season.

Gabrielle had no idea about most of that. She didn't even realize that a number of days when he had been calling her from the road, he hadn't just left work, but one of his other girls' apartments. The only thing she knew right now was that Dante was home; he was feeling down; and she was aching for him. So, she lay with him in silence, and comforted him throughout the night.

# # #

In the morning Dante shot up in bed when he heard commotion in the kitchen. He asked himself out loud what was that, as he slipped into some shorts to go out there. Gabrielle woke as he was dressing, and told him it was her girlfriend and her daughter. He whirled around and frowned up.

"Who?"

Gabrielle explained to him that one of her girlfriends had come out to visit her, but that she never had a chance to tell him because of everything that had gone on with him. He didn't hear her saying how she had missed her friends, or how they just wanted to check on her, he only told her that her friend had to go. Now. He told her to go out there and let her friend know that she would be leaving. Today.

Dante had a wild and resolute look on his face, so Gabrielle didn't bother to say that if Yvette left, she would go back too; she simply told Yvette that some things had come up, and she and Dante were having some problems. Yvette got even more worried, and didn't want to pack their bags without taking Gabrielle along too. She had always been protective over Gabrielle, especially when it came to guys. She took up for her when they teased her, and she would even defend her against Dante if it were necessary. Gabrielle assured her that it wasn't.

She drove them to the train station with Yvette constantly on her case. She hated to see them go, but she was relieved to be rid of all Yvette's questions about Dante. Jasmine tagged behind Yvette the whole way into the train station. Jasmine kept looking around at Gabrielle, who couldn't park and go in, because she needed to get back and run some errands for Dante.

The days that went by made Gabrielle wonder how right Yvette was in saying that Dante was just "real selfish." He had chased her friends out, but for the past few days he was never even at home, and when he was, he was complaining about everything he could. Her weight was now one of his main issues. School was starting in just a week more, so it didn't make sense for her to go all the way home and have to do all the packing, explaining, and then traveling back and forth by train. He surely wouldn't let her take his car. So, Gabrielle stayed with Dante and just tried to be patient with his changing behavior.

Dante was in and out all night and day. Altruis had called one night to check up on him, but he was gone. Altruis told Gabrielle not to worry, that Dante was just going through his first experience with a team cut, and he was going to be upset for a while. He told her he'd seen it happen to guys a lot, but that she just had to hang in there with Dante and keep him up. Altruis believed that Gabrielle was really good at heart and loved Dante. And he knew that Dante was prone to showing off, but that deep down inside, Dante was one of the most genuine guys he had ever known. Gabrielle also knew that Dante's heart was good. She saw from the beginning that he was prone to show out, but his heart always made him convicted enough to bring the good side out more than the bad. He really was a good guy. He was just having a bad time.

Altruis also helped to clear up Gabrielle's doubts about Dante's staying out all night. He told her that Dante wasn't anywhere but at the pool hall somewhere.

It was a good thing that Altruis had told Gabrielle where Dante was usually hanging out because one night she had to call there. When the owner of the pool hall called Dante to the phone, he flew into a rage after hearing Gabrielle on the other end. He told her that he had already asked her to stop calling around and paging around looking for him. But, she explained that she didn't have a choice. It was late night; she didn't know if he was coming home, and his agent had called earlier saying that Dante needed to be in Arizona first thing in the morning. The team wanted to take a look at him.

He asked if she had his stuff packed, and she did, so he closed the conversation with: "Alright then."

Dante made it home by midnight that night. This had been the earliest since he came back from camp. Gabrielle was in the bed already, and he climbed in next to her. She was so sweet in her sleep, and even more so when she was awake. He felt bad for how he had been treating her. He knew he was taking everything out on her. None of the other girls he was spending time with saw the side of him that he streaked in front of Gabrielle. He felt bad. He wanted to feel close to her again. He was lying in his own bed like a stranger, next to someone who had given him all of her heart, but he was scared to touch.

He didn't even know if it would feel the same for her, but he wanted to rub her: arms, face, hair, it didn't matter. He just wanted to hold her or comfort her and make her know that everything would be okay. She felt Dante next to her from her sleep, and she rolled over to face him. She looked up to him, and he looked into her eyes. She smiled at him uneasily and placed her hand briefly on his cheek, then rolled back over. She was hurt, but she hadn't totally shut him out. He wrapped her up in his arms and they slept until they got ready to part for the airport.

chapter thirteen

Dante was pulling his bags out the backseat as Gabrielle sat in the drivers'. Her tears were spilling over, and she couldn't stop herself from crying. Dante kept telling her that everything was alright, and that they would be just fine. He told her that Arizona wasn't that far, and that she would be coming out there to see him all the time. He told Gabrielle he couldn't leave her unless she would be alright, so she promised that she was, and then he promised something that he hadn't expected or intended.

"Look Gabrielle, me and you are going to be together forever. Tempe ain't nothing but a plane ride away. We're going to keep seeing each other, and things are going to get better. You'll be right out there at my side before you know it."

He hadn't even realized it before, but in his heart, he did want it that way. He hadn't ever thought to any great extent that he wanted Gabrielle with him, but when he said it, he did realize that he didn't want to be without her in his life.

School had started back, and Gabrielle thought that would be enough to get her back on track. All she had to focus on was academics. She wasn't working, and Dante took responsibility for that so he sent her an allowance almost double what she was making at work. She was staying in the apartment still, and had his car to get her back and forth to campus, yet she wasn't making it to classes most of the time. She was sluggish, starting to argue with Dante more, and getting depressed.

For the first few weeks when the Season started, she thought that maybe jet lag was wearing her out. She had been going to see him every weekend. It seemed like every time she had decided to study, he had something for her to do.

One week she couldn't make it to his Monday night game, so she piled all of her books in the bed with her and tried to watch the game between studying. Instead of doing either, she fell asleep.

He called right after the game, then called three times back to back because she hadn't answered the phone. When she finally answered the phone and told him that she had drifted off, he was heated. After that, whenever he wanted her to make it to a game, she turned around weekend to weekend and went. October was here and midterms were coming, and she knew that this would be her last chance to redeem her grades, but that was also the Bye-week for his team; they would get 3 personal days, since the team had gotten off to a solid start, and Dante had planned for him and Gabrielle to go to the islands for a couple of days. There was one stipulation, she had to lose the weight.

By this time, she knew that she couldn't. She had called Yvette at midnight, starting off with a *hey girl*, like it was the middle of the day. Yvette was curled up in bed with one of her nieces and her daughter. Gabrielle tried to sound perky, but besides the fact that it was the middle of the night, Yvette knew Gabrielle's voice well enough to know that something was wrong. Yvette asked was it school, was it Dante, did she need money to get home. Gabrielle denied that anything was wrong. Then she started off with the fact that it was school, and that she just couldn't keep up any more.

Yvette knew Gabrielle was smart enough, so she probed and found out that Gabrielle had been in Arizona a lot. Gabrielle didn't want to admit how the trips were a problem. Instead, she talked about how pretty Arizona was. Yvette was trying to be patient, but that wasn't one of her attributes. So she forced Gabrielle to move on to what was going on with Dante. Gabrielle painted the picture perfectly, but when her voice started to crack, and she could tell she was breaking down, she switched to something she was trying to be happy about.

"Yvette, guess who's going to be an aunt and a god-mother?" she asked.

This launched Yvette straight up in bed. She knew instantly what that meant, and she went driving directly into Gabrielle. Yvette needed to know what did Gabrielle think she was doing. Yvette asked if Gabrielle realized what a mistake she was making, having a baby at this point in her life. Gabrielle was the least happy about it, but she didn't know any other means to cope by now. She had tried everything, and she had run out of ways.

Dante was furthest from supportive. He didn't even call about the weekends or games now. He acted like he barely wanted to know she existed. This was his way of dealing with it, because he had already told her that he wasn't ready to be a father, and she knew what that meant. Gabrielle was too scared of an abortion. When she asked him how was she going to go to the clinic alone, he told her that plenty of people have done it, and asked if she thought he was going to be able to take off from his games to go hold her hand through that. He was flipping back to the side of him that she hadn't realized was there, and didn't want to know.

Now Yvette was giving her the business. Through Gabrielle's sobs she responded that she knew Dante wasn't her husband. She listened to Yvette rant about how even when a man was your husband, you still couldn't be sure if he was going to stick by you in raising your children. Yvette calmed down after a minute, and asked the particulars. Gabrielle told her she was due in January, and she'd probably have the baby back at home since she'd be there for the holidays. No, Dante would not be there. It looked like his team would be in the playoffs, and he said if he missed any games he would be fined, plus lose his game day salary. Yvette said Dante had to be lying; she didn't believe the penalty could be that stiff if he was going to the birth of his first child, but Gabrielle felt that his penalty was nothing; she was the one who seemed to be paying for everything.

By Christmas Gabrielle had made it home. She had given birth to her son DJ, lost her scholarship to school, and faced countless questions of her own, and her mother's about what she was going to do.

Danielle was irate that Gabrielle had lost her scholarship. She screamed and hollered about that continually. The one thing she had to do. The one thing she had to do was go to class and keep a 'B' average. Gabrielle could have done that with her eyes closed, and much easier with her legs closed. Her mother hurled these comments and those about how she didn't know how Gabrielle thought she was going to make it, or where she thought she was going to stay.

Danielle said these things constantly as if she wished Gabrielle and DJ would get out of her home. Gabrielle's room was certainly too tiny for the two of them to stay there long term. It was barely large enough to fit the twin bed, desk, and night stand that it had. Now, a baby bed, a stroller, all of these things that came with the extra added burden Gabrielle had brought.

She and her mother were in constant arguments about her baby. Danielle made Gabrielle feel like she saw DJ as a piece of junk. It wasn't that, but Danielle was beyond disappointed in Gabrielle.

Her junior year. It was Gabrielle's junior year in college, and she chose then to start messing up. Danielle told Gabrielle she wished that she would have just messed up in the beginning or never went, then she would have known not to get her hopes up on Gabrielle.

The rift between Danielle and Gabrielle was constantly growing. Danielle had made it clear to Gabrielle all her life, that at 18, she would be on her own. There was no taking that back.

Gabrielle couldn't understand how after all the years she had lived up to her mother's expectations, Danielle couldn't forgive her. Gabrielle didn't know how to look at it. She couldn't say that her son was a mistake; although she never intended to be pregnant, she had carried and comforted DJ through the nine months of turmoil they both went through with his father. Now that DJ was here, his father was rejecting him, and even worse, her mother was on the verge of throwing them out. All because Danielle wanted to keep her word that Gabrielle had to make it on her own. It didn't make sense to Gabrielle.

But there was more to it than that. Danielle saw Gabrielle traveling the same road of being a teenage mother as she had. Danielle had already struggled to raise Gabrielle, and just when she thought she had done everything right, Gabrielle came home, bringing even more burdens to her. Two extra mouths to support, when Danielle had prepared to finally start taking care of herself. Danielle's mother had thrown her out at sixteen for being pregnant, at least she had given Gabrielle 18 full years and sent her off to college.

Danielle's line of reasoning hurt Gabrielle. Plus, Danielle made no secret what a burden this was. Even worse, she said these things when friends and family were around.

Michelle and Yvette were visiting one day, and they were all in the front with Gabrielle and DJ. One of Danielle's co-workers had stopped by with a gift for DJ, and asked Danielle how it felt to be a grandmother. She said flat out that it didn't feel good. That was compacted by the phone ringing, and Danielle demanding to know why Gabrielle wouldn't come take the call. It was Dante.

Danielle felt that Gabrielle should go beyond taking the call to trying to make up with him so she and DJ could go back there. Dante had never officially put them out, but Gabrielle just didn't want to be around him. He had been so resistant and non-supportive when she was pregnant, that she didn't want to deal with him now.

She added to that how he gave her such a hard time during early December that she went into early labor later that month. If it weren't for Altruis and Roni, she would have been out there by herself when she gave birth.

Today when Dante's call came and she heard her mother making a fuss about how she needed to just pick up the phone, Gabrielle marched back to the kitchen and announced that she was not taking his calls. Her mother started the same argument about how they better do something, because they needed some place to go. Her mother had made those comments before, only this time the phone was still off the hook. Dante was right there on the line and could hear this.

Gabrielle slammed the phone down and started screaming for Michelle to get her and DJ's things. That was enough. It was bad enough that her mother made it known to friends and family how she felt about Gabrielle, now Danielle made sure that Dante knew Gabrielle and DJ were being rejected right here, by her own mother. Somehow, her mother thought that would make Dante come and get them, since they were his family now. "Married or not," her mother had told her, "Dante now has a ready made family." And Danielle felt that Gabrielle should be right there with him.

Gabrielle almost felt like she had no place to turn. Yvette would have taken her in, but her brothers, sisters, and nieces and nephews were all at her mother's. Dante wasn't even a consideration at this point. Danielle didn't really want DJ and Gabrielle out. For the most part, she just wanted to express her disappointment continually, until she had come to terms with it. But Gabrielle wouldn't stay in the house with it one more day. Michelle had already offered the extra room in their condo, and Gabrielle didn't want to intrude, but she felt that she and DJ had nowhere else to go, and her baby deserved to feel welcome in this world.

Yvette helped load the things into Michelle's car. Gabrielle and Yvette made just a few trips in and out. When everything was all ready, Gabrielle just sat in the car. Michelle was still in the house trying to reason with Danielle and tell her that Gabrielle could stay in her condo *until*, but that she just wants them to make recompense, regardless. But, Gabrielle was her mother's daughter, and they were both stubborn. While Michelle was in the kitchen trying to get Danielle and Gabrielle back to an understanding, Gabrielle was outside blowing the horn, and ready to get her baby home.

chapter fourteen

It didn't make any sense to Dante why Gabrielle wouldn't come back out there with him. He had made his mistakes while she was pregnant, but the Season had been over for a month, and he was headed back to Minnesota. He called her mother's house every day, but could never talk to Gabrielle. Finally, Danielle gave him Michelle's number, and he called there daily.

Gabrielle made it clear to Dante that she was just going to start her life over in Wisconsin. She was going to enroll in a small college near Michelle's house. She could have gone Winter term because she hadn't flunked out of college; she had just dropped below 3.0 and lost her scholarship. Nevertheless, she had decided to wait out more than the six weeks recuperating time, and spend it with DJ, and when Spring came, she'd be back in school.

She had it all planned out. Her life, and their son's life, without him. Dante hadn't even seen his son. Almost two months had gone by and he hadn't seen him. He had asked Gabrielle to just bring DJ back so he could see him. Gabrielle's answer was that it was too cold to tote DJ out there just to be seen. It wasn't show and tell. They weren't children. They had a child. They were parents now, only Dante wasn't man enough to behave like one.

Michael wanted to ask Gabrielle if she thought it was fair keeping Dante from his son, but he knew he'd be out of place. So, he talked to Michelle, and she presented the idea that Gabrielle didn't have to go anywhere, but maybe she should at least let Dante come so he could see his son. Gabrielle was livid.

Dante had every chance to be a father from the time she realized she was pregnant. And, he had a choice to come see DJ as soon as the season was over, but he went to Dallas for Christmas or stayed in Arizona, maybe with someone else. She couldn't be sure what he had really done. But she wasn't inconveniencing her son for Dante's desires.

"Let him have his way on his team, or in the club, or wherever he has a comp card. I have a son to worry about, not a grown baby."

Snapshots

That was the end of it. Michelle felt that was fair enough. There was only one more time, and one more reason during Gabrielle's stay that Michelle got involved with the matters between her and Dante.

Late one night, the phone was ringing, and Michelle picked it up. It was Dante, and he had already told her what the situation was, so he asked her to put Gabrielle on the phone. Michelle went to Gabrielle and DJ's room with the cordless in her hand. Gabrielle was already up, walking the floor and bouncing DJ. Michelle handed the phone to Gabrielle and she asked Dante what did he want.

Dante explained that he wanted the two of them back there with him. He was at the airport and had already bought their tickets. He said he was going to wait there until morning to pick them up. If he didn't see them stepping off the plane, he was going to take the 10 a.m. flight out to Milwaukee himself, rent a car and drive to Kenosha to get them. He was distraught. He couldn't stop thinking about them, and how this whole thing had gone wrong. He wanted her to come back. She could start school there in the Spring, and he'd cover what her scholarship had paid, but he couldn't keep going from day to day knowing that two of the biggest parts of him were beyond his reach.

Dante was in tears. He was so sincere that for a moment Gabrielle heard him as the person she had known before, a sweet, genuine and giving person. Her anger waned. And with a part of him and a part of her resting in her arms, she caved in to him. She agreed to take the flight out in the morning.

chapter fifteen

Michelle and Gabrielle parted extra early in the morning since the airport was a distance. DJ's eyes were looking brighter than ever. Michelle's theatrics made her say that DJ could tell he was going to his daddy today. Gabrielle was happy to hear that. She was happy to think about seeing Dante and having their family together.

Gabrielle got to the airport anticipating a lot of good.

At the gate Michelle told Gabrielle to take good care of herself, and reminded her she would always be there whenever Gabrielle needed her. Gabrielle knew she could always count on Michelle and Yvette; they were like family. With a warm feeling from home, Gabrielle and DJ made their way onto the plane, and back to his father.

Dante had changed the back guest room into a baby's room. He had made everything ready for their coming. Surprisingly, he had gotten rid of the leather furniture. He had replaced it with a cream sectional. Dante wasn't crazy about this style or material, but he felt it would be the most comfortable for Gabrielle and the baby.

Things were going well for them, but they weren't exactly the same. DJ was still having his 3 am wake ups. As a result, Gabrielle was pushing Dante's arm from around her almost every night so that she could go check on DJ. Some nights Dante would go for her, but she went so often that she just had Dante put a bed in DJ's room for her.

Dante was prone to his *lonely* spells, so some nights while Gabrielle was down the hall with DJ, he picked up the phone and made *how are you* calls to an old girlfriend of his. Gabrielle was unaware of that. She didn't start noticing that they were having problems until it was nearly summer.

She had enrolled in school again and the problems started off as minor. Dante wanted to go hanging out a lot more. He said that baby sitting while she was in classes made him need just a little time away. Just a couple hours a day. That turned into him staying out later, and even coming up with an idea for cutting out his baby sitting role all together. He would hire someone, or pay for DJ to go to the day care center at her college, that way she would be more comfortable knowing he was right where she could check on him.

In some ways that sounded like a good gesture, but Gabrielle was starting to learn Dante. She didn't like knowing that he wasn't ready or willing to really be responsible. But she didn't want to fight with him, so she accepted the day care situation, but then he started coming with more. He was hanging out late into the night, and bringing home numbers in his pocket. When she confronted him about it, he turned into the department store Dante, and started constantly telling her things like:

"You ain't running nothin' in *this* house...I can do whatever I want...you ain't paying no bills."

And, as the arguments escalated, one day he told her that she could get out.

Michelle received a letter from Gabrielle late in the Spring. Gabrielle wasn't sure what to do because Dante had put her out two or three times, and she had stayed with his former teammate Altruis and his wife. But for one thing, she didn't know them that well to stay for more than a night at a time. And the last time she had gone over there, Dante came and made such an embarrassing scene, that much like her job, whether or not she was welcome back, she was far too ashamed to return.

Furthermore, Dante had taken all her credit cards, and she didn't have any resources to do anything but stay there in an increasingly bad situation. She couldn't think of anything.

Child support, was Michelle's answer. She had wired Gabrielle train fare, and picked her and DJ up from the station. On the ride back home Michelle told her that Michael didn't deal with child support cases, but some of his friends handled them. Dante would have to give 25% of his salary for child support depending on which state he was claiming as legal residency. Even if he was low down, and Michelle suspected he was, he would try to shelter most of his salary in an annuity to make his payments lower, but it wouldn't matter. Michelle would get Michael's colleague to set up the payments so that Gabrielle could get a bulk of the money now, since football salaries weren't guaranteed. Gabrielle didn't know anything about any of this. And she didn't want to take Dante to court.

"Do you want a roof over you and DJ's head Gabrielle?" Michelle demanded. She was normally theatrical at the most, but she also had a shark's tooth when it came down to handling business.

"Now don't get me wrong, you and DJ can stay with us as long as you like, but Gabrielle, you're going to want a place of your own, and you deserve that. Ain't no sense in you and my baby nephew going from pillar to post or being told to come and go by him when he's living it up just how he wants to. This is his son, and your life. Girl no."

Michelle was furious. Almost more angry than Gabrielle, but that was because Gabrielle was worn. She had been through a lot during the last few months so she didn't have the energy to be angry.

"That's what friends are for," Yvette and Michelle told her. Friends were there to pull up the rear, when you felt like falling flat. When the three of them pulled together, the unified force helped Gabrielle face her most challenging days.

Yvette had not completed one quarter of post secondary studies, but she wanted to make sure Gabrielle made it back to school, so Michelle kept DJ while Gabrielle went to enroll. Yvette hit the roof when she found out that Dante had never paid off Gabrielle's tuition from when she went back to him. As a result, Gabrielle's college in Minnesota wouldn't release her transcripts and she couldn't enroll as a continuing student. The only classes she could take as a new student were ones without pre-requisites, that meant freshman or sophomore level classes, and she needed classes for her major now.

Michael was a corporate attorney and he knew some people who handled cases for a few of the major magazines. It wouldn't pay much, but he said he could probably get Gabrielle an internship with one of the magazines. Maybe by that time the child support would be in settlement, and she could pay off the tuition. Or, as Gabrielle was hoping, the magazine would hire her on and send her back to school.

Things weren't coming together quickly or easily. There weren't a lot of job opportunities in this small area, but while she was waiting for the internship, she had to work on something. Gabrielle had always had some money of her own, so she took a part time job at a day care center. She watched the kids during the evening shift. That job was perfect because it gave her a chance to keep DJ with her. Michelle wouldn't have minded watching DJ, but Gabrielle felt that she was imposing on Michelle's family enough.

Gabrielle's relationship with her mother could have

improved. When Danielle found out that Gabrielle was back in town, she asked that they come stay with her, but Gabrielle refused. It was hard for Gabrielle to forgive Danielle, especially since she could only remember desperately needing her mother one time in her life, and at that time, her mother threw her away. She vowed she would never stay there; nevertheless, she did start keeping in touch with her mother and dropping by with DJ.

Gabrielle's spirits were slow in lifting. She was working in the day care center full-time and sometimes overtime by early summer. The only pleasure she had was watching her son learning new things and doing new things. But the fact that she felt her hands were tied, and that she had no other employment options than this made her increasingly sad while she was there.

She didn't even like to look back to how much promise her life had just a year ago, and what a difference there was now. She went from being in college, looking forward to a tangible and rewarding career, having an apartment at her disposal, riding or driving the fanciest car in the area, to this: strolling through a nearly deserted parking lot, 9:00 at night with her son on her arm. No place to take him that was really his home, and no way to get him there.

Michelle couldn't come get them tonight; she and Michael were attending a dinner party. So Gabrielle walked with DJ to the bus stop; she could feel that she was being followed. High headlights were on her, and she would have been scared, but she noticed the truck. A Hummer.

Almost two months had gone by since she and DJ left. For the first month after they left, Dante barely called at all. He had rediscovered the joys of being single, and wasn't in a rush for them to return; but, after that wore old, he started his daily calls to Gabrielle. The difference was, he wasn't apologizing. He was telling her that all of the arguments had been her fault. She was being difficult to get along with, and he had just been reacting. After that conversation, Gabrielle didn't accept any more of Dante's calls. That was over a month ago. Maybe he had been calling to see how she and DJ were, or maybe he had been calling to ask them to come back, but every time she had found out Dante was on the other end, she hung up.

Now he was here. Dante pulled the truck along side of them and asked her to get inside. She kept walking as if she hadn't heard him. He followed at her side for a while longer, then he put his truck in park and walked to catch up to her.

"Gabrielle, I know you're mad at me," he began.

"Mad? Dante, I don't have time to be mad," she said and quickened her steps.

"Come on boo, come on. I know you're mad," he said uncomfortably and unsure of what to say next. "Boo, please, just come on with me. You and Dante don't need to be out here like this man. Gabrielle, boo. I...I'm sorry. I'll be right."

Gabrielle had been walking away from him all that time, but she stopped in her tracks and stared him in the face with fire.

"Dante...Dante...you think I got time to keep playing these games with you?"

"It's not a game Gabrielle."

"It is. It is to you. I mean, does your job end when you come off the field? Do you know that after the fourth, fifteen minutes are up it's real life and not a game anymore?"

"Gabrielle..I..."

"Dante, I don't think you do know when it ends. I think you just keep on thinking that everything is part of a game. That's your life right? That's how you make your living right? Well you don't get a crowd here, no fans and no cheers. It's just me and your son and I have to try to find out how I'm going to make a life for us."

"I'ma do right by my son Gabrielle, I am."

"Well you just do that then. When you figure out how you're gonna do right, you just let me know. I'll be right here. In the mean time, I don't know what you're even doing here."

Dante's spirits shrank. He was almost out of things to say, so he told her why he had driven out. "I got an off season trade Gabrielle."

She didn't budge.

"I'm going to Miami next week. I just wanted to see you and my son before I left."

"Well, you've seen us now, so bye. Maybe next time you'll think to have your son a roof over his head so his visit won't be in a parking lot in the middle of the night."

That was enough to break him to his knees. She meant that, and was walking off. He did the only thing his instinct would allow, he chased behind her and caught her by the arm.

"Listen, I...I want you to come with me," he pleaded.

Gabrielle didn't even realize that she had asked:
"Come with you where?"
"To Florida Gabrielle, I promise, it'll be different."
There was no way, no way she would go with him there. Not that far to be sure. And she made sure he knew it. She had plans to start on an internship, at least by Fall. And his resolution was that he would put her on his payroll. Her response was a question: "For what? To fire me when you get ready. No Dante, it's not going to work like that. I'm getting my own so I can take care of me and mine. And I'm not chasing behind you any more."

"It won't be a chase Gabrielle," he promised.

He laid out how everything had been settled. He had bought a home in Dallas. He just wanted something stable, because for all he knew he could be with a different team in another year. He wanted something comfortable and back home so he would have his own place to fall back on. He would get an apartment for Miami for as long as he'd be playing out there, but whatever happened, there would be the home in Dallas.

Gabrielle made sure to point out that it was his job, his home, his apartment, and that she had been thrown out with his son one time too many not to know that what was Dante's was his alone. The only way Gabrielle was going anywhere with any man was when it was her husband, and a real family.

"That's what it takes?" Dante asked.
"What?" Gabrielle snapped at him.
"You want me to marry you?"
Gabrielle sighed. She was getting really impatient with him now.

"Right now, I don't want anything but to be able to take care of myself and my son, and raise him right."

"That's not what I'm asking you Gabrielle. I'm asking you is that what it takes in order for us to be a family. In order for you to give us a chance. Marriage?"

"Yeah Dante, I guess in order for me to recognize you as family at this point we would have to be married."

She was nearly disgusted with how he behaved at times. She couldn't believe that she had never seen how childish he was before. With baby DJ on her arms she walked away from the senior. She was all prepared to let it go at that, but Dante pulled a box from his pocket and asked her to marry him. He told her he was coming back for that anyway. He didn't say it outright, but he hadn't been sure what it would take to get her back; so when he had left Minnesota that day to look for her, he vowed to be prepared to do whatever it took.

He went into a confessional about how many things he had realized since the last time she and DJ had left, and how he knew he couldn't make it out there in Miami without them.

She wasn't sure if it was her state of need at this point or his level of repentance this time that made her give in. Maybe it was a combination of both. But a few days passed, and against her friends' objections, Dante, Gabrielle, DJ and the few friends and family they invited were at the ceremony. Dante and Gabrielle were married.

She had given him the one ultimatum that she was sure would send him running out of her life forever, but as it turned out, it kept him in her life permanently.

chapter sixteen

Dante and Gabrielle would be headed to Miami. There were some things he had prepared for, like locating housing, ordering furniture, and having the cars shipped by train; still, there were other things he wasn't certain how to prepare for. Those were the old events with people who had been a part of his life since college. However, they could potentially bring problems into his and Gabrielle's life, putting the wrong ideas in her head.

He didn't want that. He wanted their start to be brand new, but it would be hard for him to distance himself from parts of his past that had been so close to him, for one, his best friend T-Dub.

Tony Williams (who some people called three-four or T-Dub) had been so close to Dante that they were like mirrored images. The only difference was: physically, T-Dub was a much shorter, light skinned, high strung running back; and emotionally, Dante was trying to show much more commitment to his marriage.

Tony and his wife Janiece were both from Miami, went to college in Miami, and didn't leave until he got drafted to an NFC team in the South-west.

It would have been great to say that all Tony's problems started when he got to that team, but they had started long before then. The South-west just ended up being the place where years of the rocky road Tony and Janiece had traveled, brought T-Dub's career to a crashing halt.

Life in the League had been good and bad for Tony. His first three years with the team continually lead them to the playoffs; their quarterback was stellar and offense was steadily improving. But the one area where they needed help was on defense.

That's where the good part came. Tony's younger cousin, Rayshawn Smith, was entering the League that year. Rayshawn's performance had earned him a spot at the Combines, and once he got there, he "blew up the spot." There had been no doubt, people would be shuffling draft picks trying to get him on their squad.

Even the owner of Tony's team had become aggressively involved. Of course, the owner had always given direct input on who he wanted on his team, but he was going the extra mile, flying Rayshawn to the South-west in his private jet to meet with him. Taking things a step further, the owner had invited Rayshawn to his home for dinner with his wife, son-in-law, and his only child, a daughter, Carrie. The amazing part about this particular get together was that it broke from the owner's tradition. It was a best kept secret, this owner liked to keep that really elite line drawn between players, coaches, and administration.

He understood that players and coaches would sparingly co-mingle, but as for him, he would be more than highly selective which players would be in his presence. It was as if he was all for making his money off the players' backs, but didn't want them eating off his plates.

The players weren't really bothered, possibly they weren't even aware of his underlying feelings. The owner, Mr. Jacobson, interacted with them moderately. He was certainly out of his box and on the sidelines to congratulate them when they had pulled off big wins. By the same token, he would come down and go ballistic from time to time if things didn't go well. As far as anyone could see, he was in tune with his squad.

But, it was at home where things manifested themselves differently, and all of her life, Carrie, the owner's daughter resented the comments he made behind closed doors. She could have taken on any aspect of the empire he had established, but she chose to do something which felt more rewarding. She opened a youth center in the inner-city where she could help some of the people that her father had made inflammatory statements about.

It was fine with her father that she worked at an inner-city center. He even paid for it to be built. She felt like she was "giving something back," so he supported her in that. Carrie didn't want her youth center to be a part of her father's "good guy" media blitz, but because so many of the players volunteered with her, it was inevitable; her center was flagged as being a community based part of the Jacobson's team.

# # #

Carrie had come in a little early from the Center the night that her parents, Mr. and Mrs. Jacobson had set up a dinner party for Rayshawn. Her own husband, Ed, wouldn't be there. For years her father had prepped Ed in League matters, and had now made him second in command, Chief Operating Officer and Vice Chairman of the Board. Ed knew these positions were usually reserved for immediate family or life-long business partners, so he worked hard to stay in Mr. Jacobson's favor. The fact was, he worked harder at pleasing Mr. Jacobson, than he did at pleasing Carrie.

Dinner tonight would be grand though. Rayshawn was already seated in the parlor, talking with her parents. At intervals she could hear him laughing and making some aphoristic statements. It wasn't until Rayshawn approached the dining area that his real qualities manifested.

There were many dynamics of Rayshawn. He had personality, Southern charm, and a smile that could feel like July sunshine on a frigid January morning. His face reflected innocence, yet he had strong sex appeal, without even realizing how much. Rayshawn was easily six foot seven, two hundred ninety pounds; he was coal black, with beautifully straight teeth, and dimples that almost out-shined his smile. Moreover, he was a walking contradiction. He was focused yet diverse; confident yet humble. And, a glance at his future showed a guy who always took a back seat to others.

No matter how trivial other people would have viewed it, Rayshawn devoted full interest in the lives of friends or family who called him; and what was big to them, was big to him. He would listen to them talk about their very simplistic days, and when they'd pause to ask what he had done for the day, he'd just mumble: "Nothing. Cleaned up the house." This statement could be easily followed by the fact that he had cleaned up so that ESPN or Fox Sports could come over and do an "at home with Rayshawn Smith" interview. But that wasn't important to him. The most interesting and important things in his private life were how well his friends, but mostly, how well his family was doing.

The first night at dinner, Mr. Jacobson brought up "the remarkable challenge that" Rayshawn was taking on for the sake of his family. For Rayshawn, there was nothing challenging about it. He had come to this city with seven children, three were his younger brothers and sisters, and four were the other cousins who had lived in his grandmother's house with them.

Growing up in Miami with his grandmother, the poverty couldn't have gotten any worse, but the love couldn't have gotten any better. His grandmother gave her life, working every day, trying to keep them together.

Early in life Rayshawn had lost his mother to a violent death, and his father had been in and out of prison until finally one day, the streets or the prison sent him to a violent death. Rayshawn had been so young, he couldn't remember how it happened. What he did remember was his grandmother, and how she had raised all of them in the church. Faith and the discipline of being in church whenever the doors opened, created the backdrop of his life.

As soon as he was old enough, he got out there, mowing grass, cleaning the grounds of Coconut Grove Estates, whatever honest work he could do to help bring money in, he did. As soon as he was old enough to get a work permit, he stepped up to getting fast food jobs.

Rayshawn stayed on the right track during his youth because he never wanted to break his grandmother's heart. She was counting on him to make something of his life. She recognized that he wanted to help financially, but she only allowed him to work so much.

The first priorities were school and church. Football practice was his release. But, his grandmother would make him give up all extra activities when it was time to go to church. There was no compromising the Word.

His grandmother knew, it was her faith that had been able to keep them together all those years. Rayshawn felt it was her love that made her choose to struggle for them. Because of that, he wanted to show his most sincere gratitude by getting her a home in Miami, where she could continue to keep the family together comfortably for years. But just when he was coming close to being able to, his grandmother passed.

Now, his goal was to take on what she had left behind. That would be his greatest tribute to his grandmother. To play ball at the top of his game, raise those children as best as he could, and keep them in the church where she had brought them up.

He would have plenty of help if he inked his deal here. His cousin Tony was already playing for the team, and even though Tony was having his share of problems, he and his wife would certainly help Rayshawn out with the kids. Plus, Carrie, the owner's daughter, had a growing interest in Rayshawn. During the dinner conversation that night, she stated that she would love to have Rayshawn and the kids at her Center.

Snapshots

One thing Carrie liked about her position with the Center was that she had an opportunity to partner many of the inner-city kids with some of their athletic heros. A large number of the guys did their volunteer service hours, and donated extra time, right there at her Center. As a result, she had gotten a chance to talk to many different players throughout the years. This allowed her a behind the scenes look at many of the guys as the caring, human beings that they were. Not a lot of people got to see the guys behind closed doors.

Usually, from an outside perspective, the players were either heros, gravy trains, playboys, or sometimes criminals. But, Carrie had the fortunate angle of seeing the other side. She didn't allow cameras in her Center, but she was always quick to point out to the media there are plenty of good guys in the League who, underneath their helmets, are just regular guys with families, children, and people in the community they care about.

She was tired of seeing the few bad incidents plastered all over the news. With the numbers game, player infractions were inflated. There were roughly 1,600 players in the League. If people compared that to the hundreds of thousands of lawyers, brokers, or even teachers who committed the same crimes, they couldn't harp on the players as much. Other professions did the same things and worse, but it was the players who were often portrayed as bad guys.

Carrie didn't defend players because she was part owner, but because she knew too many of them got labeled as play-makers or law-breakers. That bothered her because there were plenty of straight-laced players who came off the field, sometimes for good, and never received credit.

Rayshawn was one of the guys who would undoubtedly continue to do well, in and out of the public eye. He was active with his siblings and cousins year-round, and during the off season he stayed busy with his church.

The coaches had been worried about whether or not he would be able to handle League adjustments and pressures, along with trying to care for his young family. Fortunately for him, an NFL schedule only required that he be gone one night a week. And, even more of a blessing, Rayshawn had been warmly embraced by his new church community. Several members of Bethel Baptist had adopted him and *his kids.*

On down the line, one of the young ladies at Bethel, Monique

Harris, would become his right hand.

Monique was the daughter of Deacon and Mother Harris, a couple who had kept their children on the front pew of church every Sunday. For more than 25 years, Deacon and Mother Harris had been escorting neighborhood children to church and inviting new church comers home with them for Sunday dinner. At some point, almost everyone had found their way to the Harris home. From the youth group in the basement, to the high officials who sat, sang, or preached in the pulpit, people went home to the Harris' hospitality.

Monique's background in the church had prepared her for the life she was leading. When Rayshawn first entered the picture, Monique was away at law school. She had a promising career developing. She was sharp and articulate, which she attributed to her upbringing.

"Everything I ever needed to know, I learned it in church." Monique told that to everyone, then she gave her list of comparisons.

"How to sit still and listen...the sermon. How to talk in front of crowds...Easter speeches. How to study...Sunday school. And how to use words to cut into my opponents...the Bible. You know the Word is a two-edged sword." And, Monique always closed by saying she could use words to cut people "going out and coming in."

Monique was an erudite young lady, but intimidating to most. Her parents had seen a cast of characters come in and out of Monique's life. She dated when she felt it convenient, but she didn't have the time to concern herself with anything other than her primary goal, success in her career. Nothing outside of that received precedence. Monique's social life was replete with attending countless functions for judiciary and political figures; but even in those settings, she was out there networking for business first. There was nothing second.

Rayshawn had never seen Monique in person. He had only heard of her through her parents. They shared the same news with everyone, whenever Monique was doing something new. For months, the most he had seen of her were the pictures on the mantel piece.

Rayshawn was typically at the Harris house on Sundays, picking up the Smith team, as he called them. In the same way that the Harris's had gathered up neighborhood children throughout the years, they had been gathering up Rayshawn's siblings and cousins on Saturdays so that they made it to church every Sunday. With Sunday being game day, Rayshawn couldn't make it to church during the season, but he was always able to stop by afterwards to pick up his kids, and the home cooked dinner that Mrs. Harris had waiting for him.

To his surprise, one Sunday when he went to pick up his family, Monique was there too. He had walked in the back door to find Mrs. Harris in the kitchen, drying out a glass and putting the last few dishes away.

"What's going on ma?" he asked, leaning down, just slightly to kiss her warm and rounded cheek.

It was a surprise for him to see that his "team" wasn't crowded around her. He asked where they were, as she removed his plate from the oven.

"Oh they're in the front with the little Ms. Harris. She's home you know," Mrs. Harris began.

No, he didn't know. Actually, no one had expected Monique's visit home. Even though it was Fall break, she was usually maintaining her studies or out of the country. But, she was home, and Rayshawn's eyes showed heightened curiosity. This was partially because of the thrill that was in Mrs. Harris's voice, and partially because of the thrill he could hear in the little Smiths' laughing and talking.

He held his plate loosely; he was unsure whether to finish removing the foil and sit down, or place the plate on the table and walk to the front. Mrs. Harris took the plate and told him to: "Go on and check on them."

He walked up to the front of the house and tried to just peek his head in the living room, but one of his cousins spotted him and shouted: "Come on in Ray-Ray."

He stood frozen for a minute. Rayshawn had seen Monique countless times in the pictures, but there was nothing like beholding her in person. She had the same creamy brown skin and tall frame as her mother, only Monique was far more slender. But, more than her nice looks, Monique had a presence that filled the room. He had already known she was three years older than he; but, next to him she looked like she was five years younger. Monique was sitting in the middle of the floor with his kids. She looked pure but powerful, high-ranking, but humble.

He smiled his brilliant smile. To Monique his smile just looked gorgeous, but Rayshawn's little sister knew differently.

"Ooooh, he likes you," his little sister giggled while looking at Rayshawn, and then to Monique.

His throat moved up, and he smiled a little more, only nervously.

"Be quiet Sandra," Mrs. Harris instructed. She had walked in shortly after Rayshawn to make sure the introduction was appropriate. She could tell he was a little nervous, and to her surprise, Monique was too. Maybe it was because Sandra's comment had taken Monique by surprise.

Monique was never uncomfortable around anyone, even when she was working the political and judiciary circuits. But, some sort of awkward wave was flowing right there, in Monique's own living room. It was as if she were already a part of something that had been there for a while, yet it was just catching up to her. She and Rayshawn had of course heard of one another plenty of times. They were almost aware of each other, like brother and sister, yet their instant attraction was more than family, and far less than romance.

Monique rose from the floor, and Rayshawn said out loud: "Let me help you," then extended his arm and helped her up.

Of course then, his whole team began "Ooohing."

Mrs. Harris smiled and said "Y'all stop that," and rallied them to "come on" with her.

Monique suggested the kids stay with her, where they had been all day. So, along with Monique and Rayshawn, the little Smiths were seated in the living room.

"Okay," Mrs. Harris began. "Play nice," she closed as she walked away, talking to both the children, and the adults in the room.

And they did. From that day on, whenever Monique was in town, the children, and Rayshawn were full of excitement. It was as if Monique brought a whole new dimension to his world. It had always felt complete, but with Monique around, it was really full.

He began noticing that after months of conversation with her, and the few visits she made here and there. According to her mother and father, Monique's visits had just about tripled since Rayshawn entered the picture. He smiled within and often without because he did feel that many of her visits had been special, so that he and she could spend time together.

Snapshots

Still, he didn't push the relationship idea on Monique. She had made it clear that she could make those extra visits only here and there. With her completing law school, and taking the Bar on the East Coast, she couldn't guarantee that she'd be back down South too often, and clearly not for good.

But, Rayshawn wanted that. Visit after visit, call after call, he longed for her to be around even more. And, the kids' anticipation, along with his anticipation, often made her visits like a hero's welcome.

The problem would come in their staying power. Rayshawn was realizing that he wanted her around for good. They were in each other's world, but the distance made things hard.

chapter seventeen

Going to see Monique was tough. Even the off season didn't provide any opportunities for Rayshawn to go visit her. He had completed a dynamic rookie season that had afforded him numerous front cover magazine stories, and interviews with sports' channels. Moreover, as a big play maker on the field, and a generous person in the community, he was a fan favorite. This afforded him a trip to the Pro Bowl.

The coaches and even the owner had called Rayshawn to congratulate him on his performance. The type of accolades he was getting, and the type of contributions he was making were rare, especially so early in a player's career. The great part about Rayshawn was that it didn't go to his head.

The owner congratulated him on making it to the Pro Bowl. From the very beginning, Rayshawn had come into the League being compared to Hall of Fame defensive players, and the expectations were high. He was living up to them. Although the owner had seen countless players from his team go to the Pro Bowl, he told Rayshawn that he was ranking with the League's elite.

Rayshawn's response simple; he thanked the owner, but pointed out: "You know, the Pro Bowl is one of those individual honors; but, the greatest thing for me will be that team honor of being in the big game."

From the owner's perspective, there could be no disappointment in their investment in Rayshawn. He was young, unrehearsed, and a productive team player. The coach and owner could easily see how in a few years, Rayshawn would be an integral part of leading them to the Super bowl.

In the mean time, he was headed to the islands for the Pro Bowl, and he was taking Monique with him. She had been anticipating this trip would come for Rayshawn, since all her colleagues ranted and raved over what was in store for him. Still, when he approached her to go along with him, she was unprepared.

Monique and Rayshawn's relationship had been developing at a steady pace, but with the children in the picture, it had been more rounded out. They had all become close like a family. Even when it was at the personal level, with just Rayshawn and Monique, there was more warmth of friendship than the magnetism of a relationship. Besides, Monique was doing her own thing in New York, both with her career and on the dating scene. Rayshawn had been doing his own thing too, and when time permitted, he had taken a couple different girls out himself. Still, when the trip to Hawaii came, he couldn't think of anyone he'd rather take than Monique. It took some convincing, but Monique agreed to break away from New York and go along.

T-Dub was all for the idea. He had been worried about Rayshawn's personal life and his capacity to keep things up at this pace, virtually as a single parent. Rayshawn either needed someone stable in his life, or he needed to send a few of the cousins to live with some of their relatives. Tony already had many issues to confront, and he and Janiece had three children of their own, but maybe she would agree to do it for just a little while.

"The Lawd'll make a way," Rayshawn interrupted T-Dub's concerns by making his favorite statement.

He had heard his grandmother say it and sing it all through his life. And, even when things seemed to hit rock bottom, the sun would come out, and something brighter than his smile would come into that Smith household.

"You remember them days, dog," Rayshawn reminded Tony.

"All that praying she did down here. You know mama ain't up there being quiet now. She still up there petitioning God for her youngins. Man, come on now. How you think any of us down here makin' it? Mama up there..." he said pointing toward the sky, then continued "...makin' sure all of us gon' be alright."

Rayshawn smiled after that. Just thinking about how his grandmother had looked out for them for so many years, and knowing that she was still up there looking over them made him feel good. He shook Tony by the shoulders a little bit to get him involved.

"Come on man, I know you ain't forgot that," Rayshawn closed.

"No, I ain't forgot," Tony conceded. "Cain't forget."

The times Tony and Rayshawn had shared growing up as a family had been harder than they'd ever like to think on, but the one thing they had was family unity. Most of them were all living under one roof, and their grandmother's prayers kept them together, not only physically and spiritually, but also mentally.

It was hard for Tony to think back on the financially barren days that were filled with so much love, and be where he was now. The point where he and Janiece were financially stable, but emotionally shaky.

He would come to terms with that later. For now, he wanted to do the least he could for Rayshawn, keep the kids for just a few days while Rayshawn got a chance to get away.

Tony and his wife would keep the little Smiths, and for the first time, it would be just Rayshawn and Monique.

# # #

Nothing could have made Monique foresee what was coming, but the trip to Hawaii was only the beginning of the time she and Rayshawn would have together.

Each time he could be with her, on the phone or in person, he realized more and more that he wanted her to be in his life forever. He saw the way the kids wrapped around her, but more than the kids, he knew how complete he felt, especially when he and Monique would run out of conversation at night, but still linger on the phone. He would lie on his back, staring at the ceiling wishing that she was next to him, but satisfied that at least he was feeling her presence just by holding the phone.

He wanted that feeling of completion with her daily. He just didn't know how to approach her with it. He knew she wouldn't be willing to just stop what she was doing to get deeper into him.

She cared for him, that was clear, but she also was a full-fledged business woman with a career that she seemed driven to get to. There was no turning her away from that, and as much as Rayshawn admired her, he couldn't see asking her to be anything different than what she was destined for.

All the success and good things were coming to her. She had planned for that. She and her family had known that. But, did they ever know she was destined to be his wife?

Rayshawn hadn't even known who was meant for that role. It hadn't ever been a thought, not even when he first saw her in his circle of kids on the living room floor. But, he knew it now, and the more that time passed, he wanted her to know it too.

Snapshots

#

The difficult part of it all was that Monique would not be willing to give up her career, or even put it on pause. He didn't know how it would sit, the idea of her taking the Bar there, where he was. The possibility was certainly there. For Monique however, it would mean that she would have to spend more time in school, getting the logistics of the variance of law there. It wasn't that she was being selfish, and she clearly recognized that she had begun to love Rayshawn. The problem was, no matter how small the fraction of time would be for her to finish school and pass the Bar down there, she had just about finished that aspect of her career, and was ready to step into what she had long been dreaming of. There was little resolve for that.

Her mother would have easily told her: "Baby, you'll have the rest of your life to practice law." Though Mrs. Harris never interfered, she saw something good waiting for Rayshawn and Monique. Even though everyone who came into the Harris household was family, there was a deeper sentiment of family with Rayshawn, Monique, and the children. The question was, could Monique walk right into a ready made family.

The answer was, she already had. The Smith children had made her a part of them, long before Rayshawn and Monique realized they were coming together. In their relationship, there hadn't ever been a bridge that needed to be gapped, only one that needed to be walked over. And sooner, than later, Rayshawn was hoping that he and Monique would cross the threshold and they would become man and wife.

chapter eighteen

The road to marriage for Rayshawn and Monique was almost a sure path, but it had broken up some things that were near and dear to Rayshawn along the way.

His family and his career had always been a priority for him. He would have never let go of any aspect of his family. He knew his career, with the salary he was bringing in, would allow him to keep the family together comfortably, and provide for them a long way down the road.

The problem came when he realized that, even though everything had seemed complete in his life, he had been missing that personal touch, not from just a woman, but from what he found in Monique. She brought more than companionship and conversation, she brought her spirit, which was the most powerful part of her.

There was no question about it, she looked good. His boys never failed to stop saying that. And Monique had some real business about herself. Rayshawn was lucky to have that kind of girl on his side. The guys always notified him of that. Monique was no-nonsense, and on the ball. Everyone could see that. Rayshawn saw that and more in Monique.

He wasn't losing sight on his own life, but the two years on their path to marriage, caused him to need her more than he wanted to. He couldn't stand not having that missing link put into his chain, especially when he knew where it was.

In his heart he had decided that he wanted to be traded from his team. If she couldn't be where he was, he wanted to go there.

T-Dub had to intervene:

"The East coast? Man, are you crazy? There's not a team out there that can offer you the chance at what you are building out here."

He was giving Rayshawn advice and beseeching him to get it together.

There was no sense in what Rayshawn was crying about, wanting to be where his girl was. It took some players years to rally for a trade. And even then, the trade was usually about the bottom line—the dollar bill. Those were the players who had proven years of performance and just wanted more money. Even then, most of the players wanted to stay where they were and just get the financial recognition.

No one wanted to spend years with a squad as a top player and then get traded. But after just one year, for a player to make the kind of request that Rayshawn was making, that was crazy. Guys might do it for the money, and in a really rare situation they might do it for family, but for a woman, never. T-Dub had never even heard of anyone going off the deep end like that.

"Nobody in their right mind leaves a situation like you got here with this team. And voluntarily. Dog, you fallin' off man. Is she givin' it to you that good? You can't get your grip? Look, I'll take you somewhere; I'll put you on to something."

T-Dub said it, and could do it. He had plenty of access, and easy access to the best times anyone could want; even if they were momentary thrills, Rayshawn could get them so often that they would feel like they were permanent.

That wasn't the issue. Rayshawn knew what he wanted, and over the next two years, he put it out there that he wanted to go on with a different team. He was willing to go to a team that would pay less, where he didn't know the area; it didn't matter. Plenty of teams had been jockeying for position to get him, long before the draft, and since he'd entered the League, his performance had almost every team licking their chops at the prospective. He could go to any franchise out there, if his team would make him available. Rayshawn was outspoken about that, and the owner resented him for it.

Rayshawn's level of ingratitude was like him spitting in the owner's face. After all they had done for him, the owner couldn't even speak Rayshawn's name without wanting spit fire.

Rayshawn was still young, and though his publicist advised him against it, one day he answered a reporter's question about the team and his trade: "I can't feel guilty about what all they have done for me. I have done plenty for them too."

The owner was livid. Underneath, he realized they had been mutually beneficial; so the point wasn't what Rayshawn had done for them. The point was what the team had intended to see Rayshawn do. That was why they had invested so much in him. But, the kind of ingratitude he was showing did not sit well with the owner.

Mr. Jacobson didn't even want to look Rayshawn in the face anymore. He had gone beyond out of his way, ten times over, allowing Rayshawn into his home, having a few private chats with him, and obviously none of this registered to Rayshawn. The owner was done even putting in any time showing kindness. Rayshawn would go on the trading block. As soon as they could, they would start negotiating a deal to get him out of there.

It was a relief to Rayshawn. He had still been performing at the top of his game, so it would be open arms from any team. It wasn't quite the end of his contract, so he might have to return some of his signing bonus, but he wasn't worried about that. Incentives in a new contract could make up the loss. All was well, except what it was doing to T-Dub.

The defensive side of the team had become increasingly important, and had carried them since the offense seemed to be self-destructing. T-Dub had been *falling off* himself, even though he had been questioning Rayshawn's focus.

T-Dub's home life was distracting him on the field. Dealing with Janiece wasn't easy anymore. Nothing seemed to satisfy her. They had struggled the first few years of their marriage, because he could never get enough of whatever seemed to be out there waiting for him.

Time revealed, things would be different for Rayshawn.

Things had settled down with Rayshawn; and Carrie went to bat for him with her father. They had to realize, his first year had been a big adjustment for him, and maybe he had been overwhelmed raising the children alone. He had just lost his grandmother; he found someone who seemed to be a big inspiration; he realized he went overboard, but he would pull it all together.

Carrie had every answer, and she was adding-lib wherever necessary. There was enough good housekeeping on that team. Even his media statements could be cleaned up.

The team wasn't ever able to whole-heartedly embrace him again; but, Rayshawn regained about 90 percent in their good graces. Over the course of the next few years, his performance outdid most of the damage that his comments created, so on the field, things worked out fine.

Off the field with Monique, he wasn't so lucky.

It was true, Monique did realize that she had become a big

part of Rayshawn and the kids' world. And in the very depths of her heart, she knew that she could never let them go. She would be family with them forever. But, at the same time, she was also deeply involved in the course of her own life. She was working toward something she had been dreaming of for years.

Monique was more torn than Rayshawn could have ever imagined. Although Rayshawn and the kids were new to her life, they were still a big part of her heart; nevertheless, she couldn't break away from her own world.

Most of all she felt guilty because even as much as she loved the kids, they were something of a complication. There were seven children she would be responsible for. With her legal cases, and Rayshawn's road trips, raising the children would be too overwhelming, even if she had a nanny.

To top it all off, even though she hadn't ever seriously thought about being a mom, if she was going to settle down and be married, she would probably want children of her own. With her career, and the children they already had, it would be too much to even add one more. Those were issues, but she loved Rayshawn too much to ever bring them up; she knew how much it would hurt him.

She had repeatedly told Rayshawn that she would never turn her back on them. But for Rayshawn, that wasn't good enough. It was hard for Monique to say it, and it was even harder for him to accept it, but she told him he needed to go on with his life.

#

Monique had promised to always be there for him. And even when the day came, and it did come, when Rayshawn had slowly allowed himself to find love with someone else who he married, Monique was there. She had slid into the back of the Chapel, long enough to hear the vows, and it tore her up inside when she watched him place a ring on someone else's finger.

The longing Monique had felt to be with Rayshawn herself, but the knowledge she had that she couldn't let go of either part of her life, came crashing down on her. The inner-most parts of her heart seemed to be ripping out. Monique had always felt she would be giving up too much either way if she had married Rayshawn, but on his wedding day she saw it was all gone. There would never be another chance for them.

No one ever knew the anguish it caused Monique. During

the wedding, her parents were seated front and center, and never even knew she had shown up. One of the Smith children thought they had seen her, but before anyone could approach, Monique slipped out of the Chapel, and headed back to her life, more broken than she had imagined.

By the time Rayshawn turned to the back of the Chapel, he was heading on with his life, and his new wife.

The countless years ahead proved that Rayshawn acquired nothing less than the love and success he deserved.

For a while, his cousin Tony wasn't so lucky.

chapter nineteen

Tony had been catching hell from Janiece the first three years of their marriage. He and Janiece had been dealing with each other since college, and things didn't totally improve once they married. He had always been undecided about where he should be, and when he left her behind after college, he had decided that he just wanted to *get on with his life and leave the past behind*. Once he got with his new team though, he found himself reaching back for what he had left "behind." Things with the team weren't going nearly as well as he had expected they would, so he was constantly in need of comfort, uplifting, and ego stroking. He called Janiece for the first two, and went stalking the streets for the latter.

It was funny how he ran into all types of women in the clubs. His air pretty much dictated that he played ball, but unlike many players who would deny it, Tony often volunteered the information that he was a "baller." When he told women this, it often earned him some instant action, but a few times it just got him "checked."

There were plenty of girls who were *schooled* in players' schedules. They didn't have the whole routine down packed, but they knew enough. Tony found that out the hard way.

One night in the club, he was macking on a girl who looked like she would be impressed when he told her:

"Yeah, I play with the team."

The girl's friend quickly butted in:

"Well, then why aren't you with them? They have an away game this weekend."

It was Saturday night, and for sure he should have been on the road with the team, but he was listed as inactive, so his team had left him behind.

"Man, what kind of groupie are you?" he said rising from his seat, and yelling at the girl who had burst his bubble.

But the girl wasn't a groupie; she was a stripper, and she always knew when and where to find the guys, at home or away. Sometimes she traveled out of town with them, but guaranteed, she had a couple of regulars that she took care of during home games.

The girl really didn't know anything about being active or inactive, all she knew was what she told her friend:

"Girl, he is frontin. If he was really a player, he would be gone with the team."

There was nothing he could say to that. Either way, he was humiliated.

The girls turned their noses up at him, and snickered as they shuffled away and left him standing there, nursing his pride.

Those were the kind of nights when Tony was glad he could go home and call Janiece. He could forget about the groupies in the club and how they made him feel up or down. When he went home and called Janiece, she made him feel real again. He would easily pretend that he had just rolled over in bed, thought about her, or that he had just watched a movie that made him think back on them. When she would ask:

"Well where were you earlier when I called?"

It was simple; he had worked out so long and hard, he didn't hear the phone ringing. He had been "knocked out."

If her questions started getting too direct, he would yawn heartily, and tell her:

"Well, I was just calling you to see how you were doing. I'ma go on back to sleep now."

Those were the games he was used to playing, but there was something bigger waiting for him in the wings.

Between running game on girls in the streets, and running back to Janiece, he met Nadique, who he sometimes called "Deek-Deek."

Nadique was the type of girl that he couldn't easily place in a category. She was "hot to death." And in his own words, she had the best body he'd ever seen in his life. But, she wasn't the type of girl he could easily "get down with." Nadique was high post, but at the same time, she was down to earth. Even more striking to him was the fact that she wasn't even attracted to him.

Nadique didn't know anything about football. She didn't even know it was possible to see players out in the grocery store, which was where they met. When Tony approached her, she thought he was a body builder, and she was turned off because she didn't like guys who were "all into their physiques." But, Tony had pursued Nadique aggressively and eventually won her over.

Snapshots

Still, it wasn't an easy situation for him. Nadique was always busy. She was constantly juggling her studies while working toward certification as a practicing psychiatrist; but she always found time for Tony.

Whenever she would tell her friends about him, they suggested she wait until she was a "real" psychiatrist, because the few stories she told about Tony made her friends say he was *insane*.

Tony wasn't crazy; he just seemed to have a hard time making good decisions. In so many ways he was just unsure of himself and needed to get grounded. For Tony, that's where Nadique came in and was most helpful. Nadique provided roots for him. She was strong and focused. She had her mother's good looks and her father's ambition, but she wasn't trying to sell herself to him. Tony admired her for that. But what he couldn't admire or maybe what he couldn't understand was why Nadique didn't demand any commitment of his time or his heart.

She wanted to let things be. It was apparent to Nadique that things were developing for her and Tony, and she wanted to just let it happen naturally. So, she wasn't making any demands. There were no questions when he was out late and never called. No yelling and screaming if she found out he had been out with someone else. She believed the bond they were building was stronger than that. She knew that Tony could tell she had something special to offer him and she felt he would always be back for that. She felt that bond was stronger than whatever he was seeking out on a date. Tony knew Nadique was a good woman, and she thought he knew that she respected him enough not to wash his face in it.

Nadique had seen from his personality, Tony was the type of man who had a hard time making up his mind, but she also knew that he would have to make his own choices. If she would have tried to influence his decisions, he would always resent her. Tony had always denied that there was anyone else for him. Whenever he had done something questionable, he would come back to her pleading forgiveness before she could say anything. He was constantly sorrowful and talking about "the changes" he was "going through." Part of Nadique just took Tony at his word that he would grow "through" and hopefully, "out of" whatever he was doing. Nadique mistakenly continued to think that Tony was trying to work some of his more private struggles out on his own, and when he was ready, he would step up to the next level of their relationship. What Nadique didn't realize was that Tony knew she would never turn her back on him, and he also knew that she would never force his hand.

So, this gave him time to play games. Nadique was just sympathetic and easy going. He wasn't taking advantage of her. There were a lot of things that Tony liked about Nadique, especially the fact that he knew where her heart was. For Nadique, it was all about being on his side, and having his back. He needed that from her, but secretly he did not admire or appreciate it. In so many ways, he took her nonchalant ways to mean that she really didn't care for him. And, even when he knew she did, he took her love for granted.

He realized she was full of support and love for him, but at the same time, he had no respect for her laid back approach to a relationship. He needed a woman with more backbone. Someone who could straighten him out and make him do right. Nadique was too slow for that. She was sitting back believing that he needed to and would straighten things out for himself. But really, Tony felt he needed "a real woman" who could do that for him.

There was too much confusion playing Nadique's game, especially when he had his home-town heart throb who could and would battle with him to make him do right.

That's what he really wanted. So, sometimes he would disappear from Nadique and fly Janiece out for weekends or weeks. Nadique never questioned him about where he had been. She would just be sitting there thinking that he was going to pull himself together. Whenever Tony came back, a weekend or week later needing something from her, she was still there with all her support, and no real questions or demands.

Tony almost hated her for that. The disdain he felt for Nadique confused him. He knew that she brought many good things to him. She was strong, savvy, articulate, and sexy. But she was also making him conscious of his own defaults. He knew she could read him well enough to know that he had those defaults, yet she wasn't woman enough to try to change them; instead, her silent persuasion was demanding that he do it himself.

He didn't need that. There was something more and better about Janiece in his eyes. Nadique was too new school with her thoughts and actions, but Janiece was old fashioned. She could get him to buckle down and do right. Plus, Janiece was in the church.

Even though they had been sleeping together for years, either one of them could bring up how guilty they felt about that. And, when Janiece got pregnant, he brought up his moral obligation, and she had no intention of turning the option away. He wanted to marry her, then and there. It would make things right, all the way around.

They loved each other and had surely gone through some things. They were soon to be family. Why not make the commitment? There was no reason. Things with Janiece were much more simple than they were with Nadique. Nadique had a lot going for herself, and it was true, she had his back and would always be there for him, but Janiece had already been there for years while he battled with himself. Nadique "had it going on" and she had a lot to offer him, so he took as much from her as he could; but Nadique was complex. With Janiece things were simple. And, with the baby in the picture, the equation was solved. In his mind there was no other decision; he would marry Janiece, and just "leave the past behind." The only question that remained for years was, had he made the right choice.

It seemed that Nadique never gave any more consideration to what Tony had done. She had always known, his choices had to be his own. When she heard through the grapevine that he had gotten married, she never even bothered to question it, and that nearly burned him up.

That was the one thing Tony couldn't stand about Nadique. She was too nonchalant. Even with his marriage, she wasn't showing any degree of upset. So, he had been right. She didn't care. If she did, she would have wanted answers.

Secretly, Nadique was broken inside, but there was no need for her to question him. The fact was, he had said "I do" to someone else, and there was no answer more sufficient than that.

She wouldn't give Tony the satisfaction of knowing that he had shattered her hopes of him pulling it together, and them building toward something. When he came to her to tell her about his marriage, she just stared at him with that sharp look of hers which had always seemed to peer into the core of his being. He hated that look. It was like her eyes could slice through his skin and read the depths of his heart.

It was too bad for Nadique that they couldn't. For all the time she had known him, Nadique had only seen the good in Tony. And, even what others deemed as awful in Tony, Nadique saw as simple potential; she always thought he would clean up his act and start growing with her. But, Tony couldn't do that. He hadn't been able to figure her out. Even the day he went back to see her and say that he had gotten married, he still couldn't tell why Nadique was so nonchalant about his decision, and he couldn't tell where her head was. And for some reason, he still needed to know.

Constantly he had struggled with himself, and found himself in the arms of some old girlfriend. He was looking around to figure out if he had done the right thing. Maybe there was something else out there for him that he had overlooked.

Tony was always bothered about how things were left wide open with Nadique. He had to see if maybe he had overlooked something in her. That was the hard part. Nadique was not going to give him the chance to find out. She had always believed that she and Tony would end up together, but he had made a permanent commitment, and there was no resolve for that.

It took some time, but Tony wore away at Nadique. He worked his way back into her life, knowing that she had never kicked him out of her heart. He knew that she loved him, and he used that against her.

He came around, and called from time to time to see how she was doing. And just when he caught her in a vulnerable moment, he walked back in. And once he got his feet in the door, he trampled all over her emotions and thoughts.

She had been constantly warned by her friends to "cut him loose," so that he would never have the opportunity to turn her world inside out; but none of them could have known Tony the way she did.

For a while, even her friends were fooled. His emotional outpourings, and his inability to just "let go and leave the past behind," made everyone think that he had to be sincere. He wasn't mean spirited enough to be manipulative. But, they had forgotten, and Nadique had known it better than anyone. Tony was a person who could never prepare a sound judgment. He had always been confused about his choices; but after he went back to Nadique and wore her down for years, it was easier.

He could make his choice then. He had gone back to Nadique trying to make sure he hadn't made a mistake closing her out of his life. Every time he tried to re-enter and she put him out, he

Snapshots

was wounded like a lost puppy and told her how much it hurt, and how confused he was that he just kept finding himself coming back to her. Nadique didn't understand it either, and decided to stop being so hard on him, and give him a chance to be heard. She took a laid back approach to his actions, but before she knew it, things had drastically changed. And that was exactly how Tony had wanted it.

This last time he had entered her life with intentions. Though he said he "didn't understand why" he "just couldn't let go," he secretly knew that he had gone back to Nadique just so that he could prove to himself that there was nothing left for him there. When he went back to Nadique, it wasn't because he "just couldn't get rid of all the love" he had for her. It was because he was working hard to get rid of it.

As much as Tony hated it, Nadique had a grip on his heart. She was miles and miles away from him, but she was always on his mind. He couldn't get rid of all the thoughts and memories and regrets he had that he hadn't chosen her to be his wife. But, now that he was married to someone else, he had to get rid of Nadique, and there was no better way to do that than to sneak up on her, run her down, and then show himself that there was nothing left of her.

And that's what he did. It was a such relief for Tony. He worked hard at taking all that he could get from Nadique. And once he felt that she didn't have anything left to offer, he had proven that he had been right. There was nothing left out there for him, not even in someone like Nadique. So it was settled; he could go back to his life.

No one could have ever believed that Tony was that malicious. He had always seemed to have a tough time making choices, but with Nadique, he had been deliberate. He had decided to go back and do whatever it took to get her wiped out of his system, and now it was done.

He could go back to his life and finally make it work. All the pieces were already in place. He had a loving family; he could lose himself in them and find himself there. That's what family was for. He had built this family because he wanted to, and he would be a loving husband and a good father. It felt good now. All of his mistakes were behind him.

Tony had carried on plenty of extra-marital affairs, and had gone to countless ex-girlfriends to see if there was anything left. All he could see, time and time again was how much he needed to get right, and get himself together for Janiece and the kids.

No one would have understood this, but within Tony, he needed something to make it all make sense. Cheating made him realize what he had at home. It made him value it more, and start putting things in perspective.

Whenever he cheated on Janiece, he was overwhelmed with guilt. The thought of what it did to her, to the kids, and how it would just wreck his world if they ever left him...these things came to him full circle whenever he cheated. He faced losing them. So, being out in the streets made him place more value on his family; being out there made him see there was nothing really out there for him. It made him work harder toward his marriage. With Tony, it was all about family. It was all about making things right at home, building and growing there. And it wasn't too late. There was no way it was too late for that.

He could concentrate more, and make all the contributions he needed to make in his new life.

But, only time could tell. One thing was for sure, Janiece was tired, and she was never going to forget all the years of all his cheating and all his lies.

Tony could have been satisfied if Janiece had just found comfort in friends and family during the times when things weren't good for him. He had done so much dirt to Janiece that he could have even comforted himself if she would have had a one night stand. He could have told himself that he was reaping what he sowed. He had done it enough times to her, and she had stood by him and kept the kids and him a family. He deserved that once or twice, or maybe even a few times. If Janiece ever cheated, he would be able to just suck it up. But there was something more eating Tony up about Janiece.

It was that, somewhere in Tony's heart, he knew Janiece had found comfort somewhere else. His suspicion was that Janiece had found it in the arms of another man who had never really left her life. It was Eric Lucas that Tony was suspicious of.

Janiece had always found comfort in Eric, even when she and Tony were having problems in college. Janiece could turn to Eric, and he was always right there waiting. He had been Tony's only competition. But, Tony was able to stretch out far beyond Eric. Janiece had seen the promise of what was coming in Tony's future, and she want-

Snapshots

ed to be a part of it. Way back when Tony had pretended to be playing it cool, he would "confide" his fears to Janiece. He would talk about how scared he was that entering the NFL might change things for him. Most of his "fears" dealt with how he didn't want the money or new lifestyle to change him. Janiece knew that it would change many aspects of his life for the better, and she had always hoped to be a part of that, if Tony would give her the chance.

Eric knew that he couldn't financially compete with what Tony would be able to offer Janiece on down the line. Eric was a regular guy. He was in college with them, but he had the humble ambition of becoming a social worker. There was no way he could compete with the "glory" Tony's life would bring, or even the popularity it offered back in those days. Janiece would base her choice on a number of things, but she would surely leave Eric behind.

When Tony had settled down and gotten into his own life, he began to realize that maybe Janiece hadn't ever left Eric behind. Maybe she couldn't. Tony couldn't play games with himself about that. He couldn't stand having to live with his suspicions that there was someone else hiding in Janiece's heart. There was someone else that was able to touch her in places that Tony never could. Even though this was mostly all his fault, Tony couldn't bear being shut out. He did not know for sure whether his suspicions were right or wrong, and that was the part that ate at him the most.

#

As the years flipped by in Tony's life, he had learned to find comfort in many ways.

It was true that he had his family and kids at home, but he had never given up on working his volunteer hours at the Center with Carrie. His work there provided a level of fulfillment that had been gone from his life for years. He was appreciated there. His own children would always tear across the field and greet him after practice, screaming "daddy!" And during the games, his children gave him the only recognition he got on the field. There would be thousands of faces in the crowd, but he could always scan and find his kids. When his eyes met theirs, he would pound his chest three times and point to them, and they would do the same thing back to him. Nothing could match how good that made him feel. Nevertheless, he needed other kinds of attention. And, the attention he got from the kids at the Center provided yet another degree of gratification.

At Carrie's Center, Tony was a different kind of hero. When he walked in the door, he was rallied around by a group of kids who were strangers to him, yet needed him desperately. This gave him a chance to see how much he meant to others. It also made him see how needed he was in his own life at home. He would never want his kids to be without the guidance and leadership he could provide. And, Tony was a good father and provider for his children.

Carrie understood him. He often talked with Carrie about how emotional it made him that:

"Kids—kids are out there suffering, and needing some guidance."

He told Carrie that he just couldn't stand to see kids hurt and abused; he would give anything in the world to make sure his own kids, and other people's children didn't suffer.

That part of Tony moved Carrie.

There had to be things going on in his own life, but he never talked about them. He was just always concerned with others first. In his heart, Tony was convicted, and he made Carrie believe that he just needed to be able to give back. He had to have a place where he could make an impact, other than on the field, and other than just doing it for self. He was glad that the Center was there, and that Carrie always made him feel welcome.

More and more often, Tony found himself there. Carrie was a comforting listener. She believed in what he had to say. And she was easy to talk to. She never asked direct questions, so it never felt like she was prying into his personal life.

Her initial conversation with Tony was about how noticeable his efforts on the team were.

That struck him as odd because Carrie had been known for rarely getting involved with the business side of the game; still, she had taken notice of his hard work on the team. He appreciated her recognition.

During all of his marital unrest, his performance in the game had been shaky. But, now that he had settled down, he had been putting his whole heart in to everything that he did. The team wasn't going to fold without him, so he had been hoping the improvements he was trying to make were at least registering with the coaches. The coaches did recognize his contributions, but having Carrie notice was even better. Her support could certainly be helpful. Tony didn't want to use her, but he did want her to put in some good feedback for him. That wasn't a problem for Carrie. She had backed the guys up plenty of times when the players' performance was being evaluated in tight decisions.

In rare instances, if she had been really moved by someone, she would step up to defend a guy; she could do this for Tony, just as she had done for Rayshawn.

It was incredible how grounded Carrie was. She was the equivalent to a queen on the throne, and she could have just basked in the glory of being the owner's daughter. Or, she could have wielded her power, and run things in that organization. But, she had decided not to do either. She was out there in the trenches, and working to improve life for other people who seemingly had little in common with her. She had come from nothing but a privileged background, yet she understood the needs of every child who walked through her doors.

Tony admired and respected her for that. He felt that she was the one who deserved a lot of credit.

She blushed when he complimented her. There was nothing more rare than the closeness they had been developing with one another.

From a series of events in her own life, Carrie had been finding herself needing the Center to fulfill or complete her. She was thirty five years old, and married to a husband who had placed more value on keeping the salary cap open enough to take in the "big dogs" than he did on loving his wife. It hadn't always been that way.

Ed and Carrie had started off in real love. But, throughout the years, the power that her father had entrusted to Ed was consuming him in ways that allowed Carrie no other release than to be at her Center. She was finding herself there, later and later, as the months went by. But, she wasn't always there alone.

Tony had found his way to the Center many nights. And, one of those nights he had accidentally found a way to scoop Carrie into his arms.

It all started out sincerely. One evening after almost all the children had slowly cleared out, he found himself hanging around saying good-bye's to the rest of them with Carrie. One of the last children leaving was a little girl who had torn away from her mother's hand and ran back because she had forgotten to give Carrie a "big good-bye hug." Carrie always liked to give those to the children.

Tony smiled when he saw how elated the little girl was to get a goodbye hug from Carrie. Furthermore, she had walked outside the doors of her Center to give the little girl advice about being good in school the next day.

When Carrie turned to go back in and clean up the last few things around the Center, Tony offered to help her. He started by telling her:

"Wow, I can't believe what an impact you have on the kids."

"It's nothing really," Carrie smiled a little nervously. She never liked to be over-compensated for the work she did. The kids' thanks was enough, but hearing it from Tony made her blush.

"You get that all the time right?" he began. "I know everybody who sees you working with the kids has to give you credit for being dynamic," he finished.

The truth was, Carrie did get a lot of compliments from the guys, the parents, and of course her real fans, the kids. Still, there was something so warm about the way Tony complimented her. She knew how he felt about the children, and she saw the level of gratitude he had in his eyes when he approached her.

"You're doing a great job at what you do Carrie. You're making a lot of people happy."

As Tony spoke, he placed his firm hand gently on her right shoulder.

"I mean it. You really make them feel great," he finished.

"Well, you do too Tony," Carrie returned the compliment.

"No, for me, sometimes I think it's just being selfish. You know. I love the reaction and response they give. Knowing I'm needed and making their day...that probably makes me feel better than I make them feel," Tony said with confidence and sincerity.

He was unbelievable, this guy. Here he had a family, a full career, still found time to come to the Center, and he felt like *he* was being selfish, just because he found his work rewarding. He was amazing in Carrie's eyes.

"You're incredible," she blurted out.

"Huhn?" he asked, confused. His perplexed, but amused look really added to how bewildered he was.

"Me?" he asked, pointing to himself.

"Come on, Tony," Carrie began. "You're giving and giving

and giving. You have a full family at home. You're coming down here giving more and..." before she could finish, Tony interrupted.

"Well. You know..." he began. "We're not talking about me right now," Tony continued.

"We're talking about...You!" Tony said, pointing to Carrie, and touching her shoulder slightly.

Everything could have remained light hearted, but he did something that he had intended to be innocent, yet it turned into the beginning of the end for them.

Tony reached around and placed his firm hand on her right shoulder as he stood to her left. This time he rubbed up and down on her arm a little bit, then continued talking.

"Come on, let's head on out of here. I know you're ready to get home. Your husband is probably thinking one of us hoodligans done got you."

Tony was trying to be funny and Carrie could tell, so she smiled. But she assured him that Ed knew better than that. The people in this neighborhood had always been on the look out for her and made sure she was okay.

The truth was, Ed was still in the office, and probably hadn't noticed how late it was. She didn't mention that, but she did tell Tony that he was the one who probably needed to hurry home. Tony had always talked about how he loved to be there to tuck his children in.

So, when she reminded him about that, he placed both of his hands on the back of her shoulders, and said "Yeah, you're right."

They had begun to walk toward the front door, but a few steps with Tony's hands on her back made Carrie stop in her tracks.

There was something about his strong hands; they were both comforting and firm at the same time. Something about his touch made Carrie slow down to recoup herself. But, she couldn't shake the warm, rising feeling that had moved from her stomach to her chest. It made her tingle then shiver a little.

He could feel it too. He slid one hand down the side of her left arm, and held her hand when she turned to face him. Carrie looked into his eyes, and then straight ahead.

Tony thought he had made her feel too uncomfortable and loosened his hand a little, but she squeezed it and he tightened back up. She huffed out a short, discontented breath, looked toward the ground, and shook her head. Tony placed his right arm on her shoulder, then slid it around to her back. Carrie buried her forehead in the top of his stomach, since at 5 foot 4, that's where her head peaked on him.

He rubbed her back for what seemed like forever. She was in his embrace, and before she knew it, she was rubbing all around his lower back too.

She couldn't look up at him. It felt too unreal for her to look at any part of him and know that this was real, and that this was really happening. It felt like a dream, and she would have liked to have kept it that way.

Carrie closed her eyes, and sunk deeper into Tony's presence. No music was playing, but they found themselves standing in place and swaying slightly, with the increasing darkness wrapping around them.

She breathed him in. She could feel his heart pounding through the movement of his stomach. He was nervous too, and knew that something was happening.

She should just let go, and he should just move on, but they couldn't find the way to break free from each other. Tony began rubbing through Carrie's hair with one hand, and as she breathed in and sighed out some slight delight, he felt it happening more. He began tussling through her hair with both hands, until he found himself placing both of his strong hands on her soft, cool cheeks. He lifted her face, and lowered his body and began kissing her on the lips.

It was an awkward approach, but it created a rising and tingling heat inside of him. It was there, all up the middle of his tightening stomach, in the fist-like feeling that was grabbing the inside of his throat. It was there. The cooling nervousness that started running down the back of his legs and into his knees, which were quivering. The only part of Tony that hadn't tightened up was the newest addition to him, Carrie. Her soft lips were still massaging his. Even though his own lips had scrunched up, and he was kissing her, harder and harder, grabbing her more and more, in places he hadn't ever dared to dream of.

This couldn't be real for him either. He had never even looked at Carrie in a physical way. In many ways, he still couldn't see her like this. There was a heat and a presence clouding the room, and it was more than physical; it was almost spiritual what was happening to them. They were wrapped into one another, and her mouth

Snapshots

was opening to invite him in further and further. His mouth and his tongue were no longer in his possession. If they were he would have told her:

"We should stop."

But he couldn't. Carrie was stroking his tongue with her lips and moving them in and out and all around on his stiffly curled tongue.

She kept her eyes closed as she slid further down his stomach, kissing him on his shirt and rubbing as much of him as she could touch. He ran his hands through her hair, but was quickly shuffling to lift his shirt, and unbutton his pants.

She was right there. She was licking and massaging the base of his stomach with her firm tongue and soft lips. She was right there. Caressing every part of his body that he began to reveal. She was right there as he loosened his buttons, and his slacks fell from his waist. She was right there, and he wanted her to do it. He knew it was wrong, but his heart was pounding, and she was right there at the base of his stomach. He began gripping her head from the sides, and her lips—her lips felt so good that his neck arched back toward the sky. He had to let her do it. He had to let her take him in. Carrie was going to let him journey through her world. Her tongue was guiding the road map.

He was going in, as far as she would take him. Tony was going all the way in her, and it felt so good as he slid his way into the shaded remedy of Carrie's world.

As she took him in deeper, he spilled his joy all over her, and warmed her in parts that neither of them had expected. He trembled from the base of his belly; his knees quaked and his body shook so violently, he thought he would collapse on her shoulders.

He peaked so high that his voice seemed to screech like a chirping baby bird. Then his screaming rose to the pitch of a squawking bird taking morning flight. His ears seemed to be ringing from the inside out, and his eyes couldn't stay open for long. They couldn't focus. He kept blinking and shaking his head from side to side. He couldn't believe it, whether he was here or not, whether it had happened or not. So, he kept blinking and shaking his head, trying to get the ringing out, and trying to focus.

Tony had to get his balance. He felt around through Carrie's hair and then kneeled down by her shoulders to get his grip. When he slid to his knees and could hear again, there was Carrie, sobbing on her knees, and crying with her face now buried in his chest.

He wrapped his arms around her. He tried to comfort and caress her, but she had begun to cry out uncontrollably. Tony could understand it all now. This was real. They were here, and it had happened. He knew that. The way Carrie gasped and cried in his arms, he knew it was all too real, and unbelievably for Tony, he nearly felt like crying too.

This was wrong. Really wrong, and he didn't know how he was going to handle this. He had gone far outside of his world, and this was far beyond control.

If she had been a groupie from the club he could have handled this much easier; everything would have been "all good."

The groupie chic would have known what the deal was. She could have been black, white, Puerto Rican or Asian, but she would have known how he "gets down." The bottom line for a girl like that would have been easy. Tony could have "spit it" like he always did:

"Baby, I'm a married man. There can't be no strings attached."

Tony had used that line countless times, but this time he was in over his head. As he sat on his knees holding Carrie, he could feel his toes starting to sting. But, he couldn't rush to his feet. He held her head closer to his chest and kept shaking his head, knowing this was deep trouble, for the both of them.

For different reasons, neither of them could bear to move from where they were. As much trouble as they were in together, they knew that they should definitely tear apart. Parts of both of them were realizing this never should have happened. Yet, parts of both of them were also realizing that it would happen again.

Tony held Carrie that night for as long as he could, and as long as she needed. When the time came, he helped her to her feet and they held one another again, by the arms this time. When he had stroked her hair and they had cleaned themselves up, they left with a silent understanding that they had started something new.

Meeting after meeting, month after month, they had begun to fill something of a need in one another.

It was more than emotional. It was physical and mental, the way they needed one another. Time and time again, they comforted each other on many different levels—what was going on in their lives, what was going on in themselves, but they rarely talked about what they had going with each other. They just let that be. It "was what it was" now, and it was growing in ways that, underneath all the things they knew were wrong, still made it feel right.

Tony always met Carrie at the end of her night at the Center whenever they were getting together. Tony wasn't spending much time there with the kids anymore. He was usually just pulling up and waiting for her to close things out. When Carrie would get in his truck, they would always kiss, then hold hands and begin their continual journey to find some place where they could be alone.

They had to be extra careful not be noticed, and for the longest time it seemed to them that they had achieved that degree of privacy, but, someone had been noticing what was going on.

It was Ed, Carrie's husband.

He couldn't put his finger on it, but something about Carrie was different. She was changing. She was becoming much more lively in spirit, yet she was growing even more distant than she had ever been at home. The distance wouldn't have struck Ed so much, but her new, awakening spirit was making him curious.

Tony's wife didn't have time to notice the changes in him. In fact, there were no real changes. He had mastered the game enough throughout his years of infidelity, so even his patterns of that had started to seem normal. Tony loved to "break up and make up," mess up and then work like a dog to get things back together. Janiece knew this all too well, but to her, it didn't even matter anymore.

For Ed and Carrie, this was all new. Even though as a rule, when Carrie was out late, Ed was out even later; his reasons were legitimate in his eyes. His time was devoted to improving the empire her father had established, and he didn't really have time to worry about anything else.

From time to time, they went to award dinners for the team, and sometimes they would steal away on a special trip. At those times, things were wonderful. Sometimes when he had been able to make it to a few dinner parties, Ed had wondered if Carrie was exchanging looks with a few of his colleagues; but he could readily dismiss those fleeting thoughts. That only lasted for moments, when they were out interacting. Carrie was good at being a social butterfly, and she could sincerely charm almost everyone in the room by making them feel special, just with her smile. But this feeling Ed had been having lately was different. Carrie's new behavior was lasting, and they weren't at any parties or get togethers. As a matter of fact, he had only been at work, and she had been devoting more time and late hours at the Center. He had wondered this time, with a sick and disgusting feeling, if her new vibrant behavior didn't have more meaning to it.

One thing was for sure, Carrie had only been spending time at the Center, so there was only one type of man she could be getting involved with. It had to be one of the players.

# # #

There had been nothing calculated in what was developing between Tony and Carrie, not even the risks. But, when the equation was balanced: Tony plus Carrie, plus Ed driving to the Center one night, equaled nothing but trouble, especially for Tony.

Ed had left the office early one night, but what was early for him, was still a late night for Carrie and Tony. They always returned to the Center around nine o'clock in the evening, and as usual they were just pulling up so that Carrie could get in her car and go home. They always drove in Tony's truck so they could maintain a lower profile.

When Ed had pulled up earlier, he had seen Carrie's car. And though she didn't know it, he had always kept a key to her Center, so he had used it to go in looking for her. When she was no where to be found, he was livid. He did not even get nervous. For one thing, he knew that the people in this neighborhood had "nothing but love" for Carrie. They wouldn't have ever let anything happen to her. So when he saw her car and the empty Center, Ed knew Carrie was off somewhere doing what he had suspected. He just had to see for himself who and what it was. So he waited. He had parked his car in the distance, and he waited and watched.

When Tony pulled up to drop Carrie off, they had no idea that anything was different. Tony was his usual, playful self. He walked her to her car, and stood with his hand resting on the ledge of her window as he talked to her for a few moments. He never kissed her outside in public, but before he walked off, he reached in her window and slightly pinched her cheek. That was his goodnight kiss.

Carrie rolled up her window after that and pulled off. Once she was gone, Tony pulled off. Shortly after they had both left, Ed turned on his head lights, rounded the corner, and headed home.

# # #

There was no greater outrage expressed than the violent words Ed spewed when he got home.

He screamed, he yelled, he broke things. He shook Carrie up, and told her that if he could have, he would have attacked her and Tony earlier, right there in the street. His rage had been that full. But fortunately for them, he knew he had to contain himself. This team was big business and he wasn't going to mess anything up by being emotional. Foremost in his mind, even more than what had sickened him, was that his position and his team were a top priority. Because of that, he knew he had to avoid a public spectacle at all times. If the media had ever gotten a hold to a scandal like that, the PR department would have been working overtime and still couldn't have explained it. The rage that had filled Ed that night would have caused every police man, camera man, and news man from miles around to come and see what was going on. He didn't need that, so he waited. He waited until he got home, then he let it all fly free.

He flipped around and whirled and knocked things over. He lost all his composure. But in all of his rage, Ed still remembered that Carrie was the owner's daughter, and because of that, there was only so much he could do. So he tempered his rage by saying how much she had betrayed him as a wife, and how much she had betrayed her father. He talked about the sick feeling he had just knowing who she had been with and what she had done. He could hardly live with himself knowing who had been inside of her. He almost didn't want to touch her anymore.

Carrie's emotions had bubbled to the top. She had been screaming through her tears that he didn't know what he was talking about. She had been defending herself with words the best way she could, but more than anything, it sounded like she was defending her reasons. Ed was never involved in her life or her civic activities; he hadn't been for years. He was too busy working hard to make the team bigger and better, trying to satisfy her father. If he had been paying more attention to her and their lives, none of this would be an issue now.

Her words didn't matter to Ed. Through their screaming and yelling, her crying and his rage, he knew one thing underneath—it all had to be taken care of immediately, and he would have to move forward from here. He kicked into administrative mode. He would solve everything. This scenario would never be looked at or discussed again. He would make sure that Tony was out of their lives, and out of his way.

Tony was getting traded. If Ed could have, he would have just had Tony black-balled so that he could have never played another day in the NFL. Ed could have easily put in some work to keep Tony off many teams, but that would cause too much pressure on Tony. That might even make him talk one day about how the demise of his career and his affair with Carrie were linked.

Ed didn't need that. He would just rather see Tony ride out a few more years in the League some place where he could forget all about them. Putting Tony out there for a trade would solve all Ed's problems at once.

Carrie could have contested Ed's decision. She was still part owner in this team. She had gone to battle for players in the past, but this time she knew, the battle would be more for herself. And what was it all for? Tony had his life, and she had hers. No matter how angry or disgusted Ed was, he wasn't going anywhere. He wasn't leaving Carrie or the team, and no matter how high he ranked with her father, he couldn't be sure that leaving one didn't mean leaving the other. Carrie could branch out and choose another Mr. Carrie Jacobson, but Tony was taken; so, why not let him just go on with his life.

All along Tony had been telling her how guilty he felt about being with her. His wife, his kids. He was doing wrong. It was eating him alive. And just months into their relationship, after he had enjoyed her in many ways, he started in on her about her own scenario. Her life—her husband. She couldn't keep going on like this either. They were both wrong. Tony had started in on her, eating away at her conscious the minute he was ready to move on.

Carrie didn't know this, but it was constantly his way—to get involved with someone, make them feel sorry for him, then make them feel guilty. He had done this innumerable times, then moved on back to his life. This was the part Carrie didn't see.

She had only seen the side of him that seemed special and good. She had seen the side of him that had been painfully aware of how wrong it was for both of them to be together. She had seen how torn Tony was that he was married and so was she, but he "just couldn't let go" of her. Carrie had seen the Tony that was so tortured by what he was doing that he needed to be constantly reassured by her that he was really okay.

And he was okay. Carrie believed that. He had always told her how he felt he was just dividing himself between her and his family, and it was hard facing the fact that one day he might have to let her go. Carrie felt compassion for that, even though she had grown to need him. Maybe the trade would be best. It would give him a clean break and allow him to start fresh with his wife and life and family. He deserved that.

Carrie had decided she wouldn't fight with Ed about the trade. Secretly, she would do this for Tony. She would be unselfish enough to just let him go on with his life.

Carrie had that much compassion for him, and she wanted to let him go. Tony had told her countless times that he couldn't be the one to do it. He had cried on her shoulder about how confused he was about their whole situation because he "didn't normally do things like this." Carrie had complicated his life, and his soft-hearted honesty made her feel too guilty to continue to do that.

So it was settled. Tony would be moving on. He would have a new team, and another new start.

When things ended here, he would head back to Miami with Janiece and the kids. They would stay there until he left for camp. Then he would go on to a new city and have another chance to start all over—again. Or would he?

# # #

Tony had it set in his mind that back in Miami he would be able to think clearly again. He and Janiece would be back at their roots, and maybe this time they could really grow.

But, unlike many times in his past, things weren't going to be that easy this go round. Things had changed a little bit and life was swinging the full pendulum around for the balance of actions and consequences.

Janiece had not walked into her relationship with Tony blind. She had been highly aware of how much she could give and how much she could get, and she never stopped making sure there was something in it for her. Everyone in her family; her brothers, mother and father, had been reaping in some of the benefits of Tony's labors. She had established a few trust funds in her children's names, and she had managed to establish a foundation that would place a substantial amount of Tony's income into a non-profit organization, for which her children would one day be president, vice president, and chair. For now, she was the legal guardian of that. It took some legal manoeuvering, but she was the sole overseer of the fund.

When the children were old enough to assume positions at the foundation, they would have handsome salaries waiting for them. She explained it to Tony, so that he understood. This was another level of smart business for life after football. They had plenty of investments and stocks, but with this foundation, their children would always have a job waiting for them, plus Tony would be decreasing his tax base, so it made sense on many levels.

That was one of the things that Tony loved about Janiece. She was about business and looking out for their future and the children's future. She was always on the ball, and he didn't have anything to worry about in her. Janiece was there and had his back. That was true, but at the same time, Janiece had looked, learned, listened, and lived through enough of Tony's actions to know, she also had to look out for number one; there was no two, three, or four, because in her eyes, her children were one with her.

Eric's brother had handled all the legal matters for Janiece. Although Eric had chosen the social work field, everyone else in his family was in to some aspect of corporate law.

When Janiece established her foundation, she was doing corporate things; she was also ensuring that she and her children would have a substantial portion of Tony's income when and if she ever decided to leave. That hadn't ever been a concern of Tony's, even when a couple of his close friends and team mates had tried to warn him.

Tony knew his wife well enough, and he had seen how time and time again she had been there for him. And it wasn't like he was getting off easy when he did her wrong. Janiece was a big boned girl who had a quick temper. She had grown up with three brothers that she either fought or defended all her life, and that said a lot because her family had lived on tough grounds when she was a kid.

There was no question about it, when Tony came through the door he knew what he was in for, if he had been out doing wrong. She fought him, scratched, argued, and beat him with words so tough they could have killed somebody; but she never left.

Snapshots

In Tony's mind, that was because she knew him, and she knew that he was trying to do better. She knew how much he really did love her and the kids, and he knew how much she loved him too. So, he was going to keep trying harder, and each time he was getting more sincere. In his mind, the cheating was decreasing to so little, that he was almost done. But for Janiece, she was almost done in a completely different way.

For every action Tony had made, Janiece had packed another piece in to her mental suitcase, and she was filling it to the point that it was almost time for her to go.

When they went back to Miami, Tony had finally pulled the straw that broke the camel's back.

chapter twenty

Janiece was relieved to be back in Miami for many reasons. She felt right back at home with her family and friends. She was spending as much time with them as she could, and Tony was on edge thinking that she had a little too much of her own life going on there. He felt left out. He still had plenty of family and friends there, but he wanted to be a part of whatever Janiece was doing.

She was taking the kids with her all the time, so he knew she wasn't cheating, but then again, who was to say that she couldn't leave the kids with a relative and disappear for a couple hours. He was all giddy yet tied up in knots whenever she would head out the door on her own way. He wanted to go with her, so she started letting him. Janiece didn't have anything to hide, and she knew why Tony was sticking to her like glue. It was because of Eric Lucas. He was from right there in Florida, and Tony had the silly feeling that she might cheat on him with Eric, so he stuck to her like glue, side by side. Whenever she went somewhere Tony was there, smiling and interacting with whoever was in the bunch. He wanted it to show; he was interested and in tuned with her life, and they were a happy couple.

The few close friends Janiece still had knew that she and Tony were not the show room floor couple. They always looked picture perfect, especially when they would get together with friends in the old neighborhood. Janiece would sit one of the kids on her lap, and Tony would keep the other two close to him. Still, it had been evident for years, even during college, that Janiece wasn't totally happy with Tony. But she married him, and her friends felt that she had full knowledge and intentions when she did that. So, they had no pity for her. Even when they would periodically listen to Janiece's mounting problems with Tony, her friends secretly buzzed the question, one to another:

"Is she bragging or complaining?"

A lot of Janiece's complaints were founded, but she knew that many people weren't sympathetic, so she had learned to just turn to the few people she could trust. Her friends were still great people to meet up with now that she was home, and they could talk and interact about things for hours. There was enough going on in everyone's lives, from children to marriage, working and dating; the future and the past, could be talked about for hours in the backyards. Janiece was going to enjoy this, and Tony was right there by her side whenever she did; they were talking about the good times, the joys, the different events and things they had seen. Everyone could contribute in these surface level conversations because they all had plenty going on in their lives.

But when it was personal time, and private time, Janiece knew to talk to the few people she could trust. Her parents, her eldest brother, and her best friend and lover, Eric Lucas.

Years had gone by since she had physically touched and made love to Eric, but she had always called on him whenever she needed to talk. She could do this with him for hours, and he had never let her down.

Eric had opened up the doors to a new relationship with a woman he met through his job. As the years rolled by, he had considered settling down with her before it got too late. He wanted children and a family, and he wanted to do it the way he felt was right, marriage first. Things with Angie, the woman he was planning to marry were going okay. The only problem they had was when Janiece was entering their lives, and that seemed non-stop. She would call in the middle of the night, sometimes when Angie was there, and Eric would never turn her away.

"Where is her husband?" Angie would argue out loud. But the answer was simple, Tony was in the streets, and Janiece was on Eric's shoulder. She always knew where and when to find him, and he knew he would always be there.

Janiece hadn't been in his arms for years. She loved the comfort that Eric could provide when he was just holding her, and she loved the feel of his movements, all around and inside of her. He could go so deep that it felt like he was touching her soul. But, that was behind him now. Eric had made love to Janiece only once since she had been married, and the guilt he felt overwhelmed him. He couldn't do it again. As much as she had needed him, and as much as they felt complete when they made love, they weren't a whole. He was partaking in someone else's life. Janiece was not just Janiece anymore. Now she was married, and when she made that bond, she was

Tony; they were one.

Eric had the same religious background as Janiece and Tony, only he took it a little more seriously. He saw the vows as what they were, a covenant before God. A contract could be breached, but a covenant could only be broken, and he didn't want to stand before God after violating such a sacred thing. So, he stopped it. After one time, it was enough for Eric, and he promised to never turn his back on Janiece, but he could never lay down again in their bed, unless they were man and wife.

Janiece had begun wanting that throughout the years. There was a part of her that could never let go of Eric, and the more he rubbed around on the inside of her heart, the more she understood why. In many ways it was a blessing that he had refused to violate the laws of God with her. She respected him even more. Eric was a serious man. There was no changing his mind about certain things or compromising the Word. So, Janiece had stayed as close as she could to Eric. For inspirational, spiritual, and emotional reasons, she had needed to keep Eric in her life.

Tony was increasingly aware of this, and he knew he couldn't battle with it. He and Eric were two different kinds of men. Still he hated that Eric had something he could never seem to master, a distinction. Eric had a high level of integrity and respectability with everyone who knew him, including Janiece. Though that bothered Tony a lot, he did have one thing up on Eric. He hadn't ever been man enough to walk away with the one thing Tony did, a booming career and Janiece as his wife. So, for all of Eric's moral uprightness, he was still just a "self-righteous punk" in Tony's eyes.

Nevertheless, Tony was smart enough to know that Janiece and others were taken by Eric, so he tried hard to never show his disdain for Eric, especially when they were around him. Tony had been preparing himself for the day that it would happen. He knew it was coming. As soon as he found out that he, Janiece, and the kids were headed back to Miami, he knew they would eventually run into Eric Lucas.

#

Tony and Janiece had been back in Miami for little more than a month when they ran into Eric and Angie.

Tony and Janiece had stopped by the old neighborhood to visit Cora Lee and her husband Jeremy. The Lees had been highschool sweethearts, and later when they got married Cora didn't even have to change her last name. Tony had started that as a joke way back in grade school. It was really just a brutal tease because for years Jeremy had been forced to sit next to Cora, since they had the same last name. In the early days, Jeremy hated to be labeled as Cora's boyfriend, especially since he and Tony were two of the most popular guys in their school. Jeremy used to get tons of those "Do you like me? Check yes: Check no," letters everyday, and usually the pretty girls liked him.

Cora Lee didn't stand a chance. She was scrawny and puny and grew up looking old. She wore an "old lady's" hairstyle, and outdated clothes that were always a size too big for her dreadfully skinny frame. Most people said she wore her mother's clothes and pop bottle glasses. They even said that the only boy who had ever kissed her was her older brother Carl.

Jeremy knew those things were false. Even though he never bragged about it, he had spent plenty of time at the Lee's house, and they were nice people.

Jeremy and Cora had been study partners for years in school, and even after school, Cora and her brother often tutored him at their house. Behind closed doors Jeremy had been hanging out at the Lee's house, having dinner, great conversations, and getting to see what they were all about.

The Lees weren't as poor as people thought. As a matter of fact, they were probably a lot better off than most people in the neighborhood. The difference was, whatever money they made, they tucked it into savings. Cora's mom worked as a paralegal for Eric Lucas's father, and her dad worked as a janitor. They wanted to see their children off to college, and they wanted to make sure the money was there. If scholarships came through, that would be great, but the Lees believed in having a back up plan for their children. New clothes, shoes, and styles weren't important to them. The chief priority was placed on the impact that their children could make on the future.

The days that Jeremy had been spending at their house caused him to start getting a lot heat. In the early years, people wanted to know why he was always hanging around with "the girl who smelled like pee."
He didn't know exactly how to defend Cora back then, but as he

grew to know her, he grew to like her, and he learned how. Cora was a good person with a wholesome nature, and he didn't want people to continually make up lies and abuse her just because she was different and shy. When Jeremy started saying things like that, the rumors started running that he and Cora were boyfriend and girlfriend.

Jeremy was popular, and he was a football star; from grade school through highschool, he was great on the field. But he wasn't going to let his popularity get in the way of him taking up for someone who had been so good to him, and so helpful to his academics. If it hadn't been for Cora spending years tutoring him, he would have never even been eligible for his athletic scholarship.

So, he appreciated Cora, and by the time they were in highschool, she had been his girl for years, secretly. He had liked her more and more as they were leaving middle school, and by highschool, he had asked her to be his girl as soon as she could start dating.

Cora never blossomed in to a beauty queen, and she was no where near ready to start setting it out like some of the other girls, but she had won Jeremy's affection, and he knew she was his girl.

When highschool was ending, Jeremy had been convinced that he wanted to marry her. But, that was impossible. Cora was headed to Atlanta and he was headed to a Division 1 School in Ohio. Cora had deep feelings for Jeremy too, but she knew she had to go to college. She would be attending one of the exclusive schools in Atlanta. And, just as her brother had done four years earlier at the other exclusive school there, Cora would be graduating with honors.

Cora's four years in college had opened up a world of new doors to her life, but one door she had never closed was the one to Jeremy Lee. They had stayed as close as they could, calling one another and visiting when they could.

In all of the things they had explored during their years in college, they had found one thing; they still wanted to be together. However, the distance was going to grow even further.

After graduation, Jeremy was heading West as a non-drafted free agent to try out for a team, and Cora was staying in Atlanta to teach. Both things were equally important to both of them.

For Cora, education could have either made or broken her. She had always been extremely smart, but because she was different, she was picked on by students, and overlooked by teachers. She could have easily gone by the way side if it hadn't been for her parents, and the couple of teachers who finally took interest in her, and tried to help build her confidence. Throughout school, Cora had always done exceptionally well. With her skills in math she could have easily entered then opened her own securities firm. Or, with her expertise in science, she could have become a chief of staff surgeon one day; but she desired a career that would allow her to help other kids who might be going through the same things she did.

Jeremy admired Cora's rationale; still he had hoped she would go West with him. But, Cora couldn't commit to going with him. She had signed her teaching contract and decided to stay in Atlanta.

It wasn't until Jeremy's first year in the League was over, that Cora agreed to go away with him. At that time the distance was truly getting ready to come between them.

Jeremy's team had slated him to return for the next season, however, they felt he needed to develop some structured skills during the off season. As a result, they had allocated him to NFL Europe. He would be heading to Scotland for nearly three months, and he had asked Cora to go with him. She agreed to go. She had promised to meet Jeremy there for one week, during her Spring break. That was the week that changed their lives.

He wanted her to marry him. They had spent years together and neither of them were looking for anything more than what they found in each other. The years had gone by; the distance had been between them, still they were with one another and in love. There was no way to argue against that. Jeremy and Cora had set a date and when he came home from Scotland, made it through camp, and faced a new Season in the Fall, he would be doing it with his wife.

Cora hadn't ever envisioned herself as an NFL wife. She had always felt those glamor girl spots were reserved for prima donnas or cheerleader types. But Cora was drastically wrong. Behind the scenes, most of the guys wanted a mate who was down to earth and who they could count on. They wanted someone they could laugh with, talk with, and grow with as an equal in friendship and love. Cora definitely fit the bill for that. So, when Jeremy returned to the States, and Fall rolled around, he and Cora got married and headed West with his team.

During the years they spent with his team, their relationship flourished, but his career did not. Jeremy had lost a part of his dream after two Seasons, but he was glad to still have Cora. Moreover, he was glad to have the new addition of their first child, Cameron Jerome.

Cora had been so active as a wife, then mother, that Jeremy couldn't understand why she also insisted on having a job. But Cora was determined to work and save, and make sure they spent far beneath their means. Her financial plan would have stayed in place even if he had played a full ten years in the League. So, when his career ended after two, their lives didn't change much. They simply headed back to Miami and made a modest living right in their old neighborhood.

When they got back to Miami, Cora had been a big influence on Jeremy. She had encouraged him to go through the teacher certification process, and use his degree in sports management to become a gym teacher and coach. She had started working in the school system already, and it would be easy and rewarding for Jeremy to enter that arena also.

Back in Miami, they got settled in to their own one level, three bedroom, bungalow style home. It had a patio, and just enough land out back to entertain the few friends who would drop by on Saturday afternoons.

It was no surprise to see Eric and Angie on the weekends. They both lived in a neighborhood that was just a few blocks over, and Eric was a school social worker in the same district as Cora and Jeremy. Eric was also a celebrity at Cora and Jeremy's house. When their son, Cameron Jerome was born, Cora had decided that Eric would be CJ's godfather. Eric's family had always been close with hers, and Eric had often come to her defense, long before Jeremy had been interested in her. In some ways, Jeremy felt that he should have had some say in who his first son's godfather was going to be, but the fact was, his choice would have never worked for Cora.

Although Jeremy and Tony had gone distinctively different ways in college, they were still relatively close friends. They had stayed in touch throughout the years.

When Tony found out that Jeremy was getting married to Cora, he had been mature enough to be glad for him. During grade school Tony had been obnoxious and one of the people who had taunted Cora, but by highschool when he realized how much Jeremy cared about her, he had laid off and had actually started genuinely supporting their relationship.

Tony hadn't been able to make it to Jeremy and Cora's wedding, but he did send them a nice wedding gift, and a few months later, he sent them an announcement of his own marriage. He and Janiece hadn't planned out anything elaborate. They had just kind of "jumped up and did it," in his own words.

Jeremy respected him for getting married, especially since Janiece was pregnant. But, Cora didn't respect or accept anything about Tony; she simply tolerated him for Jeremy's sake.

Cora wasn't one hundred percent healed from all the years of jeering she endured; but she was savvy enough to realize a few things. For one, so many people had teased and prodded at her during her youth that if she had held a grudge against them, she would have never been able to speak to half the people in this community. Furthermore, many of the "popular" people had been so comfortable in who they were then, that they never grew into the better people they could have become.

And, as for Tony, he had endured early years of teasing and taunting himself. It wasn't until one of his gym teachers introduced him to the possibility of going pro that Tony started lifting weights and developing some confidence in himself. That had been very early on. And, when he had struggled and gained enough confidence in himself, he started shooting it down in others. Cora had seen that aspect of Tony a long time ago.

Now that Tony and Janiece were back in Miami, they were stopping by Cora's from time to time. Jeremy loved to hear Tony's stories about the League. His time had come and gone far too soon for him to know about all the changes that were going on, but Tony was up on everything, and shared it. He told Jeremy how teams would eventually get rid of the Play Book, and start using the strategies laid out on lap top programs. The widespread use of computers was making it easier for coaches and players to review "film." They could even run certain plays as video games, and let the players "strategize" that way. This was big news for Jeremy, and he would often sit back and nod his head, excited about all the things that Tony knew.

It was nothing for Tony to offer to come speak at Jeremy's school. Jeremy and Cora's kids could definitely benefit from hearing a "stay in school" speech from him; or, the kids on Jeremy's team could certainly use some pointers from a pro athlete like him. Tony wasn't shy about saying things like:

"Hey man, it's nothing. I could do that for you," then he would smile graciously and say how good it felt that he was in a position to "give back."

Tony was in the middle of one such conversation when Eric and Angie walked up Cora and Jeremy's driveway one Saturday afternoon. Eric had stopped dead in his tracks when he got to the backyard and saw Tony leaned back in a lawn chair talking. Cora's eyes froze with Eric's, and before she could tell him to come on back, Tony had stood up, opened his arms, and invited Eric and Angie on back.

"Hey, come on man. You know you're welcome here. We're all friends, right?" Tony began.

Eric was visibly uncomfortable so Tony turned up the pressure.

"Come on back E-El," Tony said, extending his arm, and then waving Eric and Angie over.

With Angie tugging at him, they walked in closer and Angie sneered over at Janiece. She lifted her eyebrows, smirked, and then slipped her arm even tighter around Eric's. Angie had never met Janiece, but it was easy to tell who she was. For one thing, there were only three other couples there. The only one Angie didn't recognize was Tony and Janiece. When they had walked up, and Eric accidentally cursed right before saying Tony's name, Angie instantly knew the brown skinned girl seated next to him was most likely Janiece.

Cora was split seconds from stopping any confrontation, but she should have been quicker. Tony was feeling more and more full of himself.

"Hey E-El. Long time no see buddy," Tony said, then shook Eric's hand, and reached around him for a tight hug. "Yeah man," Tony continued, "It's good to see you."

Tony looked around and added a little drama. "We all know each other here right?" He began. "This is my wife, you know. Janiece."

Tony was emphasizing certain words and definitely trying to take a stab at Eric. Tony recomposed himself and played off his hostility by looking at Angie, and saying. "You two probably haven't met."

Just as Tony had been waiting to take jabs at Eric, Angie had been waiting for her turn with Janiece.

"Oh, no. I don't believe we have—at least not formally. But I'm Angie," she began.

She looked in Tony's face but extended her hand to Janiece, as she continued:

"I'm Angie...Eric's fiance," she closed while she had Janiece's hand in hers.

It was clear to everyone, Angie's last comment was directed solely toward Janiece.

Eric had sternly placed his hand on top of Angie's shaking hand, and said out loud: "Maybe we should go."

There were dozens of comments telling Eric and Angie to stay. Eric placed his hand around Angie's shoulder and he reiterated the fact that they should probably leave. His eyes glanced over to Janiece's as he said: "I'm sorry. I guess we shouldn't have stopped."

"Don't be silly," Tony began. "I'm glad you came. I mean, I'm glad to see you." Tony started looking around the crowd for support, then placed his hand on his wife's shoulder. "And I know, Janiece here is glad to see you."

Janiece rolled her eyes, and was getting uncomfortable in her seat. She was fidgeting and unsure if maybe they should be the ones to get up and leave.

"Tony please," she said without wavering. "Sit down and be quiet. This isn't even your house, and it's definitely not your place."

Janiece had regained herself, and had risen from her seat.

"Look, Cora, I'm sorry. I don't think this is a good idea. We're just going to be going," Janiece said and then turned her eyes sharply to Tony.

"What? What?" he was asking.

"Let's go Tony," Janiece demanded.

"Why?" he demanded. He had already slid back down in his seat, and was trying to act like everything was normal.

Janiece turned her head back toward him again, and he seemed resolute that he was going to stay there and smooth things over.

"Look now, everyone just calm down. Just chill. It's no big deal. We're all family around here," Jeremy had begun, and then reached for Janiece's hand.

Cora was pretty good at restoring order in her classroom, but this was a scene that she couldn't have scripted or erased. Luckily, Jeremy was trying to bring things under control, but had beads of sweat forming as he tried to cool things down.

"Now, we're all friends here..." Jeremy reiterated, but then Tony jumped in.

"Yeah, man, that's what I'm saying. Everybody's cool. Janiece stop trippin. We cool right E?"

Tony was being a little more compassionate now. He could tell he was losing the crowd and he didn't want to be shown up as the bad guy next to Eric, so Tony sincerely started trying to be nice.

"Come on Niecey. Sit down. For real. I'm sorry," he said reaching for her hand. When she respectfully slid it away from him, he leaned over to shake Eric's hand.

"Yo man. For real. No harm intended bro," Tony said sincerely.

Eric shook Tony's hand and nodded his head. Everything was okay. He and Angie would stay for a while. Janiece was in an awkward position. She wanted to just reach over Tony's legs, grab her purse, and leave. Her mother's house was right down the street, but Eric had leaned over her shoulder and asked:

"Janiece, why don't you just stay? We haven't had a chance to talk with each other in a long while."

Eric had already pulled out a chair for Angie, and had planned to get seated himself. But he wouldn't relax until he was sure Janiece was okay.

Eric was genuine, and it was the only thing that was softening Janiece. She dropped her bent elbow, and Eric patted an open seat for Janiece that was between him and Tony.

If Tony hadn't already made himself look bad, he would have demanded that Eric mind his own business, and let Janiece go back to where she had been sitting before...on the other side of him. But, he had started enough trouble and would let that go.

The conversation picked back up, and things seemed to be going well, until they started talking about marriage.

It began when Cora's parents were dropping CJ off, and Mitsy, one of Cora's friends, commented on how nice their baby, home, and marriage was. Tony was trying earnestly to be entertaining and friendly and he chimed in how he had been partially responsible for the marriage. He mentioned how Cora and Jeremy were always sitting next to each other "back in the day," and he knew love was on the horizon for them. He said he "could take credit for a lot of the fact that Jeremy and Cora got married." His comments were getting tired, but it only got worse when he turned the question over to Eric.

Tony had felt that everyone had forgotten his earlier commotion. It had died down so he felt he could take another shot at Eric. Tony leaned around Janiece and in toward Eric and asked:

"So man, when are you going to do your thing? When are you going to get your own bride to be?"

Janiece's face tightened. Her temperature dropped ten degrees with the thought of Eric naming an actual date, and not to mention, right there in her face.

Eric had a low pitched and mild mannered nature already, but his voice softened even more as he answered:

"We're working towards May..."

"May...what?" Angie demanded.

"May fifteenth babe, you know that," Eric continued.

"Yeah, but I'm not the one asking you. Tony is. He's interested in our wedding. Maybe he wants to come with Janiece," Angie said, toying with Janiece and rubbing on Eric's arm.

"Oh, yeah man? May 15th hugh? Well, I am happy for you. Every good brotha needs a good sistah in his life...permanently man, and it looks like you got a good girl there," Tony closed.

Eric agreed by saying that Angie was great. Tony jumped right on that by replying:

"Of course she's great man. She's yours. Anytime you got somebody of your own, that's great. You sure can't count on what's out here in the streets. Man, any girl you meet, nine times out of ten, she got somebody and you're just playing with somebody else's stuff, and sending her home to her man. Shoot dog, everybody wants their own," Tony finished.

Janiece was sick on her stomach, literally. Tony was sending out multiple messages, and she knew it, and so did Eric. Most of all Angie knew it too, but she was well pleased and agreeing with it.

This was so incredibly uncomfortable for everyone, but the worst thought of all was for Janiece. In three months, Eric was getting married. He hadn't even told her, and she hadn't even known how badly it would hurt her to find out. Janiece finally choked out her comment. She couldn't even say congratulations; all she could say was:

"You didn't even tell me, Eric."

"And, why not?" Angie turned toward Eric. She wasn't even angry; she was just smug and teasing. "Why didn't you tell the world Eric? And most of all, your good friend Janiece. I would have thought she'd be the first you'd tell," Angie whispered her last statement to him; "You're always talking to her, aren't you?"

Tony butted in and offered the congratulations on his and Janiece's behalf.

"Hey man, like I say. I'm happy for you dog. Ain't nothing out there in them streets," Tony finished.

Janiece felt like crying, and Eric's heart was broken. They were sitting right next to each other, in Florida's unseasonably warm temperature, but he could feel the chills that were running through Janiece's body. Part of her had gone drop dead cold, and he couldn't even apologize.

Angie was the one to say thank you for Tony's congratulatory comments. Eric couldn't say anything and the rest of the patio was relatively quiet. Mitsy was the first one to speak. She didn't know everyone that well. She had entered this circle by marrying Cora's friend Joe, who had always wanted his kids to be light skinned, so he married Mitsy to ensure it. Mitsy thought she was changing the subject by talking about her and Joe, and how marriage is great, but how she and Joe had their own set of problems being a mixed couple.

Everyone tried to focus on the travails of Mitsy and Joe's scenario, but Angie found a way to weave the conversation back around to her and Eric. She talked heartily about how Mitsy should just be glad that Joe was so devoted to her that he would withstand anything to keep their marriage together. Angie went on to say how:

"So many couples seem like they are doing fine, yet there's so much cheating, deception, and desperation that some women can't even find comfort right at home with their own husbands."

Angie made sure to say that Mitsy was lucky she had someone like Joe who gave her all his attention and support rather than pushing her into the arms of someone else's man.

That did it for Janiece. She was choked right into tears. She couldn't believe it herself. She never let anything or anyone get to her. She was a fighter, and she could sling fists as well as words at the best of them. But now, she was feeling the hot tears streaming down her cheeks. The only thing she could feel good about was that she was releasing hostile tears. She was so angry that she could have reached over and twisted Angie's scrawny, little, smart alack body into a tighter bind than a dish rag. Angie didn't know who she was messing with. Janiece had always been one of the toughest kids on this block. Of all the guys and girls who had grown up around this street, she had been one of the contenders, and she could have polished Angie up, down, and around this block, but her restraint was on full blast.

"Hey...babe..." Tony had begun, and reached out for her hand. Up till now he had been reasonably enjoying the fact that Eric would be out of their lives, and that Angie was letting it be known to the world. But when Tony saw how it was hurting Janiece, he really started feeling bad.

Even Cora was getting vocal now. She was upset at the way this whole afternoon had been going, and started voicing her opinion to both Tony and Angie.

Janiece set it all straight. She told Cora not to worry about it, and she got up to do what she had intended to do an hour or so earlier. She reached across Tony, grabbed her purse, and started walking away.

"Wait a minute Janiece," Tony said grabbing her arm as it went across him. "I'll get that for you."

Tony was trying to take his wife's purse up, but, at the same time, he was trying to get a hold of her.

"Babe...babe...come on...we can go now," Tony said standing up.

Janiece shoved his arm away from her, with the same force she would have liked to use to snatch Angie up close to her. Angie needed a good whipping from Janiece, but she was not even going to go there today. Tony had been as responsible for disrespecting Janiece as this girl she didn't even know. So if anybody deserved a few blows from Janiece, it was Tony.

As he tried to leave with her, she pushed him away and began walking down the driveway.

Eric had stood up too, and tried to get Janiece to calm down.

He reached for her hand softly then called her name. She snatched her hand from him, and her cracking voice revealed all the hurt in her statement.

"No Eric, you let me go too. Thanks a lot. And good luck on your marriage." With that she snatched away from him, and continued toward the sidewalk.

"It's not even like that, Janiece," Eric had begun to whisper. "It's not like that...I...I was going to tell you...and...I'm..."

He couldn't finish because Angie's questions were constantly interrupting his comments:

"It's not like what?" she was asking. "And you're...what? What are you going to tell her?"

By then Eric was walking toward Janiece, and Janiece was walking even more quickly in an effort to get away. She was not paying any attention to the fact that both Tony and Eric were trying to plead a case to her.

Since Janiece was ignoring both of them, Tony wanted Eric to back down, and move away.

"Man, this is my wife!" Tony said, emphasizing "wife," to Eric as he placed a firm and intimidating grip on Eric's shoulder.

"I don't care man," Eric began, and would not back down. "This is my girl," he finished then caught up to Janiece.

Eric stood in front of her holding her gently by the shoulders.

"Janiece...Niecey...calm down...just wait," Eric said as he rocked her a little bit.

Hot tears had begun spilling down Janiece's face again. She hadn't intended a scene, and this had gone too far. It was simple; she was married to a man who she was very unhappy with, and Eric was about to marry a woman who he obviously loved. It was clear why Angie was being so malicious with it. She was bitter because Janiece had never given them any space...at least not when it came to matters of the heart. Janiece could still pull on Eric's heart strings, and he was dancing like a puppet. There was no greater proof of it than now, when Angie was in the background demanding to know why Eric was chasing behind Janiece, and wanting to know what he meant by the statement: "I don't care; this is my girl."

Angie was pulling rank now and telling Eric he better leave Janiece alone and worry about his own wife to be, before he didn't have one. Tony and Janiece had enough problems of their own, without him sticking his nose in it further. Wasn't it enough that Janiece was calling there every other week complaining. Maybe if she talked to her husband as much as she talked to Eric about him, she could get her own marriage straight. They didn't have time to worry about a marriage that was on its way out the door; they needed to worry about their own business.

Even though Angie was getting out of pocket, and yelling all these things near the sidewalk, all her comments made sense, even to Janiece. Although she could have easily knocked Angie to the ground, Janiece just stared at Angie. She wasn't going to have a confrontation with this girl. As a matter of fact, she wasn't going to say one hostile word. Everything Angie was saying was true. The only thing that Janiece didn't like was the disrespect factor. She had grown up in this same neighborhood, and though she wasn't a child anymore and didn't have to impress anybody, Janiece could see a crowd gathering catacorner to the end of the Lees' driveway. A lot of the guys on the corner had always known Janiece as Janiece Jamison, Jawaun, Darrell, and Cedric's little sister. No one had ever been tough enough to terrorize them as a family, because they all stuck together. That's how it was when they were kids, but not too much had changed. The respect factor for the Jamisons was still there in the neighborhood. Jawaun and Darrell were running things on one side of the law, and her brother Cedric was running things on the other.

Jawaun had plenty of foot soldiers in this neighborhood, and a few of them had disappeared from the growing crowd to go get him. With Angie in her face, Tony pulling her one way, and pushing on Eric at the same time, Janiece could see how this was getting out of control. And it wasn't worth it.

She had ruined Cora's get together, and had been trampled on during the course of it. Moreover, she had chosen her own route in life with Tony, and sink or swim, this was her man. Eric was Angie's. Janiece was willing to concede that, so she told Angie:

"You know what? You're right. Everything you said was right."

Janiece turned to Eric and said: "She is right Eric. You need to just leave me alone, and worry about your own life. She's your girl, and Tony's my husband, and I'm the only one who has to deal with my life."

Angie wanted to put Janiece in check, because she didn't like anything about her. She didn't even like the fact that Janiece was supposedly on her side.

Eric only made matters worse by saying:

"No Janiece, I'm not going to leave you alone. Not now, and not ever." The words slipped off his lips like cool water.

By then Jawaun was walking up, and headed toward Eric asking: "My sister tell you to leave her alone, and you're not?"

"Naw man, it's not even like that," Eric began.

Janiece got Jawaun's attention by saying: "It's not, Jawaun. He hasn't done anything to me. I'm just ready to go home."

That was all she wanted, and this made Tony happy. He placed his hand on Janiece's arm, then spoke:

"Good baby; let's just go home."

Janiece looked at him with a mixture of compassion and contempt, then shook her head and spoke.

"Tony, I'm not leaving with you. I'm going home...to my mother's."

It was a low and humiliating blow, but Tony couldn't argue. Jawaun was demanding that he let go of Janiece's arm. Tony knew, wife or not, the Jamison's would fight to the finish over what they felt their own, and Janiece was always going to be a Jamison in their eyes. Tony was sometimes crazy, but he wasn't a fool; he didn't want to get into a street fight with Jawaun, especially in this neighborhood. Tony slowly released his grip on Janiece's arm, and asked would she be in later. She simply told him: "I'll call you." But, she never did.

Days had turned in to weeks before she was willing to speak to him. Tony was no stranger at her mother's house, and he was free to come and go, as long as he was there to see the kids. Everybody knew that Janiece didn't want to have any communication with him about the status of their relationship. The few times he over stepped his bounds by trying to talk to her about it, he was escorted out by one of her brothers.

Tony couldn't believe the way things were going for him and Janiece. All he wanted was one more chance to prove himself to her, but she wouldn't give it. And what made things even worse was her brothers; they were always somewhere around, waiting to kick him out if she said the word. More and more often Janiece was asking Tony to leave her alone, but sooner than either of them had imagined or intended, Janiece was saying a permanent goodbye.

# # #

The afternoon they had spent in Cora's backyard made her realize just how strong her feelings for Eric were. She had never been faced with really losing him, because he had always been there; but, when she heard he had set a date, and both Tony and Angie washed it in her face, Janiece had been forced to realize that for the first time, she was going to have to truly let Eric go. She couldn't face that. For all of the ups and downs she had experienced with Tony, at least she had always been able to confide in Eric. Janiece didn't want to lose that. She also didn't want to make any hasty decisions.

She and Tony had children together, and no matter how many things he had done wrong, Tony had always done right by his children. He loved them, and he would battle her left and right behind his kids. In the past, she had only threatened to leave him one real time, when he was at an away game in Denver, and she had found receipts from him buying some things that weren't just for her. It was clear what he had done because he had bought Janiece and another girl the same piece of jewelry on the same day. When Janiece came across the receipt, she called him to say:

"Don't bother coming home. Me and the kids will be here, but you better find some place else to go."

He lost it. He did the hard work; he paid the bills, but when Janiece said something, it was the law of the land, no matter how much he did in the household. So he begged her to let him come home.

"Baby, as soon as this game is over, let me get there and talk to you about everything. It's not even like you're thinking."

"And what am I thinking Tony?" she yelled. "Am I thinking what I know has to be true? If there's one receipt you left laying around, there's at least 3 others hidden somewhere else? Huhn? Is that what I'm thinking?"

"Niecey...come on now..."

"No tell me Tony, am I thinking that you're behind my back doing what you're famous for? Disrespecting and..."

Before she could finish, he cut in. He had halfway put together an excuse.

"Janiece. I'm telling you. It's not like that. Me and my boy were out when I bought that for you, and he wanted one for his girl but couldn't afford it. I told him I'd get it..."

"Tony save it okay? You don't even hang around anybody who makes less money than you okay? You have the least money of anyone in your whole clique."

He had his pride broken, but more than that, he had his heart pierced. Janiece was so unforgiving, and when she was mean, she was exceptionally mean.

He was glad in some ways that he was only on the phone getting this abuse, because he knew if he had been at home when she found the receipt, she would have been swinging on him left and right. He was nobody's punk, but he was never going to swing back at her. He tried to restrain her, especially when he knew she was the one in the right, and he tried to walk out on her on the rare occasions when she had been wrong. Most of the time, he just tried to deal with her. He knew he was often wrong, but more than that, he knew there was always a chance that if he walked out, he wouldn't be welcome to come back.

Janiece wasn't playing with him this time. She hadn't ever put him out, but now that she was on the other end telling him not to come home, he could only imagine what was going to happen if he tried.

"How long is this for Janiece?" he tried to negotiate.

"How long?" she sneered out a laugh. "How much was that pinky ring? Count up the number of dollars you spent, and those are the number of days you can stay gone."

There were 365 days in a year, and he had spent a couple of thousands on those pinky rings. He didn't have to add or multiply anything. The facts and figures made it clear; she wanted him gone a long time.

He couldn't do it, and he wouldn't do it. But, the more he tried to explain, the more hostile Janiece got, and when she had spit enough fire, she hung up.

Tony didn't sleep all that night, and he almost brought everything to an end.

He had stayed out all night, missed the team meeting, curfew, and the breakfast. He stumbled into the lobby the next morning as everyone was gathering for the busses. His eyes were blood-red and he reeked of marijuana. He knew he was in trouble with the team, but he was just thankful that he had even had a reason to show back up at the hotel. He had spent the entire night out, rounding curves in the Colorado mountains, and calling Janiece threatening that he would end it all. He didn't want to lose her and the kids, and if he had to lose them, he may as well lose everything. He warned her that if he couldn't come back home, he wouldn't come back at all.

Janiece had listened to his erratic conversations all night, and by morning she had convinced him he could have another chance. With her on the line, he drove back to the hotel, feeling like nothing could go wrong.

He entered the lobby and his coaches were all over him, while his team mates just shook their heads, but none of that mattered to Tony. The most important thing was, after the coaches were done yelling, after the police escorted their busses to the stadium, and the game was won or loss, he could go home to his family.

Janiece had never lied to him. Throughout all their years together, everything Janiece had said, she had meant. So, when she promised to let him come back, he knew she would.

But now, they were back in Miami, at the end of a heated debate, and she was telling him she didn't want to be bothered, and Tony knew she meant it, so he was getting worried again.

He just wanted her back. But Janiece was not going to budge. There was her stubbornness, her brothers, and worst of all, there was Eric Lucas. As the weeks rolled by, Tony was trying everything he could to get Janiece back. He was blaming everybody, and everything, and he couldn't help blaming most of his problems on Eric. But it was no use. The more Tony brought up Eric, the more Janiece warned him: if he started confronting Eric, he would never have a chance to see her or the kids.

Janiece wouldn't take his kids from him, and he knew that. They would get things right again, and then this would all be behind them. Tony had decided it would be best to just lay off Janiece for a while, and concentrate on gaining sympathy elsewhere.

He couldn't call on most of his friends because his braggadocios ways had isolated them from him. And most of his family in Miami didn't want to be involved in Tony and Janiece's problems anymore. He rarely called on them when times were good, and for years, they had been learning to live without him. The only listening ears he could find were Rayshawn's and Rayshawn's wife Brandi. They were always listening to Tony and counseling him as best they could. Tony could wake them up anytime of day or night, and they were right there dishing out Scriptures, and verses to help him get back on track. But Tony wanted more than that.

He wanted his wife back, and he wanted to hold her in the middle of the night, instead of rolling over and calling Rayshawn. It was getting too hard, and too lonely without a woman in his life. Well over a month had gone by since Janiece had spoken one word to him. He wanted to hear a kind voice; he wanted to hear a woman who would comfort and snuggle up to him, at least on the phone; so, he rolled over one night and lay on his back. He found himself thinking, and staring at the ceiling from a cool and empty bed. And before he knew it, he found himself dialing the digits of the one woman he knew would never turn him away. Nadique.

She was still back there in his last town, probably doing the same thing she had been doing when he left her, working a little bit, studying hard, and somewhere between those things, thinking of him from time to time, and at least wondering why they couldn't last.

He called her with that comforting thought in the back of his mind, but from the moment her answering machine picked up, he was in for one surprise after another. It was Nadique's voice on the recording alright, but the message "we're not in right now" was a little disturbing. Fortunately for him, Nadique picked up the phone before the whole message played, and it gave him a chance to ask her a few questions.

He started by asking how she was doing, and then he let her know that he was just calling to make sure she was okay. She had to convince him that she was fine, and even then he had asked:

"You sure now? You don't need me to come down there and deal with anybody for you, do you? Cause you know I will. If somebody's doing you wrong, you know I'll be right down there."

Nadique told him that she was doing alright, but Tony didn't let it go at that; he went on to ask: "So that means he's treating you right, huhn?"

Nadique found herself huffing out an indignant laugh before she answered: "Sure, sure Tony. That does mean he is treating me right."

"Good, good...that's good. I'm glad to hear that. I mean, you deserve that...somebody good in your life. Sounds like you got that." He sucked in some air then breathed out the question: "So, uh, you living with him?"

Nadique didn't make any reply.

"Deek?" he questioned.

"Yeah Tony."

"You still there?"

"You know I am," she said in her ever patient way. It reminded him of old times.

"So, you gettin treated right now?" he asked again.

"What difference does it make to you?" she wanted to ask, but she couldn't reply before Tony rammed in another question.

"So you living with him?"

"Excuse me?" Nadique began.

She had never been indignant with Tony but somehow in these first 5 minutes of conversation he was getting on her nerves, and getting too far beside himself, but this was just the beginning.

"Look, its cool with me. I mean, it ain't nothing to be ashamed of. If the brotha is treating you good and helping you out, ain't nothing wrong with living with him. Just make sure his intentions are good—you know. As far as marriage and all. You know. I'm sure you want to be married one day."

Nadique was between disbelief and grief. She was heartbroken that he was sitting here talking about her odds at being able to get married, when all along she had one day hoped to marry him, before he shocked her into her senses. And it was that level of disrespect that was once again shocking her back into reality. Who did he think he was, sitting on the other end of her line, giving her advice about her life, and acting like she needed his approval. Somewhere, in her lost thoughts, he had continued on talking, apparently thinking she was too ashamed to admit her status as a shacker to him.

"Look Deek, you a big girl now. You can do what you want. Just make sure he ain't out to take advantage of you. I mean. You're a beautiful girl and all, and I just don't want to see you end up getting hurt. You deserve the best."

This was going too far. Nadique didn't even know where he was getting all his notions from, but it only took a few seconds to figure it out. Tony had heard the "we" message, and thought that she was living with someone now. But, she didn't have to explain anything to Tony. She had really done it as a safety precaution, but if he wanted to take it further and get bent out of shape thinking she was shacking, engaged, or even worse, she had moved on, forgotten about him, and found someone who made her happy, let him think it. It couldn't hurt any worse than all the things he had done.

Just a few years ago, he had left her high and dry without caring how much that had really hurt. When she wanted an explanation, he had very little explaining to do. Maybe he felt he didn't owe her one since she had never really grilled him before, or maybe he was just as obvious as they came. He didn't give one because he didn't have one. The best he could offer to all of her "Why did you do this? How could you do this? Why did you even come back?" questions was to return a simple question to her.

"Do you realize East can never meet West?" he demanded.

In all of her upset, she couldn't get her thoughts together in order to respond quickly enough, so he repeated it while she was gasping in air, through her tears.

"Do you realize East can never meet West? Do you Nadique? Answer me?"

"What is that supposed to mean?" she questioned. It wasn't that she couldn't understand the concept, it was that his statement had nothing to do with the way he had come back into her life, only to trample all over her then leave.

"What does it mean?" he asked. "It means that we are headed in two different directions Nadique, and East can never meet West. I'm heading one way, and you are heading another," he closed.

Somehow in Nadique's distress, she had pulled herself together enough to dart out the reply: "Well, you just remember Tony, I'm East, and you are West."

There was a mouthful of meaning in that statement. She didn't know where Tony had gotten his faulty concept that East never meets West since at the prime meridian those points do come together.

And, if he had thought about Nadique's comment more carefully, he would have realized that East was the symbolic place of success; it was the place where all things started rising; and conversely West was the place where things began to go down. When she told him that she was East and he was West, he hadn't even realized the weight of her words.

That had been years ago, and he had apparently forgotten—they hadn't ended on good terms. He was sitting here on the other end of her line, getting comfortable, and feeling good that they were about to embark on this long distance love—relationship type thing.

She was still there, and Tony knew, she would still be there for him. She may be living with someone or even engaged to someone else, but she would never let go of Tony. And now that he was back, she couldn't even bring herself to admit that there was someone else. He really had her heart, even after all these years. Those were his thoughts, but Nadique's were different.

She was not going to bring him up to speed on her life. She was not going to make it easy or hard for him. She was going to be as polite as she could. Nadique let Tony go on and on about a few things in his life: how well things were going in Miami, how good it was to be back home, how glad he was about the relationship he had with his kids. Nadique congratulated him, and told him she was happy for him, but then she also told him she had to get going. He said he understood, but that he would call again.

Much to his surprise, a few days later when he snuggled up in the bed to talk to her on the phone, he dialed the same number twice and then twice again, but it had been changed. Nadique had cut him out of her life without so much as a goodbye. And nothing felt worse than that. He had been counting on her, and he began thinking out loud:

"Maybe I should have been honest with her and told her I called because I need her..maybe I should have told her how much I need her right now. Maybe she's thinking I'm really doing alright, or maybe I hurt her even more by rubbing it in her face that I'm happy with my life... I know how much that has to hurt her."

His assumptions were both wrong and right, but the fact was, Nadique had not grown angry or bitter, but the last time he had cut her, the wounds almost bubbled over when they were healing. She hadn't ever thought she would hear from him again, but when she did, she decided it was time to make sure he could never get in touch again.

Tony sat up in his bed that night and thought about a lot of things. He thought about taking a flight out to see and talk to Nadique; he thought about trying to go see Janiece; but it was too late at night for either of those things. He could have called Rayshawn, but that would have meant talking to him and Brandi and facing the fact that they were so deep in love, and he was separated from his wife, cut off from Nadique, and lying in bed alone.

He couldn't stay in here like this another night. He rolled out of bed and found himself driving the town over. Hour after hour, Tony had been contemplating what he should do. The more he was out there, the more he wanted to go to Janiece's mother's house and beg Janiece to come out and just talk with him. But it had gotten later and later, and he knew that it wouldn't work. Her brothers would be there waiting for a fight, and he didn't need his kids to see that again. Still, he needed to find something to occupy him until morning, by then it might have been safe to stop by the Jamison's and try to talk some sense into Janiece.

After a few more hours, Tony found himself in one of the best places he could be. He had pulled up by the Neighborhood center, where a few of his old buddies were gathering to play midnight basketball. The community had started this league to keep guys out of trouble. Some of them had been down on their luck or in trouble with the law, but by having this outlet, they could do something positive during the night, rather than hang out on the corners.

Tony parked his car, and went inside the gym just intending to speak, and watch a few games; but, a few of the guys invited him in on a pick up game. Tony was a natural born athlete and could hoop with the best of them. He had bragged about playing and winning against a few NBA contenders in the past. This made their midnight basketball game all the more interesting. Not just for the trash talking, but because they all agreed to see if Tony could "put his money where his mouth is."

Each team decided to bet on their games, and at the end of the night, Tony's team had won. All the players had expected that the others would pay if they lost, but when the night ended and no one was willing to pay, they argued for a minute, but then let it die down. Tony was the only one who was slow to just let it go. The way he was riding people about the money made them start riding him about how much he must need the money. They told him he wasn't acting like someone who made "millions." But Tony had the money, and just to let it show, he promised to not only drop his argument about the money, but to also treat the guys to a night out.

They didn't even have to wait. They could go directly from the midnight basketball game to Grace's, the most exclusive, exotic, entertainment spot in Miami.

Snapshots

Most of his home boys hadn't even heard of Grace's, but even if they had, they couldn't have ever gotten in. It wouldn't have mattered if they put on their best suits, took their whole paycheck down there, the management wouldn't have let them in. The owner had a certain clientele, and didn't want to jeopardize it. Tony could get in because he had celebrity status. Ten of the guys who had agreed to meet him down there were his guests for the night. He would treat them all to a few drinks and one lap dance with the girl of their choice.

The late night at Grace's was full of hot action. Even though they got hassled a little by management, once they agreed to let Tony and his friends in, they were in awe of how "sexy" the girls were.

The club was exclusive. It was filled with "exotic chics" from almost everywhere, internationally. Miami was known as a hotbed for culture and diversity, but this club took it to the limit. They had girls from almost everywhere: Asia, Italy, Portugal, Brazil and more. The guys enjoyed the best time they'd ever had out in a club, and Tony had flossed for them just enough to show them, he had knowledge and access to things they didn't even know existed. His boys were impressed, but Tony wasn't done showing off for the night. He left them in the main room, while he exited to the Champagne room with two of the girls that had been entertaining him all night.

It had been a long time since he had gone to a strip club, and it had also been a long time since he had gotten "laid." Tony had whispered that to one of the two strippers swaying a hot pink, shiny thong in his face. The girl had placed her feet on his lap and was doing the butterfly in front of his nose. She kept tantalizing him—rolling her pelvis up from his lips and around to his nose. She wasn't even holding on to him for support because her partner, a girl in a shiny silver thong, was directly behind Tony. This girl had climbed on the back of a chair, bent over, and was doing the butterfly on the back of Tony's head. Her exposed cheeks were rubbing seductively all over the back of his bald head. The only thing that either of the girls had for real support was each other. The girl in front had reached around Tony's head and gripped her partner's waist. The girl in the front seemed to be guiding the movements of the girl in the back, but from time to time, Tony could feel the girl's hands sliding over his head, and up and down the thighs, pelvis, and breasts of the girl in the back. They were turning him on. They were with each other as much as they were with him, and he was heated. The smell and movement of something hot and fresh, and something he hadn't had in a long time was literally dancing all around his head. And, he had to have it.

He was cupping his hands all over the front girl's behind, until he forcefully, pulled her waist down to his lap. She was beginning to grind on him like a lap dance, but he got demanding:

"Huhn-uhn," he began. "I want more than that."

He licked his lips slightly, and the wetness gleamed on them. He was staring her in the eyes and playing with her nipples.

"Come on," he said, with a little hostility "let's go on back to the Champagne room."

The girl looked him deeply in the eyes, then leaned into his neck. She kissed him slightly, then ran her tongue on the bottom of his ear lobe before she whispered to him.

"Not without my friend." She paused, then started quickly tickling his ear hole with her tongue before she continued: "We go everywhere together," she finished then leaned back to glance in his face.

"Everywhere?" he asked.

She only moved her lips and replied in less than a whisper: *everywhere.*

"Well, let's go," Tony said, ready to get up.

The girl in front of him had never let go of the girl behind him. She had been continually rubbing around the girl's exposed cheeks, which meant that she had been brushing by Tony's ears, each time she had reached back to pull her girlfriend's bottom in closer to his head.

He hadn't asked their names, but during the course of all the activities they had been calling out each other's names. The one on front of him was named Asia, though she looked Brazilian. And, the girl behind him was named Rockie. He hadn't seen much of her, so he had no way or care of knowing much about her. She had huge breast implants which might have accounted for her last name, Mountain. He only picked this up because Asia had been rubbing and commenting on them a lot during the night. But there was only so much they could do from this spot, and he was getting tired of playing with them.

Asia was still seated on his lap and he stared aggressively

into her eyes, then looked back and forth into them. She followed his eyes, but her eyes were twinkling so much, they seemed to be laughing at him. He gripped her chin tightly and steadied her stare, then demanded again:

"Let's get up from here and head to the back."

She tossed her hair wildly and let out a small but uproariously silly little laugh, then slapped both thighs of the girl in the back and said:

"Come on; let's get back there. You heard what he said."

Asia was getting aggressive with Rockie, and Tony liked what he heard and saw. It was a nice chain of command. He was going to run it down to Asia, and she was running it down to Rockie. They could go at this all night long; there was no doubt in his mind, they were going to have fun tonight.

When his boys saw him heading into the Champagne room they couldn't think of anything but "how much juice" Tony really had. The "two freaks" were going to get in there and "serve" him all night if he wanted them to.

Tony was going to eat this up, one hundred percent. Part of the fun of the strip clubs for him was the fantasy and the mystery. The fact that when you went in, you never knew what you might get out of it. Going in to the Champagne room took it to another level. In most instances, you could honestly say that you get what you pay for, and tonight, Tony was willing to pay.

He wanted to see the two girls do whatever they did to each other, and then he wanted to "lay back, relax," and let them do whatever they were going to do to him.

When they got in the Champagne room, the first girl slightly pushed him backwards in to a reclining chair. She was a little rough, a little aggressive, but he liked it. She danced and pranced all in his face while grabbing and rubbing his face randomly. He didn't know what to expect next, whether she was going to grab or rub his face, but it made things all the more intense. She flipped her legs over his shoulders. She had curved her back like a crescent moon, and her shoulders were sweeping his knees. Her breasts would have been flopping in her face, but she had been holding and rubbing them once Tony placed his hands beneath her arms to balance her.

"Can you keep it up?" he whispered to her.

But, with her knees at his shoulders, and her head near his

lap, she couldn't hear anything. All the blood had rushed to her head. His words were impossible to hear, but the sensations were intensified. He had slid his hands down the middle of her back and toward her hips. He was grasping them roughly back and forth toward his face, and each time he got her center toward his face, he bit a little through her thong. The rush was so deep and the feelings were so frenzied that when she tried to open her eyes for a moment, she thought she had gone blind. All she could see were abstract shapes and a spectrum of fleeting colors.

Her moans and grunts didn't sound like panic, but it was enough to make security zero their surveillance cams in to take note of what was going on in there.

Tony was licking and biting right through Asia's thin, shiny thong. She could feel the firm grip from his teeth, and they felt sharper than a wolf's. There was no question, she loved it. But more than that, she liked the way the other dancer was soothing the middle of her legs. While Tony had been biting aggressively at Asia's top, Rockie had slid into the middle of Asia to rub continually and gently.

Tony wanted Asia to take off her thin pink thong, so he demanded that she do it. He looked her in the eyes, turned up his nose and sniffed in aggressively. He was licking his lips at her, and she knew what that meant. He wanted to taste her and he was tired of biting all over the thong. To prove how good it would be, he dropped his eyes to her thong, then looked up into her face as he licked across her friend's fingers. Rockie had been playing between the band of Asia's thong, but Asia was not ready to give in just yet. She was seated on his lap and her friend stood behind her. So, Tony did the next best thing. He pulled Rockie's arms around Asia's shoulders, and placed Rockie's slippery fingers in toward his mouth. He used her fingers to circle his lips, then began licking his lips, and sucking her fingers. They tasted more like Asia than Asia herself, and he stared Asia in the face licking faster and sucking harder. Then he pushed Rockie's fingers away, and said sternly:

"Get back up here."

He wanted Asia to flip her legs back over his shoulders, but this time, without her pink garment.

"Take 'em off," he said snapping the elastic on the sides of her thighs.

Asia rolled around at his center a little before rising to stand in front of him.

"That's going to cost you," she whispered as she leaned in toward his chest.

"Baby, I got whatever you need," he replied.

"You sure?" she asked, as she slid her hand, palm first, down the middle of his stomach toward his center.

"You sure you got what I need?" she smiled, playing with the stiffest part of his body.

"I got that for you too," he replied. He had taken the sides of her thong, and pulled then twisted them so tight, she would probably bruise if he just snatched them off.

"Oh, you're such a good boy. You know that?" she said, calming him down a little. "I'm going to give you what you need, as long as you give me what I want."

"You got that," he replied, and told her to lay down in the chair. He was going to stand up, and then get into her, nice and deep.

"What about my friend?" the girl asked.

"Oh, I got something for her too," Tony turned around and rubbed the breasts of the second girl. He was ready for both of them, and had laid his money on the table. They were going to give him what he needed, but he was in store for much more than he had paid for.

The only thing Tony had played with on Rockie was her breasts and her fingers, but as Asia stood behind him, loosening his pants, and pulling them down, Tony began to run his fingers down Rockie's stomach. She was pencil thin, but her frame felt ultra firm. If he hadn't been so close to getting his way with both of them, he would have asked something corny like: "You work out? Your body is real tight."

But, he felt no need for small talk. That was the kind of talk that chumps used when they were trying to get to where he was; he was close to *breakin' them off*, so there was no more to be said.

But just when he thought he was going to get what he came for, he got more than what he bargained. The doors of the Champagne room flung open, and the only words he heard were:

"Freeze."

It was security coming through the door, and Tony was caught, right there, between the two girls with his pants literally hanging down.

They were saying a lot of things to him, but he was only catching bits and pieces. He heard them say something about the charges they could bring against him...soliciation...they had him on camera...there was a tape...

The rest was a blur, because while they were talking, all he could think about was his wife and kids. The last thing he heard them say was that everything could be forgotten, if he just promised not to come back. There would be no charges, and no repercussions, the owner just didn't want him showing his face there again.

In all the commotion, Tony had been rushing to get himself out of Grace's, and get himself together. It wasn't until he got outside that he started thinking in a distorted, yet clear frame of mind. Grace's was known for allowing the free flow of activity with the girls and the clients. But, as Tony and his friends stood out on the curb, it became apparent why they had singled him out that night. No one else inside or outside of the club looked anything like him or his friends, so he started shouting a round of protests. Partially to impress his friends, but partially because he was angry, humiliated, and then the mixture of those two emotions created another one, rage.

It wasn't long after he started making outbursts that people were taking pictures and jotting down notes, and it wasn't long after that, that Tony's face was in the paper, along with the headlines about his "Fall from Grace." There were other articles: "Goodness, Graceshush...when will we stop hearing about troubled athletes."

And to top it all off, there was something that made it worse. Janiece. She and the kids were right there, in their hometown, and suffering the humiliation of Tony's latest round of improprieties. But this time Janiece had had it. She was finally finished with Tony, and there was no convincing her otherwise.

In the past, Tony had done more than his share of wrong, but she had never gone anywhere. She had fought him tooth and nail, and she often felt bad that sometimes her kids had seen her swinging fists at him or slinging anything she could get her hands on. They had heard Janiece get tougher with Tony than anyone who listened to her in the Sunday morning choir could have ever imagined. But, in the past, all of those things had remained behind closed doors. Now, she was suffering a very public humiliation, and this could have been enough to make her turn her back on Tony for once and for all.

Snapshots

But, there was something more than Tony's actions that was eating away at Janiece. It was the fact that Eric Lucas would be out of her life soon, and from the first day she heard it, Janiece knew she wasn't ready to see him move on with someone else and have him permanently out of her life.

Throughout all of Janiece's ups and downs with Tony, she had at least one person she could rely on, and that was Eric Lucas. Even during this latest episode, that hadn't changed. Eric had been by Janiece's side since the day she walked away from Tony and headed back to her mother's. Eric and Janiece, and then Eric, Janiece, and the kids had begun spending more and more time together; and this had become a problem for both Angie and Tony. Angie was hounding Eric, and on his back every chance she got. But, she did not get many chances since most of his time was being spent with Janiece. This made Angie call an ultimatum. Eric would either leave Janiece or forget about their wedding; there was no postponing their marriage until he could sort through his feelings, but Eric wouldn't have needed time anyway. He had made up his mind. The wedding was off. All along, he had secretly known where his heart really was, and so had Janiece. As soon as her divorce was final, she would be planning her new life with him.

Tony wouldn't let things rest so easily. He had made his mistakes, but he had been man enough to own up to them, and all he wanted was one more chance. But, he had married the Janiece he had always known--the one who said what she meant, and meant what she said. She wasn't giving him another chance. She was leaving him and moving on to do something she had meant to do a long time ago, be with the one man she had known would never have put her through so many changes.

The kids would present a problem though, because the kids loved their father, and he loved them too, with all of his heart. The one thing he had never wanted to lose was the relationship he had with his kids; Janiece understood that, but she would not back down. She would never keep the kids away from him, nor would she distort the image they had of their father, but for everyone's sake, she felt it was time for her to move in a new direction. She had been unhappy with Tony's actions for years, and his latest actions just brought the head to the pimple, and he pushed it until it popped. But this time, Janiece wasn't going to stick around and be the cotton ball wiping things up.

Tony pled his case repeatedly. He had explained over and again how this last time he did not mean to do what he did. If she had eased up on him just a little bit when they got into the last fight, none of this would have happened. He could have gone to her that night and asked forgiveness, and tried to get things on the right track again. But, for weeks, nearly months, she had kept turning him away. He hadn't meant to make such a mistake this last time; he really hadn't; but none of that mattered to Janiece.

Janiece believed that somewhere in Tony's heart was the intent to do wrong, otherwise he wouldn't have kept doing it all those years. But, she couldn't have been more wrong. Locked away in Tony's heart somewhere was the intent to do right, and the key had been turning--sometimes very slowly--but he had been opening up more and more, trying to let everything come out. He wanted the good things, the right things, the real love he had for them to come out and grow into its fullest potential. But it was too late to do this with Janiece. She was tired, and had been for years, and before he could have imagined it, she was gone from his life.

That part was settled, but the task was to get Tony out of Miami and ready for his new team. That part was the hardest of all because no one could get through to him. Janiece was right there in Miami, 15 minutes away from him, but she didn't have two more words to say about her decision. And though his best friend Dante was on his way to Miami, he was coming to get his new family set up in the city, and then head off for camp, which was exactly what Tony should have been preparing to do in his next new city. But no one could get this through his head, until Rayshawn stepped into the picture.

Janiece knew Tony had probably talked to Rayshawn a thousand times since she had made up her mind, but Janiece had finally called Rayshawn herself. He was just about the only who could get through to Tony. Rayshawn was aware that the list of actions Tony was compiling for himself were going to make him less and less attractive to the new team. Calling Janiece, following Eric, and refusing to accept what was now his reality, were slimming down Tony's chances of getting to camp or even making it through those six intense weeks.

He had to get his head on straight and realize that no matter where he and Janiece stood, his kids would need him to be strong enough to take care of them, all the way around. And, one of the first starts he had was getting back to work, and making sure they'd be okay financially. In some ways Tony understood that, but what he was feeling financially and emotionally were two totally different things. He or his kids would always be able to recover from financial losses, but he would never be able to overcome his broken heart. His kids made him whole, and leaving them behind for any reason made him feel like he was poorer than any man on the streets. No amount of money he made with any team, business, or organization could replace what value he had on his kids. To lose them meant he had lost everything. But he wasn't losing, Rayshawn had to explain. He was just re-grouping, re-focusing, and getting himself straight so that when he came back he could be an even better, and even stronger father.

But as the pages flipped forward in Tony's album, they revealed that life had brought about many changes.

He had always pictured himself being a good father to his children, and fortunately he had been able to frame that image. On down the line his album showed his kids were at his side as often as they were at their mother's. He hadn't lost them, but he had lost her. Tony's break up with Janiece brought so much haze, that he thought he would never see again; he had almost lost his vision, and his desire to look ahead to the future. But, he hadn't lost everything just yet.

When the clouds rolled back, there was something waiting for Tony on the horizon. It was the promise of something to come.

No one had anticipated it, and least of all Nadique, but on down the line, East did meet West again, and it gave Tony the chance to start over on something that had never left his heart or mind, but something that he had almost given up hoping for, a real chance with Nadique.

So many things had gone wrong for them in the past that he couldn't see how they would be able to make their way. But, through all of his ups, downs, and turn arounds, he had begun to find balance. He had begun to get grounded, and wanted to walk into his new life with Nadique at his side. As time passed, he had set out to find her. He wanted to finally open up his heart and give them a chance, only this time he would make it work. He would have to.

Tony knew it would be a long road; but, he was still ready to take the step, and this time he would put one foot forward at a time. He was sure of where he was going, and he had made up his mind that he wouldn't start running to or from anything, ever again.

When the pages flipped forward in Tony's life, he had found Nadique again, and they had been able to start placing vibrant photos in their album. Their pages were full of many bright shots that would one day tell a story all of its own. But for the time being, they were well on their way. Tony had finally gotten his one last chance. And, this time he would make it work. Everyone who had ever known him had hoped he would.

chapter twenty one

When Dante, DJ and Gabrielle arrived in Miami, they were in another world, and well on their way to another sort of start in the city.

They moved into the Everglades Townhouse complex, a series of free standing, two story buildings, and Gabrielle was in love with the place.

Upon entry, there was a guest restroom to the immediate left and the coat closet to the right. Two footsteps later was the winding staircase that overlooked the downstairs. The first bedroom was right at the top of the stairs, and when you turned left, there was the master bedroom, hallway bathroom, and then a third bedroom at the front of the house. That would be DJ's room.

Gabrielle walked through the spacious upstairs. She had taken her shoes off at the door to run her toes through their plush white carpeting. Everything was so bright, spacious and beautiful. Their new home was more wonderful than Dante's first apartment. His first one had been plush, but this was upstairs, downstairs and more like home. Most of all, this was their first home, together, and they had moved in it as man and wife. Everything about Miami's heat and sun with all the bright days it would bring felt right. Dante called Gabrielle downstairs so she could finish looking at the house.

When she went back downstairs, Dante was out on their elevated balcony, holding DJ and showing him around the neighborhood. Some tenants were on roller blades and waving at father and son as they were gliding by. The way the town houses were built made the first floor of each tenant's home one story above ground. They had built them up higher as a safety precaution. That was one of the things that Dante liked about this building. He would feel safer when he was away from his family knowing that no one could just enter from the ground level.

The balcony was only big enough for three or four people, but it was perfect. It was set right off the dining area. To the front of that area was their living room with it's marble fire place. It almost didn't make sense in Florida, but it was a beautiful addition to the house. Back up the hallway, toward the downstairs washroom, was the kitchen, which they could get to from the dining room or front hall. Dante followed Gabrielle as she visited each room again, and he was pleased that she loved everything.

The furniture was going to be delivered later that day, so Dante didn't want to stick around in the house too long since they had no place to sit or lay. All they had were clothes and toiletries. Gabrielle was fine relaxing on the living room floor and watching DJ make his way all around. Dante said that would be okay for just a little while, but they were leaving shortly. One of his new teammates and his wife had invited them over for a welcome dinner. So, that was on their agenda for the day.

Dante would be leaving for camp in the next few days, but a few of his teammates' wives or girlfriends had volunteered to come over and help Gabrielle get the smaller things set up. Dante would take care of the furniture when it came, and the automobiles would be coming by train next week.

Life was promising a lot to the Jacksons. In Miami, the air was more than warm, it was soothing, and it seemed to blow those breezes into Dante and Gabrielle's life. They were a couple again, and he was warm and sensitive like she had known him to be in the first months of their dating. Everything in Dante's life was centered around his son and his wife.

The first night that Dante and Gabrielle lay down as man and wife in their new home gave him a chance to hold in closest esteem the woman he had chosen to spend his life with. He laid on his back facing the ceiling and put his arm around the top of Gabrielle's pillow. She laid to his right relaxing and thinking nothing in particular except how good it felt to be home. This was the perfect place, and it seemed like where they were always supposed to be.

Dante curved his arm down her pillow and rubbed his fingers around the edges of her left ear. Gabrielle's body seemed to sink into the bed beneath her. He moved his fingers back to the top of the pillow, then stretched his fingers repeatedly from the top of her scalp toward her forehead and back. This was one of his usual strokes, but it didn't feel old and it didn't feel new; it felt familiar. Dante leaned over and kissed Gabrielle's right cheek, then slid his body down so that his face was resting at her chest. When he crossed his arm over her body, he laid his head on her chest and looked up to her face.

"I'm sorry I couldn't take you on your honeymoon," he said rubbing her up and down her side.

She smiled back at him and told him that it didn't matter where they spent their first few days; they had a life time together now.

She had endured quite a few changes with him in the past, but even after being apart for so long, they wouldn't have to do things all over again, or make things right. The things from the past were nearly forgotten, and their new days were full of emotion. Gabrielle's happiness was set on their future and not measured by their past. Dante was himself again. He was warm and endearing. He was the Dante she had always known.

The flash and flamboyance, the quick temper and overwhelming mistakes were a part of him too. But they were such a small part. His actions seemed to stick out more to everyone else because they were so extreme, and so unpredictable. When he was good, he was extremely kind, caring, and gentle; but, when he was upset, a small slice of rage overtook all 320 pounds of him and made him a beast. But as they lay together now in their new home, he was a lamb and warming Gabrielle's skin by rubbing and rolling his head across her sides, stomach and legs. He didn't even need to make love to her. He could feel everything from within her exchanging with all of him, and they could have lain and loved that way for days.

Gabrielle turned on her side and he on his. They faced one another, kissing and touching and playing mild games with their legs and feet. The love they shared was wonderful, and it should have been like this forever.

Gabrielle slid one hand between his pillow and ear, then placed both of her hands on each of his ears and kissed him passionately. It was his honeymoon night, and all he had wanted to do was drink in his wife's presence. The majority of him had wanted to just lie there next to her, reveling in the fact that they completed each other. But the tiny part of him that had been silent for so long, was being reminded of her feel.

She stroked his back with her fingertips and made him curl in. Her lips and her body were the essence of what made him quiver with delight and quake with fulfilment. Dante needed her, and had for a long time without even realizing how much. He pulled her into him, and she received him well. They were one now, as they had never been before. They were man and wife.

chapter twenty two

In the morning when she woke, Gabrielle slid out of bed from her husband's embrace to check on DJ. She had been surprised during the night that he hadn't been fussy or irritated. He was in a new environment completely, and he didn't have his mother all to himself anymore. Her maternal instincts told her that he knew this. But his instincts must have told him he was home.

Gabrielle had been worried about making his bedroom so far down the hall. She had thought the best place for him would be in the guest bedroom right next door to her and Dante. But that room was the tiniest, and Dante had decided it would be better used as an office space. He wanted little Dante to have the room on the front because it was larger, and it caught all the morning sunshine.

When Gabrielle walked into DJ's room that morning, she stopped in the door way. He was in his crib, singing and playing. His arms were going up and down and he giggled when he saw his mother in the door. She was walking over to him, but she wasn't alone. Dante had been standing right behind her peeking in on both of them.

Gabrielle walked in and lifted DJ out of his crib and Dante walked up right behind her, then put his hands on her waist. He kissed the top of her head and rubbed his son's cheek. He tried to teach DJ how to give a pound, with one fist on top of another fist, but DJ was waving his fist like a magic wand. This made Dante laugh.

"You a cool little dude, man" he said, then gripped his wife's waist and kissed her cheek.

"You know I got to go boo," he said as he turned to clear out of the room.

"I know," she said, picking up a few of DJ's things from the crib. She fiddled around his room a little more, and grabbed his baby bag, then headed down the stairs to see Dante. He was on his way to a pre-camp meeting. He would be leaving for Davie in just a few more days, and she and DJ would have to get used to the city by themselves for now.

Gabrielle made it to Dante just as he was on his way out the door. She would have kissed him in the doorway, but his teammate was pulling up outside, and Gabrielle was in her robe. Dante pointed his finger at her for her to shut the door, then he pulled it shut. She stood ready to peek her head out and give him a "Hey." But, he had opened the door again quickly and carefully, sticking just his head in, with his lips poked out. She kissed his lips, then pushed the door shut and locked it.

She and DJ began their day with her picking up things around the house and him following behind her. The phone rang around ten, and it was Ma'Leesa, one of the teammate's wives. She was offering to come over to help Gabrielle straighten up. Ma'Leesa wouldn't be able to make it until about two, but Dante would be back by twelve. Gabrielle graciously declined for that day, but the days that followed their husbands' departure allowed them more time to spare.

Not every one of the wives was on the welcoming committee. In fact, there was no such thing, but Ma'Leesa, Dawntel, Amile, and Charelena were unofficial volunteers. All of them except Amile had experienced the changes of cities with their husband's changes of teams, and knew how difficult it was. Everyone of them had experienced the similar isolation that comes with being away from home and friends and family in a place where nothing is certain, even after the roster has been cut to 53.

Ma'Leesa and Dawn were both from Dayton, but they hadn't known each other while they were younger. And, it wasn't until husbands and friends felt comfortable enough talking about things as personal as where their wives were from that the two of them found out about each other's common strand. They had been friends ever since.

Charelena and her husband had arrived in Miami about a year after Dawntel, but they had already known each other because their husbands had played together for two years in Seattle. When they got to Miami, they met Amile. She was the least socially outgoing of them all. She had been thrust into the role because her husband, Lonzo was a Mississippi boy at heart, and had never changed. He was goodly and kind and always inviting new players and old team mates to the house. His hospitality went a little too far sometimes; he would let some of the guys stay at their house when they were new to the city, until they found an apartment or condo.

Amile ran everything else in the house and made all the decisions about finances, but the one thing she couldn't strong arm her husband out of was his southern charm. Most people who knew Amile wouldn't have thought that she would be so upset about Lonzo's southern hospitality. They would have thought that Amile would have been satisfied, just as long as she could be shopping in Coconut Grove or Coco Beach or any of the places she went spending his money. But, what bothered Amile about socializing was it cast her into the hostess role for all sorts of people, who she wouldn't have otherwise even given the time of day to.

What people misunderstood about Amile was that beyond money, she liked control. Her husband's money, so she made people think, meant little to her; she had been spending other men's money for years before she met Lonzo. She had grown up right in Miami, and though she came from Liberty City, her bronzed-tropical looks had thrust her in all the areas where the power players were. Being with Lonzo, was nothing so special for her. She didn't even have to tell him; he knew when he met her because she was on some film director's arm; she was used to being with people who could do things for her. When she took the time to show interest in him, he was nothing but intrigued that he could get a girl like her. He met her his rookie year, seven years ago; their anniversary was marked by four months after that initial meeting.

Amile was slowly falling into the social role. She liked Dawntel a lot. It was probably because in contrast to Ma'Leesa's down-to-earth, home-girl ways, Dawntel seemed to be sophisticated. But Dawntel and Ma'Leesa came as a package. So, despite Amile's dislike for Ma'Leesa, she tolerated her for the sake of Dawntel. And once Charlena arrived, they all were rounded out into friends. Now that Gabrielle was joining them, there would be three in the group with children, and one with a baby on the way.

Ma'Leesa already had three children and Dawntel had one. Charlena fell into the ranks of an expecting mother as a result of pre-camp warm ups. Her husband, like most, wanted to concentrate on making love as much as possible his last few days before camp. Gabrielle experienced the same long love making sessions with Dante, and he was such a powerhouse that she didn't see the girls for days after he had left for camp.

Once he was gone, she did venture out to the sites around

town with the girls. Though they didn't see each other very often, Gabrielle, Dawntel, and Ma'Leesa, by virtue of being mothers, spent the most time together. Most often, they ran into each other at the beaches, walk ways or splash parks when their kids were out playing. The girls liked to make it to the Grove for the outdoor cafes, but that was a rare treat because the kids didn't enjoy the confines of such close quarters. Dante was fine, because he was fine just about everywhere. His early life probably made him easy to adapt to wherever he was, as long as he knew his mother was near.

Ma'Leesa's kids were a little wilder, probably because they were older, so they couldn't sit still too long; but then again, neither could she. And, according to everyone they knew in common, her husband was the same way. They used to laugh and joke about how wild their household would be, probably until they were in their eighties.

Dawn had a daughter who clung to her, and like every move, La'Shae was her mother's shadow. But she couldn't have been sweeter or prettier. She and her mother both had almond colored skin with a touch of honey; they both had jet black, long and wavy hair, except Dawn kept La'Shae's hair swinging in two pony tails or wrapped around in a ball on top of her head. Though La'Shae was just three years old, it was obvious that she would have the same paper thin build as her mother. The way La'Shae clung to Dawn reminded Gabrielle of Michellene and Michelle. Gabrielle missed them and all the rest of her hometown friends.

Yvette had called her on occasion. She kept in touch often in comparison to Michelle. Yvette felt that Gabrielle would make the right decisions. For all the time Yvette had known her, Gabrielle had made bad choices only a few times, but Yvette was sure that Gabrielle would finally decide on the right things to do.

Michelle was snappy in pointing out that she had never known Gabrielle to make poor choices, nor had anyone else including Yvette, until Gabrielle met Dante. Ever since then, it seemed like Gabrielle was compiling a list of poor choices and big mistakes. One of Gabrielle's ultimate mistakes, in Michelle's eyes, was the decision to marry Dante.

Gabrielle was just "too forgiving, naive and innocent" Michelle had scolded her. She was very severe in telling Gabrielle how big a mistake, and even "stupid" it was for her to walk into a marriage with Dante as if she was blind. Gabrielle seemed to be able to believe in Dante when no one else could, but that was because she had experienced a side of him that none of them could have ever believed. She had been through a lot of things with him before they had DJ so she understood him. She knew that when life seemed to throw unexpected changes at him, he reacted as if he was a kid swatting at bees. He didn't know any better, but when he got stung enough, he would learn to be still. Most people learned that quickly, but Dante hadn't quite figured it out completely. Still, Gabrielle knew his heart and knew that he could, so Michelle's advice on the marriage had been well heard, but not taken.

Her mother was a background player in the wedding decision. Gabrielle hadn't been on real close terms with her mother since the Christmas incident, though she had started taking DJ around to visit when she moved back for the second time. Even though she had clashed heads with her mother much less than she did with Dante, Gabrielle had been slower in forgiving her mother.

When she gave birth to DJ, she had needed her mom, more than she had needed anyone else. Gabrielle knew that her mother had invested a lot of confidence in her ability to complete college and be successful on her own, but when she fell, she thought that at least her mother would help her recuperate. She hadn't ever dreamt of the double edge of rejection from both her mother and her son's father. But she was past that now.

Gabrielle and her mother had redeemed their misunderstanding of one another, even if they hadn't completely restored the relationship. Her mother wanted the best for her, and told her before she married: "Now that you have a child of your own, you'll see it's not easy to be a good parent. Nobody gives you a rule book for it Gabrielle, and you will try to prevent some mistakes for your children, but that might mean you make some even bigger mistakes while you're trying."

Her mother apologized for the mistakes she had made with Gabrielle. Danielle made it clear that every mistake she had made was in an effort to prevent Gabrielle from going through what she had. But the marriage would change things. It would give Gabrielle her first chance at a family unit. Something that Gabrielle had always longed for but could never seem to get. Her mother prayed that things would work, because DJ and Gabrielle deserved to know what

Snapshots

it was like to have two parents who cared and shared in raising him.

That was something Danielle had never been able to give Gabrielle, and with her having to work so hard all her life, she was barely able to give of herself to Gabrielle. That had been her real reason for wanting Gabrielle and Dante to stay together. If Gabrielle had been able to finish college, then she would have been fine by herself; but once she had DJ, Danielle felt they should stay with Dante. Danielle couldn't have supported Gabrielle in any way to allow her to go back to college. She didn't have the money, nor could she change her life around to become a baby sitter while they tried to figure out a way for Gabrielle to make it back to school. Once Gabrielle became a mother, Danielle wanted DJ and Gabrielle to have time to grow and know one another in a way she had never been able to do with Gabrielle; Danielle had believed that being with Dante would best afford Gabrielle and DJ that chance.

That understanding had made things much easier for Gabrielle and her mom. They began to know each other in a way that they hadn't ever before, but it was mostly over the phone. With Gabrielle being so far away, visits were limited. She had her life to make in Miami, and her mom was working many and varied hours which made it difficult to plan a trip out there. Even when the season was over, Gabrielle wouldn't get a chance to go back to Wisconsin. Dante and Gabrielle would be heading to Dallas. Gabrielle had never been there, not even to meet his parents.

She had met his parents over the phone inadvertently when she and Dante had been dating; Gabrielle had mistakenly picked up the phone to make a call while he was talking to his parents. They didn't like to get involved in his personal life, but they knew he dealt with plenty of girls. From what they knew of Gabrielle, she was just one of the few who had been able to come close enough to exchange words with them.

Dante had always told his parents how difficult it was for him to settle down with anyone because of how girls chased him for his money and fame. He had always been a little over taken with himself, and they knew that much about their son. But then the problems started coming with Gabrielle, like when she "trapped" him with the baby and he was under so much pressure from that, he was calling them almost every night from Arizona. That's when they knew she had to be up to something. Then, when he called at the last minute to announce his wedding plans, so fast that they couldn't even make it to Wisconsin for the wedding, Dante's parents believed Gabrielle was truly a manipulative girl who was out to get their son for everything she could.

He hadn't staged it to go that way but he didn't do anything to change their perception of Gabrielle either. In the back of his mind, it really didn't matter because they were two entities that never had to be matched. They were his family, and Gabrielle was his wife.

The Jacksons had been cordial to Gabrielle because they were good Christian folk; yet they were skeptical of her, even though she was unaware.

Gabrielle had experienced a life with Dante that was much different than the one he painted for his parents, so she didn't know what they knew, but from the way they treated her over the phone, she had no cause to believe they were anything but accepting.

Gabrielle had every reason to believe that they would become close once she got to Dallas with the two Dantes.

chapter twenty three

The off season stay in Dallas would be ideal for many reasons. DJ had so many cousins there who he would get to meet. He would be surrounded by family and friends who would broaden his already growing interest in people. Gabrielle looked forward to her son having a good life in which he was constantly surrounded by people who loved him. He had come into the world at a cold time, and had been met with some cold events, but he never seemed to notice it. And for his early development that was good. She wanted him to grow in love and laughter and be able to remember those things the most.

The trip to Dallas would also be good for her and Dante. He was her husband now, and though Dante did everything he could as the man of the house and as a family man, Gabrielle wanted time with him as her husband. They had spent time one on one when they were dating, but they never really had time to themselves to just get to know each other as man and wife.

DJ and Dante went for walks or rides together. He took DJ shopping with him or running errands sometimes. She and DJ did things with each other. They spent their days together, visited daddy's practices or games, visited neighbors and friends. And she, DJ and Dante did things together, but Gabrielle and Dante had not had time to be with just one another. One of the main reasons for that was because Dante had forbidden Gabrielle's having any baby sitters.

Now that they were married, he felt strongly that only he or Gabrielle should watch DJ. Dante pointed out that when he was growing up, his mother had never allowed anyone to baby sit or watch them, not even other family members. There were too many of them to leave with one relative, and his parents didn't want them scattered around and subjected to too many different influences. So if they went anywhere, it was as a family. Usually that meant just church, but that was fine. It wasn't until Pauline, his eldest sister, was seventeen that she was able to babysit for them; so it wasn't until then that Dante's parents went places with just each other. Even then, they never went too far.

Gabrielle didn't object to many of Dante's regulations. He had a few, but he had them with such conviction that she tried to respect them. He didn't want her out at night, so most of the last minute shopping or evening errands, he ran himself. Even though they lived in a nice neighborhood, he didn't want to take any chances with his wife and son being out alone at night.

He also chose to manage his own money. Dante had observed from one too many teammates that their wives were managing or mis-managing their money, in his eyes. Ma'Leesa had told Gabrielle about the financial training seminars that the League offered for the wives, but when Gabrielle brought it up to Dante, he went into a fury. He demanded to know who she had been talking with about how to manage and spend his money. No doubt, he said, it was Amile. He had observed her one too many times with Lonzo and saw how she had reeled Lonzo's wallet into her purse by holding his heart in her hands. Dante wasn't going to have that happen to him.

No woman, wife or not, was going to get in his way of having money for what he deemed priority. He had a family to take care of back in Dallas. He had made good on his early promise to his sisters and parents that he would be good to them. Even when his parents insisted that he didn't, he sent money and gifts. He knew that his parents and sisters would have his back no matter what became him, but he couldn't say that for anyone else. So he did for them first, and he did for Gabrielle and DJ too; he just made sure he did it through her weekly stipend, because no one was going to spend his money in any way that was lavish, except for him.

That was one of their first marital arguments. And with that came the fact that he was still keeping a couple of separate credit cards and had his own P.O. Box at one of the mailing stations. That could only be for dirty things, Gabrielle was sure of that. There was nothing that could be so secret that she shouldn't be able to at least take it out of the mail, or see what had been billed, even though he was writing out the checks. They had fussed about that, and Dante ended the argument by slamming the door on his way out. He wasn't dressed for the evening. He was actually in shorts and a worn out t-shirt, but when he left, he left for the night. He came back after 4 a.m.

Snapshots

She could tell where he had been when he walked into their bedroom and leaned over her to see if she was sleeping. He was breathing heavily, and the hot gusts of air blew liquor all in her face. When he was satisfied that she was sleep, he knelt down next to her from his side of the bed. He tossed and turned for a while that night, knowing he had to be up for practice in just a few hours. When she couldn't take it anymore, she got up and walked downstairs to watch the morning come to life from the couch; but, she curled up and fell asleep, until both the Dantes woke up.

Her husband came down the stairs before he dressed for work, and was extremely apologetic for staying out all night. He explained that he had only been out with his boys. She wouldn't have even believed that he had been in a club that night because of the way he was dressed when he left, but athletes and celebrities could get into most clubs in any city she had been to, no matter how they were dressed.

He promised he would never do that again, and that the next time they had an argument, he would stick around through the end. She knew him better than that. But what she didn't know was how guilty he really felt about the things he had said to her before he left. He had no intentions of handing over his money, but he would get rid of the mail box. He called her on his way to work to say that. And, he called her a couple hours after that to tell her that he had met with the player coordinator for the team. The financial seminars were available for the wives. He missed out on that information when he was a rookie, because he hadn't ever planned to be married nor handing over his accounts.

He also rediscovered the information about the continued education program for players and their wives. He wouldn't be going back to school; he was sure of that. But Gabrielle did deserve to finish her degree, so he was going to start that up. He gave her the name of the team's player coordinator and told her to: "Call Cindy from now on, instead of Amile. Cindy will put you on to some stuff that's legit."

Gabrielle wouldn't be able to start school then because the Season was ending. She had actually started packing their clothes for Dallas since they would be leaving in a little more than two weeks. She didn't need to take anything else because Dante had already established everything for their house out there. As soon as the

Season ended, all they would need to do was close up things in the Miami house and head for the airport to Dallas.

DJ celebrated his first birthday right in the midst of all the packing. Dawntel, Ma'Leesa, and the other girls had made it over with their husbands and children to celebrate the birthday, and the fellas enjoyed their rap session out front. They had combined that time as a Christmas present exchange day as well because they would all be away in New York for the final Christmas day game.

Gabrielle was not looking forward to spending Christmas day away from her home. She couldn't even put up decorations because they were packing to leave, plus after the game, they would only be back in Miami for a few hours until their plane left. Still, she was glad that at least after the game, she, Dante and DJ would be together as a family this Christmas holiday. She was also glad that they did have to be in New York on Christmas day. That meant DJ would get to see some snow. It wasn't much like Christmas with palm trees and sun.

chapter twenty four

Dante more than made up for their being away at Christmas. When they made it to Dallas, not only was their new home fully furnished, but it also had a Christmas tree with gifts underneath, and a fire place with named stockings hanging from it. His sisters, Erica and Erin, had come over and put on the crowning touches before he and his new family arrived.

Gabrielle walked in the Dallas home, and was fully amazed. It was even more beautiful than their first. It was a ranch style home with hard wood floors and wide space. The kitchen was at the back of the house and spread from one end to the next. She had an island in the middle, cabinet and counter space all over. The pantry and downstairs restroom were to the front and right of the island, and through the kitchen to the left of the island was the day area for the kitchen table. The entire back wall of the day area was a floor to ceiling window that looked out onto the back patio. The sliding door that lead to the patio and back yard was in the kitchen.

The dining room was in front of the day area, and to its right were the stairs going up. If you kept straight past the stairs there was the large, open den with the fire place and Christmas decorations. And straight ahead, beyond the den was the living room area, which was even more spacious and lavishly done. Above the fire place in the living room, Dante had a picture of him, Gabrielle and DJ hung. The mantle had 'what nots' on it. The floor was carpeted, and had a few statues standing on it. Toward the back of that room was a guest bedroom and restroom, and when you walked back out through the den, you could turn left and go back to the kitchen, or you could go straight and a little further left to go up the stairs, or if you got to the stairs and turned right instead of left, you would be heading out the front door.

Gabrielle had walked back through the den and was going left up the stairs, but DJ crept off to go straight and into the dining room. Dante had placed some statues of elephants at the entry of the dining room area. And DJ thought those were his toys, or at least that they should be played with. Gabrielle scooped him up, and tossed him over her shoulder on the way up the stairs. She knew that would distract him enough to keep him from crying about the elephants.

They reached the landing and the stairs split the upstairs, but not in half. Two bedrooms and the office were on her right. Directly in front of her was the hall bathroom. To the left were the three other bedrooms and she walked through them. She and Dante would take the room on the front of the house this time. Their master bathroom connected to the next bedroom over, so that would be DJ's. The other rooms would be for guests when they had them. Dante had known when he had the house built that she would want her mother to come out and visit, and he had family there, so they would be entertaining whenever they were in town.

Dante had really thought things out that day in July, just like he said he had. Things were just as he said they would be. Gabrielle was done exploring the upstairs for now, but DJ would not want to leave any time soon. He had found his room and was sitting in the floor with some toys he had pulled out. Gabrielle watched him play for a while, then lured him out with the only thing she knew would be enticing: "Daddy's going bye bye. You better come on so we can see him."

She knew her son well enough to know that nothing else would appeal to him as an incentive for leaving a room full of toys. Dante Jr. grabbed one of the animals from the room and Gabrielle attached him to her hip. She walked back down the stairs, quickly but carefully. The floors looked so waxy that it seemed you could easily slip and fall. Dante was sitting on a stool in the kitchen where he had been all this time talking on the phone. DJ had slid down from her hip, and had gone over to play with the refrigerator magnets. Gabrielle walked up to Dante and wrapped her arms around him, hugging and kissing him so tight that he almost lost balance from his stool.

"What is it boo?" he asked, already knowing; she loved the place.

It wasn't quite as hot as Miami, but it was warm enough that there was no sign of snow. Even without the snow, it felt like more than Christmas here; it felt like home.

Dante's older sister Pauline, her husband and three children were coming by this evening. They didn't celebrate Christmas because Pauline's husband felt it was too materialistic. He had grown

Snapshots

up in a home where they could hardly afford any gifts, so he learned early to appreciate the holidays just for the aspect of family. Dante couldn't have disagreed with that more.

Dante and Pauline argued many times about her husband's concept of the holidays. They made enough money to make sure that his nieces and nephew had a nice Christmas. Regardless to what her husband didn't have, there was no need for him to deprive the kids of the joys of Christmas and opening toys. Pauline and Dante had grown up in a house where there wasn't much spare money either, but their parents always had at least one gift for each of them, and as far as he could remember, it was usually the one gift they had each wanted the most. But he was tired of arguing with Pauline through the years, so for this year, he would make sure things were different.

Gabrielle was a little unnerved that she had just found out in the last fifteen minutes that Dante's family was coming over. She had not met any of them in person, and though it was only one of his sisters and her immediate family, Gabrielle wanted to make a good impression. She hadn't cooked anything. Pauline would probably think she wasn't a good wife. Two of his other sisters had already gotten the house ready; surely Pauline knew that. Gabrielle hadn't done a thing in this new house.

"Relax, baby." Dante told her as he took her hand and held DJ on his hip. He walked her up the stairs. They stopped to put DJ down for a nap, then Dante walked through the halls of the upstairs with Gabrielle, asking her if she liked this room and then the other. He pointed out a few small changes he wanted to make here or there in the different rooms, but when they got to the threshold of their own bedroom, he stood behind her and bumped his pelvis to her backside and only said: "Go in."

She turned her face back to him and smiled.

"Go on in," he reminded her, looking at her seductively.

Once they walked into the room, he asked her what she thought. She glanced at the clock on their black lacquer dresser and told him that she thought she should hurry up and get ready.

Gabrielle walked to the dresser, and began pulling out things to wear, but Dante had already flopped down on the bed. He was stretched out on his back like a snow angel.

"No boo, come over here and tell me what you think," he said, and placed his fingers behind his head.

"Dante," Gabrielle protested. "Your sister will be here any minute. I want to get dressed and ready before..."

"Come here boo," he had already interrupted.

He knew that Gabrielle would start walking to him pretty soon, but he still sat up and eyed her with a look to rush her along. But before she could turn all the way around to face him, he had slid up from the bed and was behind her with his hands on her waist. He stood for a moment, rubbing her sides up and down, then running his hands across to her breasts. When he massaged to the center of each breast, he pinched just a little and her body fell back into him. He still knew how to make her weak.

Gabrielle turned to face him, and he smiled down at her, kissing her forehead. He held each of her arms and slowly moved his hands on them from top to bottom. After about the third time that he had gone down her arms, he placed his thumbs on her wrists, giving just a little pressure, then massaged the insides of her palms with his finger tips.

He slid his fingertips over hers and walked backwards, leading her toward the bed. He fell into the bed on his back, and pulled her on top of him. He caressed her repeatedly. She kissed him slowly all over his face. Her tongue neatly circled his nose, then ran wildly around his cheeks. Her elbows rested on his shoulders, and her fingers massaged then tightened the skin on his forehead, cheeks then chin. She was so engrossed in her husband, that she had forgotten to nag him a little more about his sister coming. He began kissing her, then rolled her over onto her back.

"Do you love me?" he asked her, looking into her eyes.

"You know I do," she said with her heart sinking in.

"You love me with all your heart?" he continued.

"I love you with everything I have in me," she answered, trying to lift up.

He smiled down on her, and kissed her neck from ear to ear, then around to her cheeks and up to the center of her lips. He stared at her then said:

"I know you do."

He smiled then licked between the middle of her slightly opened lips.

He scooped his hands under her shoulders and sat her up then rolled her back on top of him. He lifted her skirt slightly, then slid her to his center. She placed both of her hands on his cheeks, rubbed them, then shook her head 'no.'

"Your sister is going to be here any minute," she whispered.

"Listen, my sister won't be here for hours."

"Dante..."

"Gabrielle, be quiet. Please. I know what I'm talking about.

She protested a little more, then he choked in:

"Listen, Gabrielle, I know what I'm talking about. Those are my people."

He was getting irritated, and pretty soon they would be arguing because she didn't like the way he had said they were his 'people;' it sounded like he was excluding her from being family. She leaned back a little and he knew she was upset so he tried to smooth it over.

"Boo, look. Pauline hasn't been here to see my mother in two months. That's an eternity for them. She's busy yapping with my mother and Erica and Erin like she's never seen them before."

That wasn't enough to convince Gabrielle, but she knew there was no point in starting up the same argument of how she still wanted to get dressed, so she blurted out another thought.

"Dinner. What about dinner? I haven't..."

"I'm running out to Papadeaux," he asserted. Then, laughing he continued. "Unless you know how to make up some fried alligator, yea. Pauline's a Louisiana girl now, and even before that, she wasn't eating none of your Wisconsin stuff. We Southern bred baby."

Now her feelings were hurt. Gabrielle was too sensitive. He knew she wanted to start whining and ask what he meant about her not being able to cook right. But he was going to be patient this time. He wasn't even going to fuss with her. Obviously, meeting one member of his family was so important to her, definitely much more important than it was to him, but he would try to respect that. He sat up on the bed, placed her to the side, and told her to forget it.

"Are you mad?" she asked him.

"Nah. I ain't mad," he said getting up and walking into their bathroom.

"You are. You're mad at me aren't you, Dante?"

"Nah, Gabrielle. I told you I ain't mad."

She heard a little more irritation in his voice, so she got up to follow him. He shut the bathroom door almost right as she got to it.

He opened the other bathroom door to peek in on DJ, and Gabrielle came through the door he had shut on her.

She walked up behind Dante, placed her hand on his waist and peeked through his arm to see what DJ was doing.

DJ had gotten out of bed to play with his toys after they left, and he had fallen asleep on the floor. Gabrielle told Dante she would go get him, and put him back in his bed. But Dante held her arm, telling her to just let him stay there and rest. DJ's floor was carpeted just as plush as most mattresses. Besides, if Gabrielle moved him he would wake up, and he probably needed the rest. They'd had a long day. Gabrielle had slipped underneath Dante's arm, and they both stood for a while admiring their sleeping son, who had piled an army of toys around him. Gabrielle turned into Dante and asked her second question while running her fingers up and down his stomach. "You sure you're not mad at me?"

He smacked his lips together as if she were being ridiculous. "Nah Gabrielle. I told you man, I ain't mad."

But as he pulled away to walk back toward their room, she shut DJ's connecting door, and pulled her husband down to his knees. Right there, next to their black lacquer bath tub, she slipped and slid all over the floor with him. He tried to restrain his grunts and roars, which always let her know how good she made him feel.

When they had reached their peak, Gabrielle's head was on his chest, and he was rubbing through her hair. He looked up toward the ceiling, repeating: "Whew." "Girl." He looked down to her, then back to the ceiling. He smiled a double smile. One, because she had made him feel as she always did, better than the last time. And two, because he had known that walking away from her, even though he really wasn't mad, would make her come after him even more.

She had fallen right into his trap. He knew she was right earlier; they should have been getting ready; but, he just wanted his way, and he knew that acting mad at her would certainly get it.

He placed his hands on the sides of her head, and lifted her face up towards his: "Baby, we got to hurry up and get dressed."

He paused for a minute to give more impact to the last part of his statement.

"You know Pauline will be here any minute."

Gabrielle's mouth dropped, and she was ready to argue Dante down, but he was laughing, and wiggling underneath her so that he could get up. She pushed and swatted at him before going into their bedroom, pulling clothes out of the closet and fussing at him. Dante was still in the bathroom, and he told her she would have to yell at him louder because he couldn't hear her; he was running their bath water.

He let the tub fill up, then snuck behind Gabrielle who was still in the bedroom yelling things to him. He grabbed her from behind, tossed her over his shoulder, then placed her in the tub. He got in behind her and they splashed water with their hands and feet then bathed each other down, and slid into a long, deep kiss.

"That's why we're running late now," she reminded him.

He breathed out a short laugh, then picked up his towel and stepped out. She followed.

When they were dressed, Dante rushed out to Papadeaux and Gabrielle roused and readied DJ.

Pauline was about another 30 minutes in getting there, and when she arrived, Dante's earlier words had been confirmed; she had been catching up with her mother and sisters. Pauline went on to talk about how difficult it had been for her to leave her family and go to Louisiana; but that was her husband's birth place, and he had a job offer, so they had to go. She surely regarded her husband as family, but much like Dante, she seemed to truly regard the Jacksons as her first family. The difference was, she honored her husband and did what was best for her new family. Dante's choices were always based on what was best for him.

Pauline and her husband, Deshawn, had met at the city University. She told Gabrielle about their beginnings, and wanted to hear Gabrielle's version of her and Dante's. Pauline had already decided two years ago not to believe Dante's version of what was going on with him and Gabrielle. Though she had never met Gabrielle, Pauline knew her brother well enough to know that he always wanted things to go just his way. Dante had a way of appealing to people's sympathies and making them believe that when things went wrong, it was because someone else had done him really wrong. And, you could actually end up hurting for him.

It wasn't that Dante was manipulative, but his appeal came from his big heart. Anyone who knew him knew that at the very center of Dante was a loving, warm heart that poured over. He was sweet, funny, and charismatic. Those were the parts of him that shined out, so those were the parts that you remembered even when he was at his worst.

Most of the time, Dante seemed to be the best person in the world; he was kind and caring and warm almost all of the time; but, when his temper flared, the incidents were so overwhelming that it made you wonder if he wasn't just all bad. Still, everyone who knew him saw beyond those bad streaks to the Dante they knew was within. When he was good, he was so good that you always wanted to find the real him again when he had done wrong.

Gabrielle had slowly begun to understand Dante and his ways. Pauline knew them, but she realized that she only knew them as his sister. So, she didn't get involved with his early complaints about the "situation that Gabrielle had put" him in. She knew there had to be a lot more going on, and so did her parents. But they were mom and dad, and he was their baby boy, so he could always appeal to their sympathies. He drew his mom in, though his dad didn't believe things as readily. Still, the two of them had always allowed Dante to get away with more than any of the other children.

His mom knew Dante the best, so when they were children she disciplined him; and, when he was older she protected him, even though sometimes she knew her son was in the wrong.

Pauline had always been the mediator. She was the eldest child, and always kept an eye over all the other children, especially during the rare occasions when her parents left the house for a few hours. She not only disciplined Dante when her parents were gone, but she told on him when they returned. Dante would sometimes bully or blame his sisters and brother for things he did when his parents were gone, but Pauline always set it straight the minute they came through the door.

With Gabrielle, Pauline was certain there would be no need to explain away anything Dante had previously said to their parents. Gabrielle's personality was genuine and sweet. This emanated from her heart and gave her a glow of sincerity. Gabrielle was a simplistic person, yet her inner beauty illuminated her outer.

Pauline's children were immediately taken by Gabrielle. When they had walked in the door earlier that evening, the children stared at Gabrielle with bright eyes, wanting to know who she was. And Shayonna, who normally said whatever was on her mind, became shy and whispered a question to her mother. Shayonna wanted to know if Gabrielle was Nia Long.

Gabrielle lifted the slim eight year old Shayonna into her arms, kissed her cheek and told her that she wasn't Nia Long; she was just 'auntie', but Shayonna was the sweetest little girl in the world for the compliment. With that, Shonyea and Deshawn Jr. began telling Gabrielle they were sweet too. Gabrielle agreed, and Pauline swept them toward the den where Shawn, her husband, would keep an eye on them.

Pauline and Gabrielle headed back to the kitchen to talk, but Gabrielle had to go between the den and dining room a few times because she could hear DJ pushing his father's statues through the hall. His cousins were helping him. Shawn had dozed off on the couch.

When Shayonna understood that 'auntie didn't want them playing with these things,' she walked to the kitchen repeatedly to tell on the other kids; but after a while, she decided to stay in the den and just boss them around herself.

With Shayonna in charge, the den was calm one minute and chaotic the next. Gabrielle had quit going back to the den. She had taken DJ to the kitchen with her the first time he was crying, but he wiggled away from her and rushed back to be with the other kids as soon as he could.

That was the part that had been missing for DJ, being with kids and people he was familiar with. Gabrielle remarked about that and she and Pauline talked about family and how important it was to be close. Pauline missed being around her mother and family here, but with her husband's job, she had to be gone. Even with it being the holidays, they would only be in town for a few days.

Shayonna was a grandma's girl, so she would want to be with Pauline since Pauline would be with her mother almost the entire visit. DeShawn Jr. was introverted like his father, so he'd be staying close to his parents, which meant they'd all be at the Jacksons', except Shonyea. She was Dante's baby. Shonyea was quiet and shy, except when Dante came around. Then she had almost as much personality as he did. Shonyea would surely want to stay with her 'Uncle D.'

Gabrielle told Pauline that it would be fine, to just bring Shonyea's things over. Pauline told Gabrielle:

"You just don't understand the Jackson nieces and nephews

yet. If I pack Shonyea's things, Shayonna would all of a sudden want to stay."

Gabrielle told her that would be fine, but Pauline added further explanation that:

"Then Erica would be sending her children too, and you'll have a houseful."

Dante's sister Erica had four children, who were always at their grandmother's house. Once Pauline went back to pack Shon and Shay's things, Erica's children would be coming too.

Dante walked through the door just when Pauline was talking about who was staying at his house.

"Who's staying here?" he asked, ducking his head in to the kitchenette area. "You staying here?" he asked, hugging Pauline sideways and kissing her on the cheek.

The sound of his voice sent Shonyea running to the kitchen and the other kids following with excitement.

"I'm staying here..." Shonyea said shyly grabbing the leg of Dante's jeans.

"You are?" he asked and scooped her up into the air.

Then Shayonna, DeShawn, and even Dante started repeating that they were staying. They bombarded Dante with tugs and hugs, and he lifted them up: two on one arm, one on another, and walked into the den dragging Shayonna who was hanging on to the back of his pant's leg. The children swung arms and legs all over Dante until he dropped them dramatically on the couch, where he fell down on top of them.

Shawn was wide awake by then and trying to get his children into some order. They had climbed on top of Dante and were pushing and punching him down. Dante sat up from under the pile of children and reached his hand across the end-table to speak to Shawn.

"Aw, no man, they're alright," he said.

Shawn explained how he just didn't want them tearing up the new furniture, but Pauline yelled out from the kitchen and embarrassed him: "Well, you should have done something about that an hour ago. They were climbing over you and the furniture while you were in there asleep."

Dante yelled back in the kitchen and playfully told Pauline that she just better be in there getting his food ready. Pauline was walking to the doorway to tell him that she would send him upstairs with no dinner, just like in the old school days. He hadn't forgotten; she had always been the one in charge.

Dante walked to the door way, which Pauline was blocking. He held her chin and looked toward the dining room where Gabrielle was setting the table.

"That's why I got my baby in here. She ain't gon let nobody take advantage of me."

Gabrielle smiled up from the table, and he headed into the dining room and stood behind her.

"Are you baby?" he asked hugging and kissing her from behind. "You ain't gon send me to bed hungry?"

Shonyea had arrived in the dining room holding her father's hand, and the rest of the kids were with Pauline. Shonyea's eyes were glued on Dante, whose attention was all on Gabrielle. When he noticed Shonyea, he put his hand out to her.

"Come here baby," he said to Shonyea. "You wouldn't do your uncle D like that either would you?"

Shonyea shook her head "no."

Her uncle picked her up and held her on one side, while his wife stood at the other. He asked Shonyea if she liked Gabrielle, and told her that Gabrielle was her aunt. Shonyea shook her head 'yes' that she liked Gabrielle.

Shayonna stole Shonyea's spotlight and said: "I like auntie too uncle D. She's nice and pretty. She looks like Nia Long."

"Whoa," Dante said laughing. "Well uncle didn't do too bad then. Uncle loves Nia Long."

Gabrielle playfully cut her eyes at him as he hugged one arm around her shoulders then got everybody seated. They all took hands at the table and Dante lead the grace. Shonyea, who was seated on his lap, chimed in with the Bible verse afterwards.

Dante showed proud surprise and thanked Shonyea for her big addition to his grace. Dinner was going around the table, and so was good conversation and cheer.

chapter twenty five

Everyone retreated to the den after dinner was cleared. Deshawn felt they should start heading back across town to the Jacksons' household. Pauline was in agreement. It was nearly midnight, and her children had been running all day, and now they had just pooped out on the den floor. Dante was on the couch with his head tilted toward the ceiling and Shonyea across his lap. He had to be exhausted because he was usually refueling the light at any party.

Everyone was tired, but the minute Pauline said "Come on, let's go," and started getting the kids up, they whined and cried that they wanted to stay. Shawn was helping her get them up, and thanking Dante who had now drifted back in. Gabrielle and Dante were both telling them that they should just go on and stay the night.

The kids could sleep in the guest bedrooms, or if they wanted, they could stay down in the den. Shawn didn't want it to be any trouble. And Pauline certainly felt that it would be. This was Gabrielle and Dante's first night in their new home, surely they should sleep in it alone. But Dante insisted that they stay, so Gabrielle held Shayonna's hand and walked her and Pauline up the stairs. She would put the two little girls in the second bedroom on the right, and Pauline and her husband could stay in the first.

Shayonna was not ready to go to bed once she was upstairs, so she asked if she could see the other room, where Deshawn Jr. would be sleeping. Pauline was getting impatient with Shayonna's stalling technique, but Gabrielle didn't mind. It would give her a chance to show Pauline around. She hadn't had a chance to show Pauline around earlier.

"We'll see it tomorrow," Pauline said to Gabrielle. "I'm tired. You're tired, and Shayonna is going to bed."

That was supposed to finish it, but Shayonna had one more question. "Where's Shonyea? When is she coming upstairs for bed?"

That would have been enough to earn Shayonna a spanking, but Shonyea was downstairs crying. So, Pauline walked back toward the stairs, and called down to ask what was going wrong. Then she started heading down.

Dante was trying to yell back: "It's nothing. It's nothing," but by that time, Pauline was already in the den.

"What is wrong with you?" She began demanding from Shonyea who was holding Dante's hand and sniffling.

"Aw, it's nothing Pauline. I don't even know why y'all trip on these kids like you do."

"What are you talking about Dante? Don't you start with me like that about anything that has to do with my kids."

Shawn handed Pauline a partially opened gift box that Dante had given to Shonyea. Shawn shook his head and Pauline frowned up at Dante.

"What do you think you're doing Dante? You know we don't celebrate Christmas like this," she began.

Dante waved her off. "I'm not trying to hear all that Pauline. I'm..."

"You're...going to hear it!" she interrupted.

The argument was on between the two of them.

"You can't just rush in and give my kids gifts when you know we don't do that," she began.

"I ain't asking what y'all do Pauline. I'm doin' what I do while I can do it," he exchanged.

"Dante, I don't need your thoughts, actions, or opinions about what I say goes for my kids. They don't get gifts like that."

"Well, they gon' get 'em from me!" he yelled.

"I say they aren't. These are my kids, and my rules!"

"And this is my house, and my..."

Before he could finish, Pauline interrupted with: "Well, maybe we'll just leave."

"Maybe you should!"

Dante and Pauline were at a stand off, and Gabrielle wanted to say something to break them down. It was Christmas. Things were supposed to be warm and endearing, but Dante and Pauline had made it hotter than July.

Fortunately, Deshawn, Jr. chimed in a word or two:

"But mommy, it isn't Uncle D's fault; Shonyea started opening it first."

Pauline whirled around and didn't know whether to slap Deshawn, Jr. in the mouth for interrupting, Shonyea for opening the gift, or Dante for encouraging it.

Dante was telling Pauline that it was his fault and that he had bought all of them something, and that he intended to give everybody their own gifts.

The more Pauline yelled at him, the more he started lifting things from the tree and throwing them back toward the couch saying whose gift was whose. Pauline grabbed up her children and told her husband that they were leaving. Gabrielle had picked up DJ because he was among the crying children. At the same time, she was trying to grip Dante's arm, and begging him to stop.

Pauline and her family were heading out the back door. She was still yelling back at Dante about how she couldn't believe him. Gabrielle wanted to ask her to please stay because it was so late now and they were all tired, but Dante and Pauline's words were the only two lighting up the air. All Gabrielle could do was follow them to the door. She was yelling out to Pauline that she was sorry. Dante's eyes were fire red.

"What you got to be sorry for? This ain't got nothing to do with you," he started with Gabrielle; then he continued to yell out to Pauline how ridiculous she and her husband were.

Pauline and Deshawn had made it to their car, and Shonyea was in her mother's arms wiggling, with her hands stretched out for Dante to come get her. Pauline was yelling back to Dante how ridiculous he was, and slapping Shonyea's hands for her to put them down.

Dante kept repeating that:

"Yeah, I am ridiculous."

Then he started throwing the boxes of gifts he had bought for them toward their car. Pauline was the last one to get in the car. She was standing on the inside of her open car door looking at her brother as he flung the boxes toward the car. He wasn't even aiming to miss.

If it would have been the old days, she would have charged right back at him from where she stood. But she had stopped yelling now, and her husband had fastened the kids in their seats. They were still crying, and her husband quietly asked her to please just get in the car so they could go. Pauline's eyes couldn't even lock with Dante's because his were glazed. He was still yelling, but he had run out of things to throw. Gabrielle had already turned and gone back into the house.

Pauline agreed with her husband; it was best to just go. She sat down in the car so that he could pull off.

chapter twenty six

Gabrielle had put DJ to sleep upstairs and walked back to the den to begin picking things up. Dante stormed back into the house kicking the few boxes that he had dropped in the kitchen. When he made it to the den and saw Gabrielle picking up things, he took a box from her hand and threw it back on the floor.

"Come on Gabrielle and go upstairs. Leave that stuff alone."

He had snatched her hand and started walking upstairs. She wanted to cry; she was so hurt. Pauline was his sister; surely she had seen Dante's obnoxious side before, still it embarrassed Gabrielle that he went into such a rage. And it hurt her more than it frightened her. She was humiliated by his actions and sorry for her son to have to see his father acting this way.

The night was quiet. When they had gotten upstairs and laid down for bed, both of them were quiet, and the house echoed that. Outside, the sky was blue black. Dante had their window cracked and they could hear the insects.

He laid in the bed on his back, and she did too. He wanted to say something after a while of just lying there. He knew she was still awake. Even though both of their eyes were facing the ceiling, he could tell that Gabrielle's were probably filling up with tears. He wanted to tell her that he was sorry, but he laid there stubbornly for a while, and instead of telling Gabrielle how sorry he was, he started thinking of how angry Pauline had made him.

Gabrielle rolled over on her side and faced the window, looking out at the sky. Dante stayed still until he intertwined his fingers and hands above his head and rested them on his pillow. By the time he rolled over toward Gabrielle and wrapped one of his arms across her, she had already finished crying and was well into her sleep.

In the morning when she woke up, DJ was at her bedside, and Dante was gone. She had thought she heard the phone ring a couple hours earlier, but she was drifting in and out of sleep. Now, it was almost 10:30, and her son was tugging at her for breakfast. They walked down stairs and past all the mess from the night before. Gabrielle fixed DJ's breakfast and then seated him at the breakfast bar while she cleaned the den up.

It wasn't long before DJ had climbed down and come into the den with his mother. He was asking which gifts were for Shonyea. He pointed to different boxes asking: "For me? For Yea Yea?"

Gabrielle couldn't explain to him what had happened last night, but he obviously remembered and was bothered by it. She was too.

Gabrielle became increasingly bothered as the day went by, and she had not seen nor heard from her husband. There wasn't even a note saying where he had gone. DJ wouldn't want to stay in the house much longer. It was bright and sunny outside, so she got him dressed and they went outside walking through the neighborhood. The land was so massive that they only made it past two or three houses. This area was full of new properties and developments, and the homes being built were on sprawling acres, much like their own. DJ went wild over a pony he saw in one of the neighbors' yards, but they didn't have the type of neighbors that would let him even pet it. So after a while of him looking and crying to get on one, she headed back home with him.

When they got back home, she laid him down for a nap.

There wasn't much for her to do around the house now, so before she knew it, she had dozed off for a nap too. DJ was upstairs and she was on the couch in the den. She woke up to the phone. It was her mother. They talked for a while, and Danielle wanted to know all about Dante's family and how they were getting along. Gabrielle couldn't offer anything much because she still had only met one sister, and Dante had turned that into a disaster. So, she just told her mother that they were still settling in.

Gabrielle wanted her mother to come down to visit. She volunteered her husband to spring for the trip. Her mother really wanted to visit, but her work schedule still wouldn't permit it. Danielle wanted to wish her grandson a happy belated birthday, so Gabrielle got him to the phone. She also wanted to wish her son-in-law happy holidays, but Gabrielle explained that he was out running errands.

The phone beeped and it was Pauline. Gabrielle took down the number to Dante's mother's house, and returned to the line with her mother. When Gabrielle called back, Pauline was gone, and Dante's youngest sister Erin answered the phone. She asked when they would get a chance to meet Gabrielle and why she hadn't come

Snapshots

over for the family dinner.

Gabrielle hadn't even known about the family dinner, so she didn't know what to say. This made the situation more awkward, and it made her seem as aloof as Dante had depicted her.

There was a lot of background noise, and Gabrielle thought she even heard Dante's voice, but Erin had ended the conversation by saying she would have Dante call Gabrielle back because one of her aunts needed to use the phone.

DJ and Gabrielle spent the next few hours alone. She let him open a few of his toys and play with them, and she made a few calls to wish happy holidays to Yvette and Michelle. Talking with her friends made the afternoon to evening transition a little smoother, still, when Dante walked in the door after 8:00, she was heated.

He was in an upbeat mood, but her instant confrontation set him off. She was demanding to know where he had been all day, and why he hadn't told her anything, nor called, nor left any way for her and DJ to get around. He wanted to know just where she had been planning to go.

"To your mother's for the family dinner, for one!" she screamed.

He almost banged his hands through the kitchen counter. He had told her when they were living together not to be calling around looking for him, so he demanded to know why she had been calling over to his mother's. She reminded him that they weren't living together anymore. She was his wife now, and she had every right to call looking for him.

He told her that when he wanted to be with his family, he had a right to be. So Gabrielle warned him to stop separating the Jacksons; she and DJ were his family too.

For some reason, he sighed as if they didn't count as family, as much as his parents and siblings did. That created a bigger confrontation. Dante ended the argument by just telling her, as he stormed up the stairs: "You just better quit calling over my mother's house."

chapter twenty seven

Gabrielle stayed to herself for the next few days. It was just her and DJ in the house mostly. Dante was in and out, and when he was there he was hardly speaking. He played with DJ a little, but usually by the time he got in, DJ was ready for bed. He always wanted to stay up to play with his daddy, but Gabrielle would usher him up to bed, with few protests from Dante.

Dante's absence and his minimal interaction with his son angered Gabrielle, but she would have been even more angry if she had known how much time and energy he had been giving to his nieces and nephews throughout the day while he was gone.

It wasn't that Dante didn't want to take DJ with him to be around his cousins; it was more that he was simply being spiteful toward Gabrielle, and choosing to reinforce how he would make the decisions about when she would be in contact with his family.

The first day he had gone over to his mother's he had gone to apologize to his mother for what happened between him and Pauline the night before. His mother had called early that morning and wanted an explanation, face to face. He went over there to apologize and had forgotten that the family dinner was later. He ran around visiting old friends and made it back to his mother's in just enough time for the dinner, but without Gabrielle. Instead of telling them he had forgotten about the dinner, he said he came alone because Gabrielle was tired from the night before. No one else in the household understood why Gabrielle would be too tired to come. They had all pitched in to get the house ready so that Gabrielle wouldn't have much to do once she and Dante arrived. Dante didn't try to help them understand either. That made his family think that Gabrielle was just too 'sa'ditty' or 'plain funny acting.'

Only Pauline came to Gabrielle's defense and explained that things had really gotten out of hand the night before and maybe it had taken a toll on Gabrielle or DJ. That helped some, but Dante's parents, and his other sisters, Erica and Erin still had reservations about Gabrielle.

After a few more days passed and Pauline hadn't even heard from Gabrielle, she began to wonder. She called Gabrielle the day before she and her family were leaving, and asked why they hadn't seen her yet. Gabrielle felt comfortable with Pauline but didn't want to tell her about Dante's forbidding her to go over there, nor did she want to tell Pauline how Dante had been gone for hours at a time and she had no way to get around. But, Pauline somewhat guessed it.

They had seen Dante at the house a few times, but mostly he was running around in the neighborhood visiting. Pauline wanted to see Gabrielle before she, Deshawn, and the kids left town, and the kids had been asking to see Gabrielle too.

Pauline explained how she had vowed never to step foot on Dante's property again after what had happened that night, but Gabrielle put her at ease. She really wanted to see Pauline and the kids, and the fact that she had no way to get around, nor had she seen anything else in the city, made Pauline decide to come over and get her.

Pauline arrived alone. She had been running errands and left the kids with her parents, so she, Gabrielle and DJ headed over there. When they first arrived there were sparks, then a flame, and then an explosion.

Dante's parents didn't know how to receive Gabrielle. From the beginning they had heard so many things about her from Dante that they didn't like. Pauline had initially given them a much different impression, but the fact that Gabrielle hadn't shown up for the family dinner, nor was she willing, according to Dante, to come with him when he came by every day made his parents reticent about accepting her whole heartedly.

Pauline, DJ and Gabrielle walked onto the back patio, and the minute Shonyea saw Gabrielle, she ran and leaped in her arms. Shayonna followed suit, and before Gabrielle knew it, the crowd of Dante's nieces and nephews had surrounded her. Pauline was calling them away from Gabrielle, but Gabrielle told her the children were fine. She kneeled down slowly to let Shonyea down, and then one by one went through each of the children's names.

Dante's mother was standing in the door watching. She had intended to call the children in and away from Gabrielle, but Gabrielle was devoting such attention to the children that Mrs. Jackson tried to wait until Gabrielle was done. Even though the children were in a crowd around her, Gabrielle gave special attention that made each one feel like the center of her focus.

Once Gabrielle knew all of their names, she introduced them to Dante, Jr. and answered questions about whether she was their auntie, how old she was, where she had been. The list would have gone on, but Mrs. Jackson could see that Gabrielle wasn't experienced enough with these children to cut them off.

"That's enough..." Mrs. Jackson announced as she walked out to the patio. "You all can get down off of this patio and go in the back yard and play."

The children had grabbed DJ's hand and ran off to the back yard. Gabrielle apologized that she hadn't had a chance to introduce DJ to his grandmother. But Mrs. Jackson told her that Dante had brought DJ by before, besides that, she knew children well enough to know that DJ wouldn't have paid any attention to her when there were ten other children playing.

Gabrielle felt very uncomfortable finding out that Dante hadn't ever told her that he had taken DJ to meet his grandparents. But she covered up her shock and Mrs. Jackson moved the conversation on to other things.

The next break in the conversation came when Mrs. Jackson said she was glad that Gabrielle was feeling better and had finally made her way over there. This time Gabrielle looked at her puzzled, then replied that she hadn't ever been sick. Mrs. Jackson would have thought Gabrielle was the one lying, but Gabrielle's face no longer looked puzzled; she looked hurt.

They couldn't go any further into the conversation because there was loud music at the end of the driveway. This prompted Mrs. Jackson to walk down the driveway and toward the front. Gabrielle was getting up from the table, but Mrs. Jackson asked her to stay in the back and keep the kids there.

The children started running toward the front. Three of them knew the loud music meant their dad was there; the others wanted to get in line for the money that their uncle Torrence liked to pass out. But Mrs. Jackson was trying to head Torrence off before her husband came from the neighbor's porch.

Pauline had been up front talking to a neighbor, so she was already at the door of Torrence's candy apple red Cadillac. He stepped out and placed one hand on the beige rag top, and rested his foot on the side panel. He extended one arm to his sister and smiled with most of his teeth matching the gold rims on his car. He was no where near as tall as Dante, nor was he as big, but he always prided himself on probably having as much money as Dante. That didn't matter to his parents, nor to Dante, but it did create constant friction.

Torrence had chosen the wrong path as far as making his money, so even though his parents didn't like to accept money from Dante, they refused to accept it from Torrence. His three children had three different mothers and none of the mothers knew where Torrence lived; so when one baby's mother found out that another mother had dropped off her child with Mrs. Jackson, the others followed suit. That meant that in addition to Erica and her four children constantly being at his mother's, Torrence's children were always there too. As a result of that, he felt the least he could do was compensate his mother for her time, feeding, and baby sitting them. But Mrs. Jackson refused his money, and Mr. Jackson demanded that Torrence get himself together.

One time he came down so hard on Torrence that their verbal debate turned physical. Torrence had argued that his father wouldn't have ever been as tough on Dante. That lead to Mr. Jackson comparing the two boys which turned the confrontation into a fight. The only thing was worse than the fight itself was that Dante had shown up to break it up. That had been years ago, but the feelings of resentment never died.

Today Mrs. Jackson made it to the car and she and Pauline had convinced Torrence to turn down the music. But, Mr. Jackson was already on his way. He got to the car and confronted Torrence about why he would even pull up playing such loud music, knowing that this was a good Christian home, and that they had good Christian neighbors, and that there were children for whom he was being a bad role model. The four members of the Jackson family were soon joined by the children. Gabrielle couldn't keep them in the back any longer. Even Shayonna, who was the oldest grandchild and loved to boss the other children into order, had torn off to the front. They stood at a distance, but they could still see the commotion. Gabrielle called for the other children to come to the back, but even DJ who was in her arms, was kicking and yelling to be let down.

More loud music filled the air, but stopped immediately. It was Dante's car, and his music stopped the minute he pulled up and saw the scene developing. When he approached it, Torrence demanded to know why they weren't saying anything to him. The confusion got even more out of control, but Torrence threw his hands in the air and yelled for his 'youngins' to 'hop to it.' He got them in his car and screeched off.

Dante continued to ask "what was going on here?"

His mother was shaking her head briskly, just repeating: "That boy, that boy..." as Pauline escorted her toward the porch.

Dante continued to ask his father what had happened. A few of the children shouted out to Dante that they knew what happened, but their grandfather silenced them and told them to go on to the back. They stood looking for a minute, but Dante yelled at them:

"You heard what your grandfather said."

Dante continued to ask his father questions about what had just happened there with Torrence. Mr. Jackson answered Dante's question about Torrence by shaking his head and saying:

"Sometimes I wonder if Torrence ain't doing more than just selling the 'stuff.' Maybe he's using it."

Understanding their children's irrational behavior was difficult for the Jacksons. They were quiet, church going people, and had raised their children in a God-fearing, church going home. But some of the behaviors the children developed as adults made them seem like strangers.

Gabrielle had gone back to the patio and was standing in the opposite direction of the back door, so she could watch the children while they played in the yard. A few minutes passed before Dante had stepped out onto the patio behind her. He did not come quietly.

"What are you doing over here?" he demanded.

chapter twenty eight

Gabrielle couldn't even explain herself before he had started growling at her how no one had told her to invite herself over to his parents' house. He fussed on telling her that he didn't want DJ around all of this commotion, and that she had no business nosing into his life and being around his family. It had come up again. The divisive notion that his family was separate or didn't include her and DJ. The tears were welling up in Gabrielle's eyes when Pauline stepped out onto the patio with the cordless phone.

Erica was on the phone and wanted to speak to Gabrielle. She would be at the house soon with Erin, but wanted to say hi before they saw each other. Erica said that Erin would probably monopolize all the time once they arrived, so she would have to talk to Gabrielle now.

This made Gabrielle laugh some, and put her at ease. Pauline sat down with Dante as Gabrielle stood to the side and talked. She asked why Gabrielle had been crying, and Dante explained how Gabrielle always cries when there's a bunch of confusion. Pauline understood that, and felt bad that once again, Gabrielle had to witness a Jacksons' fireworks in December.

Gabrielle began walking toward the table with the phone stretched out to Pauline. When Pauline got ready to take the phone, she asked Gabrielle who it was. Gabrielle explained that it was just a beep. At the same time Dante was about to reach for the phone, Pauline waved her off and told her to answer it, then briefly continued the conversation with her brother while sitting at the patio table. When Gabrielle clicked over the phone line, she stood above Dante.

"It's for you," she said staring him in the eyes. "It's a woman, who says you missed her mother yesterday, but they're all home today, and they're waiting for you."

Dante looked at Gabrielle for a while, with a half smirk, half sneer. His emotions were wrangling, and part of him wanted to snatch the phone, and another part of him wanted to snatch Gabrielle.

"Tell her I'll call back," he snapped.

Gabrielle would have just hung up the phone, or at this

point, slapped Dante with it. But this was his mother's house and phone, and she wasn't inclined to disrespect it, so she laid the phone on the table and walked out to the back yard where DJ was still playing with his cousins.

Pauline gave Dante a sharp look and he picked up the phone to speak to Sa'Lissa. Pauline walked to the backyard to catch up to Gabrielle. Dante's phone conversation was brief, and after it, he walked out to the back yard and looked at Pauline as he said to Gabrielle: "Come on, we're leaving."

They walked to the front and met his parents on the porch. Dante's parents noticed how somber Gabrielle was. They had all been drained by the day's event, and felt that maybe it had just taken it's toll on her as well. They started to apologize to her for what happened, but Dante stopped them.

"This is family," he emphasized. His parents took it to mean that they were all family, and Gabrielle understood. Gabrielle understood it to mean, that it was his business and she was excluded.

Gabrielle carried DJ to the car and he was crying and wanting to go back and play with his cousins. She was silent along the ride home, and Dante should have been; but, he insisted on going over and over with her how she was not to just go showing up over his parents' house.

"You don't know anything about them Gabrielle, or the things that go on over on there," he yelled.

"I don't want you or DJ in the middle of any mess," he paused and could tell that Gabrielle did not seem to be listening.

"I mean it. You and DJ better not ever be over there unless I am there with you."

Dante ranted and raved about the incident that had just taken place.

"You don't know what you are getting yourself into. You saw what just happened with Torrence. I'm telling you now. It could have been worse. It could be somebody outside of the family he's gettin' raw with next time."

Torrence was a hustler. Anything was subject to go down at any time when he was around there. So, most of what Dante was saying was true, but Gabrielle didn't care what he was trying to explain at that point. While Dante ran his mouth about how she should respect the things that he asks her to do, there was only one thing dancing around in her mind. The phone call.

She stared ahead the whole time that Dante ran down his rules to her. He looked over to her sharply a few times and demanded to know if she was listening. The first time she didn't answer he repeated:

"Oh...oh...alright then,"

The next time, his question was:

"It's like that? You can't even answer me?"

And the third time he told her that she better say something to him.

That was when she sizzled out the question about who was the woman on the phone. Dante tried to escalate a temper so that Gabrielle would back down, but she didn't even turn her head to look at him. She questioned him again in an even more severe manner, but by then they were pulling up in their own driveway.

When the car stopped, Gabrielle's eyes shot fire over to Dante, and she demanded again to know who the woman was. He had set in his mind to tell her that it was none of her business, and that if she hadn't been at his mother's in the first place, she wouldn't have anything to say about it now. But this was the first time since the night in the parking lot in Wisconsin that Gabrielle had seemed so furious. He pulled DJ from the backseat and told Gabrielle that he wasn't even going to answer because she was being ridiculous. He gave a slight explanation that the girl was someone from the church and someone he had grown up with, but not seen for years.

"And now you're making it up by seeing her everyday?" Gabrielle said standing in the door of the car.

Dante was walking into the house with DJ in his arms. He looked around behind him to tell Gabrielle to come on into the house and that she was acting silly. Their eyes met, and he could feel the fury beaming from them, so he turned his eyes from hers, trying to dodge her.

She made it into the house a few steps after he had set DJ down on the den floor. He walked into the kitchen and stood on the other side of the refrigerator where she was pulling out sandwich things for DJ. He peeked his head around the door, and then grabbed her arm.

"You're not going to make anything for me, mommy?" Dante asked Gabrielle, rubbing up and down her arm, then trying to smooth her heated cheek.

She turned her body from him and continued making DJ's sandwich. She called DJ to the kitchen, and when he didn't come, she realized it was because Dante had put on the Barney tape, and DJ was engrossed. She walked to the den and sat on the couch with his plate in her hand.

"Come on boo. Mommy has your dinner all ready."

When DJ still didn't come, she took him by one arm and walked him back toward the couch. He stood next to the couch with his eyes still glued to the tv; but periodically she was able to get him to take a few bites.

Dante walked into the den. He had started an explanation now about how it wasn't what she was thinking. Then, he got ready to sit next to her, but she lifted DJ and sat him next to her so that Dante couldn't. Gabrielle continued feeding DJ and talking to him while Dante was trying to explain. Every time Dante paused to ask if she was listening to him, Gabrielle either continued talking to DJ, or said nothing at all.

"Oh, you trippin," Dante snarled and then stormed up the stairs.

Gabrielle never looked up, even though Dante continued to stare down at her during his walk up the stairs. He came back down shortly and had changed clothes; DJ was napping on the couch, and Gabrielle was at the kitchen sink. Dante walked past her back, and when she turned to ask where he was going, he had slammed the back door shut.

For the next few days and nights Dante was in and out of the house before Gabrielle knew it. She didn't have a chance to say anything to him. He came home every night, but it was always so late that she was asleep, and if she woke up and tried to talk to him, the smell of alcohol was so heavy that she knew nothing would make sense. But those were just the few nights when he made it upstairs to bed. Often, his resting spot was in the den.

She had cornered him there one afternoon while he was sleeping. DJ was in the kitchen riding his toy truck, and Gabrielle had slid down on the couch at her husband's feet. She rubbed underneath his blanket and up the sides of his calves. That woke him and he sat up and stared at her angrily for a while.

"Dante, we have to talk," she began.

His body language gave her the answer. He snatched his legs from her fingers, pulling his knees toward the ceiling then dropping his feet to the floor. Gabrielle placed her hand on the blanket, but he pulled it toward him, and looked beyond her when he answered.

"We ain't got nothing to talk about," he returned.

When she persisted that they did, he grabbed up the cover and stood up.

"Dante, please don't leave again," she asked. "We have to talk. This just isn't right."

"When I wanted to talk to you, you didn't have nothing to say, alright? So, now...ain't nothing for us to talk about."

He had begun walking toward the upstairs, but when he saw that she was following him, he turned around, tossed the comforter on the couch and headed for the back door. DJ started to follow Dante on his truck when he came through the kitchen, but Dante walked right on by, so DJ got down to follow after him. Gabrielle was standing in the kitchen asking Dante didn't he see his son, and wasn't he going to at least take time to spend with DJ. Dante turned around and said: "Hey little man," then gripped and rubbed DJ's head, and told him:

"Go on back with your mother, it's too cold for you to be in this door."

Gabrielle was now heart broken watching her husband walk out like this.

"Dante, we have to talk," she pleaded, approaching the door.

"Go on back in the house Gabrielle. It's too cold out here for you to have this door open."

He was still in his clothes from the night before, but she was in her bed clothes, and ready to walk out the door after him. She plead with him to come back, and began taking steps outside.

"Get back in the house Gabrielle. You can't be out here like this." He paused and watched her sink inwardly and her tears start rolling. "Go back in the house Gabrielle. We'll talk later. I promise, we'll talk." He paused again to make his last statement more emphatic. "I'll be home early tonight. I promise."

With that he was gone. And she now had to turn to DJ who was at her side calling for his daddy, and knowing that something was wrong with his mommy. All she could do was pick him up, close the door, and hope that tonight would bring the opportunity for a new understanding.

chapter twenty nine

Dante got home at ten o'clock that night. It was at least two or three hours earlier than when he had been coming in, still Gabrielle was asleep. She was lying on her left side with her right arm stretched out. She normally didn't sleep that way unless they had been in an argument, and she was turned her own way, away from him.

Tonight, her face looked so sweet and placid that it was hard to imagine that they had been battling for nearly two weeks. He sat down on the far right side of the bed and stared at her, taking her fingers into his hands and rotating them. She pulled back slightly, but he knew it was only because she was asleep, so he rubbed her cheek gently to wake her. She sat up somewhat startled, and he settled her down quickly. DJ was on the other side of the bed, Dante's side. He had started sleeping in his mother's room because he was having bad dreams.

Dante lifted DJ to carry him into his own room, but Gabrielle explained that DJ had been having rough nights and she wanted him to stay there, so Dante laid him back down and said that they've probably all been having some rough nights. Still he asked that she stay up tonight and talk. Mostly, she listened.

He started by saying how wrong he had been for not talking with her sooner, but that it was difficult for him, and it was all so new. She understood that Dante had a hard time talking sometimes, but she didn't understand what was so new. The longer she listened, the more it hurt.

Dante told Gabrielle how the whole concept of him, DJ and her being there all together was new. It was true that they had been a family before, and for years. But when they were in Minnesota, they were just living together and there weren't any ties. Even when they moved to Miami and were husband and wife, he had his own space.

During the week, his schedule required that he be gone to practice, and often on Saturdays he was headed out of town for away games. But, even when they had home games and Gabrielle and DJ visited, they could only stay until the team's curfew. That meant he had some part of his life that was still his, and he could come and go, at least to work. And, when he had away games, if Gabrielle didn't come out, he hung out with the guys to eat or club. When he got tired or got in for the night, he could always go back to his room and call his wife. She was his safe-haven when he had enough of the fellas or clubbing. But now, he didn't even have the freedom to hang out with the fellas, or even drop in the club from time to time.

During the season, he had a right or reason to leave. Now, if he walked out the door, he had questions to answer. He was tired of that.

He just hadn't thought about what it would be like to be with someone night and day. His son required his attention, and his wife required his time. It wasn't that he didn't want to give them what they needed, it was just that he wanted to figure out what he needed.

Maybe he just needed time to be single again, and able to do what he wanted, like he had always done—without answering to anyone about his choices.

With marriage, he had given up more than he thought he would.

During his talk, Gabrielle's emotions had risen and fallen, and now everything was tied up in a knot. She wasn't sure if Dante was too childish to realize that he didn't have a girlfriend anymore. She was his wife, and she was due his respect. There wasn't supposed to be anything for him in the clubs. Still, he claimed that he liked to hang out there with his friends from time to time, so she rarely hassled him. He felt that he needed to be able to do the things he wanted, but Gabrielle knew that he was doing what he wanted. Whenever she confronted him, he was either sorry, but did it again; or, he was unrepentant and walked out.

She couldn't see how he could have any complaints about their marriage. Nor could she understand how he felt that he "had given up more than" he thought he would. She was the one who had repeatedly changed cities, changed schools, changed her focus, given birth and had her entire life changed. So when he made his statement about what he hadn't expected to give up, she shrieked out:

"You've given up more?"

He conceded that: "Well, maybe we both have. Maybe we just didn't think things through."

Dante had paced the floor, and was resting on the window

sill across the room. Gabrielle had been sitting on the bed watching and listening to him, but she walked over to face him.

Her voice started in a whisper, but grew to a roar: "We didn't what? We didn't think? You didn't think? What was there to think about Dante, huhn?"

If Gabrielle could have been rational, she would have kept her voice down since DJ was asleep. But, fury was racing and the heat was on too high for her to cool down.

Dante slid down into the leather couch chair that they had near the window. She stood over him, and he talked to her in a whisper asking her not to get loud. He looked out at the blue-black sky and the glaring white moon. He was filled with a sense of calm, even though he could tell that Gabrielle was ready to explode all over him. Still, he knew what he had to tell her was the truth, and somehow that comforted him, even though he knew that it was going to set her off.

Dante couldn't answer most of her questions. He wasn't sure about anything. He wasn't always sure about himself or his decisions; sometimes he made mistakes. He did know that he loved Gabrielle. And, when he came to Wisconsin that night, he did know that he couldn't have made it in Miami without her and DJ. He would have been too lonely going home by himself every night. Sure, he could have taken different girls with him, but he would have ended up calling Gabrielle anyway; he needed the feel of something constant.

But when he went to see her in Wisconsin, Gabrielle had made it clear that she wasn't going to Miami with him nor was she going to take any more of his calls, or keep being there when he needed her unless she was his wife. She wasn't going to visit or live with him, until they were married, so he did what he had to in order to make sure she stayed in his life. He married her, but now he wasn't sure what he wanted.

He only knew that she hadn't done anything wrong. He knew that he still didn't want to lose her. Still, he didn't know how long he could go on feeling tied down and trapped. Maybe they needed time apart, or maybe they needed to get away together. They hadn't had time for a vacation or to just be with each other. Maybe that was it. Maybe it wasn't. He didn't know what they should do. He was young, made quick decisions, and now he was confused.

Gabrielle was furious. She wanted to know how long he had been feeling that way. He wasn't sure at first. Then he decided, it was when they got to Dallas. In Miami, he came and went, but now that it was the off-season, he had realized how boxed in he felt. It wasn't every day, but there were a lot of days when he just felt he needed to escape.

The last statements cut her. All of Gabrielle's pride was stripped. Her voice screeched into a scream and her elbows dropped to the window sill. Dante had hurt her many times before, and she had maintained a tough exterior, but her pride couldn't keep her standing. Her elbows wobbled on the window sill, and her legs dropped beneath her.

She collapsed to the floor and was slumped over crying. She drew in a deep gust of air, and Dante knew that she was going to let out a shrill scream. Immediately he grabbed her up from the floor, almost throwing her over his shoulder, and ran down the stairs. Dealing with Gabrielle would be enough; but, if she woke DJ, Dante wouldn't be able to stand it.

They got downstairs and he placed her on the couch where she sprawled out and cried for hours. She didn't even know where she was or what had happened by the time she stopped crying. She only knew that something was tragically wrong. Dante was at the end of the couch with her feet in his hands. He was rubbing them slowly, but staring out the den window into nothingness.

When Gabrielle sat up she began to ask him questions about their marriage. She couldn't believe how desperate she felt, and must have sounded. She needed to know was he leaving her.

The Yvette in her said *let him leave*, but she honestly wanted her husband; she wanted her marriage with him to work. She had left him before; pride had laced up her shoes and sent her walking. But it was deeper than pride now; they were family.

Dante didn't know what answer to give her. He didn't know what he had done or why, but he only knew that he was feeling a lot better now that he had been open about that part of his feelings toward them.

She wanted to know if it was the other girl. No, it wasn't that. She wanted to know if they needed to separate for just a little while.

He wasn't sure about that. She needed to know if he thought they could get it together; he couldn't answer that. She didn't know what to do.

She knew that Michelle would have told her to just take everything he had; she was his wife now and with a child in the picture, even a pre-nuptial couldn't keep her from taking most of what he had. Yvette would have gotten up from there, slapped him, snatched her son from upstairs, and went out on her own. But this was Gabrielle, and the only sincere thing she could do was ask why he had even married her.

He had told her before that he didn't want her and DJ out of his life. The bottom line was, he loved Gabrielle and he had realized back in Wisconsin that if he didn't get it together, she would pick up the pieces and move on. He had spent too many nights in Minnesota realizing that he might lose someone who sincerely loved him. He knew back then why he married her, and now he couldn't figure out how after he had come to his senses years ago, he was sitting here making the same mistake.

"I love you Gabrielle," he said, looking into her swollen face. He wanted more than anything to draw her into him and hold her until she felt right again.

The weight of his words didn't hit Gabrielle the way it should have. Normally, she understood Dante better than he understood himself. So she could put up with or walk away from his actions and not be confused. But now, she didn't understand anything he was saying or doing. She didn't even know him.

"I love you Gabrielle," he repeated and pulled her into him, but she wasn't giving. Even his explanation of how he didn't know what he was doing sometimes or where he was going, didn't help her. She was still in a daze. But he continued holding her, in silence almost until morning came.

When she woke up, she was still somewhat confused by everything that had happened. Dante was still seated on the couch nodded into a light sleep and Gabrielle was still lying across his lap. His arms were wrapped all around her. Their son was at the top of the stairs, crying and looking for them, and then it all made sense.

chapter thirty

Dante and Gabrielle decided to spend more time with his family and let DJ have more time with his cousins. The issues about Dante's comings and goings were few. He still went out some nights, but he always promised that it was just to hang out with his boys. And, he made it his business to come in at reasonable hours, and without the alcohol-drenched breath. Gabrielle went to church with his parents, DJ and the other grandchildren. That was a family standard. They were glad to have her as a part of them, and began to see her true attributes. She was a good mother, and she loved their son. She was honest about that, without ever having to tell them once.

Things could have continued perfectly for them well into Spring, but Dante's program got changed in mid-Spring, and that sent all of their lives in a different direction.

He had spent the last year as a free agent again, and Miami did not renew his contract. He had stepped up in seven games from backup to starter, while the first string offensive guard had been out injured. But the team still waived him. The draft had been full of offensive line men that year, and he had some idea that his contract might not be renewed. Still, he thought they'd wait until after camp or at least give him a chance to go through mini-camp. But these things happened.

His mother had been there for countless years to lift him up when he almost gave up from all the changes. Gabrielle had been beside him, and always would be, no matter what his career or life brought him. Still, no one knew how frustrating it was for him to go through these continual, humiliating cuts, commentaries, speculations and accusations from the teams, papers, and sports anchors who raved over his shortcomings in comparison to the once high expectations for him.

The articles and commentaries were far behind him now; people hardly noticed him anymore; but, there were the inward reminders of what he had once expected to be: front page news, chief endorsement guy, and now that ate away at him. He had been reporting to camp for years, and he was getting tired. There were star players who barely had to try out, and there were young rooks holding out for more money before they'd even think about reporting to training camp. But Dante was there, year after year, and he had to struggle just to make the team as a back up player.

The reality was, he was no longer prime time. He wasn't headline news. The only time his name was in the paper was when he appeared in the 'Deals' section. No full article, just his name among the many who had been cut, traded, or waived.

Gabrielle knew there was nothing much she could say to him during these times. She was just there for him, at home trying to keep things as normal as possible without mentioning that they could make it without football, or how important other things were. She just tried to be silently supportive, and keep DJ out of his way because Dante was in his own world: being family oriented for days, and then slipping away for hours into his own thoughts about what was ailing him the most, his career.

Gabrielle had never seen him weep, but some mornings when she made it down to the kitchen, she thought she might have just walked in at the end of his mourning.

She rubbed his back one morning, longer than she had on the others, and kissed him on the cheek and told him how much meaning he brought to their lives. DJ and Dante had been spending a lot more time together, and that gave Gabrielle time to study. She had taken Pauline's advice and enrolled at the city University. It was Gabrielle's choice, but once it was seconded by Dante's mother right in front of him, there was no other vote to be cast.

In a lot of ways, Dante was glad to be home with his son so that Gabrielle could go back to school. She had asked if his mother could baby sit while she was in classes, but Dante had really been sincere in what he said about not wanting DJ to be at his grandparents' home without him or Gabrielle there.

His parents were good Christians and had raised them right, but Torrence was into too many things in the streets and involved his parents just by virtue of him going over there.

Dante tried to move his parents to a newer and what he felt was a nicer area. But his parents couldn't think of any place better than where they had raised their children and helped their neighbors. Besides, as long as Torrence would come around, it didn't matter where they moved; his lifestyle could potentially follow him and cause them problems anywhere.

That was bad enough. But then Torrence was prone to fight verbally or physically with their father, and Mr. Jackson vowed to never succumb to a 'butt woopin' from one of his children. That meant anything could happen. And, despite the fact that Dante was prone to behave excessively, there were certain things he didn't want DJ involved in.

So, he would be home and babysit DJ while Gabrielle went to school. Dante had been enjoying the time he had with DJ; this made it difficult, but not impossible for him to leave later that Spring when he got a call from Washington. He was heading to a new team just to condition for a few months. There was no need for DJ and Gabrielle to be uprooted yet. He wanted to make it through conditioning and then camp. Perhaps when Fall came, they would head out there, or if Gabrielle wanted to stay at the same school and keep DJ in their homestead she could.

The Spring had brought new life for both the Jacksons. Gabrielle was taking classes at the University. She and Dante had agreed that once he left, DJ would stay at the University's day care center while she went to classes.

The first few days of returning to school with a child were hectic. But once DJ adjusted, the first few weeks were invigorating. She was back in a setting that required her to explore her feelings and emotions then translate them into poetry or stories. She hadn't even realized how stifled her imagination had been during the last year or so. But now she could dream, imagine, and create things, and she felt good about that. She felt good about herself.

She established writing hours for herself when she was at home. Things were busy at the house. Dante knew what time she got out of classes, so he called periodically during the day to see how things were going. They never really got a chance to talk for too long, because she always had to keep a close eye on DJ. He was feisty and always getting into things, much like his father. Dante was usually frustrated with the interruptions in his calls, so he'd talk for a moment then let Gabrielle chase behind DJ or take him outside or to the park. That was DJ's favorite place. Most of his cousins were usually there, and it was hard dragging him away from them. But once she finally got him home or settled into bed, she made time for her husband's evening calls, and then her writing; she usually didn't get to that until eleven.

One night, she was curled up in bed writing with DJ sleeping on the other side of the bed. The phone rang at two in the morning and she reached over DJ to pick it up. It was Dante. He said he couldn't sleep, and that he'd been tossing and turning all night thinking about her and how much he missed her. She thought that was sweet, but assured him that everything was fine there. She told him what she and DJ had done during the day, and that she was just sitting up writing.

Dante didn't have much to say, but he kept hanging on the phone. She could tell he just wanted to be there with her. Dante wasn't going to admit this but he had gone out for a few drinks earlier, even though he told her he was going to bed. While he was out, he had met a few girls, and took one back to the room with him. After he had let this girl do all the things he didn't want Gabrielle to do, he wanted the girl to leave; but, she insisted on sleeping there for the night since she had no ride and it was too late for a bus or cab, especially in her condition. So he was stuck with her for the entire night.

He couldn't stand it. He looked at her, lying across his bed with one arm north and the other arm west; her hair propped up in a stiff french roll on one of his pillows. She was a pretty girl when the night began, and he was attracted to her. She was in graduate school in Georgetown, so she was smart, but she wasn't what he wanted for the long term, not even for the whole night. So, as she lay there sleeping, he felt disgusted, not only with the girl, but also with himself. So, he called his wife to talk about more pleasant things.

This wasn't the first time he had done this. He had taken girls into VIP rooms, limousines, or just let them sit under a table to satisfy him. When he did those things in the past, it made his conversation more hostile to Gabrielle because when he came home, she was usually starting an argument about where he had been.

When he'd try to walk by her and say that he had just been 'kickin it with the boys' she followed behind him still fussing. That made him sometimes pick up the phone and tell her to call a few of his team mates; they had all been together in the limo, or just drove themselves somewhere to meet. He came home didn't he? So, obviously there was nothing out there for him; he was just socializing with his boys. This was his attitude in the past. But now, he felt guilty. So whenever he had a rendezvous, he either called to say how much he loved and missed her, or he sent extra special gifts, sometimes in blue boxes; that made him feel better, and made her think that he just cared that much.

Tonight was the first time Gabrielle was inclined to believe something was wrong. Just as she was getting ready to say goodnight, she heard a woman's voice in the background. Gabrielle questioned Dante about it, but he said that it was the tv; then, he turned his tv on, and continued the explanation. But, Gabrielle was certain that she had not only heard a woman's voice, but also that the woman had mentioned Dante's name, and had asked was it morning yet or something.

Dante had never had this happen before. Usually, if a girl stayed the night, he slept on the couch or told her to be quiet while he made a phone call. If the girl demanded to know why she had to be quiet, he would simply stop dialing, hang up the phone, and call Gabrielle later, or tell the girl that she had to go. This time it was different, because this girl woke up talking, and for the first time, Gabrielle had a real reason to be suspicious.

Now that the girl was sitting up in bed getting ready to ask more questions, he shook his head 'no' at her, and then made the 'Shhh' sign with his finger to his lips. She looked like she was going to give him trouble and start asking why she had to be quiet.

He couldn't just get off the phone with Gabrielle, since she was already suspicious. He decided to eye the girl down, and then pointed his finger for her to lie back down.

She bowed her head, and looked at him from the side of her eye. Did he think she was crazy? She pushed the covers back, started picking up her clothes, and saying how she didn't need this. Dante wasn't saying anything. He turned up the tv and wanted to convince Gabrielle that it was a movie scene. But Gabrielle heard everything the girl said, then she heard the door slam. Dante was at a loss for words to explain, but it wasn't necessary; Gabrielle had hung up the phone.

Her writing and class work could have suffered during the next few days. Her spirits were low, and she couldn't even take any of Dante's calls. DJ was keeping her busy during the day, but at night, she was committed to writing. She turned all the ringers off on the upstairs phones, shut herself away and explored words and emotions, and how mystical it was to write things away.

Everyday there were countless messages from Dante that she

had erased. Frequently, he sent boxes that she refused to sign for. One day, he sent his sister over to check on her. He didn't like to involve family in his business, but he was starting to wonder if something might have happened to Gabrielle. He told his sister that the phone lines were out at his house and he couldn't reach Gabrielle, maybe something had happened to her, or maybe she had gone to visit her mom. But, his sister told him that she had seen Gabrielle at the park several times, and at his mother's on occasion.

For a few days the constant calls had stopped. For the past three days, Dante hadn't called at all. While Gabrielle sat in class, she was distracted by thoughts of whether or not she should call to see if something was wrong with Dante. When she picked DJ up from day care and they headed home, he noticed before she did; his daddy was home. Gabrielle looked up the driveway and saw Dante unloading his things.

As soon as he was unbuckled, DJ made his way from the car to his daddy's arms. Gabrielle walked over to the truck.

"What are you doing home?" she asked softly.

"The pre-conditioning is over. I don't have to go back until camp," he paused and rubbed one hand up and down Gabrielle's arm. "I just wanted to come back and be with my family."

She couldn't even look in his face. She reached her arms out for DJ, but he wouldn't come. She patted his legs and said "Oh, alright then. You're being a daddy's boy now, huhn?"

She smiled at her son, didn't look at her husband, and walked on into the house.

Conversations weren't easy in the house. Gabrielle cooked and cleaned, and slept in the same bed with Dante, but things weren't the same. For one thing, DJ was sleeping in the bed with them, and Dante had a problem with that. His wife was barely speaking to him, wouldn't let him touch her, and that was frustrating him. On top of that, he was burning to ask her why she had been at his mother's, but he knew he was in no position to demand any answers from her.

Finally, the ice broke. Dante had come to her school one day with a few of his nieces and nephews. He wanted to pick DJ up and take all the kids to the circus. When he walked through the halls looking for Gabrielle, he found her in the student lounge talking and laughing at the vending machine with Austin, one of her classmates.

Snapshots

Dante stood behind Austin, who was barely 5 ft. 7. He placed his hand on top of the vending machine and talked across Austin to Gabrielle who was on the other side of him.

"Gabrielle...have a word with you?" Dante demanded.

"You see I'm talking, Dante," she replied and eyed him for a moment.

His face tightened and he shook his head. "No, Gabrielle, now!" he demanded. "I want a word with you." He reached across Austin and took Gabrielle's hand and pulled her toward the sofas.

"What is wrong with you?" he demanded. "You gonna disrespect your husband like that. In front of all these people?"

"Disrespect?" she began.

He vigorously ran both of his hands across the top of his head. "Don't start with that Gabrielle."

"No, what's to start? You did it. You did it. And there's no denying that. You're the king of disrespect, so don't you come here talking to me about it."

"So... What? That's your little boyfriend now or what?"

Gabrielle had almost forgotten herself. She was at school. There were people around, and she didn't want to fight publicly anywhere, much less in a place where she wanted academic respect.

"Not now Dante," she began.

"Oh, what? So that is your nigga, huhn?" Dante was rising to his feet, and she knew his next move would be to go confront Austin. She got up to speak to Dante, who was already turning around looking for Austin, and saying: "Where is he? No. Where is he?"

"He is not my boyfriend," she said and grabbed Dante's hand. Dante was barely listening.

"Look at me Dante. He is not my boyfriend. And you can't do this up here. I am at school."

He turned to look at her. "I don't care where you are Gabrielle; you are my wife. And any body whose messing with my wife is taking a beat down."

"What makes you so sure that I am that kind of person, Dante? That's not me. Even if it is you."

He looked at her, and though her words were true, they hurt. "Gabrielle, that's not me," he began.

"Well, you're the one who did it, and has been doing it. I've come to that conclusion."

"Are you leaving me?" he asked.

"It's not the time to talk about that."

"Are you?" he asked again.

"No. I'm not." She paused because he was waiting for more. "I have thought about it Dante. But we'll have to work through it. And that has to be later. I'm in class right now, and I have to get back."

"I understand," he said. "But we have to talk G. And it has to be tonight. No more of this silent treatment man. I can't take this."

"Okay. Fine," she said and began walking away.

"Hey G." he called after her. When she stopped and looked back, he continued. "Hey G. I love you baby. I do."

She smiled at him, nodded her head and kept going. She knew he did, but there was a lot they had to work on.

She made it back to class, and shortly afterwards Dante showed up at the door. Austin seemed to notice him first, but nervously tuned in to the professor. Gabrielle saw Dante opening the door and walked to the back of the room to ask him "What is it?"

He had forgotten to tell her that he was coming to get DJ. She directed him toward the daycare, and he left.

Later that night when they talked, all of her issues with distrust came up. She told Dante how if he lied about one thing, he would lie about another. He promised her that he hadn't been lying, even though he only confessed to cheating a few times.

She had asked him about all the nights in the club; he denied cheating. When she probed further, he admitted to letting a few girls 'go down' on him. But that was cheating, Gabrielle notified him. She demanded to know about Sa'Lissa, the squeaky voiced girl who seemed to call his mother's house all the time for him. The one he seemed to visit a lot.

He told Gabrielle that they used to date in high school, but their families are just tight like that, and he only stopped by to see her mother. Now that he had been home for a while, that was a visit he rarely made. He felt he had cleared himself enough to bring up the visits that Gabrielle had been making to his mother's house, while they "were on the subject of visiting."

He asked casually, and Gabrielle answered as if she saw nothing wrong with it. She had gone by a few times when his mom needed a ride to church. A couple times after church, his mother invited them for dinner; she couldn't see telling his mother that they wouldn't come in. Dante pointed out to Gabrielle that he had specifically asked her not to go over there. She reminded him that his mother needed a ride, and that she wasn't going to refuse his mother's dinner offer when they were already right there.

Dante had a solution for that. He made up in his own mind to go drive his mother and father's car to a dealership, trade it in, and buy them a new one. That killed two birds with one stone. He always gave big gifts to his family; furthermore, that would alleviate the need for a ride. He didn't mention this to Gabrielle, because he didn't feel he had to. But he felt better already, knowing that he could reissue his demand that she visit his family only when he's with her.

The conversation could now end on a good note. He felt things were settled, but Gabrielle wasn't finished with her questions. She wanted to know how many times he had been unprotected when he was cheating. He was shocked at her. They began arguing about that, and the end of the conversation was that she wanted him to have an Aids test. He couldn't refuse. She wouldn't let him inside of her until he did.

He was almost ashamed that she mandated the test for him. And he was even afraid because he knew that he had been out there for quite a while: before he married Gabrielle, and even afterwards.

His test came back negative and that made things better. Still, Gabrielle made it very clear that from then on, if he ever cheated again she couldn't say that things would go so easily.

Those mistakes were behind him now and he was so glad to be in the clear with his wife, and with himself. His was free of diseases, worries, and restrictions from his wife. They could make love again. Once he was able to feel her again, he melted and poured all of himself into her.

The friction and frustration that they had for weeks was now calmed, and they could love once again, in bed and out. He knew things were coming to an end though. In a few weeks, he would be going back to Washington for camp. He wanted to spend as much time with his wife as he could.

She would not be going to Washington with him. Even though he had asked her to come, she said it didn't make sense. There would be six weeks of intense work outs and scrimmages, and there was no guarantee that he would be staying with that team.

Gabrielle and DJ would visit every week, or maybe every two weeks; it made more sense to do things that way. She had decided to enroll for the summer session at the University and get another term out of the way.

None of her friends knew about Dante's cheating, but Cassandra and Angelique would have told her to stick to him like glue from then on and make sure he never had another opportunity to cheat.

Yvette and Michelle would have told her to leave him, and Michelle would have been pushing for a huge settlement. But Gabrielle had to trust her own feelings, even if she wasn't sure that she could completely trust Dante ever again. The best thing for her to do right now was finish school. She didn't need any distractions.

But a few weeks after Dante left, she realized that she would have a new diversion in less than nine months. She was pregnant again. She didn't find out until she and DJ had gone out for the first team scrimmage.

They had planned to spend the morning going for breakfast and then meeting him at the game, but Gabrielle was too sick. She thought of everything that could be wrong, but it was Dante who realized that she had to be pregnant. He could just feel it he said. And there was no mistaking, he was very unhappy about it.

Things weren't going well for him. It was his sixth season in the League, and all the announcers' comments about his promise had changed to speculations on whether he could even make it as a third string player. He was 'on the bubble' was the word, and he couldn't think of anything else but his career and how displaced he felt now that it was ending.

He knew that he could get picked up off the waiver wires, but that wasn't what he had ever seen for his future. Besides, the humiliation of being asked for your play book and being sent back home were overwhelming, no matter how many times you had been through it before. The rejection still took something away from you.

And it happened. He was cut from the team before training camp was even over, and he was headed back to Dallas, less than a week after Gabrielle and DJ had been out to see him. Gabrielle and DJ were glad to have him home, though Gabrielle understood how anguished he was to be there under the circumstances. She got behind Dante and told him that there were more important things in life than the job. His career wasn't over; another team would certainly call. But even when the time came that no teams were interested, he would always have his wife and children there. That raised a new issue.

DJ was with him almost all day, everyday, while Gabrielle was off at class. And, at night DJ was still sleeping in their bed. That had to stop. He was too old for that, and Gabrielle was setting up a bad mistake letting him think that he could come between them anytime he felt like walking in their room and crawling into bed.

Dante didn't want to hear about how he was gone most of the time, and DJ was used to it being mommy only. Dante was back now, and DJ needed to give him and them some space. On top of everything, he couldn't deal with the fact that Gabrielle was pregnant again. He couldn't understand how she could make such a foolish mistake at this time.

They could have been in continual arguments about the pregnancy. Every day that Gabrielle was sick, having complications, or needing assistance, he refused to help her with anything. If DJ wanted something while she was there, he demanded that she do it. He had DJ all the other times, and since she was so set on being a mother, she would have to at least "be woman enough to be a mother while" she "was sick or well;" he wasn't going to do everything. He made it clear that he didn't want to do anything for this new baby. He was constantly raising abortion as an option. She didn't want to hear about that.

Dante began to deal with his frustrations the only way he seemed to know how; he started hanging out late and being difficult to get along with. Gabrielle was approaching the end of her first trimester, and with school, raising DJ, and being stressed by Dante, the baby was distressed.

After a few full weeks of Dante's wild and selfish behavior, and his demands for an abortion, Gabrielle left the house early one morning. She had been in the bathroom clutching the toilet and knocking things over while she was in there. When she looked up she saw Dante standing in the door way. He lifted her to her feet.

"What are you going to do man? You can't keep getting like this every day. And, I'm not going to always be around. My agent just called and I'm probably leaving for Cleveland in a couple of days. How are you going to make it like this Gabrielle? Out here by yourself, with DJ and trying to go to school."

She couldn't answer. Not only didn't she know an answer, she was simply too sick to speak. She held on to the threshold of the door for support and heard him ask the same question about what she was going to do. She found the strength to go downstairs and out to the car. When she backed out of the driveway, she didn't know where she was headed, but when she got back home, Dante was waiting with a question.

He was in the den with his legs propped up on the coffee table, and he was talking on the phone to Sa'Lissa. When Gabrielle came in she saw the den was in a mess. DJ had strewn things all over, and had juice and food spills all over him. She was too weak to even walk, so she decided not to concentrate on the mess in there. She approached the stairway, and instead of Dante asking where she had been all day, because it was late evening now, he removed the receiver from his mouth to ask:

"Ey, did you do that for me?"

No one would have known what he was talking about. But Gabrielle remembered his last question that morning had been would she just go on and get an abortion.

She was holding on to the rail and trying to make it up the stairs slowly. She saw DJ at the bottom of the steps with his arms stretched out for her to pick him up. All she could say was: "Mommy can't."

She gripped the rail tighter and went to the first bedroom at the top of the stairs. She collapsed onto the bed and wept violently.

Dante walked up the stairs after telling Sa'Lissa that he would talk to her later, followed by:"Yeah, I'ma see you boo."

He was ready to walk down to their bedroom, but realized immediately, that the crying was coming from the first guest bedroom. He walked in and lay down next to Gabrielle and rubbed her back. "Boo...it's going to be okay," he said, and sat up, lifting her upper body onto his lap. "It's going to be okay," he repeated.

He stroked Gabrielle's hair and rubbed her face. She couldn't even look at him. She would have pulled away from him, but her heart was so weak that she just let him hold her. The baby was gone. He knew that; what he didn't know was that she had miscarried, and against her doctor's orders, she drove herself home because she had one son she wanted to get home and care for.

Snapshots

Dante's plans to leave for the night hadn't changed. He didn't know what his wife had been through that day, and she wasn't up to talking. He made dinner for her and put Dante to bed, then showered and got ready to head out, but something killed his spirits. The phone rang, and the deal with Cleveland was off. They had negotiated a better deal with a veteran player who had less years, so it would cost them a little less to get the same results.

He was upset for the night, but during the next few weeks, he tried not to sulk.

Gabrielle had been quiet and distant. She wasn't even angry, and she was beyond hurt. She just said whatever things she needed to say to Dante. She was kind and gentle, but she wasn't the same. He wanted to be close to Gabrielle and know who she was becoming. She was his wife still. She was understanding and supportive about his last let down. She was affectionate, and even against her better judgement, she let him make love to her before the six weeks were up. He was gentle and compassionate then, and even in the days that followed, but something was missing from them. The hollow space was Davelle, the son she had named, but lost due to her complications with Dante. She tried not to blame him. She was deferential with him, still she could not feel close, and he wanted that.

During the months that passed, Dante did more around the house. He found little to complain about. Gabrielle resumed school full-time in the Fall, and had a double load of work. She had requested 'incompletes' as grades for the summer courses, so she was now doing the equivalent of two terms in one. It was worth it though, because by the end of Winter term, she would have senior credits. Dante did most of their cooking, took them out to eat, or brought home meals from his mother's. Once again he had become very involved in her studies.

He had talked with Gabrielle about how they would have to cut back on some things, because he was not working, and wanted to be able to spread out his finances for the years to come. One thing he didn't want to cut out of the budget was her schooling.

He was committed to making sure she finished. He was already planning their trip for after Winter term. He wanted to celebrate the fact that she would only have one more year before graduation. She suggested they go to the South of Spain, where they could not only enjoy Andalusia and Malaga, but they could also take the ferry to Morocco. She had heard of trips like that ever since she was in high school and some of her classmates took them. Dante's thoughts were on a cruise to Jamaica or the Bahamas. Most of the people he knew were big shots once they made these trips.

It was the thought that counted. The fact that he was trying to budget, but still wanted to take her on a cruise was extremely considerate. He had slowed down his spending, and Gabrielle knew he had to be concerned about finances, because he had never really put himself on a budget. Things would probably get tight. She was glad that she would be finishing school soon.

Even though her career might start off slowly, she knew that in time she would be able to help in the household if he would let her. She would stand by Dante no matter what they had to face, and he was really doing his best to care for her despite his past mistakes. He loved her and he did want to make her happy. They made it through Fall and part of Winter. Gabrielle had finished her classes with top marks. But when it came time for the celebration cruise, their plans got delayed.

chapter thirty one

Danielle, Gabrielle's mother had finally saved up enough vacation time and money to make it down for a visit. In the past, Dante had insisted on paying for her mother's visit, but Danielle wouldn't accept any money from him. When he picked Danielle up from the airport, DJ and Gabrielle were still at home straightening up. It was the holiday season. His mother had made plenty of food, and they would be over there for dinner at least a few days, but Gabrielle insisted on cooking dinner for her mother's first night in town. Danielle would be staying for two weeks, and Gabrielle wanted to make sure every day was perfect.

When Dante and Danielle arrived at the house, Gabrielle was coming down the stairs. DJ could scarcely remember this grandmother, though he talked to her on the phone at least once a week, and saw her pictures in one of the guest bedrooms. Gabrielle lead Danielle upstairs to her room, and DJ followed.

After Danielle got settled she returned to the downstairs den where DJ was relaxing with Gabrielle. She tried to get DJ involved with his grandmother, but he was watching his favorite tv show. The only thing that caught his attention about Danielle was the purple stuffed animal she had for him. At first he tore off with the toy, but Gabrielle made him go back and say thank you. When he did, his grandmother also had a Barney story book that she showed him and wanted to read to him. She lifted him onto the couch next to her. He was convinced that he could read the book himself, so he took the book, and followed the pictures. Page by page, he told her the story, with 'songs' and 'hoorays' and plenty of sound effects and mumbled words.

Dante had run out for an errand to his mother's. He had a few things to pick up from there. While he was out, he also stopped down the street at Sa'Lissa's mother's house to drop a few things off. He had bought gifts for her mother, Sa'Lissa and her son. He only stayed long enough to drop the gifts off, and he put the ones they gave him in the trunk of his car, then headed home with pies and a cake that his mother had made for him.

He made it back home in just enough time for dinner, and after they finished he sat with Gabrielle and Danielle in the den. DJ was between the kitchen and den with his toys. Long after Dante had put DJ to bed and had fallen asleep himself, Danielle and Gabrielle sat downstairs talking.

The next few days were busy. Whenever Gabrielle didn't have something planned for her mother, Dante's family was getting together, so they visited there a few days. Gabrielle's life seemed to really be in order, and her mother was happy to know that there was a lot of family and love surrounding her daughter. In the middle of the second week, Danielle realized two things: it was nearly time for her to head back home already, and that her daughter was pregnant.

One night in the kitchen, Danielle was admiring the pendant necklace that Dante had given Gabrielle. After she complimented the necklace, she informed Gabrielle that she was pregnant. Gabrielle's body hadn't felt or looked pregnant, so she wasn't sure what her mother was talking about. Danielle could tell by the double pulse at the bottom of Gabrielle's neck. Gabrielle dismissed it as a wive's tale, but Dante, who was breezing through the kitchen toward the den was alarmed. Gabrielle perceived this, and tried even harder to dismiss her mother's claims. Danielle didn't push it, but she did want to know why Gabrielle wouldn't be excited. She was married now, with a large home, plenty of space, and a wonderful husband.

Gabrielle explained it away by saying that she would think more about it when she found out for sure, and that for now, she just wanted to concentrate on her last few terms of school. Danielle respected that, but told Gabrielle that within the sanction of marriage, having children would be a wonderful experience, especially with the supportive people she had around her.

Danielle had gathered a lot of pictures of DJ, Gabrielle, her husband, their home, the cousins, in-laws, family and friends. She would be taking them back to share with Michelle, Yvette, and others in the town. The snapshots were nice, but they didn't show the whole picture.

Dante was fuming when he heard the whole pregnancy talk. He couldn't say anything though until Danielle had left. He tried hard to cover up how angry he was about the slightest possibility that Gabrielle was pregnant again, but his actions started to show. Danielle wasn't aware that when her door shut at one end of the hall, and the Jacksons' shut at the other, Gabrielle was on her side of the bed, and Dante took the covers and wrapped up like a mummy on his side. In the morning, everything seemed fine. He would come downstairs after Danielle and Gabrielle had started having breakfast, kiss Gabrielle on the cheek, and be on his way to his mother's, the store, the gym, or some place with DJ. He always asked Danielle if she needed anything while he was out, and even though she said no, when he returned later that evening, he always brought something for her.

On the last morning of Danielle's stay, Dante had made it downstairs before anyone. He made breakfast and called them down. They ate together, then left together for the airport, but after they said farewell to Danielle, Dante and Gabrielle began going their separate ways.

When they got back in the car, his first words were:

"Gabrielle, tell me you're not pregnant."

"I'm not Dante," she replied.

"No, tell me you're not, and mean it. Don't just guess about it."

"Well, I'm telling you from what I know. I don't think I am," she responded. "How can I tell you something I don't know?"

"Then why are you guessing about it? Why didn't you go see?"

"First of all, I didn't have time to go see, and you asked me a question, so I answered."

She was firm and he was firm. There was no compromising in either of their statements. Gabrielle hadn't intended on being pregnant at this stage. She was coming too close to completing her degree, and she knew from the last pregnancy that she would have to be in a stress free situation to have a healthy delivery.

"Well, we'll settle this," Dante announced.

He got off at the next exit.

"We'll just get the test and see," he said as he pulled up directly in front of the drug store's door and jumped out the car.

He came back with the box in the bag, and said that they would see once they got home.

They walked in the door, and DJ was asking was his mommy pregnant. She cut her eyes at Dante for being so irresponsible as to have brought up that conversation in front of DJ. Dante almost shrugged it off.

"Here Gabrielle, take this box with you," he said reaching his arm out toward her, even though she was facing the other way and walking away from him. He caught up to her and put it in her hands.

"Take it Gabrielle. I want to know."

She had reached the stairs and was heading up, but he grabbed her arm from the other side of the railing and made their eyes meet. "You are, aren't you? You are pregnant."

"Yeah," she answered without even knowing whether she was or not.

"I am," she said, because she was tired of him and didn't want him rushing up the stairs for an answer. She wasn't going to take the test immediately, nor was she going to have him upstairs harassing her to hurry up and get it over with. If she was pregnant for sure, they would just have to deal with it, so answering 'yes' right now, would only give him time to think. If it turned out she wasn't, then fine; life would go on as usual.

But it couldn't. Dante didn't take a minute to think about anything. She was near the top of the stairs now, and he was already behind her.

"You're getting an abortion," he said when he got to the landing.

She stopped for a moment and looked around at him.

"You're getting an abortion," he repeated. "I don't know how you're going to bring a child into this world and ain't got means the first to take care of it. That's something you come to me first about. You ask me about that. I'm the one that's got to take on the responsibility for it."

"Oh, you are?" she asked.

"Yeah. I am. And you see how things are going right now. I haven't worked at all this season, period. Did any more teams call for me after my last deal went up? Did they? You think we're going to live on a partial pension and my savings forever, huhn? With you popping out babies left and right?"

"Oh, I'm popping out babies left and right? I'm planning this? I'm in school Dante. Just like I was when I met you. I never had any plans to do anything but graduate. I didn't expect to start having children."

"Well neither did I."

"Well, it's been just a little harder on me than it has been on you."

"Why? Why? How's it hard on you? You're the one who's making the come up from it!"

"The come up? What are you talking about?"

"You know just what I'm talking about. You keep having all these kids and decide to leave me one day. You can take everything I got."

"Dante, what are you talking about? I'm not planning to go anywhere."

"Yeah Gabrielle, that's what you say now. But I guess a little insurance never hurts."

"Insurance?"

"Yeah. You already got one kid. The more you have, the more you take."

"That's how you look at it?"

"No, that's how you look at it. I ain't stupid Gabrielle, and neither are you. And, I know your little friends have filled your head with all kind of dibs about how you can slice into my dough."

"So, our marriage, child and children, mean that to you...how much I'm going to take?"

"No, but it means that to you. You're the one plotting and scheming to keep having 'em. And, you're walking around knowing you're pregnant and wouldn't even tell me. That really shows you're scheming something."

"Dante, you're just so stupid and childish. It shows that I just went on and answered yes. I don't feel like being bothered with you coming to me door after door, minute after minute demanding that I take the test."

"If I do it minute by minute, or hour by hour, door by door or whatever, it's my house, and I have the say so of what goes on in it, when and where."

"Your house?"

"My house."

"When we got married, all that 'my' stuff was supposed to change. It's we, ours, us."

"See, see. That's just how you thought. This is yours. Baby, this house is in my name. I knew to be on the look out from the beginning. Chics are always out looking for a come up. I knew you weren't any different, way back when."

"First of all, I'm not a chic; I am your wife. And even before then, when you met me, I was in school. I didn't need you. I was well on my way to making my own living."

"Oh yeah, but it wasn't gonna be no where near the living you knew you could have with me. I don't even know how I let you trick me."

"Trick?"

"Trick, trap. Call it what you want, but I don't know how I let you catch me up."

"And do you know how much you have cost me? Do you realize how much I have sacrificed and lost with you?"

"Well, don't lose no more Gabrielle. Here, I tell you what. You take this test, right now. And if you're pregnant, you get rid of it, or you get rid of me."

"That's the way it goes?"

"That's how it is. You take this test and if you don't want to get rid of it, you can get out."

She was heated enough to tell him that she wasn't going anywhere. But, hurt was taking over her conversation.

"Dante, I can't believe you. After all that I've been through with you, after all I've given to you, this is how you feel about me? Like I'm out to get you. This is how you respond to something, a baby that's a part of you and me, that will be a part of our lives forever. You haven't even thought about how I feel about it, or what I want or wanted. You haven't thought about anything, or anybody but yourself. What about..."

"All the talking in the world is not going to change anything. I told you, I don't want no more kids. Not now, and probably not in the future. You can't calculate and think I'm gonna be able to support you and a bunch of kids. I already got a family to take care of."

"What are you talking about? You have..."

"My momma and my sisters. That's what I'm talking about. You listening to your mother and friends about how successful I am, and how big and nice this house is. For all I know, this might end up sold somewhere and I'll be back at my momma's. I got to make sure she's taken care of because you might be somewhere else, with your momma or one of your little smart alack college boys."

"You sound crazy Dante. You really do. Me and DJ are your

family. And whatever comes we're going to be here."

This was one of the longest arguments they had ever had, and Dante was getting tired of talking. Gabrielle was either going to do what he told her, or she was getting out. Gabrielle knew that she wasn't ready for another child anyway, but she was not going to let Dante make any demands on her body.

She wasn't done talking to him either, because she wanted to know how he had come to the notion that she was out to get him. After all the love she had given and shown, and after all the times he had shown how much he loved her, she couldn't believe that somewhere, these thoughts had been lurking within him.

She wanted to talk about that, but when he began hollering for her to take the test right now, and DJ was climbing up the stairs, she just walked down the hallway toward their bedroom. He followed her.

"Are you going to take it?" he demanded.

She shook her head no. He grabbed her tightly by her arm and stared at her through squinted eyes, and said through his teeth: "Then, I want you out of here."

He pushed her arm away, and she almost fell to the bed. He flung open the doors to their walk in closet and continued mumbling about how he was doing the best he could to provide for them; he didn't have any way to make a living right now, and all she was doing was adding more problems and troubles. He began throwing her clothes toward the bed. Some made it; some dropped to the floor. He went to their dresser and started flinging her jewelry toward the bed.

"Get your suitcase Gabrielle," he roared.

She could only stare at him as her body shivered from head to foot. She was sobbing from the pit of her stomach.

He marched past her to pull out her suitcase, and began tossing her things in it. He crossed through their bathroom into DJ's room and started pushing some of DJ's things to the hall, then down the stairs. Gabrielle got up to go get DJ who was sitting in the hallway at the opposite end from Dante.

She took DJ to the room with her, and began putting things into the suitcase as quickly as she could. Still, she was moving in slow motion. None of what was going on seemed real. She could hear a few things banging down the stairs and Dante in the hall, but it didn't seem like this was really happening.

She got the things in the suitcase and had made it to the bottom of the stairs while Dante was still rummaging around in DJ's room. When he headed back to the stairs, ready to hurl some more things down, Dante's eyes met with his son's; Gabrielle was facing the door with DJ on her hip facing Dante.

When he saw little Dante staring at him with teary and questioning eyes, Dante was filled with guilt. He dropped the things he had intended to throw, and saw for the first time what a mess he had made.

He called Gabrielle's name, but she wouldn't look back. He called her again, but she was turning the knob and walking out the door. She had already called a cab, and the driver was pulling her things to the car.

Dante was frozen watching his life fall apart in front of him. When he gathered himself enough to walk down the stairs and out the front door, Gabrielle and DJ had already made it down the front sidewalk and into the cab on the street. He was calling her name, and she could hear him, though the window was up. Still, she just stared ahead.

The radio played "They say I'm Hopeless" and it seemed like fate that the verse: 'good bye yesterday, you just won't do me right. I've cried just a little too long, and now it's time for me to be strong' was playing. The cab driver asked her 'where to' and they headed toward the bank.

chapter thirty two

She withdrew all the money from her savings. It wasn't much. It was the money that Dante had been giving her as a weekly stipend. She had saved almost every penny of it, still, it wouldn't get her by for long. She had to find an apartment and furniture, at least for DJ's room. She would have to buy utensils, pots, pans and whatever else she would need for her first apartment. Then there was tuition for school, costs for transportation, not to mention the new baby.

She hadn't taken the test. She had answered 'yes' to Dante just to get him off her back, but she now knew that she was pregnant. The stress was effecting her body, but much like the last time she was pregnant, the baby was even more stressed.

Gabrielle found an inexpensive one bedroom apartment. The bedroom was in the back, and she gave that to DJ, though he often made his way to the plaided cloth couch in the front where she slept. Between setting up the apartment, taking care of DJ, and enrolling in school, Gabrielle had to find a part time job.

She had been surprised in the college's business office when they told her that her tuition for the term had been paid. She couldn't understand how, until they pulled out the receipt showing that Dante had paid in full for that term.

That had been a nice gesture, but she wouldn't be able to count on that for the next two terms, so she found a part time job waitressing near the campus. DJ could stay at the daycare center while she worked or went to school; she would only be 10 minutes away from him when at work, and five minutes away when in class.

Dante insisted on baby sitting, but she told him that she didn't want to trouble him. He asked for her and DJ to come back home several times, but she refused. She called weekly to let him know that they were fine. But she wouldn't allow him to know her phone number, nor would she tell him where she lived. These things broke his heart.

Gabrielle had changed so much. She was softer and quieter. She didn't have many conversations with him except to say how DJ was doing. Whenever he asked about her or the new baby, she told him she had to go. He wanted to talk to her and spend time with her and have them back in his life, but Gabrielle was moving on. She wasn't even angry with him which made him wonder if she still cared.

Some days he went to the school and visited DJ in the day care center. The woman who ran the center, Mrs. Pritchard, had been his Sunday school teacher. She didn't even know that Dante and Gabrielle weren't together anymore, and Gabrielle never notified anyone, including her own mother or friends that they weren't. So, from time to time when Dante would take DJ from the day care center to spend the day with him, Mrs. Pritchard would tell Gabrielle what a wonderful husband she had."He wants to be with his son day and night, and hates to even drop him back off at daycare."

Gabrielle wanted to tell Mrs. Pritchard to stop letting Dante take DJ out, but she couldn't do that without making him look like a villain, and she had no interest in that.

When her mother or friends called the house for her, she had asked that Dante just take a message. He often wanted to at least tell her mom that Gabrielle had left him. He thought that maybe her mom could push Gabrielle to come back to him. But then, he or Gabrielle would have to end up telling Danielle why they were apart. He wasn't trying to be secretive or portray himself as a saint, but he didn't want anyone to know how terrible he had been; he couldn't even come to terms with how contemptible he had been himself.

So, for months they were apart. She wouldn't let him come to her new place, and she refused to take DJ to their old home. Sometimes she felt that she ought to go back to her husband for DJ's sake.

She and DJ were in a low income apartment complex. The noise and scenes sometimes made her keep DJ inside even when he desperately wanted to go out to the jungle gym or sandbox where the other kids were playing or fighting. She hated to deprive him of the outdoors; he loved being outside, but with her working and going to school, she couldn't take him to the park any more. She felt bad, but the only recreation he got was at day care, or when they were walking to and from the bus stop.

School and work were becoming more difficult tasks. By late August she had to quit her job. She was due in October, but her doctor was predicting a September delivery. He was correct.

Davis Jackson was born September 23rd. The minute that Dante found out Gabrielle was in labor, he went to the hospital to be at her side. He stayed through the night, and had Erin pick up DJ and keep him at her apartment.

After Gabrielle delivered Davis, their second son, Dante did and said everything he could to convince her to bring the children back home with him. He had converted one of the guest bedrooms into Davis' room, and had even put a crib in their bedroom in case she didn't want Davis down the hall yet. He painted the picture perfectly, still when it was time for her to leave, she headed back to her own apartment.

The only thing that changed was she did allow Dante to know where they were living. She had asked Dante to bring Davis' crib and whatever else he had purchased for Davis to the apartment. When Dante walked across the plots of dirt that had only patches of grass, and saw his son, DJ, on the nearly rusted jungle gym, he decided not to take Davis' things in. Instead, he knocked on the door and Gabrielle turned the knob immediately. She had peeked out the window just behind the couch where she was sitting and nursing Davis. She knew it was Dante.

"Why are you living like this?" was the first thing he asked Gabrielle.

"Dante, please..." was all she could find to say.

"And why is DJ out there unsupervised on that broken up toy set, swing gym or whatever?"

"Dante, DJ can't sit inside all day. I didn't want him out there either, but I've kept him in here for more than seven months. Our next door neighbor took him and her daughter out there, and I can see him from the window."

Dante still hadn't sat down. Besides the couch, there was only a small tv stand in front of her, a lamp stand next to her, and a small card table with a couple of red vinyl chairs in the dining area.

"This isn't right man. You can't keep living like this Gabrielle."

"I won't Dante. I won't."
"So, you're coming back home?"
"This is home for now," she replied.
"I mean with me Gabrielle."

"The lease is in my name here," she answered.

He thought for a minute, then remembered what he had said to her about the house being his.

"It's both of ours Gabrielle. I was just angry that day. I was just...you know how I get when I'm mad. I was just saying things."

"Maybe you said too much."

"Come on Gabrielle. You've got to come back home."

"I'm not going anywhere for now. Maybe in a year when I get my degree and I can afford better, I'll move. I don't plan to stay here forever."

"I can't have my kids here. My wife. Man. Gabrielle you are my wife. You can't be out here like this."

Gabrielle knew that she didn't want to raise her children here. But she wasn't just being stubborn. Dante had torn into her one time too many, and she couldn't be moved by his promises anymore. His apologies and explanations hadn't really changed all that much since he first started making mistakes. She thought about those things, but:

"I can't come back," was all she could say.

"So, you're leaving me?" he asked and she looked at him puzzled. "Well, you know what I mean, are you divorcing me? It's been almost a year now."

"Why, are you worried about a settlement? I haven't asked you for anything so far."

"Man stop being ridiculous man, Gabrielle. I'm not thinking about that. I'm thinking about your safety, our kids. And I'm tired of lying. I'm tired of lying to my family. Your mother, your friends about where you are. I'm tired of lying to myself; I need you. I want you to come back home with me."

She stared at Dante, and she knew he meant it, but all she could repeat was: "I can't."

He stared at her dumbfounded and looked around at the way she was living. He was desperate for some way to convince her to come back with him. But there was nothing he could say.

"Are you bringing Davis' things in?" she asked as she rocked him.

Dante's head dropped, and he told her yes. There was nothing more he could do. He brought the things in, and placed an envelope on the lamp stand next to the couch. She heard something jingle when he set the padded envelope down.

"Just come back home when you're ready," he said and walked out the door with his eyes on the ground.

Moments later Gabrielle's neighbor dropped DJ off. When DJ came in the house, he saw the envelope on the lamp stand. He always noticed anything new, different, or out of place.

"What's this mommy?" he asked picking it up.

"Give it here," she said patiently. The envelope was padded with some money and her set of house keys were also in there. She picked up the phone with the intention to call Dante and ask him what was this for. But she knew him well enough. The keys were for her to come back home. And since he apparently saw how stubborn she was being, he realized that she might not come back; so, the money was for her to take care of her expenses.

She let some days pass before she called Dante to thank him. She hadn't heard from him in a while, and when she called to talk to him, she had to leave a message. Almost minutes after that, he called her back from the airport. He was just returning from out of town, and had forgotten her number at home. He had gone to Minnesota to meet with Altruis and a few other former players. They were contemplating opening a soul food restaurant since there was nothing like that in the area.

"Bros get tired of Morton's you know. Especially when they're way out there, and there's not too many of us. You need a little home cooking then," he was laughing and telling Gabrielle.

She told him it sounded like it could be a big success. He told her that Roni was asking about her and the kids, and that she and Altruis would probably be out to visit them in the next few months.

Gabrielle told him she'd be glad to see them. He asked if that meant she was coming home. She paused, and he knew that meant she wasn't ready. He talked for a while longer, then told her he'd call once he got to the house.

It didn't take long for him to get home, and he called her when he walked through the door. It became a daily thing again. Now that he had her number, he was calling all the time to check on her and the kids. Everyday he told her how lonely he had been without them.

She told him that she was sure he had found plenty to do, but he convinced her that he hadn't. He said that he just couldn't go on living in that house alone without them. So she asked if that meant he was ready to move back in with his mother like he had predicted it would happen.

He told her that was a low blow and then he explained that the statement meant exactly what he had said. He was lonely without them, and desperately wanted them to return.

Dante and Gabrielle began to talk more frequently and openly as the weeks went by. When he felt a little more comfortable, he often began to tell her that he knew how bad he had messed up, but he wondered why she couldn't forgive him. He couldn't understand why after all this time, and as sorry and as sincere as he was, she still refused to come home. But then, he arrived at an answer, and he couldn't have been more incorrect.

chapter thirty three

Christmas was approaching, and he had asked Gabrielle to bring the kids over so he could take them shopping. In the mean time, he had picked out some apartments that he felt comfortable with. And, if she weren't going to come back home, he would at least like to show her the apartments and help with the bills. Gabrielle agreed to bring the kids to the house, but nothing more than that.

The day that she was supposed to meet Dante, Davis got sick, and she had to cancel. Dante had been so disappointed that she didn't show up; so, he called and complained about how let down she had made him feel. The following day, she decided to try again, and surprise him. She had called her classmate, Austin, and asked him to take her to the house. She still had her keys, but out of respect, she called Dante first to tell him she was coming.

There was no answer when she called the house, and Austin was already outside to pick her and the kids up. She loaded them in, then headed to the house. Austin and Gabrielle pulled into the driveway and she saw both the car and truck in the driveway and knew that Dante was home. She got the kids out the car, and walked to the door. Fortunately, Austin had told her he would wait until they made it in.

Gabrielle and the children reached the stairs, and just as she rang the door, Dante was opening it. He was so happy to see Gabrielle and his sons that he didn't realize Sa'Lissa was coming down the stairs until she called his name. He looked back up the stairs, and breathed out the name: "Sa'Lissa."

Gabrielle saw the slim built, medium height, lighter skinned woman walking downstairs fastening her bath robe. Gabrielle could have thought that this was some one night stand or some foolish mistake that Dante was making, but when she heard the squeaky, unforgettable voice, she knew there was more to it than that. This was the same woman who had called his mother's house and asked why Dante hadn't by been to visit her mother. Sa'Lissa was coming down the stairs, and Sa'Lissa's son was charging down the hallway toward the stairs.

Gabrielle had known she would never forget that voice, and with what was happening before her eyes, she knew that she wouldn't ever put this scene out of her mind.

Sa'Lissa didn't realize who was on the outside of the door, until she was standing behind Dante with her hand on his waist.

"Gabrielle..." Dante whispered looking into Gabrielle's face. His heart had shrunk, and he could barely get out any words. He had ruined it. Any chance that he had of reconciling with her, he had ruined.

Gabrielle had started backing away from the door. She could not take her eyes off of Dante, but she knew she had to back away. DJ was crying and pulling toward his father, but Gabrielle had clutched her hand around his arm and was dragging him backwards. Davis' face was nestled close to her breast and he rubbed against her. DJ fought with her crying repeatedly: "I want my daddy." Gabrielle couldn't say anything to Dante's pleas that she not go.

He told her that it wasn't what she was thinking. She couldn't even hear DJ who had begun screaming and crying even louder for his daddy. Everything had rushed the blood to her head, and the sights and sounds were a blur. All she could do was shake her head 'no' in disbelief. Dante continued appealing to her, but she was headed toward the car and dragging DJ along the ground in a hurry to get there.

Dante was only dressed in his boxer shorts, still he stepped out onto the front ledge and started walking toward the car to beg Gabrielle to just listen. Fortunately, Austin had gotten out to pick DJ up and put him in the car. This expedited Gabrielle and Davis' return to the car. Just as Dante was approaching the car, Austin was backing away.

Dante had made the same mistake twice: he had let Gabrielle get away, right when he was close to her. First he was hurt and angry with himself, then with her. As the hours passed he couldn't stop thinking about her and what had happened this morning. He was devastated and he had to make her understand. The first step was to talk to her.

He had to explain to Gabrielle that it wasn't what she was thinking. Maybe she was thinking that Sa'Lissa was living there. Even worse, maybe Sa'Lissa's son Dontel had been visible. Maybe Gabrielle thought this was his second family. But she was wrong.

Snapshots

He wasn't going to admit all this to Gabrielle, but he had still been carrying on an affair from time to time with Sa'lissa. She had always been right there in his mother's neighborhood, looking good as ever. He had always messed around with her when he came home from college, and for years beyond that. It was nothing serious. She knew that and so did he. There was a time when he probably would have gotten with Sa'lissa, and even married her; but, she couldn't wait long enough for him to start making money. She had started messing with someone in Torrence's click who was *balling* and had as much street fame as Dante had on the field. Sa'lissa and that guy had even had a son. For the longest she had claimed it was Dante's, and he did take care of her son.

Even when she came clean that Dontel wasn't his son, Dante still did things for him and Sa'lissa. And though Dante had basically broken off the relationship since he got married to Gabrielle, he still stopped by Sa'lissa's house when he was in the neighborhood, and she still called his mother's house, but Mrs. Jackson had warned him about it and wanted it to stop.

Dante had been planning to back away from Sa'lissa; but they were good friends underneath all of the extras and it was just hard for him to let go. Whenever she had needed something from him, he had been right there, and last night was no different. Sa'Lissa and Dontel had just needed a place to stay for the night because she and her mother had gotten into it.

He should have just put them in a hotel instead of letting them come to the house. He should have explained that to Gabrielle, but she wouldn't have listened. Her 'smart alack college boy' had taken his wife and sons away before Dante could even make it to the car good.

Thousands of thoughts shot through his head. He was getting overwhelmed, so he threw on the first pair of pants and shirt he could find and headed to Gabrielle's.

chapter thirty four

The banging and yelling outside of Gabrielle's door made her glad that she hadn't let DJ go outside. The neighbors in this area were getting worse and worse. Davis had awakened to the noise and Dante Jr. had come from his and Davis' room to tell his mommy that he was scared. She reached for the phone on the lamp stand and thought to call the police, but then she recognized the yelling was coming from Dante.

He had been pounding on her neighbor's door without realizing he was at the wrong door. Luckily, that neighbor, Mr. Smith, was at work because if he had been home, he probably would have shot Dante. He always carried his "piece," and didn't hesitate to flash it or fire it at the hooligans.

One of her other neighbors heard that Dante was calling out Gabrielle's name, and asked if he wasn't Dante Jackson, the football player. He told the guy yes, so the neighbor pointed Dante in the right direction of Gabrielle's apartment.

When Dante got to her door, he began banging and yelling for her to open it. She would have opened the door, but the more he yelled, the more reticent she was to let him in. He hadn't ever yelled threats to her before, but he started yelling that he knew she was in there and that she better open up the door. Dante could hear DJ on the other side of the door crying for Gabrielle to: 'just let my daddy in, mommy.' Dante could also hear Gabrielle telling DJ to be quiet. Dante decided that she was hiding from him, so she had to be hiding something from him.

"Open up this door, Gabrielle, or I'll break it down. You know I will."

DJ continued crying, and Gabrielle shook her head 'no' to him as he placed his hands on the knob.

"Don't do that to mommy," she whispered, then shook her head even more. "Don't open that door, DJ."

She could see the door moving in with each beat that Dante gave it. She wanted DJ to move back from the door, but she was scared if she grabbed him, she might use too much force. His knees and arms were already scraped from her dragging him that morning. She didn't want to put her hands on her son, so she reached out her arm to him and motioned for him to come to her. DJ ran to Gabrielle and clung to her legs and said: "I'm scared, mommy."

Dante continued banging and threatening that once he got inside he would beat Gabrielle and the "punk-nigga" that was in there with her.

She hadn't understood how he had the nerve to show up at her house with anything but an apology, but the more he yelled, the more clear it became.

He yelled that he couldn't understand it before why she wouldn't come home, but now that he saw her and the "low life nigga" that brought her to his house, he saw that she would just rather live in a scummy, low lifed way. He told her that was alright for her if that's what she wanted, but he didn't want his kids caught in her sleazy life style. They didn't have to live like that; she could live as she chose.

Under different circumstances, she would have yelled replies back to him, but she couldn't think of anything. She was too scared to even move close to the door where the phone was. If Dante kept banging like he was, in a matter of minutes, he would break the door down, and she didn't want to be right there when he did.

In a different neighborhood, this wouldn't have gone on for more than a few seconds, but in this neighborhood, some people liked the action, some were too used to actions like this or worse, and a few others recognized Dante. One guy even had on an old jersey with Dante's name and number on the back.

It seemed like no one would be able to stop this. But someone in the neighborhood had had enough of Dante's theatrics and did call the police. Gabrielle could see the flashing blue lights through the cracks in her shades, and she could hear the police talking to him, then reading him his rights.

She cried and prayed that for his sake he would calm down so that they wouldn't hurt him. He tried explaining to the police that something was wrong with his wife and kids in there, and he was just trying to get in to see.

The police knocked on the door and found Gabrielle shaken and weeping and comforting her children. They asked if she was okay, and she tried to vouch for Dante's story. But the older lady, Mrs.

Adams, from across the driveway, was outside in her spotted head rag telling the officers that she was the one who called, and that Dante had been out here disturbing the peace.

They asked Mrs. Adams if she was sure it was Dante, and then they told her who he was. She said she didn't care who he was, that she knew who did it, and he was the one. The eye witness' word was weighed more heavily than Gabrielle's. She would of course try to protect her husband. And the 911 call did originate from Mrs. Adams' home, so they took Dante to jail.

The police had left, and DJ was asking where was his daddy. Gabrielle knew that she should be comforting her son, but instead she flung herself on the couch, buried her face, and screamed out her tears. DJ stayed with his mother, crying some, patting her on the back, and trying to see her face.

chapter thirty five

Too many days had gone by that Gabrielle had cried inwardly or outwardly alone. She had been dealing with the ups and downs of this relationship virtually by herself. She had never really been able to talk to anyone but Michelle and Yvette about the problems in her relationship. She didn't want to talk to Michelle about her marital problems, because from the beginning, there had been only one solution in Michelle's eyes, leave him and take what she could. Yvette would be much more compassionate, but she was so overprotective when it came to Gabrielle, it would crush Gabrielle to have to admit even a few of the things that Dante had done and said to her.

Danielle would find it hard to believe that Gabrielle and Dante were having so many problems. When she had seen them last, they were happy. Gabrielle didn't want to disappoint her mother, or worse yet, have her mother say something that would hurt her.

She would have to talk to her friends, and then she would have to leave Dante. They would give her the strength to leave him, though she didn't have the heart to do it.

Gabrielle still loved her husband and thought that maybe in time they would be able to pull things together. Dante had been opening up so much lately that she took a step to reconcile with him. She traced her footsteps from earlier today, and what it had lead to. Her giving him a chance, and him accusing her of doing what he was obviously doing again, being unfaithful. Added to that was the fact that he had just been arrested because she wouldn't let him in. She couldn't go through this alone any more.

She sat up on the couch and looked around her. A tiny box of a one bedroom apartment, and her friends and family thought she was living in a six bedroom home. Her husband had three vehicles that added up to the cost of some people's dream homes, and here she was taking the bus to work and school. He had offered the car to her when she first left, at least to get her and DJ around, but she couldn't have kept that car in this neighborhood. There was too great a risk that someone would break in the car or her apartment after seeing the 850ci and thinking she had money. She had nothing.

Dante had been giving her some money and paying some of her bills, still it didn't cover everything. She had actually been forced to pawn most of her jewelry months ago when she quit her job. She had to survive, and she didn't want to ask Dante for anything. If he gave it fine, but she wouldn't let his words be anywhere near true. He had accused her of wanting to take his money, so if she could help it, she had vowed never to ask him for anything.

The only piece of jewelry she could not let go of was her wedding ring. That was because no matter how many difficulties she would have to face, she didn't want to let go of the hope she had in her marriage. Now, that was fading. It was time for her to call home, and most likely head back there.

She had nursed Davis and fed Dante Jr. who immediately fell asleep.

When the children had been taken care of, she dialed up Yvette first. Once again, it was nearly the middle of the night. She choked out a 'hello' to Yvette, but after that, she couldn't say any more words; she only cried.

Yvette called Gabrielle's name and kept asking: "Gabrielle, is this you?"

Gabrielle gave an "uh huhn" to say that it was, then Yvette started in with the questions.

"Is it that Dante? What has he done? Did he do something to you? Is he beating you? Girl, I'll kill him. I'll kill him if he's out there beating on you. He's too big for me to fight, but Lord knows I'll jump on a plane and kill his big behind. I knew he was an evil son of a gun when I was in Minnesota. I didn't like him. I didn't."

Gabrielle laughed slightly through her tears. Yvette was being a motor mouth. Gabrielle hadn't said yes or no to any of Yvette's questions, since they came one right after the other. Still, Yvette had convinced herself she knew everything that was going on.

"Yvette. Yvette. Dante is not beating me," Gabrielle composed herself and began talking.

"Well, is DJ okay? Did anything happen to him?"

That reminded Gabrielle, she hadn't even told Yvette that she had given birth to Davis. And even though Danielle had a mother's instincts and told Gabrielle that she was pregnant before she knew it herself, Gabrielle never even told her mother. Danielle would have wanted to come out and help with the baby, at least during the first couple of weeks, and she couldn't have anyone out here since no one knew that she and Dante were separated. Only Austin had been around to help, and now she didn't know how she would explain to Yvette, one of her best friends, that she had kept so many large secrets during the past year. But she had to tell Yvette now. She was in a lot of trouble and needed someone to talk to, so she walked back to the days in January, almost a year ago, and began explaining what happened up to today.

Yvette's thoughts, questions, and comments were all over the place. She wanted to know a lot of things about why Gabrielle hadn't called sooner; how did things get so far out of hand with Dante, but mostly she wanted to know when Gabrielle was coming home.

They had to call Michelle. Yvette didn't feel that Michelle could comfort Gabrielle any better than she, but she did know Michelle could handle the legal matters. There had to be a divorce, and Gabrielle had to come home even if she couldn't get the divorce until later. It was too dangerous in too many ways for her to be down there alone.

Yvette called Michelle on three-way, and Michelle began listening to the story. Gabrielle asked Yvette to just tell it all. She had already been on the phone more than two hours, and she couldn't even afford that.

Yvette and Michelle continued the conversation. They had promised Gabrielle that they would not call Danielle. They agreed with one another that they would go half and half and pay for Gabrielle's ticket home.

Shortly after Gabrielle got off the phone with Michelle and Yvette, the phone rang again. She thought it was one of them, but it wasn't. It was the first Mrs. Jackson, Dante's mother, and she wanted to know what was going on with her son and Gabrielle.

Gabrielle hadn't had any contact with Dante's family for nearly a year now. She was sure that they thought pretty low of her. She had wanted to call his mother, or at least go to church with her, but she had no way of getting there, and to ask for a ride would have opened up room for too many questions. Still, she was sitting here now, and had to answer a question that she didn't know how to.

She would have wondered how Mrs. Jackson got her number or knew where she was, but she could hear Dante answering "Yes sir" or "No sir" to his father who was yelling out one question after the other in the background. Mrs. Jackson had already gotten the gist of the problems from hearing her husband tear into Dante for the past few hours. He had started his line of questioning by repeatedly asking:"What's wrong with you boy? What's wrong with you?"

Dante had sat directly across from his father in the den with his hands cupping his head, and kept repeating that he didn't know. But when his father asked him what Gabrielle had done to him, he began to talk. He started off by saying that she hadn't done anything wrong to him, ever.

Gabrielle had been the best woman and had the most to offer to him. He didn't know why he flew off the handle or showed such a lack of appreciation for her. He had been selfish with her, and that was where the main problems came in. It wasn't that he distrusted her. He had always known in his heart that she never would have taken advantage of him. Even though throughout the years, he had splurged and spent money on girls who always wanted bigger or better gifts, Gabrielle appreciated whatever he did for her or the children. And the most she had ever wanted of him was his time, or for him to do right by them. She wanted them to be a family. And when he couldn't do that, she left him and never asked for anything.

That had happened more times than he could count. There weren't gifts or money enough to bring her back when he had done something wrong. Every time he had messed up, he had to prove to her that he meant to do right in order for her to budge. He had always been sincerely sorry whenever he pleaded with her to come back, but he had never really thought about what he had done that made him have to be sorry. This caused him to make the same mistakes over and over again.

His father didn't spend the entire time scolding Dante. He had always been the last one in the house they would go to when Dante had really messed up. He had also been the only one who could get a firm enough grip to shake Dante up, and get him on track. Dante could coax his mother, and even though he didn't always have her convinced, he did always have her on his side. Things were much different with his father.

After he had scolded Dante enough, he began talking to him about what the world of fast money, flashy cars, flashy jewelry, and pretty girls could do to a person. Dante's spiritual self had deteriorated. His father had never been in the limelight, but he knew that his son and other "big-headed boys" like him could misjudge women.

Not every woman wanted to be a part of that world which could push you to the top one day, and knock you to the bottom the next. Dante had been with team after team. He had gone from commanding top dollar to barely making the practice squad. And, for the last two seasons he had sat out. It wasn't impossible for him to get picked up, but it was getting to be less likely, still Gabrielle hadn't left him yet. She had been with him through every trade, cut, and foolish mistake he had been through.

Dante had just been thinking too much of himself and forgetting that long after football was over, his children would know him as "daddy" when the rest of the world had forgotten his name. There would be another Dante Jackson in the League one day. Maybe with the same name, or maybe with a different name, taped above Dante's old number. Even if his fans remembered him, they would one day know him as a 'former.' His children could know him as the greatest, but only if he did right by them and their mother.

How was he going to face his children knowing that he hadn't done right by them? How would he face himself knowing that he let go of the better half of him, Gabrielle?

His father had given him plenty to think about; but, Dante didn't know how he was going to do anything. He had lost Gabrielle, this time for sure. Her words came back to him, and so did flashes of the good times and bad.

"Some things happen for better." He caught a mental flash of their wedding day.

"Some things happen for worse." He saw some of the many times that he had turned her away.

"And, some things happen for good." He wept then, because he saw the day that she backed away from his door and he pled with her to come back. She continually shook her head no; she would not come back.

She had spoken the "for better, for worse, and for good" statement to him a long time ago. But the scene from today made it fresh. How could this mistake be so close, yet seem so impossible to correct.

He didn't think any apology would be good enough. He had done and said things that he could probably never convince her he didn't mean. That was the hard part, knowing that she probably couldn't believe in him anymore. He would never be able to prove himself to her, unless she gave him another chance.

His father had almost given up on him having any more chances with Gabrielle.

"No matter how much she loves you," his father began "if that girl is smart, she will go on and leave you. You'll just have to prove your love at a distance by respecting her choice to go on with her life."

His mother hadn't seen Dante cry like this since he was a child. He wept and gasped, and turned into her for comfort when she sat down on the couch next to him. She held him at the back of the head with one hand, and rubbed his back with the other.

"She'll give you another chance Dante. I know she will. She's wise enough to know your heart is good."

Mrs. Jackson directed her last statement toward Dante's father.

"Son, wisdom is greater than smarts. Gabrielle is wise. She'll give you a chance."

While Mrs. Jackson consoled her son, Gabrielle Jackson walked the back room of her apartment with Davis in her arms until he could fall back asleep. He was having an uneasy night, and for some reason, DJ had awaken as well. He didn't require his mother's attention, but he watched her walk and talk with his baby brother.

In the morning, Michelle called. She informed Gabrielle that she and Yvette had put together the money for her ticket. All Gabrielle needed to do was pack her things and make it to the airport tomorrow afternoon. They couldn't get her out any sooner because the holiday traffic was so heavy with people flying in and out.

Michelle and Yvette were putting a rush on her. Gabrielle knew that she needed to leave Dallas, but she hadn't decided when it would be. Tomorrow was DJ's third birthday, and she wanted him to have some kind of party. Michelle and Yvette promised to have a cake, Jasmine, Michellene, Michael and a few neighborhood kids there.

Gabrielle also had to let the children say good bye to their father. Michelle and Yvette wondered about Gabrielle's excuse. As far as either of them were concerned, Dante didn't deserve a goodbye; he had said that a long time ago.

But, Gabrielle also pointed out, she had to tie up some loose ends at the school. It was the only excusable reason she had given.

"So, how long will that take?" Yvette demanded. "A few weeks?"

"No," Gabrielle assured her. "It will only take a week, maybe two, then I can start transferring my credits and head home."

"And what about the divorce?" Michelle wanted to know.

"That will all take time," Gabrielle sighed. "It's just going to take time."

There would have been a barrage of questions from the two of them, but Gabrielle had a beep on the other line, and had to go. It was Dante's mother. She wanted to know how Gabrielle and the children were doing, and whether or not she could come pick them all up. Gabrielle paused and didn't know how to tell her that Dante had forbidden them to go over there.

"Gabrielle, why can't you give me an answer? If you're busy I understand. If you don't want the children around us, I'd at least like to know why. We haven't done anything to you."

Mrs. Jackson wasn't demanding, but it sounded as if she were slightly upset that Gabrielle didn't agree to come over.

Gabrielle didn't know whether to lie and say they were busy, because she didn't want to disrespect Dante's demand that she stay away from his parents' house. Nor, did she want to tell his mother that Dante had prohibited her from going over there. But his mother seemed to already know.

It was hard to understand why Dante did things the way he did, but he had kept Gabrielle from his family because he felt that was the only part of his life that he had left that was his, and his alone. He explained that to his father when they talked the other night. Gabrielle didn't know any of this, and Dante's mother didn't feel it was her place to go into detail with Gabrielle. She only assured Gabrielle that Dante was just being really misunderstood. The holidays were near, and the family wanted to see Gabrielle and the kids. Plus, Pauline and her bunch were coming in, and had been asking about Gabrielle.

Gabrielle did want to see all of the family. DJ would be ecstatic about running and playing at his grandmother's, especially with all of his cousins there. Gabrielle explained to Mrs. Jackson that she had a lot of things to do around the house for the day, but that tomorrow would be DJ's birthday, and that she would love to bring the children over.

Pauline got to town and called Gabrielle the minute she finished hearing the news of Dante and Gabrielle's troubles. Pauline wanted to know why Gabrielle hadn't called her, or told anyone in the family. She and Pauline talked, and Pauline knew her own brother. She hadn't realized that Dante had tried to ostracize Gabrielle from his family; none of them knew until he recently explained. Still, Pauline felt that Gabrielle should have known that she could come to her. But Gabrielle was clear in explaining that she hadn't even understood Dante's reasons, and moreover, she just didn't need any more confrontations from Dante at the time.

Davis was being nursed, so Gabrielle and Pauline talked for a little while longer, but Gabrielle had to go. Pauline promised to be the one to pick her up in the morning for the get together. As soon as she hung up with Gabrielle, Pauline called Dante.

This was about the fifth degree of reproach he had gotten. His mother, father, Erin, and Erica had all confronted him and demanded to know what he was going to do about making amends with Gabrielle, and why he hadn't at least tried anything yet.

He was still feeling sorry for himself, believing that there was nothing he could do. Pauline told him that he better come up with something by tomorrow, because it was DJ's birthday and the whole family would be there.

When Pauline picked Gabrielle up in the morning, she realized that it would be the last time they would all be meeting like this. As Gabrielle was loading suitcases in the back seat, she told Pauline she had to stop by her college and close some things out. She loaded the rest of her things and Davis' baby items in the trunk. Those were the only things worth taking. Most of the other things she had purchased second hand, or spent very little for. It wasn't worth a shipping fee to send these things across the country.

chapter thirty six

They arrived at the Jacksons' home and DJ raced to the door when he saw Erin. She was the aunt who had kept him when Davis was born. Erin lost DJ in the crowd as soon as he got in and saw Erica, Torrence, and Pauline's children. They were off and running to the enclosed back porch.

The weather was warm, even for a Dallas winter. The temperatures had shot into the mid seventies. Mrs. Jackson didn't want the children going outside of the back patio, but her husband convinced her to let them put on sweaters or light jackets and go outside and play. The only stipulation was that they were not to go around to the front. They had to stay in the back where somebody could watch them. Their grandfather sat on the back porch and agreed to watch them. After watching them play tag, freeze, red light green light or Simon says, Mr. Jackson dozed off to sleep.

Gabrielle and Davis were surrounded by all the family who wanted to hold him, know how old he was, what things he had learned to do, etc. They passed him around, and he cried for his mother so she tried to stay near.

After Mrs. Jackson's children had been mingling for a while, they rotated in the kitchen to help her finish dinner. Then she called for all hands to come help her carry things out to the back yard. Today's celebration was even larger than most. A few of the church people were stopping by; some of the neighbors came over, and Dante was picking up his aunt Candace and her husband Joe from the airport. Candace was his mother's favorite sister, and all of the children's favorite aunt. The kitchen was a buzz with talk of aunt Candace's arrival.

This gave Mrs. Jackson a moment to slip away to the front with Gabrielle. They sat in the den, and Gabrielle watched out the front window. Even though Mrs. Jackson had assured her that Dante didn't mind her being at the house, Gabrielle still felt a little uncomfortable knowing that she hadn't heard this from him, and that he would be coming through the door at any moment.

Mrs. Jackson wanted Gabrielle to know that she was happy

to have her and the children with the rest of the family, and that she was looking forward to seeing Gabrielle at more of the family days. This put Gabrielle in an awkward position. She knew that she wouldn't be back to Dallas for a long time; maybe the children would be young people by then. She wasn't certain whether to tell Dante's mother this, since she hadn't even told Dante. But she couldn't sit there and lie, telling Mrs. Jackson that she would be at the family gatherings.

"Mrs. Jackson," she began. "I...I really don't know how to tell you this...but...I...I won't be here too much longer." With that she paused. She could see that Mrs. Jackson wanted more. Her face was asking Gabrielle 'why.'

The explanation was simple, yet it wasn't. "I'm leaving today." Gabrielle began. "I have to go back to Wisconsin," she said looking at the ground, and wrapping her fingers around her hand, then her hand around her fingers.

"Is something wrong in your family? Is everything okay? When will you be back?" Mrs. Jackson ran off her questions with her face full of concern.

"I won't be...well, I mean, I don't know when I'll be back. My family is fine. It's just that I can't keep living out here like this. It's just gotten too tough for me. I'm by myself and..." Gabrielle stopped. She was saying too much.

"You don't have any help. Right? That's what you were going to say."

"I don't mean any offense Mrs. Jackson," Gabrielle said looking up to her.

"You're not offending me baby. I'm just sorry we didn't know sooner. We didn't know you and Dante were having so many problems and that he had gotten so far out of control. Not that we could have completely changed him, because Dante's been Dante since he was born. But maybe we could have got him to talk, like he did the other night. Gabrielle, Dante does love you. And he realizes a lot of things that maybe he knew but didn't understand before. The thing he realizes the most is that he's been too selfish and immature to show you just how much he does appreciate you."

"I understand," Gabrielle replied, but still had her heart set on leaving.

There was no point in discussing it. This was the perfect

point to just agree. Mrs. Jackson's statement was right, though it didn't change anything. Nothing would, so Gabrielle stared at the ground, not knowing what else to say.

"Well, let's get to the back. I think we understand each other. Whatever you choose to do, you just always know that we do care about you here, and you are family."

Gabrielle smiled and took the hand that her mother-in-law had extended. They walked back toward the kitchen. The girls had taken everything out to the back porch. Erin and Erica had even woken their father up, and were sitting next to him talking. Gabrielle walked out on the patio with them. He patted a seat for her to sit down. She talked with them for a while but then looked out in the back yard for DJ. She saw Pauline was holding Davis, but she didn't see Dante Jr. Gabrielle excused herself, and Mr. Jackson asked where she was going. She told him that she wanted to find DJ.

"Sit yourself down and relax. Pauline's got 'em all under control. He's probably just out there behind the shed," Mr. Jackson assured her.

Gabrielle told him she had full trust in Pauline, she just wanted to run out and see about DJ. Mr. Jackson laughed and said he understood. They had been the same way when Dante was a boy. Even if they knew where he was, they liked to keep an eye on him.

"You could see why," Mr. Jackson called after Gabrielle as she walked out the patio door. She turned and smiled in agreement.

Sure enough, Dante Jr. was out behind the shed. He was wrestling with some of his older cousins. Gabrielle tightened her sweater across her shoulders and sat on one of the fold out chairs next to Pauline.

"Your dad was right," she told Pauline.

"He's right about everything, so what now?"

"He knew exactly where DJ would be. Behind the shed. Is that where Dante used to be?"

"Dante was everywhere and into everything."

"Was he back there wrestling?" Gabrielle asked.

"And then some," Pauline returned, and they both laughed. A few years ago, Pauline had been the one who gave Gabrielle her first snapshot of Dante's early life.

The longer Gabrielle had been at the house, the more she realized, they all had plenty of stories about each other.

She wouldn't be able to stay much longer. Pauline had agreed to take her to the airport, but they had at least two more hours before they had to go. Just as they were making plans for departure, Gabrielle saw the back porch enraptured with the arrival of their aunt Candace.

Pauline took Gabrielle inside with her to go meet aunt Candace. Mr. Jackson had gone outside to sit with the kids. In a matter of minutes, he was asleep again. The kids were always so active that it made him tired.

Aunt Candace was pleased to talk to everyone, but when she met Gabrielle, the porch almost fell silent.

"So you're Gabrielle Jackson, huhn? I heard so much about you the whole ride over," she began.

Gabrielle smiled graciously and blushed.

"Listen, you're all my nephew says has been going on in his life. You and his little ones."

Aunt Candace was removing Davis from Pauline's arms. "This is Davis," she began, then walked over to the back window, and pointed immediately and correctly to DJ, and said: "That's little Dante."

Aunt Candace saw the surprise on Gabrielle's face, and replied. "Oh, I know Dante's children baby. They look and act just like him. That one's feisty," she said of DJ.

"And this one has his funny acting ways," she said about Davis, who was squirming in her arms.

Dante was still in the kitchen with his mother. No doubt, Mrs. Jackson was filling him in on Gabrielle's plans to leave.

Aunt Candace called him out to the back porch to "get this funny acting boy" of his.

Dante ducked his head then walked onto the porch and took Davis in his arms. He saw Gabrielle and wanted to move in close to her.

Aunt Candace began talking to the two of them, but her sister, Mrs. Jackson knew that Dante and Gabrielle needed to talk with each other. She came out to the patio and took Aunt Candace to the kitchen with her.

This gave Gabrielle an opportunity to wander away. Dante followed, with Davis in his arms.

Gabrielle had cornered herself off toward the back of the

porch. She was watching DJ play with his cousins and the other children. Dante stood behind her for a while, watching the children play, then he asked if they could talk.

She told him that she didn't have a problem with that; and he told her that wasn't what he was asking. He wanted to know if she would give serious consideration to what he said. She told him that all she could promise to do was listen.

With Davis in his arms, Dante escorted Gabrielle to the folding chairs in the back yard, and began to talk.

"Gabrielle, I don't even know where to start with you. I have messed up so many times, and I've asked your forgiveness that many times and more," Dante paused. "You have forgiven me every time. You believed in me each time, enough to trust that I would do better."

He placed Davis' face down across his lap and stroked his son's back.

"Gabrielle, I've just been thinking and thinking all these days about how much I need you, and how I can't live my life without you. I don't want to lose you. Maybe I already have. I just. I thought about losing you, and how that would tear my world apart. And I thought about what the worst part of it all could be, and Gabrielle, I keep coming back to, whatever happens, I just don't want you to give up on me. I just don't want you to stop believing in me."

Dante had done most of the talking, still Gabrielle could only sit in silence. She hadn't ever heard him say these things before, nor had she seen him cry, and he was pulling his shirt to wipe his eyes repeatedly. She wasn't bitter, but he had watched her cry many days, or turned his back on the hurt he had caused her. She wanted to console him but no words would come.

"Gabrielle. You've got to say something. I don't want to lose you. I don't want you out of my life. I know all the things I've said before and done before that were wrong, but I loved you too Gabrielle. I wasn't always bad to you."

"I know that Dante," she said softly.

"So could you look at those times Gabrielle? Could you try to remember the times when we were in love. When I was good to you? I want that back. I want to be good to you, but I need you to give me a chance. Baby, please."

Gabrielle's lips turned down. She shook her head from side to side. This meant no. She couldn't. She wouldn't give him another chance.

"I can't Dante."

"Oh, Gabrielle please. Please. You have to give me another chance. I'll do anything in the world. I just can't...I can't make it without you," he began crying.

Gabrielle stared at him and didn't want to be cold. She wanted to place her hand on his shoulder, but her arm wouldn't move.

It was the children that snapped her into action. Some of them were staring over at their uncle. They had never seen him in tears. Shonyea came bounding towards Gabrielle and Dante, and then a troop was following her. Gabrielle called out for them to turn around and go back and play. Mr. Jackson was sitting a few feet away and woke up to re-emphasize her command by adding: "Hey, hey. Alright now. You kids better do as you're told."

The kids weren't quick to turn back around, so Mr. Jackson reached toward his waist and reminded them that if he could take off his 'strap' quicker than they could turn around, they'd be in trouble. That made all of them race back to their games, except Shonyea. She stood watching her uncle. Mr. Jackson went to take her hand, and kept her with him when he walked to the back porch where the ladies were fixing the plates.

Dante repeated how he couldn't see himself making it without Gabrielle. She reminded him that he had been making it before he knew her, and that he has been doing fine on his own since then. He told her that he had thought the same thing too, but there was no way for him to show how much he loved her and needed her unless she gave him one more chance. Gabrielle notified him that her friends had already covered her trip home, and that she would be leaving in little over an hour. He asked her to cancel her trip or at least postpone it; but, it didn't seem like she could be moved.

"Just talk to me Gabrielle, and at least tell me where your head is at. Just talk to me. Tell me something," he pled.

The minute she began to explain, he almost wished she hadn't said anything. Gabrielle's words cut to the core of him. She talked about how she had loved him, and how all the problems began to make her feel bad about him and about herself. She told him how he had devalued her goals, dreams, and her love for him.

She realized that she had lost herself in him, and tried to do everything she could to improve his world, but he kept kicking her out of it, and for a long time she had no where to go. Now, she was finding direction again. She was going to school, and she would be finished soon, but she needed help with her children. She needed an environment that was safe for them, and a place where they could be loved by family and friends.

It seemed like a paradox that she was making those statements, yet leaving the Jackson household, where the Jacksons were embracing her and the children. But this was new. She wanted something that felt familiar. She knew this was genuine, but what she didn't know was how long this could last.

His family's welcome wouldn't change, but Dante might. He might fling into a fury and refuse to allow her back over here, or he might put her out again, threaten her again, or maybe the next time he would just hit her. That would knock her out. And who would she keep calling.

Her family and friends were too far away to run to her rescue, and if she kept going back to Dante, they might even get tired of helping her. No. She had experienced enough confusion, questions, hurt, love and lost love with him. It was time for her to move on.

They sat in silence for a minute until Pauline walked out and announced that it was time. She called for the children to head toward the patio, and told Gabrielle and Dante to come on. They were all going to sing happy birthday to DJ. All of the children, except DJ made it to the back porch.

Gabrielle was the first to notice that he wasn't in the crowd. She called his name and when he didn't reply, she began asking the children where DJ was. Shayonna, Pauline's eldest daughter, took Gabrielle's hand and lead her around to the front. Dante followed. DJ was on the front porch with a five year old girl. Gabrielle and Dante made it to the porch right when DJ was placing a peck on the little girl's lips. He didn't really know what he was doing, but Gabrielle shrieked out his name and snatched DJ by one hand, and the little girl by the other. She walked them to the back, scolding them both.

Shayonna ran to Pauline to tell what happened. Dante's mother met Pauline at the entrance of the back patio and asked what had happened.

Pauline explained that DJ was 'just like his daddy. Doing the same things that Dante did.' Even though DJ was half the age Dante was when he had his first kiss, DJ was twice as mannish.

That sent the back porch into a discussion about that incident, and the beating Dante had gotten all those years ago. Gabrielle smiled when she heard the story again. That had been the first snapshot she had gotten of Dante's early days. Pauline had told her about that years ago.

The family gathered around the table, sang happy birthday to DJ, ate and talked about more clips of the Jackson children's earlier lives. As was expected, Dante's were some of the most colorful.

Time was getting away from them. Gabrielle knew that she should be going, but between one relative or family friend then the next, she couldn't seem to pull herself away. Different people had different questions about Dante and Gabrielle's lives together. This was the first real time that any of them had seen Dante and Gabrielle together. They looked so perfect together, people wanted to picture what their lives had been like. How did they meet; when did they know it was love? Aunt Candace wanted to know how Gabrielle was keeping Dante in line.

"That's taken some work hasn't it Gabrielle?" his mother asserted.

"We're still working on it now," Gabrielle bashfully conceded.

Dante placed his arm around Gabrielle's shoulder and kissed the side of her head.

"I'm gonna make it easier," he whispered to her under the noise of the crowd.

She would have pulled away from him, but she found herself slipping her arm around his waist and through his arm. Dante was standing next to his father who was holding Davis. Somehow, Mr. Jackson could tell what Dante had said to Gabrielle. He tapped his son's hand, and when Dante looked over, his dad was shaking a finger and saying: "You better."

Gabrielle was looking off for DJ who was back running with his cousins.

It would be too difficult to get him out of here tonight.

"Maybe you'll postpone?" Dante asked her.

"Maybe I'll cancel," Gabrielle thought to herself.

She wanted to give her children a chance to be with their cousins and aunts and grandparents, even their uncle. Torrence was in as much trouble as Dante claimed, but he was still family. He showed up late, but he was still there, and they each embraced him as they did one another, like family.

Gabrielle had relaxed into the scene and was taking in all the activities and conversations around her. Some of the Jacksons were on the back porch talking, and a few of them had gone up to the family room. They were flipping through family photo albums. Dante made space on the couch for him and Gabrielle to look through the pictures of the Jackson children's earlier days.

Between Aunt Candace and Mrs. Jackson's explanations about the pictures, Gabrielle didn't have many questions about Pauline, Torrence, Erica, Erin and Dante's early days. But, as she sat nestled between her husband and their sleeping son, she wondered what story their photo album would tell in the years to come.

She could hear Michelle's conversation from last night inching up in her mind, and her own words from less than twenty four hours ago.

# # #

"It wasn't supposed to turn out like this you know?" Gabrielle had laughed a nervous laugh then continued.

"I was supposed to be Gabrielle Davis, the first one in my family to graduate from college, then go on to be a feature writer, my own column...one day even have my own magazine," she paused then went on.

"Or, maybe I was supposed to be Mrs. Gabrielle Jackson, the happily married wife of the wonderful and caring Dante Jackson that I met years ago, but now I'm neither...I'm not either one of those people I saw myself being, and I don't know if I ever can be."

Michelle had assured Gabrielle that she could be happy. There were plenty of chances and opportunities still left out there for her. But, to Michelle, it just sounded like Gabrielle had given up. In so many ways, Michelle could understand it.

Gabrielle had never been as aggressive as Michelle or as assertive as Yvette. She had always just gone with the flow and did what was expected of her. So, when her mother told her that at eighteen she was on her own, Gabrielle tried to manage that. And when life thrust her into the role of being a mother then wife, Gabrielle had tried to be the best she could be at both of those, but she was failing. At least that's how Gabrielle saw it.

The problem was Gabrielle had been so isolated from the

world she had once known and when she tried to move back or forth, something from either side was grabbing on to her and pleading for her to stay. But this time, she was realizing she had to find her own place and begin discovering her own new path. She just didn't know how.

The more Gabrielle talked with Michelle, the more clear it became.

"You know Michelle, sometimes there's a little voice in my head that asks me *are you still you?* It whispers to me at the strangest times...like... when I'm on the swings with my kids, when I'm in my husband's arms late at night, when I'm up writing or studying through the night and he's on the road, maybe in someone else's arms...the voice asks me: *are you still you?* And I almost don't know how to answer it. I almost don't know what's real any more." Gabrielle sighed.

"It's like I don't know if I am me or if he's really being him, or if any of us knows just what we're doing," she paused then continued.

"I mean, here I am, moving from place to place...in and out of his world, and sometimes there's just this whole dream like state, like none of this is real. I'm meeting all these faces with names and I don't know what's behind them. I don't even know what's behind Dante's. I used to think I knew that. I used to think I knew his heart. And, when I did...I thought he loved me."

There was a pause, and Michelle knew she couldn't say the right thing at that time, and she also knew Gabrielle wasn't through saying what was on her mind. After all of this, Gabrielle needed to just let it go, so Michelle listened.

"It's just like something deep down inside of me kept saying no matter what he's done, his heart is right—his heart is good. And I wanted to believe that. I wanted to stand by him until he got himself together because I do love him. And, somewhere between all his right and all his wrong, I do believe he loves me too."

"Maybe he does love you Gabrielle," Michelle interrupted, then rephrased things. "I mean, in his own little way, Gabrielle, he does love you. I have no doubt about that, but is that good enough?" Michelle paused then continued.

"There is no doubt in my mind that he is loving you the best way he knows how, but is he loving you the way you need to be loved?" Michelle's questions continued.

"Is he loving your kids the way they need to be loved...enough to be mature and man enough to treat you the way you deserve to be treated?"

These were the questions that needed to be answered.

The only thing that Gabrielle could say was how all this time she had kept believing that things would get better, and believing that he would finally do right.

For Michelle, the task was to get Gabrielle back to something much more important, and that was believing in herself.

In some ways, it seemed to make things worse. The more Michelle reminded Gabrielle of her old dreams, the more Gabrielle questioned how real those were.

Gabrielle began by saying:

"I used to think my old world was real. My life was so simple back then. It was Gabrielle go to school, get your degree and make it out there in the world on your own. But then things changed. Dante came along, DJ came along, and my whole world went upside down. It's like I walked into a world where everybody else was running, ducking, or hiding, and I just can't catch up. Maybe I shouldn't. I don't know if I or any of these people around me really knows where we're headed," Gabrielle paused for a moment, then went on.

"It's like I look at my life now, and I don't even know if I'm walking, running, changing or hiding. It's like I've lost myself somewhere in all this madness, and I don't know which part of me to become."

Michelle closed Gabrielle's statement by saying:

"Become the part of you that you will always love."

Michelle's solution was simple. It had come slow and soft, yet firm. And it was real. This was what Gabrielle needed to hear, and it was what she would have to do. She would have to become the part of her that she could always love and embrace.

For the rest of her life, Gabrielle was going to be a mom. That was true. And Dante was going to be her children's father no matter where they went or where he went, that much wouldn't change. But other things might.

There was no guarantee that Gabrielle would always be Dante's wife; and there was no guarantee that he would ever get himself together enough to finally make things work. Anything could change, and as the future later revealed, many things did.

chapter thirty seven

No one could predict the future, but everyone who had ever loved Gabrielle had rallied for her to leave Dante that day. They had wanted this because they felt it would be best for her. Gabrielle's friends had always told her that she could have left Dante behind, a thousand times over, and done fine or even better on her own. They also told her that she had given Dante enough chances, but for Gabrielle, marriage wasn't about chances; it was about commitment.

All of her life, she had been looking at her future through other people's eyes...first through her mother's, then Cassandra, Angelique, Yvette, and Michelle's. But that wasn't an option for Gabrielle anymore, nor was following in other people's footsteps.

As the pages flipped forward in her life, she saw herself stepping into some of the things she had always dreamed of.

Some of the early snapshots showed DJ at age 6 on the basketball court with his father. Another snapshot showed Gabrielle in her cap and gown holding her college diploma in her hand; Dante was standing behind her holding Davis; DJ was standing beside her, and DeAndre, their third child, was pushing her stomach out.

As the Jackson's pages were turned, there were vibrant shots of Dante, Gabrielle, and the kids at their grandparents'. One shot captured DeAndre and Davis in their red wagon, with their big brother DJ pulling them. Their album spilled over with shots of their own happy days at home, at backyard cookouts, and countless other times when they were in laughter and in love.

But those were the last of the early shots, and Gabrielle had chosen not to save any more memories of the bad. Dante had settled down as much as he could, and he was a good father to his kids despite the periodic struggles that he and Gabrielle had. She had viewed those shots before, but there were much brighter ones to come.

In a special section of their photo album, Gabrielle kept some clippings from her first writing job. She had started out with a small commentary section called "Notes and Quotes" in the local newspaper, but went on to gain notoriety in her own nationally syndicated column on League related matters. As her career continued to flourish, she was offered a position with the local team, where she not only wrote about "Women in the NFL: a series chronicling the contributions of wives, mothers, and others behind the scenes." But the team also contracted her to host her own radio show called "The In-Zone." Each week, her show took listeners into the lives of players, their wives, families or significant others and explored their off-the-field contributions.

Because Gabrielle worked for the team, she was at every game. When they were away, she could go in and out of various stadiums without even noticing anything special about them. But, each time she reported for home games, she was overcome with the empowering sense the home turf gave her.

She got to the stadium very early, and her sons were always with her. Her sons loved to run through the empty bleachers, go down on the field and talk to a couple players they had made friends with. Her two youngest sons were almost too young to remember the days they had spent in the stadium watching their father; but week after week when their mother went in to work, they were right there in the stadium with her. To her boys, game-day was full of excitement and fun; but to Gabrielle, entering the stadium held much deeper meaning.

She always reported extra early so she could relax in the near solitude of the stadium. When it was empty, the field seemed to stretch into forever, and no matter how far away from it you stood, you could always see the markers that let players know how far away they were from their goal. But more important than that was the star in the middle of the field. This star was blue with a silver lining, and it probably had its own symbolic meaning for the team, but in Gabrielle's mind, the star pointed to success in all directions. Though it was flat and on the ground, the star represented Gabrielle's constant and rising hopes.

When opponents came, they knew, there was no greater disrespect than to stand in the center of the field on that blue star. Although Gabrielle wasn't an opponent, she wouldn't have ever stepped foot on the middle of that field. Throughout her years and experience, she had come to realize she couldn't ever place her foot on anyone else's star.

She had learned to dream her own dreams, mark her own

goals, and rise to every occasion and meet her own star, and the way things had been going, there was no doubt she was going to do it. Her lens was finally in focus, and she was developing some good rolls.

Gabrielle and Dante had faced countless challenges, and though their picture was far from perfect, they had been able to make most of their negatives clear.

One of the last snapshots in their early photo album was taken the day that their eldest son, DJ, was graduating from high school. The picture showed DJ standing between Dante and Gabrielle while holding his diploma. He had received an academic and athletic scholarship and would be attending a university in Wisconsin, which was close to his other grandmother, and not too far from the place that his mother and father had gotten their first start.

For Dante and Gabrielle, watching their son head off to college in Wisconsin was like going back and moving forward at the same time.

Acknowledgments

I must always first acknowledge my Lord and Savior Jesus Christ, who truly is the beginning and the end, and who has been the greatest source of strength in my life.

I want to say an extra special thanks to my mother who has always made my snapshots bright, and who worked so very hard to get Snapshots in everyone's hands. I love and appreciate you more than words can say; to my family and friends (especially Krista Kay), and to my brother, Dwayne J, who I love with sincere appreciation, admiration, and now, understanding. DJ, you know, you are one in a million...and I thank you for always having my back.

To my pastor, J.M. Shafer, who stepped in as a mother, mentor, and best friend, when I lost my grandmother. You knew how much it hurt, and you always loved enough to help me heal. I love, admire, and appreciate you for always.

Unmeasurable thanks goes out to each of you who took a chance on me and my work, and provided your support by buying, reading, and spreading the word about my book. I so appreciate that. Very special thanks goes out to each and every bookstore, book club, group, organization, and person who purchased and supported my work.

Special thanks to my friends at the Pier: Nefertiti, Annette, Lynne, and especially to my favorite doorman, Michael, who gave me an unforgettable measure of help.

Also to the radio stations, newspapers, cable stations and NBC for providing exposure about my novel. To R. Tatum. To all of the many authors who I have met, signed with, and who have given me tremendous support, especially Kweisi, Parry Brown, Timm McCann, Marcus Major, and countless others. To my publicist Portia C.

Much love to Art and Nikki for all your support.

To all of my colleagues who believed the biggest things for my book, I will always appreciate you.

To Eva Greenberg and Mrs. Carlton. To everyone who got with and behind my mother to get Snapshots out there, I thank you. To my #1 homegirl, Shonnie, Maggie, and Malik, for always believing in me. To all the Scotts, no matter where we are. To the Austins, Woodsons, Watsons, Brooks' and all of the others who have always been family. To Professor Hughes who knows what it means to be a part of the Scotts. To Karmika, Koran, Pook, and all the Martins who always made me family. Especial thanks to two of my cousins: Jimmy and Cheryl. To my Aunt Audrey, Uncle Raymond, Uncle Ron, and Uncle Tony for always looking out for me. To Dr. Rhimes for your guidance.

To all my Bennett sisters who got the Belles ringing, and to my extended family of sisters at Spelman, and the countless other HBCUs, and sororities who support my work.

To the guys throughout the NFL who read, supported, and gave honest feedback on my work, I thank you.

Also thanks to Dani. To my girls, Phyllis and Sherry, thanks for hanging in there with me.

For the diligence of my layout guy, B-Doc...You are the bomb! You are going to do big things...I just know you are!

Francelly, I will never forget your help; you really came through!

On a final note I want to say to every reader:

By the time you have finished Snapshots, I hope you have found something to smile about, laugh about, talk about, and think about. I hope it has entertained, but also given us some things to think about.

We learn some lessons the hard way—by living them, and we learn others more easily—by watching others. But, however we live, love, laugh, and learn, I hope that we will always share enough with others, so that their journey is a little more enlightened, and their way is a little more clear. Above all, here's hope that we all: Find something each day that we can laugh about and enjoy, as well as something we can work toward making better.

May you enjoy each day, and I'll see you again, in the next novel.

*Snapshots is a fictional novel; any similarities are coincidental or attributed to the universal experience.

Photo by Tim McGill

About the author: Jacquelyne Jermayne (J. Jermayne) is a native of Ohio, and a graduate of Bennett College. Jacquelyne holds a BA/S in Mass Communications & English, and earned her Master's degree in Education and English from DePaul University. She has taught English at various levels, including at a magnet school on the West side of Chicago, and at National Louis, a college accredited with Bachelors, Masters, and doctoral programs. Jacquelyne currently resides in Chicago, IL.

To book events, signings or speaking engagements email:
jaxsnaps@aol.com or call 312.259.5388
or write:
jaxon publishing
227 e. ontario #11664
chicago, il 60611
To contact cover artist, use same information as above.
Be sure to let others know what you thought of the novel.
You can post your reviews at amazon.com.